# Reinventing Verity

by

Sharon Sobel

**Reinventing Verity**

Cover Art by *Teddi Black*

The Wild Rose Press, Inc.
PO Box 708
Adams Basin, NY 14410-0708
Visit us at www.thewildrosepress.com

Publishing History
First Edition, 2025
Trade Paperback ISBN 978-1-5092-6220-5
Digital ISBN 978-1-5092-6221-2


Published in the United States of America

## Dedication

In honor of
Gladys and Jerry O'Neil
Heather O'Neil, Arie Belok, and Tommy Belok
Whose Commitment and Generosity to
Discovery to Cure
at the Yale University School of Medicine
has Granted Them a Place
in One Small Novel
And a Far Greater Place
in the Hearts of Those Seeking a Cure for Cancer.

Chapter 1

"I am lost, without any direction. What would you have me do?"

The plaintive question, barely audible above the incessant creaking of the great wooden ship, was not so much directed at the lady groaning on the compact bed, as to an Authority higher than any member of the lofty Harwood family. Annie Merrill looked uneasily toward the dark-timbered ceiling, feeling the full weight of despair, having learned as a child her humble prayers were not likely to be answered. But now, utterly adrift, she did not know to whom else she might turn.

"Get the ship's physician, idiot girl! And do not return to me until you have him!"

"He promised to attend to you as soon as possible," Annie patiently reminded her mistress. She was well accustomed to the lady's melodramatic complaints and demands, which rarely amounted to much. But she nevertheless summoned up her well-rehearsed voice of compassion and patience and again told her mistress why they waited so long for assistance. "Dr. Willis is with Mr. Van Houten, a very important government official and an—"

"American," Lady Verity finished contemptuously and had a coughing fit.

Annie reached for the damp linen cloth near the pillow and dabbed at her lady's chin and starched collar. Spotty remains of breakfast ruined the perfect image of the delicate invalid, and Lady Verity's chestnut hair was matted against the damp pillow. When the doctor finally came, he might be persuaded to believe his patient's complaints were genuine.

"Shall we change your nightgown?" Annie asked dutifully. Though Lady Verity was determined to be diagnosed with serious illness, it was essential she look her best. One never knew when the attending physician might prove to be a handsome, eligible bachelor or well connected to those who were.

"Stupid, foolish girl!" Lady Verity cried out with characteristic ferocity as she threw a china bowl at the door. "I am a dying woman! Put me in my burial shroud or leave me well alone! Nightgown, indeed!"

Annie rose shakily to her feet, surprised and fearful. Finally, here was evidence to sway her, to allow her to believe Lady Verity's illness had some semblance of truth about it. Never before had she known her mistress to be unmindful of her appearance, of the image she projected to both the high and low.

"Do not fret, my lady," Annie said soothingly. "I will seek out the doctor and explain the urgency of the situation. Perhaps he did not understand the importance of the note we sent him." *Or perhaps I did not understand it so well myself*, she thought.

"Such is your problem. A total want of understanding has always been your problem. It is no wonder you will never be anything better than a lady's companion, and fortunate at that!" Lady Verity gagged, but Annie did not know what to do to alleviate her distress. Circumstances had not changed, no matter the temporary trappings of genuine illness. Lady Verity would never be anything but what she was: an arrogant woman born to wealth and privilege, whose associations with those less fortunate were scarcely endured.

Annie, exasperated, regretted her honest response of compassion and concern, for it surely would never be appreciated. Of all those Lady Verity resented, none were attacked with such persistent contempt as Annie herself.

"That I will never be anything better than a lady's companion might be more the problem of the Harwood family than my own," Annie shot back recklessly. "My birth cannot be counted as my fault, but that of my parents."

Lady Verity looked wildly around, and Annie knew she sought something else to throw.

Annie backed away and stumbled against the washstand, her boldness tempered by guilt. Her late mother, for many years the housekeeper at Harwood Hall, forever counseled Annie to behave with discretion, to accept the accident of her birth as an unarguable fact of her identity. That the young girl could not be blamed for the indiscretions of her parents, however, did in no way relieve Annie of all responsibility. If she acted precipitously, spoke unwisely, she might very well be cut off from the great household that had always been her home.

But in the week since the two young travelers left the port of Liverpool in this spring of 1821, some democratic seed had planted itself in Annie's spirit; nurtured by fresh sea air and the promise of adventure in the New World, it began to grow into something resembling rebellion. She and Verity were both daughters of Lord Percival Harwood, the Earl of Westwarren. By what natural right, Annie now asked herself, was one destined to be the mistress over the other?

"You have spilled my rose water! Now the whole room reeks of a river whore! What will Dr. Willis think?" Lady Verity wailed.

Annie could not help but smile. There was hope for the ship's doctor, after all. "He will think you have disguised the natural odors of a sickroom which will undoubtedly endear you to his care."

Annie thought it a pretty fine argument. Indeed, it proved sufficient to give Lady Verity pause. The fingers of the invalid's right hand drummed meditatively on her shallow chest and she smiled weakly. When she looked thus, the resemblance to Annie was startling. They each might have both been looking in a mirror.

Then Lady Verity scowled, and the mirror cracked. "It will do no good if I am dead when he arrives," she muttered. She closed her eyes and crossed her hands upon her breast, already assuming the pose of eternal rest.

And yet she breathed.

Annie could not be so cruel, so unfeeling, to actually want her mistress dead, but she could not help but feel relief when granted even the slightest respite. The woman had been her tormentor for as long as she could remember, and the trip to America was no holiday. The rigors of a sea voyage and of the weeks-long overland journey to follow promised to be even more demanding than daily life at the great house. Annie was responsible for making the travel connections, for posting the mail, for choosing appropriate clothing for America's variable climate, where summer burned hotter than in England. If she was lucky, she might catch a glimpse of the great Niagara Falls or spend an afternoon shopping at Mrs. Trollope's Bazaar in Cincinnati.

Annie studied Lady Verity's face, stern even in repose, and wondered what her mistress wanted of this wearisome adventure. Her prospects in the marriage mart had not proved agreeable, though Lord Harwood had bestowed a huge settlement upon her. Twice she had been jilted, the gentlemen turning to ladies generally regarded less advantageous a match. More recently, Lady Verity entered into a very public liaison with a married man who had no intention of abandoning his wife and daughters. When Lord Eastbourne finally broke off the dalliance, Lady Verity acted with uncommon decisiveness and ordered Annie packing for a journey to America.

It was not for Annie to protest. And Lord Harwood, desperate for some respite from his recalcitrant daughter, dared anyone to question the propriety of two young women traveling to a strange land by themselves. Annie packed nearly all her own belongings in her mother's ancient carpetbag.

Now, a few weeks later, Annie sighed and threw her shawl around her shoulders. The sudden movement reflected in a tiny mirror, and she paused to study herself, and not the counterfeit reflection she was accustomed to seeing in her sister's pinched face. The vision renewed her frazzled spirits.

Her chestnut hair shone warmly in the yellow light and fell about her face in curls to her shoulders. Her skin retained a healthy glow even after days of seclusion in her cabin and was now flushed with worry. Eyes, blessed with darker and longer lashes than those of Lady Verity, matched the grayish blue tones of the stormy sea.

"Go, foolish girl!" cried Lady Verity, with more strength than Annie believed she could summon. "Would you have me die while you admire your complexion?"

She would not. She would not have Lady Verity die at all. But she would, very much, desire some distance between them.

Her hand caught at the damp door latch and pushed gently. The door fell open, and the cold, stiff wind of the Atlantic assaulted her. "I will find Dr. Willis for you, my lady," Annie promised resolutely, as Lady Verity weakly waved her off.

The door closed as Annie stepped down onto the salt-sprayed deck and crossed to the rail. Closing her eyes, she sucked in great breaths of fresh sea air until she was breathless.

When she opened her eyes, a man stood before her, his lips parted in an expression of surprise. He looked familiar, though he could have been any one of the throngs of people against whom she had jostled this past week while on the *Andromeda*. He nodded briefly and turned away as another man's voice, gruff and insistent, bellowed forth from a nearby cabin. In the bowels of the great ship, hundreds of people languished in swinging bunks awaiting deliverance on the shores of America.

Two worlds coexisted on the *Andromeda*, Annie reflected with some bitterness. There were those of privilege and wealth, for whom such a journey was sport, business, or—for one such as Lady Verity—a diversion from some unpleasantness at home. It did not signify where they were as much as whom they were, for their identities were inviolate and their comforts a priority.

And then there were the others, like herself, whose lives were dependent upon the whims of their employers, and for whom a sea journey only changed the setting, and not the substance, of their lives. Some might believe the rumors about the New World, and the opportunities it offered, but most travelers were as incapable of changing their fortunes as they were of steering the *Andromeda* back to England.

"Have a care, girl," came a voice, too late, behind her. Something large and hard pushed against her back and thrust her against the wooden railing of the deck.

Annie, strengthened with a sense of injustice, turned defiantly to face her attacker. But instead she faced two men, their heads so close she thought them attached at the shoulder.

"You will allow us through, please." His accent identified him as an American, which would account for his impatience. Americans were always in a hurry. "We have little time for pleasantries just now."

Of course not.

"An apology would be sufficient, sir," she said instead, standing her ground.

The other man's eyes narrowed as his mouth opened in a broad smile.

"Release me, Will," he said cheerfully, revealing his American identity as well. "It appears we must pay a toll before we can go farther."

"Perhaps the gate mistress does not realize the urgency of our mission," said his companion and shifted his broad shoulders. He also reminded Annie of someone she knew, but surely she was having delusions if she imagined she recognized every man she saw on the ship.

But the gate mistress had had enough of insults and condescension and being made to feel altogether inferior.

"It cannot be any more urgent than mine," Annie argued. But she was just a lady's maid, and they had no reason to believe her. Her words might convey need, but no authority. She paused for a moment, but the die was cast before she quite realized what she said. "I am Lady Verity Harwood of Harwood Hall," she bluffed and waited to be struck down by the hand of God. When nothing happened, she continued. "My dearest friend and companion, Miss Annie Merrill, requires medical attention at once. The situation is most desperate."

The darker man studied her for several moments, his bright eyes narrowing. "And you are Lady Verity Harwood, on an errand for your maid? It is very admirable of you. Perhaps Miss Merrill ate something that did not please her, or pricked her finger while sewing? I understand your concern, but my good friend has probably broken his ankle."

Annie chose to ignore the man's rude tone and instead studied his companion. She realized now that they stood so close together because the man called Will supported his friend's weight. She looked down at his trousered legs bent at the knees, and the booted foot angled most awkwardly.

"Do you require further proof, Lady Verity?"

Annie no longer knew what they were disputing, for all her thoughts were on the wickedness of her deception. And yet her gaze wandered brazenly upward, from the sturdy worn boots they both wore to the blue worsted trousers as common as any sailor's. Their shirts were starched but unadorned with collars or cravats. Will, the taller and broader of the two, wore a somewhat wrinkled jacket bearing a salt stain upon it. His friend, now leaning against the rail, sported a knitted sweater.

They were not dressed like gentlemen. She did not know who they were. But their need was surely as great as hers, no matter their class or station.

"I do not need to be convinced of anything," she said, sounding a bit loftier than she intended. She looked up into Will's frowning face and wavered under his dark gaze. "But you need not fear my interference, for I believe we are going to the same place. I am on my way to Dr. Willis' chambers, to bring him to the bedside of my dear Miss Merrill. Perhaps it is nothing more than sea sickness, but she is quite convinced she is at Death's door."

"And she has sent her mistress out into the rough wind to do her bidding. You are exceedingly obliging, Lady Verity. It is quite unexpected." He continued to study her, and she had the unnerving feeling he knew precisely whom she was.

"I do not know why anything should be unexpected when people are unacquainted," she said. "I do not know who you are. It displays an appalling lack of manners."

Annie thought she managed the Lady Verity part

rather well. Now, if she could just find something to throw overboard, she could be utterly convincing.

The injured man laughed, surprising in one with a painful injury. "I do apologize, but we are as distracted as you under the circumstances. I am Mr. Geoffrey Marsh, of Boston, and my friend is Mr. William Bentley, of New York. Disregarding the cautions issued by the crew, we ventured to the upper deck, where I slipped and fell. It was foolish of me, but then we would not have had the privilege of meeting a beautiful lady."

His companion did not look as delighted with either the meeting or the lady and continued to scowl at her.

Annie turned her back on him and reached a helping hand to Mr. Marsh. "I certainly forgive you, sir, if forgiveness is desired, and would be happy to assist you. As we are destined for the same place, I will take you there myself, if you will lean on me. But you must decide quickly, as I have already been detained far too long from my errand."

Mr. Bentley cleared his throat, and Annie spared him another glance. His skin looked as tanned as any sailor's, though flushed after the exertion of supporting a man probably heavier than himself. His lips, delicately shaped for a man's, were pressed uncompromisingly together, creating a cunning dimple along the line of his cheek. Annie had the impression he was younger than his more cheerful companion, though his manner and general air somehow revealed his superiority.

He left her feeling acutely uncomfortable. His unblinking dark eyes never left her face, and once again she wondered if he somehow knew she was putting on airs and letting them believe her someone better than she was.

"We will go together," he said authoritatively. "It appears my friend does not suffer as greatly as I first feared. Perhaps his miraculous recovery is due to the influence of a pretty face, though I very much doubt it."

Annie wondered if he doubted she had a pretty face, or if that face sufficient to work a miracle.

"I do not consider injured ankles capable of healing by such means."

"A pity," Mr. Marsh said sorrowfully. "I would much rather be with you than with the doctor."

"And I would much rather return to my companion than be an audience to your ill humor when the doctor attempts to set your ankle," Annie answered truthfully.

"Then we will let you precede us, of course. My friend will have to endure his pain like the brave adventurer he is," Mr. Bentley said. "Even if Miss Merrill suffers from no more than a splintered finger, a woman's complaints must take precedence over those of a man."

"You must allow me to lead the way, however," Annie insisted, "lest you collide with some other unsuspecting passenger."

"Then please lead us, Lady Verity," said Mr. Marsh and smiled gratefully. Annie saw the lines of pain in the corners of his eyes and guessed how dearly his good manners cost him. "We trust you to part the seas for us."

As Annie turned her back on them, she heard his companion grunt as boots scraped along the deck. An irregular pattern of footsteps marched heavily behind her, and perversely, she hastened her step so the disagreeable Will Bentley would need to work harder.

"We will trust her as far as the doctor's chambers," he said, only slightly out of breath. "And not a step beyond."

If Mr. Bentley did not support Mr. Marsh, Annie would have been perfectly happy to lead him over the prow of the *Andromeda*.

****

For all the time spent in the company of her new acquaintances, Annie was not apart from her mistress for more than twenty minutes. Dr. Willis stood in the open door of his cabin, reading from a pile of small notations, and stepped aside at once. He looked over her shoulder at the two men behind her and readily relieved Mr. Bentley of his burden by clearing a pile of books from a low bench, and urging Mr. Marsh to sit upon it. The doctor's understandable indecision was alleviated when his patient urged him to first tend to Miss Merrill and return when possible.

"I am incapable of leaving, sir," said Mr. Marsh convincingly and accepted a small glass of brandy. His friend declined the drink, preferring to scowl at Annie.

"Best wishes for a speedy recovery, Mr. Marsh," Annie said sincerely and turned her shoulder on Mr. Bentley as she walked out the door. Dr. Willis was beside her in a second, and they walked briskly back to Lady Verity's cabin.

"I do not have your knowledge," Annie said, a trifle breathlessly. "But I know my companion only too well. She enjoys the illusion of failing health, though can name no specific complaint. I would not be surprised if it were the sea itself that plagues her, for she has given up every meal to it."

Dr. Willis chuckled but did not seem unsympathetic. Annie thought him agreeable enough but knew Lady Verity would not be impressed by his lean figure. It suggested he had not the means to have a good meal set before him.

"I will see for myself," he said when they reached the cabin door. "I am too familiar with the symptoms of seasickness."

Annie preceded him into the room, announcing his presence to her lady. Lady Verity slept fitfully, groaning as she tossed beneath the covers, and did not acknowledge either of them. Dr. Willis walked directly to the bed and shot Annie an unreadable look.

"I will leave you," Annie said quickly before escaping to the closet between their chambers. She supposed she ought to be worried about her mistress or about the possibility Lady Verity would be so unwilling to take to the seas again they might be captive in America for the rest of their lives. She realized she ought to feel some concern for the gallant Mr. Marsh, who lay in pain while Dr. Willis comforted a healthy woman.

But Annie could only think of the arrogant and unforgiving Mr. Bentley who would have others believe he was above their company. That he was certainly above hers was of no consequence, since they were unlikely to meet again. His kindness to his friend notwithstanding, there seemed nothing in his character to recommend him.

Of course, there would be others who would not bother to look beyond his appearance to determine what ought to recommend him. Annie could not erase the vision of his dark eyes and sensitive mouth, nor forget his obvious strength. She guessed he was a man who was quite comfortable in the wind and salty air, and his rough clothes suited him very well. They certainly matched his manners.

When Dr. Willis sought her out, she was smiling.

"Lady…ah?"

"Verity Harwood," Annie answered quickly, on the assumption that a lie—like bitter medicine—would go down easier if one swallowed hastily.

"Yes, of course," the doctor said thoughtfully. "We spoke on the first night of the voyage."

Annie bit down on her lip, wondering if the doctor suspected the truth.

"Please join me," he said simply.

Annie studied her mistress as she approached the sickbed, wondering if Lady Verity had already revealed her own identity, or if the doctor knew they were connected by more than friendship. But she lay quietly, snoring slightly and twitching as if she were being nibbled by some small creature.

"She suffers from a lack of nourishment, among other things," the doctor pronounced. "It is likely the cause of her delusions, for she imagines herself Lady Verity Harwood. But this is temporary, and I believe she will do well with a steady dose of sugar water and with the occasional slice of toast. In her condition, it is necessary she eat something, even if it is very little."

Annie took a deep breath. "Will her condition improve if I take her from this cabin and have her breath in fresh air?"

Dr. Willis looked at her curiously. "Her condition will not change, though her spirits might improve. I assume there is a gentleman awaiting you in America?"

Annie felt a little sputter of alarm. What could ail her lady that her condition remained unalterable? And was it so serious help would be required in her care?

"My friend will not be alone in America," Annie said evasively. "She will always have me at her side."

Dr. Willis looked from her to the lady on the bed and back again but said nothing about the obvious resemblance between mistress and maid. What he thought of it, or what anyone ever thought of it, Annie never had the heart to guess. "I doubt neither your loyalty nor your competence, Lady Verity. I only hope your powers of persuasion are as strong as your intentions."

"Do not fear, Dr. Willis. I will get her to do what you want." Annie smiled, though she still felt some unease. "And you have another patient awaiting you, sir, so I will not keep you any longer."

Dr. Willis nodded and took her hand, looking down as he spoke. "I wish you the best of luck, Lady Verity Harwood, and ease in the care of your charge. You seem to be the true measure of a lady."

Annie blushed with pleasure, little realizing how prophetic were the good doctor's words.

\*\*\*\*

Lady Verity did not take kindly to the spoonfuls of sugar water Annie attempted to force through her lips. Twice she spat the liquid back at Annie and slapped away the hand holding the spoon. At the end of an hour, Annie's breast was damp with water and she was beginning to feel chilled.

She wanted to retreat to her own cabin, where she might change into dry clothing. But one look at Lady

Verity's pale face made Annie reluctant to leave her, and she decided instead to find something in her mistress' closet to wear. In such circumstances, it could hardly matter how it fit or if it suited.

Hanging next to its more ostentatious sisters was a simple blue day dress. Annie pulled it from its hanger and struggled to fasten it over her body. Snug at the bodice and short in length, it nevertheless gave her a certain unfamiliar confidence, as if borrowed finery bestowed some provenance hitherto unknown. Now warmer and drier, Annie returned to the bedside of her mistress.

Lady Verity's breathing seemed easier as she lay calmly against her pillows. Annie wished she understood what the doctor meant by her "condition" and resolved she would ask him about it on the morrow. She recalled some mention of Lady Sarah Harwood's consumption and knew Sir Jasper suffered from the gout. But she did not know if such ailments were inclined to be carried through families, for it was well known that Verity's parents were close cousins. If it was possible to inherit physical weakness as easily as some inherited wealth, Annie ought to have a touch of concern about it herself.

The sound of the wind blowing against the door of the cabin aroused Annie from her sleep, and she groaned in wretched discomfort. Somehow, she had settled herself face down on the covers at the foot of her lady's bed, though she remained firmly planted on the seat of a chair. Her arms lay folded beneath her, and her fingers were numb with cold and lack of circulation. Her hair was tangled and damp.

She pushed herself up, blinking into the darkness.

The candle had burned down, and the only light came from the pink dawn creeping through the small porthole. All was silent, uncannily calm.

Uneasily, Annie sat up, sensing something out of joint, and looked at the still figure on the bed. Lady Verity's eyes were open, staring intently at the ceiling. Her mouth was slack, and a spittle of blood ran down her chin. Her brows were smooth and gentle in repose.

With dreadful certainty Annie knew what she would discover even before she pressed her ear against the lady's breast, for though she knew little of death, she did not require a map to discover it now.

"Verity!" she cried, dragging the cool body from its covers. "You must not leave me! We are almost to America!"

Lady Verity's head fell back, lolling loosely like a ragdoll's. Her slim body suddenly seemed uncommonly weighty and slipped through Annie's grasp onto the bed beneath them. A little gasp of air escaped the lady's blue lips.

Annie stumbled against her chair as she stood. She needed to summon the doctor at once, for there must be something he could do. Had he not said the lady would be well soon enough? That the sea air might do her good?

At the door, Annie turned back to gaze unhappily at the form of her mistress. There was no dignity in such a death, and no justice in a life stopped so young. Even so disagreeable a person deserved a future, an opportunity to find happiness and contentment.

And now, with all hope gone, Annie's own future lacked even the glimmer of promise afforded to the companion of a very fine person. Without Lady Verity at her side, Annie's identity became obscure and unimportant. She was Nobody, adrift in a vast ocean.

Annie reached for the latchkey in her pocket, and her fingers fumbled at her side. Looking down, she remembered she had changed from her own damp dress and now wore the one she found in Lady Verity's closet. Yesterday's masquerade felt wicked now and wearing the gown only tainted her further; it was as if she assumed the soul of the dead woman and walked about in her stead.

She gasped as she caught a glimpse of herself in the small mirror, for it might have been her mistress wearing the blue gown, staring back at her.

Annie blinked and looked again.

Unbidden, the small seed that planted itself into her desperate, fearful imagination, one that was so unlikely to nurture it could never have taken root unless the ground proved profoundly fertile, suddenly bloomed. It sprang to life defiantly and vividly, growing with rapidity on an otherwise barren landscape.

She could never manage to pull it off.

There were too many people who already knew her, and who expected to host Lady Verity Harwood in America. There were matters of legality, ranging from burying the wrong woman, to drawing on funds intended for another. It would be forever impossible to return home, for no one at Harwood would be in the slightest bit deceived. And morally…Annie shuddered just contemplating the scope of her sinfulness.

But Verity was dead, and in a place where nothing could harm her. And Annie lived, facing an unhappy future of servitude and injustice.

She came away from the door, her own reflection

looming even larger in the mirror as she approached the bed. Next to it, her simple muslin gown was strewn on a chair, drying in the stale air. It looked as if the stricken woman tossed it there before she took to her bed. But there were other things that required staging if the deception was to be at all persuasive, and Annie needed to act quickly, before she talked herself out of it.

She pulled Lady Verity's arms from the covers, and saw how quickly the signs of death were already upon her. Her wrists had a clammy, cold feel, and seemed oddly disjointed. And then she took the lady's hands, strange even in life, and knew something had to be done. There were those back home who whispered that a six-fingered child was the spawn of the devil, but it was a trait for which Annie could never blame her mistress. She knew there were accidents in nature, and they were as likely to fall on the wealthy as the poor. It was pitiful, to be sure, though since Verity was likely to punish Annie for having perfectly ordinary hands, she certainly did not want her pity.

Annie went to the closet and found a pair of fine white gloves specially made for the lady. She pulled a bouquet of tired lilies from a vase on the washstand, and shook them gently until the stems were dry. Then she dressed Lady Verity's hands for the last time, crossed them over her breast and set the flowers upon them.

There was nothing to be done for the wrinkled white nightdress except to smooth it neatly around the still body. Annie's deft fingers twisted the lady's matted hair into a simple fashion very much like her own and removed the gold locket from around the thin neck.

Pressing gently, she closed the sightless eyes and spread the thin lips into some semblance of a smile. And then gazed in horror at the vision of herself in death.

The realization of what she had done finally stopped her and made her back away. She could not continue with this dreadful masquerade.

Suddenly, unexpectedly, great racking sobs shook her whole body and blinded her vision. Sinking down onto the narrow bed, Annie cried for everything she had ever wished and all that would be forever denied. Her mistress, her sister was lost to her, and with Lady Verity died Annie Merrill's purpose. The survivor of this sea journey would arrive in America bereft and alone.

Annie could not say how long she remained against Lady Verity's cold stiffening form, but when she awakened to the sound of loud banging on the door, her eyes were nearly glued shut with the crusty salt of her dried tears. She rubbed her fingers over her eyes and hastily smoothed down her borrowed finery. She glanced down at Lady Verity who, for once, was not censorious of her companion's appearance. The dead woman looked very small and insignificant in her bed.

It was she, Annie Merrill, who was alive and had a future. What she dared to contemplate in the early hours of the dawn now seemed a gift of opportunity, to redeem the humble circumstances to which she was born, and reach for a new life. She caught her breath, fearful of the awesome prospect.

The banging continued, more insistent now.

Annie stumbled to the door as the ship rocked sickeningly beneath her. A young man in uniform stood in the brightening light of a new day, his hand still aloft when Annie opened the door to him.

"Excuse my intrusion, Lady Verity, but Dr. Willis sent me to inquire as to the health of your friend."

Annie stared at him, realizing the great, irredeemable moment had arrived. Nervously, her hand went up to the side of her head and she fixed a stray pin to secure her riotous curls. She opened her mouth to speak but realized no words would come out.

She cleared her throat.

"My dear friend, Miss Merrill, died during the night. I have been trying to overcome my grief so I might venture out to bring Dr. Willis to her."

She stepped aside and revealed the composed scene within.

The young man's eyes opened wide, and he stepped backward.

"My lady!" he said hoarsely. "This can't be true."

The newly reinvented Lady Verity Harwood wisely said nothing, for indeed it was not.

Chapter 2

Lady Verity Harwood stood alone in her cramped cabin, inspecting the selection of slippers she had set out for her lady when she was still Miss Annie Merrill. At that time, she thought there were far too many of them to conveniently be included on a journey to America; now she realized she had not enough choices.

The colors and styles were fine and elegant. Indeed, they were grander than anything she ever wore in her life. But the lady whose small form would soon be lowered to the depths of the Atlantic had daintier feet, or else did not mind so much if the toes pinched a bit as she walked.

There was no hope for it, Annie realized. Though she now wore the loveliest day dress in Lady Verity's collection, she could only manage her masquerade in her own sturdier, well-worn shoes. If she got as far as the harbor of Boston without being clasped in irons, she would locate a shoemaker before continuing with her adventure.

If she got as far…

For now, she would be happy to escape to the cabin immediately after the funeral service by the ship's captain, and not worry about such trifles as dance shoes when she should be worried about the consequences of assuming another's identity.

Annie selected a warm jacket from the several

hanging in the closet and shrugged her shoulders into the smooth lining of the sleeves. Her own worsted garments offered a comforting sort of scratchiness against her skin, but genuine ladies did not prefer such rough pleasures. Certainly Lady Verity would not, though Annie was hard-pressed to remember anything at all that gave her mistress pleasure, aside from tormenting her maid.

Remembering Verity with an affection she never felt while the lady lived, Annie smiled and closed the door on the wardrobe. If she remained this cheerful, she would never be mistaken for the woman she hoped to impersonate.

****

Will Bentley was glad he was persuaded to set aside his work for a few hours, as he smiled politely at the young lady with whom he strolled along the narrow deck of the *Andromeda*. They had only recently met, but she seemed just the sort of girl who ought to appeal to him, for she professed independent beliefs and a keen sense of adventure. Indeed, it was because of her headstrong nature that she was ready to put her trust in Mr. John Reese, a fellow traveler of dubious reputation and some notoriety. Not knowing what Reese planned, but recognizing a lady in distress—even if she remained blithely unaware of any danger—Will stepped in to protect her. Geoff would have done the same, if he had been in a position to protect anyone.

However, it was not long before he realized that the young lady's sense of adventure was inspired by the journals of travel writers rather than her own experience and that he might find their acquaintance quite useful.

"I should like to explore the forests of Boston," she

said, "and live among the native people. I shall bring my own food with me, for I believe their diet consists of nothing but raw fish and seeds."

"In a land of fertile fields, they find a great deal else to whet their appetites, my dear Miss Compton," Will said patiently. "And you may realize some difficulty in finding your quarry in the area around Boston, for the native people are quite assimilated in society. For a taste of their culture, you have to travel farther west into the continent. I plan to do so this summer, along the route of the construction of the Erie Canal."

"Are you quite certain about assimilation, Mr. Bentley? I believe I must disagree with you, for some months past I read a very clever piece by Mr. Benjamin Williams of the New York Republic Society and he wrote about a sort of wild energy at loose in the New World. What else could he mean but the activities of natives?"

Will groaned inwardly. He supposed he ought to be pleased his opinionated friend was an avid reader, but he wondered if she examined much more than the opening and closing paragraphs of a piece. Mr. Williams was a writer who preferred to put a great deal of substance between those slices of bread.

"Perhaps you did not read all of Mr. Williams' piece," Will said a little rudely, but instantly regretted it when he saw the indignation on Miss Compton's face. "He is so verbose, I doubt anyone can read him through entirely. Nevertheless, I believe he elaborates on his theme with some detail elsewhere in the article."

"Ah, then you are also familiar with it?" Miss Compton's delight granted redemption.

"Passably," Will said.

"It is an excellent article," Miss Compton said quickly. "It is one of the reasons I chose to tour America. It sounds like a very exciting place, and it promises to make this dreadful sea journey almost worthwhile. It is why I have all the more pity for poor Miss Merrill, who did not live to see it."

Will would have preferred the conversation to go anywhere but here. He did not wish to speak of Williams, not even to hear praise. But in the several hours since he heard of the death of Miss Merrill, he could not escape dark feelings of guilt. His impatient abruptness, his nearly unprecedented arrogance, his barely concealed rudeness to a lady who only wished to help her deathly ill friend were all so regrettable, he scarcely knew how to atone. In his more generous moments, he reminded himself of Geoff's distress, and the lady's willingness to tarry while she flirted with them both, and how he could not possibly have predicted the dire outcome of that day.

Geoff appeared so overcome by remorse, he would not speak of it at all.

Will preferred it that way, bearing his own burden in silence and coming to terms with his unfortunate behavior. After all, he did not kill the girl.

At least, he hoped not.

It was why he now attempted to appear more gracious with others on board the *Andromeda*, lest something happen to them as well.

"Did you ever meet Miss Merrill?" Miss Compton asked in the face of his silence, but continued before Will could answer. "She hardly ever emerged from her cabin, except in the company of Lady Verity. She was a servant, of course. They kept very close to themselves and spoke to almost no one."

"I did not meet Miss Merrill," Will admitted. "I collided with Lady Verity on the way to Dr. Willis' cabin, both of us seeking help for our friends. You already know about Mr. Marsh's broken ankle. But Lady Verity also required the doctor's attendance on her friend, knowing how grave was her illness. I did not fully comprehend how dire it was at the time."

"How could you, Mr. Bentley? It would have been very indelicate for the lady to reveal the extent of her friend's illness. There are some things a gentleman ought not know." Miss Compton smiled.

Will nodded. He knew this very well, as he had grown up amongst five sisters and was frequently shut out of their conversations.

"But Lady Verity certainly did know. After all, she ventured out into the wind and cold, risking her own safety. But in times of desperation, rank must be dismissed."

Miss Compton laughed. "Why, you truly have been reading Mr. Williams, have you not? You sound very much like him!"

Will frowned and looked over Miss Compton's head, out to sea. One morning soon, the passengers of the *Andromeda* would wake up to see the vague shoreline of the New World.

"It is nearly time for the funeral service, Mr. Bentley. Shall we attend and pay our respects to a fellow traveler? I'm sure Lady Verity will be there, and you might compliment her on her sacrifice to her friend." Miss Compton smiled winningly.

"I am sure it is none of my concern," Will said.

"Mr. Williams writes that it is the hallmark of every American to make everything his or her concern."

"Mr. Williams sounds like a busybody," Will said under his breath.

Miss Compton laughed. "But you need not fear, Mr. Bentley. Lady Verity will surely talk to you, though she is reputed to be a very haughty lady. You shall honestly offer your apologies along with your sympathies, and I am sure all will be well. Ladies do not like deception, in any form."

Her voice broke off, and Will glanced down to see her reddening face and raised eyebrows. "There she is."

At the prow of the ship, some fellow travelers already gathered for the solemn ceremony of committing one of their small band to the unrelieved blue of the Atlantic. The captain stood over a long and narrow canvas shroud, fighting the stiff wind as he sought a passage in his Bible. Lady Verity Harwood remained somewhat aloof, rubbing her gloved hands as if she could not possibly keep them warm enough. She dressed very elegantly in a pale gown of some frilly fabric, and a darker jacket trimmed with fur. The wind whipped her skirt around her ankles, which looked rather sturdy in the unfashionable boots she wore. The contrast to the rest of her ensemble was surprising, but Will could only applaud the good sense of a woman who recognized the hazards of a wet and rolling deck.

The lady looked up as they approached.

Will wondered if she recognized him, though she had been most preoccupied at the time of their first meeting and decidedly distressed at the time of their second. Indeed, her reddish hair and tempting pink lips were already familiar to him, as was the blush that quickly spread across her high cheekbones. He studied her and caught a flicker of fear in her gray-blue eyes, before they turned downward to gaze upon her incongruous boots.

"Dear Lady Verity," Miss Compton rushed in. "Please allow me to extend my condolences on the loss of your companion. It is a great tragedy."

Lady Verity glanced at the captain, who still fumbled with his Bible, and turned back to them. "Thank you. I feel the pain of Miss Merrill's loss as if a part of me went with her." She paused, and Will felt sure he misinterpreted the small smile that flickered in the corners of her mouth. "Please tell me to whom I am indebted for such kindness? And is this your husband?"

"Oh, no, my lady. My name is Miss Compton, and I am only taking the air with Mr. Bentley."

Will bowed, expecting her to extend her hand. When she did not, he looked up, meeting her enigmatic eyes and seeing his own reflection in their blue depths.

"I believe you met Mr. Bentley shortly before Miss Merrill died. I am sure it is not his fault," Miss Compton rushed on.

For all Will was annoyed by Miss Compton's artlessness, he was immediately distracted by the return of the smile to Lady Verity's lips. This time, he was able to attribute it to her wit.

"It was never my intent to accuse Mr. Bentley of murder, Miss Compton, though our meeting did delay my mission to the doctor. I am sure it did not make any difference in the outcome, however." She hesitated and dabbed at her eye, though Will saw no evidence of tears. "We were like sisters, you understand, and I shall miss her dreadfully."

"I believe I saw the two of you together just once, while dining on the upper deck. I would say you were not merely like sisters, but close enough in appearance to pass for twins." Miss Compton nodded. "Mr. Reese thought the same thing."

"What does Reese have to do with this?' Will asked.

Both women gazed at him, and he realized he might have spoken a bit too vehemently.

"I do not know any man named Reese," Lady Verity said. "But Miss Merrill and I were distantly related, and so somewhat resembled each other."

Will guessed she was resisting something that was readily apparent to others and was curious enough to provoke her.

"In fact, when we first spoke on the day before Miss Merrill's death, I thought you were she. If I was rude that day, you must forgive me my error."

Something flickered again in the blue depths, but no smile teased her lips.

"Mr. Bentley," she said. "I entirely forgive your rudeness. You were in some distress, as well. And were breathless with assisting poor Mr. Marsh."

She glanced at his shoulders, and he might have felt her gesture somewhat complimentary but that she looked as if she chewed upon something that was not at all pleasant. He realized, with a start, that her sympathies were all for Geoff. And just as quickly realized he was envious of his best friend.

The ship's captain was a man endowed with little grace, either of the religious sort, or of the type that would allow him to comfortably address an audience.

Fortunately, the audience was very small, as one could hardly expect much interest in the final reflections about a young woman of no consequence. So Annie Merrill went to her watery grave accompanied by the rambling words of a man who looked as if he wished to be any place but there, the respect of a few curious passengers, the unwished-for prayers of a couple who seemed more interested in themselves than in the woman in the canvas shroud, and the dreadful sadness of Annie Merrill herself. Who would now be known as Lady Verity Harwood. Annie was gone, the injustices meted out to her throughout her short life must be forgiven and forgotten. And yet, the new Lady Verity was the beneficiary of that experience, for she would always be mindful of how power could be oppressive, and vanity an affliction upon others. She would have servants and would treat them kindly. She would have money and spend it wisely.

A splash returned her to the present, and she realized she missed the very moment of her half sister's transition. The others seemed to have been better prepared, for they were already lined up to offer their sympathies. Lady Verity thanked them graciously, even as she wondered how she would manage her new life in America. She knew the names of the banking institutions to which she could present a draft, and she had letters of introduction to several people in society. But otherwise she was quite alone.

"Do call on me if I can be of any assistance," Mr. Bentley said, breaking into her reverie.

"And on me, as well, Lady Verity," added Miss Compton eagerly. "I am to meet my betrothed in Boston and will live in the home of his aunt until we are married."

Mr. Bentley glanced down at her arm entwined with his own and slipped out of Miss Compton's knot. He bowed to the two ladies and set off by himself, carefully avoiding a slop bucket that slid across the deck.

"He is the only man on this ship who amuses me," Miss Compton confided. "He interfered with my meeting with another man, when all poor Mr. Reese intended was to show me his collection of sea maps in his cabin. Mr. Bentley cautioned me quite intently, as if he were my older brother, and warned me not to go anywhere with strange men. And yet he is a stranger himself."

"And somewhat strange, as well. In fact, he does not amuse me at all," Verity said. "I think he's prickly and aloof and a little too sure of himself to allow comfort to those near to him."

Miss Compton looked at her in surprise and, perhaps, some admiration. "My goodness! And yet you have only made the briefest acquaintance!"

"I would wish for no more, Miss Compton," said Verity. There was something in his dark eyes that attempted to pull her in, to admit confidences. He saw a good deal too much and was intelligent enough to extrapolate the rest. Verity shuddered involuntarily, already knowing the great pleasure he would feel if he managed to expose her crime of deception. She must therefore avoid his company, at all costs.

She turned around at the sound of heavy steps on the deck and knew today's trials were not yet over.

"My dear Lady Verity," said Dr. Willis. "I am so sorry for this unhappy event and wish there was more I could have done."

"Dr. Willis," Verity said in low voice, "I am so grateful for your concern. This has been a dreadful journey, and I yearn to walk upon the terra firma of America."

"You shall not be disappointed, my lady. I have been there many times due to the nature of my profession and find it a land almost as fair as our green island. The cities are nowhere in size comparable to London or Manchester, and therefore the countryside is ever so much closer at hand. We arrive at a perfect time, when the first leaves of spring appear through the ice."

"I shall look forward to exploring it all."

Dr. Willis leaned toward her. "I want you to know, my lady, that I very much admire your generosity of spirit in seeking help for your maid and allowing her the comfort of your own bed. I know many ladies who would not be so inconvenienced nor grieve at a loss of someone not of her own class. I believe you will enjoy your stay in America very much."

Verity let out a long breath. "I thank you, but do not give me more credit than is deserved. Annie Merrill was a woman of worth, loved by her mother and many friends. I will miss her every day of my life." Her last words were barely out before her voice cracked, and she began to cry.

She reached out blindly, and Dr. Willis took her hand, murmuring words of comfort. She certainly did not want anyone's pity, for the guilt would be too great. It was not her fault her half sister had died, nor could she truly mourn the loss of one who had treated her so miserably her whole life. But a young woman had perished at sea, and a life that always held the hope of redemption, of some glimmer of goodness, was forever lost. Verity looked away, to the dark rolling sea into which the *Andromeda*'s officers had cast the physical remains of her own lost identity.

"The sea is very vast," she said inanely.

"Indeed, it is, my lady," said Dr. Willis. "But then, so is the continent of America. I asked it once of you before your circumstances changed, and I shall now ask it of you: have you someone waiting for you in America?"

Verity evaded the question then, and she did now. "I have letters of introduction to several respectable people, including Mrs. Frances Trollope in Cincinnati. I will hire a hire a new companion once we arrive in Boston, and we shall travel together."

"My dear lady, have you any notion of the distance between Boston and Cincinnati? It is not less than three weeks, and that if you travel directly."

Verity faltered, trying to recall the map in the great atlas at Harwood Hall. The planning of the journey was so hurried, she scarcely had the time to do it any sort of justice.

"I am confident I can manage it, sir," Verity said a little haughtily, sounding much more like the lady whose identity she assumed than Annie Merrill.

Dr. Willis laughed. "I have no doubt you can, Lady Verity, for you seem a very resilient sort of woman. Here you are, a survivor in the most laudable sense of the word, with great plans to travel until you reach the protection of Mrs. Trollope. I must warn you, however, that aside from the distance, there are many situations in which it would be inadvisable to venture as a single lady. Pardon my interference, but perhaps you might find a trustworthy gentleman who is planning a similar journey and ask for his protection."

"A protector!" Verity said despairingly. "But everything I have heard about America allows me to understand that rank and gender do not matter and that women enjoy opportunities equal to those of men."

Dr. Willis frowned. "You have read the papers of the American patriots, no doubt. They write of the glories of their new country, and the great philosophies upon which it is founded. But in many ways, this is only a great hope. There are enslaved people throughout the land, and native-born fellows who have been robbed of their lands, and women are still not afforded all rights under the law. You are a young person and cannot be expected to know of such things. But did your mother and father not advise you in this?"

Verity paused, knowing how easy it would be to answer artlessly and give everything away. Her late mother was a housekeeper who bore a child out of wedlock and could never hope to be anything better than what she was. Lady Harwood had been a sad and sickly woman who spent her days in a fog of whisky bemoaning the fact that she never produced a son for her husband. And her husband...

Lord Harwood was as sad as his wife but, instead of escaping through drink, preferred the comfort of the private cottage on his estate, where he spent his hours writing a great book on the fauna of England. It was there Annie and Verity visited him as girls and gently handled the stuffed birds that surrounded him and studied the sketches he made of fox and deer and tiny hedgehog. In the cottage, in his company, his two daughters were treated equitably, with double doses of affection and patience.

Perhaps that was why she was resented so much by her legitimate sister. Perhaps that was where the trouble between them started.

"Lady Verity?"

"Forgive me, Dr. Willis. I am distracted thinking how ever so much more complicated my life will be than I had reason to expect."

"A strange place always challenges us, and we must rise to the occasion. I have every confidence in your abilities but felt the need to offer a word of caution."

"I thank you for your advice, sir."

"I thank you for your willingness to respect that advice. Not every lady I know would condescend to do so." He offered his arm, which Verity gratefully accepted for support and as a show of friendship.

"And do you know many ladies, sir?" she asked as they started to walk along the unsteady deck.

"I have met many ladies, though I'm inclined to remember their illnesses better than their faces."

Verity, as a maid, was better inclined to remember gowns and furbelows than faces. And, yes, she remembered rudeness, impatience, and some abuse at their hands.

"They would not be flattered to learn of this," Verity said, even as she knew the ladies would not care at all. Why would a lady of quality care in the least what a ship's doctor thought?

The sunlight slanted off the bridge and brightened Dr. Willis's face. Verity realized he was younger than she thought, and not at all bad looking. Perhaps if circumstances had been different, Miss Annie Merrill might have been interested in furthering their friendship. But Lady Verity Harwood had trapped herself into a corner; he was no match for a lady.

"It's not my intention to flatter, my lady. It is, however, my hope to be of service. And for you, I prescribe some new friendships on board the *Andromeda*. You and Miss Merrill remained very close to each other, I observed, and now you will be impatient to end your journey. Do you wish to meet some others? They will also find their trip hastened once they have the privilege of meeting you."

"That sounds very much like flattery, Dr. Willis." Verity blushed, so unaccustomed was she to receive words of such lofty praise. That they were truly not intended to flatter her real self was no obstacle to her delight. Her whole body was buoyed by the strength of it, and she held her face high into the wind.

They walked up the steep stairway to the upper deck, the small exclusive area she would not have dared to enter alone two days before. She knew who would be there, impressing the ladies and vying for their attention. But she scarcely expected Dr. Willis to steer her directly into Geoffrey Marsh's path.

"Aha! Behold my favorite patient!" Dr. Willis said cheerfully.

Mr. Marsh, his injured leg awkwardly stretched out on the low table in front of him, smiled broadly as he looked up.

"There is only one man on board who might say that, and I find him a man of infinite patience!" Mr. Marsh smiled at Verity. "Please forgive my pun, madam. I have little else to occupy my mind while I sit here bemoaning my sad fate."

"Do not apologize, Mr. Marsh," Verity said quickly, "and I hope your fate is only a temporary one."

"Ah, I forgot you were already acquainted, my lady," Dr. Willis murmured.

Verity looked into Mr. Marsh's sincere blue eyes, framed by skin crinkled with laugh lines, and wondered how much he remembered of their last meeting, when he was in so much pain.

"We met very briefly, sir, and had no time for conversation. We were both in some distress," Verity said.

"I was in distress, but not unconscious, my lady. I could not forget a meeting, however rushed, with the beautiful Lady Verity Harwood."

"Mr. Marsh," Dr. Willis said warningly. "Lady Verity has just buried her companion. This is not the time for flattery."

"It is quite all right, Dr. Willis," Verity said, and pulled her hand from his arm. "I believe flattery could be very comforting right now."

"Then as you both can manage very well without me, I will leave to look in on another patient," Dr. Willis said, sounding grateful to be done with the two of them. "You will find Mr. Marsh to be an excellent conversationalist." And with that, he bowed neatly, and left.

"Forgive me for not rising, my lady. You can understand the difficulty," Mr. Marsh said.

"It must be very painful," Verity answered sincerely. Pulling a chair close to his side, so they might talk without shouting into the wind, she sat down. "But perhaps, if you exercise your conversational skills, you would not lack for company."

"Mr. Marsh only lacks for company because he insisted we all leave him," another voice interrupted as a long shadow fell over the splinted leg. Verity tried to compose herself before she raised her eyes to Will Bentley.

"Ah, Mr. Bentley. Have you abandoned your agreeable companion? I am surprised, since Miss Compton seemed to feel it necessary to rely upon you for support. I cannot imagine how she gets on without you."

"Miss Compton manages very well. Just now she is managing very well with Lord Barrington, undoubtedly telling him about the dietary habits of the native Americans."

Verity wondered what he could possibly mean by this, but he sat down before she could respond. His brow was furrowed, and he made rather a big show of settling his long legs comfortably in the confined space of their small grouping of deck chairs. When he finally spoke, he seemed intensely serious, disconcertingly direct.

"I have met your father, my lady. I was in an audience to which he spoke, and I discovered he and I have much in common."

Dear God, but this was an unfortunate turn.

"Are you familiar with the mating habits of the wren, perhaps?"

Mr. Marsh laughed. "Oh, he is very familiar with mating habits!"

Bentley wisely ignored him. "I do not share your father's love of wildlife. We do, however, have a similar determination not to remain idle, as we prefer to be continually constructive. We are always fully engaged."

Verity envisioned her father in his little cottage, measuring the wingspan of little brown birds, and sighed. "Are you indeed? May I inquire what it is you do?"

"I am a writer of social commentary. I observe various customs and manners in both America and England and offer my opinions," Mr. Bentley admitted in the manner of a man who has been accused of spying.

"I see," Verity said slowly, though she was not sure she did at all. What could Mr. Bentley possibly have to say that might interest anyone enough to purchase an article or volume of his words? He certainly did not seem to have the wit of the famous Mr. Williams, whose thick volume of commentary she'd found among Lady Verity's possessions. "And you, Mr. Marsh? I hope you will tell me you are engaged in something very useful, like investing in railroads or something of that sort?"

Geoffrey Marsh winced, and Verity wondered if his ankle suddenly pained him.

"I am Mr. Bentley's personal secretary, Lady Verity."

Verity saw he did not like to admit it to her, and yet his more modest position would have made her favor him over his friend if his agreeable personality had not already done so. After all, she knew a great deal about sacrificing oneself for the benefit of another, a role demeaning to one's spirit and identity. She wondered if Mr. Marsh ever dreamed about changing places with his employer. Or murdering him.

She drew herself up sharply.

"Whatever do you expect to write about while in America, Mr. Bentley? I am sure most Englishmen are already passably familiar with the manners of our republican cousins. Or do you go after bigger game, and intend to write scathing reports about your President and parliament?"

"They call it a congress in America. I have already written extensively about the government in both countries." He studied his hands, and for the first time, Verity noticed the ink stains outlining his blunt fingernails. "The British audience is both attracted and repelled by life in America. It demands to hear the very worst, and yet many have some envy for those who live in the New World."

"It is a bit of a paradox," Mr. Marsh said. "Yet, it is very hard to find much to censure when walking the streets of Boston or New York."

"You look very severe, Lady Verity," Mr. Bentley said, ignoring his friend. He shifted in his seat so he was once again directly in her line of vision. "Do you not believe we might find great affection between rivals, even enemies? In this case, the relationship may better be compared to that of parent and child. The parent observes the behavior of youth and regrets the loss of inhibition and freedom. But the child understands the power that is his parents' and aspires to it. Every American child knows British history and can recite the names of Henry's six wives and offer a narrative of the Scottish intrigues."

Here, at least, Verity felt on safer ground. She had the advantage of the same governess as the former Lady Verity and proved a better student. And Miss

Drummond liked nothing better than to start each day with a cheerful recitation of the glories of England's past. Verity now realized, for the first time in her life, the texts they used might have been slightly prejudicial.

"On those themes, I believe there is very little remaining to be said," she said as if she knew. "But you tell me you are interested in recording present events, in our modern world of 1821. The people of whom you write are still very much alive. It is surely unkind to find fault with those who would suffer the consequences."

"Suffer the consequences?" Will Bentley's voice rose along with his dark brows. "Do you not think prejudice and thievery deserve some censure? While there is much that is admirable about the New World, there is much that is ridiculous. The same must be said for England. To expose such things could facilitate change." And then, as if an afterthought, "My lady."

Verity blushed and looked away. So unaccustomed was she to the deferential title, she had not even noticed the lack of its use. It was intended to be a token of deference, but when Mr. Bentley uttered it, it seemed scornful. Her first thought was that he secretly knew her for a fraud, but then, in the moments of silence that seemed was broad as the great ocean, she realized his more likely intent.

"Do you intend to make all of us the subject of your cynical pen, sir? An injured man, a harried ship's doctor, a silly young lady looking for diversion while on her way to her wedding. And a rather boring lady who has just lost her companion. What do you make of us? Nothing good, I daresay."

"My lady," Mr. Marsh began and raised a hand in

supplication. "I am sure my friend did not intend…"

"I do not find you at all boring, my lady, with or without poor Miss Merrill. The very fact you are on board this ship allows me to speculate there is a story waiting to be told," said Mr. Bentley.

Verity cautioned herself to remain silent, to ignore the provocation, to just walk away from a business she would prefer to avoid. But Mr. Marsh was not so reticent.

"Whatever do you mean, Will?" he asked. "Is a lady not permitted a sea voyage? Is she not entitled to adventure, as are young men?"

Mr. Bentley looked down at his friend, in both senses of the word. "This is not a trip for recreational pleasure, nor one any lady of quality would undertake. Therefore, I suspect Lady Verity needed to escape society or family or a young man whose attentions she found officious."

"You are insulting, sir," she said, her voice cracking with emotion.

"But even if my speculations are wrong, there is something else troubling me about your character."

"My character is none of your business."

"Everything on this ship is the business of a writer, Lady Verity. If we didn't make the world and its people our business, there would be too many essays about a favorite cat or the pleasures of a sunny afternoon." Mr. Bentley withdrew a notebook from a pocket within his jacket. To Verity, it seemed as dangerous as a dagger. "What do you have to say about your dear friend, Miss Merrill? Can there be true friendship when one is so elevated above the other? Did you expect to act as equals once in America, or would she remain your maid?"

Geoffrey Marsh cleared his throat.

Verity knew her story would be examined very closely and was determined to get it right. "This presumes that Annie Merrill wanted us to live as equals. Certainly it is a tantalizing notion, but one we will never be able to confirm. I can tell you that poor Annie was a very modest and unassuming girl and probably never aspired to be more than my companion. I can also tell you that when she fell ill, I feared she would not get the medical attention she deserved. Though she was very dear to me, we both understood that there were those who would treat us unequally."

"I believe you said you were distantly related. Was she a poor cousin or something of that sort?"

"Miss Merrill? Something like that, and yet even closer. Her dear mother, a lovely woman, was the housekeeper at Harwood, and we grew up together." Verity wiped her eyes on her sleeve, quite forgetting herself.

Mr. Bentley did not seem to notice. "And you remained friends and companions. Is that not odd, Lady Verity? That the daughter of a housekeeper should be the close companion and confidante to the daughter of an earl?"

"It may not be as rare as you think, Mr. Bentley. Gentlemen may decide on a moment's whim to travel to town or escape to an estate at the seaside. The whole business is far more cumbersome for women, and we enjoy our comforts of home. Therefore, we are content to remain in a small society, such as that which we enjoyed in Harwood. If one is too particular about friendships, one may find oneself completely alone."

Verity thought she made a pretty case, and yet knew the truth of the matter: her lady barely tolerated her and confided nothing. "As I am now."

"We are your new friends, Lady Verity," said Geoffrey Marsh.

"Dear Mr. Marsh," Verity said gently. "That is very kind, but we are yet barely acquaintances and not likely to meet ever again."

"Did you not just explain how friendships might flourish in small societies?" Mr. Bentley said, leaning slightly toward her.

"They might, if one feels a natural affinity…or affection," said Verity. Her voice trailed off as she noticed a slight deformity in one of his eyes, as the black of his pupil slashed through the brown of the iris. She was fascinated by this, until she realized his unblinking gaze suggested a fascination with her.

She leaned back. How well would her masquerade show up to close scrutiny? Verity and Annie spent all of their twenty-four years mistaken for each other, but surely when one was close enough to notice the absence of a birthmark or the slight twist to a tooth or the scarcity of fingers, the ruse would be revealed. Whom should she avoid in the future?

"I am cousin to Lord Eastbourne, my lady," Mr. Bentley said casually. Verity thought she would be ill. "I met your father not only at a lecture but also last year, when I was a guest at Eastbourne Abbey. The properties adjoin, do they not? So, indeed, you must be friends with my cousin and his wife as well?"

Verity looked past him, calculating an escape. How was it possible that the man was related to the person who might be the very reason for their flight from

Harwood, the married man with whom the real Lady Verity was intimate? Did Mr. Bentley read her mind? Eastbourne was one of the few who would know her for a fraud.

"We are scarcely acquainted, my lord," Verity said, and it was true.

"Oh, come. Did you not just remark on the pleasures of small society? I believe we met whilst having dinner with Lord Eastbourne, so you must be more than casually acquainted with each other."

"Your cousin is a pompous windbag who is overly fond of killing small animals," said Mr. Marsh. "I can understand why Lady Verity would wish to avoid the acquaintance, for it would never lead to friendship. I see no reason to doubt Verity."

"Very clever, my friend," said Mr. Bentley, his eyes still on Verity. "It is an excellent lesson. We shall not doubt Verity. Lady Verity, of course."

"I am sure I have given you no reason to doubt me," she said softly.

He said nothing, and she had the uncomfortable feeling he was reading her as he might a very difficult book, taking stock of every nuance, pausing over every difficult word. What had Eastbourne told him? Why did he not reveal the relationship before this? And why bring it up now?

Verity silently vowed to avoid the company of these two men for the remainder of their journey. As if Mr. Bentley's rudeness and Mr. Marsh's familiarity were not enough, anything that could connect Lady Verity to Eastbourne was a dangerous business. As for now, they could depart this ship and Mr. Bentley need not say anything more to his cousin than that they shared a few conversations and that she looked well, despite the loss of her poor companion. Lord Eastbourne might or might not be interested, but his indifference to her well-being would be well calculated.

"I must leave you now, gentlemen. While the light is strong, as it is now, I like to write in my journal," she said and smiled as if it had been the most pleasant of interviews.

But she said the wrong thing.

"A journal. Are you a fellow rhetorician, Lady Verity?" Mr. Bentley asked. The dark scar on his iris seemed to contract.

"I write but am scarcely a skilled practitioner. I daresay we have very little in common. You write for financial gain, do you not? And I write because I choose to do so and preserve memories that are precious. I have just lost someone who was dear to me. I must record my own reflections for future meditation."

He did not answer at once, and Verity should have made good her escape. But she knew he was readying a retort, and she had to admit a faint curiosity to hear it.

"Do you consider me less a gentleman because I enjoy some useful employment? I am in a sorry position if that is so, my lady. For you will find in America they would think me less a man if I did not." Mr. Bentley glanced at his friend, who answered him with a grin. "It seems I cannot satisfy everybody."

It was a harmless remark, tossed off by a man who was both ironic and astute. But something in his tone and in the way he looked at her made Verity's heart start to race. He was someone to avoid; she did not want to think about satisfaction and Will Bentley in the same sentence. But that he could satisfy her, in the way Lord Eastbourne satisfied Lady Verity, she did not doubt.

"I feel for you, Mr. Bentley, I truly do. Perhaps you can seek out Miss Compton. For you seemed to do very well with her," Verity said.

Bentley made a gesture of impatience, and Verity remembered something of his roughness and strength at their first encounter. She wondered how far she might provoke him.

"Miss Compton's satisfaction is no concern of mine," he said tersely.

"More's the pity," she answered. It really was time to break away. "But there are other ladies present in our little society on the *Andromeda*. And there are lots of good fish in the sea. Take care if you decide to swim amongst them."

She steadied herself before she started down the salty, wet stairs and did not look back. In most circumstances, she would have considered that she went out on the last word, but she knew it was not true in this case.

Even as she made her way to the cabin, Verity knew Will Bentley, he who fancied himself an equal to Mr. Williams, would add a page to his book this day. He surely would have much to say about ladies who were provincial and snobbish, and who could not be bothered to make the friendship of his beloved cousin.

Chapter 3

Will watched the gentle sway of Lady Verity's body until she disappeared from view below the deck and wondered what it would be like to swim with her. Not in the treacherous ocean, but in the clean, still lake at Hudson Point. And yet, one never knew where dangers lurked, and he was certain the lovely Lady Verity was deeper and darker than she seemed to be.

He tucked away his journal, vowing to write nothing until he sorted it all out. He could understand why a lady would not admit to a relationship with his wretched cousin, and yet had she not already done so to everyone else in the *ton*? The dinner party at Eastbourne Abbey, at which a belligerent Lady Verity demanded precedence over Lady Eastbourne, was already legendary in some circles and very likely the reason why Harwood needed to get his daughter out of the country. Could she imagine that a cousin of Lord Eastbourne would not know of her disgrace?

She must know that he would know. Her discomfort in his presence, bordering on rudeness, was evidence enough of that. She could not know it was mere coincidence that they were both sailing on the *Andromeda* and would therefore find his writing doubly suspicious.

And yet, there was something strangely innocent in her character, a sweetness he had not sensed in her the one and only time they met. Lady Eastbourne had hosted a picnic about a year ago, and he would have avoided the party if he had any hope of doing so. But he was traveling through and staying with his cousin, who promised him an introduction to the loveliest lady of his acquaintance. Since Will had been introduced to Lady Eastbourne some years before, he wondered at his cousin's bold pronouncement. He could only imagine Eastbourne was doing a bit of matchmaking on his behalf.

It was not the case. Lady Verity ignored everyone at the party but Eastbourne himself. Their flirtation was bold and frankly embarrassing. Lady Eastbourne looked the other way and departed early, pleading a sudden onset of a headache. Lady Verity and Eastbourne spent some time behind a very large bush, where she somehow managed to lose several hairpins and her bonnet.

Will was disgusted, both with the lady and his cousin. And yet the sight of her, with her auburn hair spilling about her shoulders and her lips reddened by something more than the strawberries they ate, haunted him for these many months. Once he got past his initial surprise upon seeing her again, he remembered her well.

Surely it was part of her insulting manner that she now claimed not to remember him at all.

"Do you suppose an English lady might throw off her inhibitions and find comfort in the company of a poor secretary?" Geoff asked.

"Whatever do you mean?" Will said. "I pay you very well."

Geoff laughed. "That you do. But I remain poor in

the way of titles, which is the consequence of being an American. You, on the other hand, have English relatives and expectations. They are sure to impress a lady."

"And yet you see they do not. Lady Verity can barely tolerate my company, and for that I am sorry. You might have made some progress with her if I had not shown up when I did."

"That is small comfort, indeed. She could barely take her eyes off you. I have seen that expression before, though you always seem indifferent to such interest."

"The lady did tap your shoulder, which is a rather familiar gesture. Perhaps she is already enjoying American freedoms." Will paused, appreciating the irony of his statement, because Lady Verity seemed to enjoy at least one too many English freedoms as well. "But if titles concern you, why not do as many of our countrymen do?"

"Whatever do you mean? Should I attempt to purchase one?"

"Nothing so expensive, my friend. In America, it seems every other man is a colonel or major. One would think half the population of our cities is composed of military leaders. Since it cannot be true, why not just assume a title? Major Geoffrey Marsh sounds very grand."

"It makes me sound like one of the old fools who bore the ladies at dinner parties," Geoff grumbled.

"It is the privilege of military honor, real or imagined."

Geoff held out his hand as he struggled to his feet. Will pulled him up slowly and made certain he was steady before releasing him.

"And now you have a war wound. I understand ladies are likely to be very sympathetic to a gentleman with a limp," said Will, already thinking about an essay he might write on the subject.

"It would have been a good deal easier to pretend to have an injury than actually have one. I would not have to suffer so."

"Well, take heart. You might feel a good deal better by the time we arrive in Boston, and then you may play act your way to Cincinnati."

"Ah, yes. If I do not leave you before then," said Geoff, gripping the railing.

Will thought he held the bar with something of the same desperation that Lady Verity exhibited minutes before. He recalled the image of her small hands clutching the rail for balance, her delicate fingers folded over each other. And then, oddly, he remembered noticing her hands when first they met, the year before. At the time, he thought them only slightly less attractive than her behavior toward his cousin. What was it about them that should make him think of them now?

"Have I worried you?" Geoff asked.

Will shook his head, as much to dispel the image as to contradict his friend. "Not at all. But why would you leave me before we arrive at our destination?"

Geoff shrugged his shoulders. "Perhaps I will marry before then and never leave my home again. I think I should enjoy living in Cambridge under such circumstances."

"You will not be able to support her if you no longer have employment."

"I am sure I can find employment or be fortunate in

finding a wife who has sufficient resources for us both."

"You are thinking of Lady Verity, I suppose."

"And you are not?" Geoff waved him off as Will reached out a steadying hand. "And are you not aware what we are facing in Cincinnati?"

"Mrs. Frances Trollope, who is a bit of a bear," Will said. Mrs. Trollope was already a well-known Englishwoman who had cut a wide swath through the cities and countryside of America. His cousin, Eastbourne, suggested that she might be a valuable source of information for his book on the western territories and provided a letter of introduction.

"Cincinnati is famous for its stockyards of hogs and the serving of ham for breakfast, luncheon, and dinner. I was there years ago."

"But Mrs. Trollope is rather grand, Eastbourne tells me. She's apparently too grand for her own husband, whom she left behind in London. She may not have known the situation when she decided to open her famous Bazaar in Cincinnati," Will said thoughtfully. He started down the narrow stairs ahead of his friend, so if Geoff slipped he could shield him from disaster.

"Lady Verity could be a cheerful respite from the weariness of travel," said Geoff.

"I doubt Lady Verity would wish to be called a respite," Will said. He thought she would rather be called Lady Eastbourne.

"Then I wonder how the name Mrs. Marsh might sit with her," Geoff said, and repeated it twice, for good measure.

\*\*\*\*

She was doomed. What did they do to thieves in America? She was sure she heard they were sent to live in malarial swamplands or worse. Perhaps just living in America was punishment enough; had not the former Lady Verity threatened her with it every time Annie allowed the fire to burn down in the grate or pulled her mistress's bonnet ribbons a bit too tight?

But was the theft of identity as egregious as the theft of property?

Verity recalled that Shakespeare believed it so. And surely it could hardly matter, for once the *Andromeda* arrived in port, she would have to borrow freely from Lady Verity's resources.

She was a thief. And she was doomed.

How had she thought she could get away with this masquerade? One needed cunning and determination and a great deal of luck. She somehow imagined she possessed the first two, but she had not reckoned with the absurd coincidence of the presence of Eastbourne's cousin on board this very ship.

Perhaps it was not a coincidence.

Again, it did not matter. Verity resolved to stay as far removed from Will Bentley as possible in such a close environment, for she did not doubt he would expose her in an instant if he could confirm the truth of her identity. Indeed, he seemed so rash in judgment she imagined he might expose her merely on an intuitive hunch she was not whom she claimed, and suffer the consequences.

But of course, it would be she who would suffer. And bitterly so.

Her resolution ought to make her feel somewhat safer as they approached the shores of America, but she was not at all content. For one, she would have liked to spend some time with Mr. Marsh, who seemed pleasant enough and for whom she felt a natural sympathy. But as friendship with him would put her in the path of Mr. Bentley, she dare not make any advances toward him.

The second source of her unhappiness was less easy to reconcile. For, even as she told herself she must avoid Mr. Bentley, she thought about him all the time, imagined him in her dreams, and revisited the spirited words they already shared. Never before had she met a man who intrigued her more, who treated her as an intelligent, thinking person even as he goaded her, who stimulated all her senses all at once. Including some she never realized she had.

But never before had she been Lady Verity Harwood, a person who might attract the attention of intelligent, thinking men.

Her unbidden thoughts were quickly dismissed even as they continued to surface, for Verity could not imagine a more unlikely liaison in the whole of human history.

She had another, more immediate reason to set her mind on a straight course, however. What she had begun on a daring impulse must necessarily be carried out with utmost care and consideration. She had left England as Annie Merrill but would arrive in America as Lady Verity Harwood, and only a great deal of skill would allow her to continue her impersonation with any degree of success. Funds would need to be borrowed until she could manage to earn something on her own, and she must correspond with her father, lest he think anything amiss. With a sinking feeling, Verity realized he might very well insist she return home immediately, for the impropriety of a woman traveling alone in the United States would be apparent even to him. She could neglect to tell him of Annie's death, but he might learn the truth from his neighbor, who would learn the truth from Mr. Bentley. Of course, if Lady Verity had already secured another companion, there would be no cause for concern.

Unless her father did not approve of her choice.

She might allow his letters to go astray.

But then she could not petition for more funds.

And to claim those funds would make her a thief.

Shouts on deck startled her out of her reverie, and she glanced through the salt-sprayed porthole. She saw nothing unusual but two gulls riding the wind, their wings dipping in unison.

It took a moment for her overtaxed mind to absorb the vision, and then her voice cried out with the others. Reaching for her woolen cape, she pushed against the door and spilled out onto the deck in a distinctly unladylike manner. But it did not matter who saw her now.

"Is that the port of Boston?" she asked breathlessly of the first person who passed. It did not look very impressive, as not more than a dozen structures stood upon a bluff. But after her sojourn at sea, Verity would have been contented with Mr. Crusoe's island and happy to call her journey at an end.

The man she hailed paused and squinted out toward the shore, as if noticing it for the first time. She studied his profile and realized she had noticed him several times before, always in proximity to her cabin. He must be a near neighbor.

"Indeed, it is not, my lady," he said in a Yorkshire accent. "You be looking at Provincetown, a tidy fishing village. If it is Boston you want, you have time enough to pack up your bags. We have to round the bay before entering the harbor and may not see landfall until late this afternoon."

"Oh, dear." Verity sighed, unable to hide her disappointment, nor really account for it. But her anxiety to escape the ship did not make her entirely sensible.

"Will someone leave without you if you do not arrive in port this day?" he asked.

"Who can leave the ship? Is such a thing possible?" Verity asked anxiously. The idea seemed suddenly very tantalizing.

"Now, settle down, my lady," the man said familiarly. "No one jumps ship in these waters. I only meant, is someone waiting for you in Boston?"

"I do not know," Verity admitted.

"Then allow me to assist you. My name is John Reese, and I am well-connected in the city. I have friends, business partners, and know of good accommodations. I would be happy to show you—"

"My Lady Verity is already spoken for, Mr. Reese," said a deep voice behind her. "I am certain she will have little time to spare for your excellent company."

Verity did not turn around but instead watched the changing expressions of Mr. Reese's face. His smile, at first so sympathetic and inviting, now seemed a little bitter and even cruel. She wondered what he had done to earn Mr. Bentley's distrust.

While she studied him, he watched her in his turn. "And yet the lady seems a bit surprised by your announcement, Bentley. Perhaps you did not inform her of your intentions? Or, more likely, she does not welcome them?"

Verity felt Will Bentley step closer, until he stood just at her shoulder. She smelled the vague odor of tobacco on his clothes, though she had not ever seen him with a pipe, and the more pleasing scent of citrus. Her logic told her she ought to refute his arrogant assertions. But, unbidden, came the impulse to lean back against him and find comfort in the warmth of his lean body.

"If there is one thing I have learned in my travels, Mr. Reese, it is that a lady never likes to be told what to do. Indeed, I would not presume to speak on her behalf. But it is my friend, Mr. Marsh, who has it all arranged, for his sister awaits us on shore. She is to be Lady Verity's companion, you understand."

"And you have accepted this arrangement, Lady Verity?" Mr. Reese asked with a keen edge of sarcasm in his voice. "You did not seem so certain of it only a few moments ago."

Indeed, Verity reflected, she did not seem so certain of anything then. But, increasingly, things became startlingly clear.

"You must forgive Lady Verity, Mr. Reese. For, as I am sure you already know, she lost her own dear companion on this very voyage. It must be the cause of her present distraction; I am not sure I would display half her composure after the death of so close a friend."

"You recall, Bentley, I have had the pleasure of sitting down to cards with you. I daresay you would exhibit supreme composure even if someone amputated your limbs," retorted Mr. Reese.

"An interesting theory, sir. I hope you do not intend to put me to the test," Mr. Bentley said coldly.

Mr. Reese looked sorely tempted, but Verity saw how he began to back off. His eyes narrowed, and he bowed his head slightly. But it was just enough to dismiss him gracefully.

"I thank you for your concern, Mr. Reese, and for your kind offers on my behalf. I will not forget your offer of friendship and may very well rely upon your help if my arrangement with Mr. Marsh's sister does not suit me," Verity said sincerely. She felt some pity for the man; indeed, she felt pity for anyone up against Will Bentley. Including herself.

"Good day, my lady," Mr. Reese said, deferentially. "It shall be a good day if we make landfall in Boston."

"I could not agree with you more." Verity smiled encouragingly, watching him edge away. As soon as he turned his back on her, she pivoted on her heel.

"It shall be an even better day if you mind your own business, Mr. Bentley. I have no intention of following your direction or anyone else's in the path I will follow in America. I trust you no more than you trust Mr. Reese and—"

"How do you know I do not trust Reese?" Mr. Bentley asked quietly and leaned his elbows against the rail.

Verity caught her breath and copied his gesture. She was not sorry for it: the sand dunes of the Massachusetts shore glistened in the sunshine, and here and there tiny human forms punctuated the white expanse.

"You made it fairly clear, I think. Though I cannot imagine the cause of your distrust. He seemed a very pleasant sort and made me a very kind offer of assistance. I would have been happy to oblige."

"I daresay you would have," Will Bentley said between clenched teeth. "Do you have any idea what sort of connections John Reese owns in Boston? The people with whom he does business?"

"Of course I do not! I only just met him when you blundered onto the scene in your usual self-righteous style! Mr. Reese tried to be helpful, and I would have taken his words under advisement if you had not interfered in business so wholly unconnected to yourself," Verity argued and gulped in large breaths of sea air. Pausing only to swallow, she turned on him once again. "Did you not preface your rude remarks to him by pointing out how you would never presume to speak for a lady? What nonsense! You are the first to break your own rules!"

"Perhaps it is because I make up the rules as I go," he murmured so softly Verity could not be sure she heard him correctly.

"And I have every inclination to do what pleases me," Verity went on heedlessly.

"Indeed, my Lady Verity? Sometimes the pursuit of pleasure can lead to unfortunate circumstances. Your new friend is known as a courier of information, someone who is hired to deliver ransom money and bribes, and occasionally escorts individuals from one port of call to another. One might say his currency is human lives. Perhaps this journey is intended entirely as a pleasure trip, but I sincerely doubt it. I do not know what his interest is in you, but I have a keen suspicion and I do not trust him." He turned to look at her, and she saw his concern. "You should not trust him either."

"Thank you, Mr. Bentley, but I am sure Mr.

Reese's interest in me is a matter of happenstance. We simply were in the same place at the same time and began to talk, much as you and I are doing right now. Is there any reason why I should trust you more than him?"

"I think you will need to trust someone while in America, for it can be a very strange place for an unescorted English lady to navigate. You will not be afforded the same privileges to which you are accustomed, for all women are ladies in America. Nor can you quite believe everything you hear, for there are those who would take advantage of your innocence."

"I am not so very innocent," Verity protested.

He continued to study her. "No, perhaps not. But you have already revealed to Mr. Reese that you are somewhat uncertain about your reception in America. Such an admission makes you an easy mark."

"Why might you—or Mr. Reese—imagine I am the least bit uncertain?"

Unexpectedly, he grabbed Verity's shoulders and turned her full around to face him. He was not at all gentle and yet his gesture felt comforting and encouraging. A familiar longing swept over her: the need to make intimate contact with another human being, even in circumstances as unhappy as this. Verity leaned her head back, feeling her windblown hair loosen onto her shoulders, and looked into his strange dark eyes.

"You could not, unfortunately, have made it more clear, my dear lady," he said gently. "Your confusion, your doubts even about your journey to those who would shelter you, and your obvious guilt about the death of your friend make your uncertainty plain to those who would use you to their advantage."

"I suppose the mind's construction is, indeed, all too readily read in the face," Verity admitted, for she knew not else what to say. It seemed impossible to fight him, or argue with one so astute. "But while you have given me suspicions of Mr. Reese's intent, I have no reason to trust your own motives."

"What makes you think I have any motives as concerns you, Lady Verity?"

"You seemed all too sure of your intent when you rebuffed Mr. Reese. Or is your talk about Mr. Marsh's sister as vaporous as class in America?"

He released her shoulders, and Verity shivered in the stiff breeze.

"Miss Eleanor Marsh is real enough, as are the discussions I have had with her brother about the possibility of allowing you to travel with us with Nell as your companion."

Verity looked at him in disbelief.

"Your arrogance does not cease to amaze me, Mr. Bentley. Surely you might have imagined I should have been a participant in such a discussion, especially as it concerns me? In any case, I might have saved you much time, for I would never agree to it."

"But why not? Mr. Marsh and I plan to travel to the Western territories, past Albany, Buffalo, and through to Cincinnati. I am writing a book, as well you know, and require the assistance of my secretary. Geoffrey, due to his injury, imagines some difficulties along the way. His sister, just out of school, longs for adventure and often begs to come with us." While reciting the steps of his argument, Mr. Bentley recounted each on his long, thin fingers. As he raised the smallest one,

Verity saw it was bent at an odd angle, but functioned just the same. "Nell cannot come unescorted."

Cincinnati! The very place where she was to present herself to Mrs. Trollope!

Reluctant to sound utterly delighted at the coincidence, Verity raised her own finger. "And so you imagine I have nothing to do but to chaperone a young girl so she might travel in your company?"

For once, Bentley looked disconcerted. He frowned a little sheepishly, revealing a dimple along the line of one cheek. "As to that, I guess you and she are very much of an age, as were you and Miss Merrill. And if you are setting out in somewhat of the same destination and no clear plan how to manage it, the arrangement would not be unfavorable to you, I think."

Verity caught her breath, realizing what he proposed might well be the solution to her current predicament. If they could only get her to Mrs. Trollope and at reasonable expense, she might have some hope to succeed in America and never have to reveal the truth about her masquerade. But in the teeth of Mr. Bentley's warnings about opportunists such as Mr. Reese, and in light of the uncomfortable relationship they already shared, Verity could not bring herself to be so acquiescent.

"You are wrong, sir, as you are about so many things. The arrangement is distinctly unfavorable, because it involves remaining in your company longer than necessary."

"I hoped Mr. Marsh's presence might mitigate your strong feelings on the subject."

Verity believed it did, though not for the reasons Mr. Bentley suspected. And so anxious was she to find refuge in the strange new land, she was tempted to agree. But then she remembered herself, and who she now was.

"Are you suggesting I have any interest in your friend but as a sympathetic companion? You may remember, sir, I am a lady of England."

" 'Tis a pity, then, the king himself could not accompany you on your journey, for I doubt anyone else worthy of your notice," Mr. Bentley said nastily. "But might I point out that inasmuch as you are immune to our charms, the propriety of the arrangement is virtually assured?"

His argument was nearly unanswerable. And indeed, it exempted Verity from very real concerns she might otherwise have. If she maintained her lofty masquerade, she might manage to travel with impunity. If she did not, she would be no worse off and possibly a lot closer to her destination.

"I should like to meet Miss Marsh," she said, without actually agreeing with him.

"I believe she would very much like to meet you, my lady. The last titled lady who circulated in our company in Boston proved to be a scullery maid from Basingstoke. I am sure Nell would enjoy making comparisons with the genuine article."

Verity's face grew very warm, and she turned back to face the distant shore.

"You have ventured outdoors without your bonnet, Lady Verity, and the sun will burn your skin if I keep you much longer. The first rule you must learn about New England is that the climate is much warmer here than in Old England, and we do not get nearly as much rain. Our crops thrive, and so do freckles upon our ladies' cheeks."

"You are too familiar, sir," Verity said, and blushed all the more.

"I daresay you will get used to it, Lady Verity. As you will the freckles and the sunshine."

"Somehow I doubt it, sir. Certain things are too intrusive to ever admit happily into one's company," Verity said coyly.

Will Bentley did not answer, and Verity slanted a glance upward to his face. His eyes narrowed against the sun, his dark hair blowing wildly in the breeze, and he looked as impenetrable as the future.

\*\*\*\*

"Where in hell are my inks?" Will muttered as he dove into a pile of unwashed shirts tossed upon the narrow desk. "If they are beneath this mess, I will need to return to the shirtmaker on Milk Street, or else dye the whole lot black."

Geoffrey Marsh put down his thrice-read broadside and glanced up at his friend.

"I suspect your inks are in the top drawer of the cabinet. Where you placed them yesterday," he said pointedly. "If you continue at this level of anxiety, my friend, you shall accomplish nothing and still be packing your belongings when the *Andromeda* sets sail to return to Liverpool. What, I wonder, might be the cause of it all?"

Will paused on his way to the cabinet and straightened his back. After these weeks at sea, it would be a pleasure to stretch his body in the wide open spaces of the American landscape.

"There is no cause. I am merely looking forward to exercising my sea legs upon solid ground. We have only an hour or so before we make landfall, and I wish to be the first man off the ship."

"Nell will like that. I suspect she harbors some vague admiration for you and hopes it might be mutual," said Geoff, as he started to fold the broadside into a pleated fan. "I promise I shall not be the one to tell her of your sudden interest in a lady who turns away every time you approach and who barely manages a polite word in your company."

Will thought about holding Lady Verity in his arms, so she could not turn away from him, and how he already wrung a few polite words from her tempting lips. It was not something he cared to explain to Geoff. "I am very fond of Nell; she knows it as well as you. But I am far too old for her and would never suit."

"Ah yes. I forget you are all of three months older than I. And it is true most men of twenty-seven or so would scarcely consider a woman seven years their junior. Absolutely unsuitable." Geoff fanned himself gently. "Do I recall your own father was nearly twice the age of your mother? By all reports their marriage was admirable."

Will nodded, recognizing defeat. But reason argued that it was not a calculation of years that measured compatibility, but a shared sensibility, a certain appreciation of like experiences. Dear Nell would always be a little girl to him, though her hair would eventually grow gray and her complexion pale. Other women, not much older, seemed worlds apart.

"But I do not intend to press my sister's interests, no matter how well they might suit my own. She could do a lot better than you, I daresay, for though you are connected to some excellent people, I do not consider a traveling writer any great recommendation for a prospective husband."

"Indeed, Nell deserves a good, steady sort of man. Someone who is tied to his property, perhaps. A farmer or a scholar. A man who raises sheep."

Geoff smiled and raised his dark brows. "Some would consider such an existence Elysian."

"Some do not find adventure in plowing the same fields year after year."

"I am right, then. My sister requires someone who is steady and reliable. Unlike yourself," Geoff said and shifted in his seat. Will hoped he would forget about the other thing, so their discussion might be deferred until later, but luck was not his today. "However this does nothing to explain the reason for your certain agitation. I do not credit the business of thumping about on dry land. I can only then suppose it has something to do with the lady."

Will took exaggerated care removing the bottles of ink from the drawer and pushing in their corks.

"And of whom do you speak?" he asked casually, though he knew he could not escape Geoff's inquisition.

"I certainly do not mean Miss Compton, for I am sure you spared her hardly a moment's thought since you were introduced. She is a pretty piece of fluff, to be certain, but so airy as to vanish altogether when out of your presence," Geoff said, and rattled the fan again. "Of course, I am speaking of Lady Verity Harwood. I daresay you attempted to make your farewell, perhaps dared a bit too much, and the lady rebuffed you. Such an explanation would satisfy my present inquiry."

Will smiled back, thinking how his friend knew

him so well, he might consider writing his books for him. Nothing escaped Geoff's notice, even when the man was confined to a chair.

"It certainly would satisfy if it were only true."

"You did not seek out the lady?" Geoff asked, a note of uncertainty in his voice.

"I sought her out and even managed to save her from the grasp of John Reese. But I did not say farewell."

Geoff looked up from the chair, the fan now abandoned next to his outstretched knee.

"Out with it, Will. You cannot be so distracted for nothing."

"I invited Lady Verity to join us in our westward travels." Will wrapped the ink bottles between sheets of waxed parchment and set them snugly in his writing case. "She has not actually consented, but I daresay she will soon see the beauty of the plan."

"As you have also seen the beauty of it. Or of her, I should say. You propose to marry her then?" Geoff sounded a bit disgruntled, perhaps believing he would soon be looking for employment.

"Marry her? Even if I were so inclined to align myself with such a harpy, why do you think she would be the slightest bit tempted to accept me? Are we not forever being reminded of her rank and position?"

"Hardly at all, I would say. But you are not without your own credentials."

Will waved off his friend's words. "She scorns me for the manner in which I choose to occupy myself. In any case, marriage was not my intent."

"How, then, do you expect a lady to travel with us? I believe the sea journey has addled your brain."

"I have offered Nell's services as a companion for her. Nell has often asked to join us on our journeys. What better way to include her within the bounds of propriety?" Will paused and listened to the echo of his own words. Indeed, though he may have doubted it at first, the logic of his argument seemed to be reasonably strong. In time, he might come to believe it himself.

"I see," said Geoffrey, undoubtedly seeing a damned sight too much. "Lady Verity gets an escort for as far as she will travel with us. My sister gets to accompany us, as she has always desired. I get two assistants, to ease my way with this blasted ankle. But what does William Bentley get? Aside from the obvious?"

Will decided to ignore the jibe. It would not do to let even his best friend see how very much he desired Lady Verity Harwood, for it went against any logic, or sense, or motive. "William Bentley, writer of fame and fortune, gets a new hook on which to hang his wearisome thesis. Think, man. Instead of recording, in acute detail, my impressions of our travels, and finding insights that should be apparent to any thinking person, I can write about our experiences through the eyes of another. Would not our readers be fascinated to learn how an English lady regards American customs?"

Geoff let out a long breath, and Will knew his friend was convinced of nothing.

"You, yourself, know how recalcitrant Lady Verity can be. Do you not suspect she will falsify her answers for the purpose of confounding you? I believe her very capable of it," Geoff argued.

Will had not considered that and had to admit to himself the likelihood of such an occurrence. "We shall have to keep our business quiet, then. We can safely interview her, and I will write down her words later."

"And what do you think will be her reaction when she discovers this, after you are published in a dozen languages?"

"If she is as much a lady as she says, I will wager she reads very little. She certainly has read nothing to prepare her for her journey to America. Why, even Miss Compton read my *Atlantic Travels* and took some lessons from it. Lady Verity would have done well to do the same."

"Perhaps she does not like your style."

Will smiled ruefully. "I am almost sure of it."

"And how do you know she is not here in America to write her own impressions for a volume?" Geoff asked.

Will looked at him in surprise. He had not thought of that possibility.

"I believe it highly unlikely, Geoff. If the lady does not read much, she does not write. And if she does not write, she would not find any pleasure in the excruciating practice of putting pen to paper and taxing her mind with reminisces of her observations."

"You feel certain of this?"

"As certain as I am of anything. As sure as she is a lady. As sure as she will torment me all the way to Cincinnati."

"Well, then, what would you have me do?"

Will smiled, knowing he had finally won his friend over.

"I would have you make the introduction to your sister and urge the relationship upon them. The farther away Lady Verity is from my person, the more agreeable she is likely to be to the arrangement."

And the more sensible shall I be, he added to himself.

****

Verity stood on the deck of the *Andromeda* and braced herself for the impact of the ship hitting the wharf. A dozen shouting men were already prepared for her entry into the port of Boston and eased the vessel in with an efficiency that spoke of skill and many years of practice.

Satisfied she truly stood at the end of her strange sea journey, Verity studied the myriad faces uplifted at the dock, awaiting the welcome of loved ones, and the sight and sound of the large city beyond them.

Here was Boston, at last. Brightly colored buildings lined the wharf, and carriages and wagons stood ready to receive the *Andromeda*'s burden. The masts of other tall ships punctuated the darkening sky, their sails bunched beneath them. Large, open crates were piled on end down the length of the wharf. Nearby, on the wet sand, a rotting carcass of some great fish almost spoiled the sense of vibrancy of the place but could not truly discourage Verity's otherwise strong impressions. She had arrived.

"It is extraordinary, is it not?" said a familiar voice.

"Oh, Mr. Reese. It is you again." Verity edged a little away from him. "It is rather wonderful, though nothing to Liverpool, I believe."

"Have a care not to let your new friends hear such sentiments," Mr. Reese whispered. "Most Americans will allow for no improvement over what they have here and no world better than this one."

"Indeed, that sounds very true to Mr. Bentley. I am

sure no opinion is ever better than his own."

"You know him well, my lady?"

"Well enough on so short an acquaintance," Verity answered truthfully. "Well enough to know we are unlikely to ever improve upon our relationship."

"I wonder, then, why you align yourself with him."

"The alignment is not between us, but between Mr. Marsh's sister and myself. Such a relationship should prove entirely satisfactory."

"I am glad you believe so. Let me say, however, if you ever find yourself in irreconcilable straits, I can introduce you to many people who might prove worthy of your friendship."

Verity studied his face but could find no trace of irony there. Of course, she only had Mr. Bentley's word on the man's scruples, and they might prove to be no worse than her own.

Verity sighed, realizing the little trap she set for herself. Her scruples? The scruples of a woman who would pose as another and conceal the death of a lady from those who would rightfully mourn her? She was a fool if she imagined she truly proved any better than a man who traded in people's lives and other people's interests. What she did was criminal, whereas Mr. Reese undoubtedly worked within the law.

"Ah, I see our friend is fast approaching. Or approaching as fast as he could with a cripple in tow. I applaud your patience, Lady Verity. The thought of accommodating a man with an injured ankle on so arduous a journey makes me already weary. But I wish you the best of luck."

"I thank you, sir," Verity said, and turned toward her approaching companions. Had they not looked something like this when first they met on the salt-sprayed deck? Will Bentley, the taller and leaner, burdened by supporting the weight of his good friend, but managing it all with physical—if not conversational—grace? Now, it seemed, she knew them so much better.

And perhaps would know them better still.

"Farewell," she began, but when she looked around, it seemed Mr. Reese already managed to escape. As she would not.

"Welcome to America!" Mr. Marsh cried gleefully. His friend grumbled something under his breath. "Is it not as beautiful as I promised?"

"It is certainly lively," Verity admitted and caught him under his free elbow. Though her effort was well-intended, Mr. Bentley still supported him.

"I understand from our mutual friend that you might honor us with your company as we travel, Lady Verity. I cannot tell you how delighted I am at the prospect."

Verity glanced up at Mr. Bentley, who stared expressionlessly ahead of him. He might not have even been in their company, for all his willingness to share in their conversation.

"I believe the arrangement might be mutually beneficial. Of course, we cannot decide anything until I meet your sister, Mr. Marsh. But if she is a tenth as agreeable as you, I am sure the arrangement will be amiable."

"Oh, Nell is the best of women. There are few who are not captivated by her," Mr. Marsh said, and glanced up at his friend.

"Then I look forward to meeting her," Verity said,

and wondered at the relationship between Miss Marsh and Will Bentley.

"You will not have to wait long," he spoke at last. "She is just there, on the dock."

As Mr. Marsh waved with a great deal of enthusiasm, Verity scanned the crowd for some clue as to the woman's identity. And then, without too much difficulty, a bright face emerged from among the others, its lips breaking into a wide grin. The eyes, the pink cheeks, the accustomed smile were a feminine version of the lady's cheerful brother. Soon, Miss Marsh's whole body grew animated, and she hopped up and down, lest she go unnoticed in the crowd.

"Miss Marsh seems perfectly delightful," Verity said, and meant it. "I fear she will be very upset when she sees your ankle, Mr. Marsh."

"Upset? Perhaps my friend has not represented her properly. My sister loves nothing so much as a worthy cause, Lady Verity. When she sees what has happened to me, I believe nothing will save me from her enthusiastic smothering."

Verity laughed politely, but Mr. Marsh's words had the perverse effect of making her feel her own loneliness. She could lay claim to no one, to nothing, not even to her own name. Who was there who would ever comfort her if she found herself in pain? Who cared whether she lived or died?

Chapter 4

"I think you are very brave, Lady Verity," Eleanor Marsh said some time later. "I have always longed to travel as freely as Geoff and Will, but I would never have dared to set off on my own."

"But I did not set off on my own and could claim no bravery, Miss Marsh. Every day of the journey, I sorely missed my good friend Miss Merrill and could not imagine how I would go on without her."

"How fortuitous it was you met with my brother, then. If you are willing to join them, I cannot think of what I should like more." Nell clapped her hands in pleasure and settled against the pillows of the huge, overstuffed bed.

Verity was not altogether sure where they were but did not fear for her virtue. After passing through the simple debarkation procedure of identifying Lady Verity Harwood's name on the ship's manifest and notifying the agent that, regrettably, Miss Anne Merrill had perished at sea, she found herself swept up onto a large carriage where her trunks were already waiting. Though she guessed Miss Marsh herself had driven the vehicle to the dock, the young woman relinquished control to Mr. Bentley, who maneuvered it expertly out of the web of similar carriages waiting to be claimed. Freed from the propriety of English society, Mr. William Bentley was now simply Will, even to young

Miss Marsh.

Verity reflected on the nature of their relationship as she sat quietly in her seat, almost forgotten, and admired the passing scenery. Eventually Mr. Bentley— Will—led them to a ferry crossing by which they arrived at the opposite shore of a modest riverway, and they then moved speedily along the bank to a settled area in the town of Cambridge. Their destination was a small clapboard house, though it was too dark to see much of it when they arrived.

A maid met them cheerfully at the door and brought Verity to a tidy room at the back of the house. Nell, who surely must have been anxious to talk to her brother, nevertheless planted herself on Verity's bed and could scarcely contain her excitement. For Verity, adult feminine companionship based on an equal footing was an unprecedented event, though she had longed for it all her life.

"Do you have sisters?" Nell asked, as if reading her mind. "Or brothers? Do you live in a grand house? A castle?"

Verity looked at her new friend and knew she must not disappoint her.

"Harwood Hall is very large and very ancient, far older than any of your buildings in America. There are many more servants than Harwoods who dwell there, for we are quite a small family. My mother is dead, and I have neither brothers nor sisters."

Nell leaned forward, her eyes wide and her mouth in an almost perfect oval.

"Then you are your father's heir, are you not? All his property will be yours someday."

The notion had uncomfortably settled in Verity's

mind once or twice before, but she had readily dismissed it. What did she know of Lady Verity's expectations other than that she would marry wealthily and to one of exalted rank?

"You are a great romantic, Miss Marsh. Women in England can expect to inherit very little, unless there are no men who claim precedence. Even now, a girl younger than either of us stands to be queen because there are no male cousins before her. My father, Lord Jasper, has brothers, and they all have sons. I have nothing but a small settlement, and some charms by which I might lure a rich husband."

"Is that your intent in coming to America?"

"You are impertinent!" Verity laughed, attempting to hide the awkwardness of the moment. If she only knew why Lady Verity, a woman of no imagination and an incurably lazy spirit, had chosen to come to America, her own direction might be made a good deal clearer. "I do not look for a husband here."

Nell looked offended, and Verity belatedly realized she had every right to be so.

"There are many excellent prospects," Nell protested.

"I am sure there are," Verity answered gently. "Is there someone you particularly favor?"

Nell looked to the ceiling, blushing. "I am sure he thinks of me as nothing more than a child."

It took Verity only a moment to guess whom she meant.

"You cannot be many years younger than me, and yet I feel very old," she said with all the wisdom of her twenty-four years. "But experience counts for a good deal, and if we choose to make this journey with your brother and his friend, then you will soon acquire it. I guarantee it. It feels a very long time since I set out for America, and so much has happened since then. I might even consider myself a new woman."

Verity could not help herself when she said such things and silently prayed she would not live to regret it. Eventually someone would realize that she was, in fact, a new woman.

"Of course. Geoff told me you suffered a great tragedy in the loss of your friend. He said he met you while you were seeking help for her and demanded the attention of the ship's doctor. He thought you very resourceful. Even Will admired that, and he rarely looks favorably on any woman."

"His responses did not seem so favorable to me," Verity said disagreeably.

Nell looked up, surprised. "And yet Geoff spoke of it most particularly. He said the weather was beastly, and yet you risked much by trying to help another woman. Was it not so?"

It surely was but was not something that ought to be applauded. After all, she now was that other woman.

"I am sorry I made you unhappy to remember that day," Nell whispered.

Verity caught herself up straight. "Oh no, not at all. I am only unhappy to think about Miss Merrill, who remained such a dear all her life and whose death seemed so unjust. As for Mr. Bentley, I scarcely consider him worthy of my attention."

"I see," Nell said flatly.

Cursing herself for her graceless blundering, Verity attempted to redeem herself.

"Oh, do not mistake me, Miss Marsh. He is a very

fine sort, clearly intelligent and industrious. It is only that I, in my position, must choose very carefully. And, as the only child of Lord Harwood, I have a great many excellent choices."

Dear God, but she sounded like a pompous ass, albeit very much like the former Lady Verity. In any case, her words reassured Nell completely.

"Of course," the younger girl said, and grinned. "There are many things you must consider. I doubt Will Bentley would suit you."

"He is, after all, a traveling writer," Verity pointed out.

"He hardly ever spends time at his own home," Nell added.

"I do not even know if his books are successful."

"Oh, they are. But hardly enough to maintain an ancient castle."

"I do not own one," Verity said.

"But he does," Nell pointed out. "It is not so ancient, but it is very grand and well situated."

"I doubt he owns generous feelings toward any woman."

Nell blushed. "I hope that is not true. But he is, by nature, censorious."

"Then I can only wonder," Verity said thoughtfully, "how such a man, who finds so many things disagreeable, can write dispassionately on any theme?"

"I would not consider Will's writings at all dispassionate. Nor is he. Under his cool and aloof exterior is a man of many passions and genuine humor. Wait upon judgment until you come to know him better, Lady Verity. I think you will discover he is not what he at first seems."

Verity turned away and studied herself in the small mirror over the dressing table. The latter might be said of her, she realized. In fact, it would make an entirely suitable epitaph.

Nell's enthusiastic gestures of friendship occupied so much of Verity's time, she scarcely had time to wash and dress for dinner. Alone at last, unattended by the sole servant in the household, Verity hung up her clothes in the empty wardrobe closet and considered what she might wear for her first night in America.

She knew the garments well, better than the lady for whom they were sewn. Muslin proved less likely to wrinkle than chintz, and cotton more comfortable than worsted. Such things would matter when they recommenced their journey.

But for tonight, in the warmth of the cozy house, Verity gave in to all temptation and chose one of the loveliest evening gowns in Lady Verity Harwood's collection, one she once hoped the lady would discard after a few wearings and donate to her companion's meager wardrobe.

Verity slipped the peach silk over her head, relishing the sensation of the exquisite fabric sliding over her body. Though her dimensions were somewhat more generous than her predecessor's more boyish ones, Verity fancied the cut and fit suited her and showed her assets to their best advantage. Indeed, never had she felt so much a lady.

What she gained in satisfaction she sacrificed in convenience, for she required a good deal of concentration to button herself into the garment. Now more than ever, she understood why great ladies required maids and why Lady Verity could never have managed a journey without assistance. When she knew Nell better, they would necessarily help each other.

Verity opened the wooden trunk containing Lady Verity's slippers, for the first time since the day after her mistress died. The rapidity with which she was whisked away from town this afternoon had prevented her from ordering new shoes with a better fit, and it was quite impossible for her to wear the black boots of a servant when she sat down to dinner in this house. She would have to do the best she could and suffer the consequences.

Her feet ached even before she reached the door of her room, but Verity determinedly walked out into the hallway and listened to the sounds of the house. She heard the tinkle of glass in the hall below.

It was a lovely house, larger than it appeared from the outside, and decorated with a very fine taste. Landscapes that might have been of the Salisbury Plain hung on the pale green walls, and a corner table was crowned with a bowl of Mr. Wedgwood's jasperware. When Annie Merrill was no more than a girl in Harwood Hall, she had broken a similar piece as she ran through a room and all-too-vividly recalled her punishment. Wincing while remembering that unpleasantness, she carefully walked down the carpeted stairs.

"Oh dear," came the first greeting from the hall. Nell, dressed very simply in a high-necked pique gown, bowed formally and a little awkwardly. "You are surely too fine for our assembled company, my lady."

Nell's form of address conveyed Verity's misstep very succinctly, revealing they were no longer two young women sharing confidences in a cramped bedchamber.

"I am sorry if I am inappropriately attired, dear Nell. You should have warned me one does not dress so formally in America as in England. I only thought this gown might be a pleasant change after the discomforts of life on board the *Andromeda*."

"You need not apologize, Lady Verity. You have brought a rare grace and beauty to our home," said Mr. Marsh, though Verity could not yet determine from whence he spoke.

She walked uncomfortably down the last several steps and looked toward the open archway of light. There, seated in a wheeled chaise and holding aloft a goblet, Geoffrey Marsh smiled at her.

Verity returned his smile and accepted a similar glass from the maid.

"Your house already owns a rare grace and beauty, sir. I have done no more than return the compliment," she said.

"You do us too much credit, Lady Verity," Nell said, coming up behind her.

"It is an honor to have you here," echoed her brother.

"Enough!" said Mr. Bentley. "If you each must indulge in such useless praise, might it be done elsewhere? At Fresh Pond, perhaps, where you are apt to meet with Narcissus admiring himself among the willows? Such is the place for such exercises. Not here, where it may interfere with our digestion."

Verity glanced at Nell and met her amused expression before she turned on the evening's spoiler.

"Why, Will Bentley, are you here as well? I would

have thought you would have retired to your chambers for the evening so you might accomplish some writing in your book. You have been on a journey and made several friends, and I daresay you have nothing positive to say about at least one of them. You must wish to record your unhappy impressions right away."

Mr. Bentley said nothing, but he held his glass so tightly, Verity could see his knuckles whiten.

"Our travels were not all taken in the excuse of Will's work, my lady," Geoff Marsh explained cheerfully.

"Ah, you went for pleasure, then. And yet, somehow, I cannot think of your friend finding pleasure anywhere. It is a mystery to me," said Verity lightly, wishing she were not always so perturbed by the man's antagonism.

"We traveled on business. There are sufficient matters concerning us having no bearing on my books, my lady. Though I do not see how they are any business of yours."

"Will is in expectation of property in England, you understand," Nell rushed in, and pulled on Verity's free arm.

"No, I did not understand," Verity said quietly as her friend pulled her into the drawing room.

"It is no matter. Come, I wish for you to see my harp. Geoff bought it for me on my last birthday. It is a wonderful thing and I do love to play, but he requires I entertain all of our guests here."

"That cannot be too punishing on such a beautiful instrument," Verity said as she ran her fingers over the elegantly carved wood. She felt perfectly giddy knowing she should never be required to polish it. "I should love to hear you."

"And I should hear you. Perhaps we may play a duet. There is the pianoforte."

Verity pulled her fingers away from the harp, suddenly chilled. Why had she not thought to bring down a shawl?

"But I do not play an instrument, Nell," she said lightly. Though she had shared the schoolroom with Lady Verity and proved a better student, music lessons would have been quite an indulgence for the bastard daughter of an earl. When Verity met with her music tutor, Annie usually retired to the kitchen, where Cook taught her the rudiments of baking. It proved a useful diversion, if not a gracious one.

"You do not play an instrument, Lady Verity?" asked Mr. Bentley, having followed them into the room. "It was my understanding all ladies received instruction."

"I suspect my education was of a more practical bent, sir. I know you must doubt it, since most English ladies play and sing, and embroider, and paint china, but I have many skills. Unfortunately, playing an instrument is not one of them."

"A pity, my lady."

"I say the same, since now I must play alone," Nell said under her breath.

"But I do not say it is a bad thing because you have charms that surely compensate for the omission. You look very…well tonight, my lady," her tormentor said with obvious reluctance.

Verity tried to look anywhere but into his eyes. Now she felt glad she had neglected to bring her shawl. In fact, her skin burned so, she would have stripped down to her corset if she dared.

"Do I misunderstand you, sir, or do I hear the faintest glimmer of a compliment there? I thought you did not approve of such things."

"Oh, I approve of compliments, especially when the subject is worthy of it. I do not cast my words lightly about, however, and save them for the appropriate moments."

Verity caught her breath. "In that case, I thank you for your rare indulgence."

Will Bentley did not answer but continued to watch her with a scrutiny that proved disconcerting. Verity glanced at Nell's demure high-necked gown and wished she had better measured the consequences of wearing the peach silk gown with its revealing neckline.

"Would you like to sit down for dinner, Lady Verity?" Geoffrey Marsh asked. He managed to wheel himself into the drawing room with little apparent effort.

Verity felt the pinch of her slippers. "Oh, very much so, Mr. Marsh," she answered enthusiastically. "It will be a pleasure to dine without the Atlantic rolling under our seats."

Mr. Marsh and his sister had the grace to laugh, but of course, Will Bentley said nothing. He bowed as Verity passed through the open door, and she felt sorely tempted to smack him on the head with her folded fan.

Mr. Marsh wheeled himself to the head of the table, which settled any lingering doubts about the ownership of the house in which she was a guest. Nell sat opposite, leaving the two side chairs to Verity and Mr. Bentley.

"Your house is most elegant, Mr. Marsh. You have

pieces as fine as any in the great houses of England," Verity said knowingly, conversationally. She unfolded a white linen napkin and saw embroidered initials that did not seem to match either of the Marsh siblings.

"We are not beyond the ken of civilization, my lady. I hope we may surprise you in many things," Mr. Marsh answered.

"As you may surprise us," Mr. Bentley interrupted.

Verity chose to ignore him. "You already have, sir. Might you tell me some of the history of this house?"

Mr. Marsh shrugged. "There is not so very much to tell. My grandparents arrived from Scotland just after the War of Independence. The mood in Boston was not altogether congenial, so they removed to the countryside and built this modest house where fresh water seemed plentiful and the distances were not so great to markets and society. It did not take very long before the desirability of the locale became apparent to others. By the time my own parents married, Fresh Pond was already a neighborhood, with its own market and school."

"Other tenants moved here?" Verity asked.

"Tenants?" Mr. Marsh laughed. "You shall have to adjust to the ways of American life, my lady. The people who farm here are property owners, one and all. Those who cannot yet afford a plot aspire to do so in the near future."

Verity at last understood why men and women of the lower classes in England spoke so admiringly of those among their equals who risked the great journey to America. It was not so much the spirit of adventure that proved admirable, but the expectation that those of the most humble origins might transform their lives. It was a notion about which she was recently very keen.

"And Mr. Bentley? Do you also have a property in the vicinity?"

He looked up from his glass, clearly reluctant to be a part of their conversation. His dark eyes glinted in the candlelight, reflecting the delicate illumination.

"I do not, though I own a home in New York. When I studied at Harvard College here in Cambridge, I rented rooms from the Marsh family, who were gracious enough to take me in."

"How very kind of them. We also have a university in Cambridge in England, you know. It is a very fine place, I understand." So Verity did, though imperfectly. What did she know of what men did while at school, but for some lively rumors among the servants?

Mr. Bentley tapped impatiently on the table, and Verity realized he had little tolerance for idle conversation.

"And is Harvard College a fine place, as well?" she asked.

"It suited me," he said tersely. "And I am always eager to experience life in another city."

"I see, Mr. Bentley, you had the heart and soul of a travel writer even then. It is good to pursue one's passions, even if they necessarily take you away from home. Are you never homesick?'

"Are you, my lady?" he countered.

Verity thought about the beauty and grace of Harwood Hall, the only place she ever considered "home." And then she recalled the rigors of her life there, an existence without any real dignity, a deep familiarity without any true belonging.

"No. Not at all," she said honestly.

"It appears you have met your partner, Will," Geoffrey Marsh said playfully, apparently indifferent to the embarrassment of everyone else at the table. "Both you and Lady Verity share an avid sense of wanderlust. A house, a castle, an estate prove nothing more than places to secure the possessions you do not wish to have about you at the moment."

Verity looked down at the lovely china set out before her and saw the longing in her own reflection. To own such objects, to care for people and things one loved and cherished, remained almost beyond the scope of her youthful dreams. It was, she might believe, the real reason she'd plunged so recklessly into her masquerade. To be a part of such a world, however briefly, was above rubies, far more valuable than rank and wealth.

"No, Mr. Marsh, you misunderstand me. I have seen great and wonderful houses, full of treasures and those of lofty lineages, and yet without a glimpse of a soul within them. The house is nothing without the people."

"You surprise me, my lady," Will Bentley said drolly. "I have known houses worth nothing precisely because of the people within them."

"I think we are talking about the same thing, sir. For example, I suspect your own house, wherever it is, is all the more pleasant just now because you are away from it."

Nell gasped and then managed a weak smile. "Hudson Point is always pleasant, Lady Verity. But we are grateful our friend has brought all his charm to our humble home."

"Do not trouble yourself, Nell. I believe Lady

Verity is so accustomed to being taciturn she would not know the difference. As it is highly unlikely she will ever see Hudson Point for herself, it surely does not matter if she finds it pleasant or not."

"Of course not, Mr. Bentley. It is certainly not on my list of destinations while on this journey."

"Shall we discuss the places we might prefer to visit?" Geoffrey Marsh asked, a little too quickly.

"Yes, please," Verity agreed, reaching for the lifeline he threw her. "I have read only a very little and should enjoy hearing your preferences and recommendations."

Actually, what she most enjoyed hearing was Mr. Bentley's grunting concession and the tinkling of silver as the first course was served. Geoffrey Marsh carried the conversation with a lengthy description of towns and cities and the great natural wonders of the American landscape. Nell interrupted from time to time with questions, and Verity played her part with cheerful encouragement. But Will Bentley sat silently indifferent, as if it were not he who aspired to be a great travel writer, but his loquacious secretary.

Verity listened less and thought about him more. She could not deny that even as she disliked him, he nevertheless intrigued her. He seemed such a contradiction in so many ways, she felt as if she gazed upon an image in the water, always changing, often elusive. And nothing she learned about him made the vision more succinct: he had expectations in England and yet was indifferent to them; he had a property in America and did not desire to return there. He was adored by his friends, but seemed indifferent to their praise.

Verity sighed and concentrated on her roasted beef. It was not so very salty as that to which she was accustomed at home, and a good deal easier to slice. Geoffrey Marsh glanced at her curiously and poured her another glass of wine.

She felt a little drowsy but certainly comfortable and warm. Lady Verity's cursed shoes were almost intolerable by now, and Verity thought it would not matter if she slipped them off. The rug beneath her stockinged feet felt plush as she curled her toes between its tufts.

"What say you to our American cooking, madam?" asked the young serving girl at her shoulder.

Verity promptly awakened from her daydream to look upon her with surprise. If she herself ever dared to speak to a dinner guest at Harwood Hall, she would have been promptly sent back to the kitchen. It was enough she was schooled with the young lady of the house; to presume upon further privilege would have been disastrous.

Verity glanced at Nell, to be certain her behavior was appropriate. But Nell looked expectant and curious and certainly gave nothing to indicate there was anything wrong.

"Why, it is all quite wonderful," Verity said truthfully. "But I am not at all accustomed to indulging so much. I shall have to get plenty of exercise on the morrow."

"Why wait until then?" Mr. Bentley said bluntly. "If you will walk with me in the garden, you shall have appetite enough for tea and cakes."

Verity looked a little desperately at the Marshes, but nothing in their expressions suggested they were interested in accompanying their guests.

"I do not know, my lord. I am somewhat tired…"

"Nonsense, my lady. It is not past eight of the clock. We do not dine nearly so late in America as when we are in England. There are hours to go before we retire." He stood up and threw his unsoiled napkin upon the table. With a smile toward his invalid friend, he half circled around the table and caught the posts at the back of Verity's chair.

"I hope we may be excused," she said hoarsely.

Nell looked like she might protest but said nothing. And Mr. Marsh cheerfully waved them off.

"Have a care for the ducks," he said. "They are nesting just now and would not wish to be disturbed."

"I am in complete sympathy," said Mr. Bentley, as he caught Verity by her elbow. She paused only to look back at Mr. Marsh, who seemed to find his friend's words very amusing.

The dining room opened into a solarium of sorts, a name incorrectly applied when the place was illuminated only by the light of the moon. Through this, they silently passed into the formal garden situated on a terrace overlooking the wide pond. It was only then, stepping down onto the smooth cold slate of paving stones, Verity realized she left her shoes beneath the dining room table.

But luckily, Will Bentley seemed intent on the ordered paths, leading Verity around a marble fountain and under an arbor not yet resplendent with seasonal fruit.

"I will confess, Mr. Bentley, you seem the very last man to indulge in a romantic idyll of this sort. And certainly not with someone you so patently dislike."

He made a little noise, which she could not decipher, and she could not see his face in the darkness, which might have revealed much.

"It is a very pretty place," he conceded. "Most of the gardens in this part of the country are modeled on the English, rather than Continental, style. But I have not brought you here to make love."

"I should think not," Verity said indignantly. Absurdly, her heart sank with an irreconcilable disappointment. "If I thought it, I would demand you return me to the dining room at once."

"But you are not so headstrong."

"Not at all," she lied, too keenly remembering recent events.

"And, I daresay, you are more than a little curious."

"I am a little curious. But only a very little."

Verity started to pull her arm from his, confident she could find her way back in the darkness, but he caught her quickly.

"My lady, I have a business proposition for you."

"A business proposition! Have you forgotten our positions? A lady does not engage in business propositions!" Verity sputtered righteously. It was the best she could muster. Her predecessor would have collapsed with heart palpitations.

"No, I suppose most do not. But you, Lady Verity, do not seem to be like most ladies."

She hoped he could not feel her shaking through the sleeve of his jacket. "What do you mean, sir?"

"You do not seem protected, sheltered from the world. You do not profess to weakness when you feel none, nor do you hesitate to act upon your genuine instincts. There appears to be very little deception in you."

Verity tripped on a paving stone which, unhappily, made Mr. Bentley pull her closer to his side.

"How do you know I am not merely playacting, to cover up a deplorable lack of confidence?"

He took a very long time to answer, and she regretted her impulsive words. Perhaps he already suspected the truth and knew her for a fraud. Perhaps he intended to blackmail her or expose her to legal authorities.

"I do not. But I am willing to chance the consequences."

She sighed into the darkness and silently sent up a thankful prayer to heaven. "The consequences of what, sir?"

"Why, the business proposition of which I have already spoken, my lady."

"I confess, I am prepared to decline. It is not merely that it is inappropriate, no matter what you say. It is also that I know very little about such matters."

She felt him study her in the darkness, but could not look away.

"You have mentioned to Geoff that you plan to visit Mrs. Frances Trollope," he said pointedly.

Unfortunately, Verity had not a clue what direction this conversation ought to take. What did she know of Lady Verity's friend but that the woman lived in a place called Cincinnati? "I am not certain what you imply, Mr. Bentley."

He made a gesture of impatience, for once possibly justified. "Mrs. Trollope, my lady, owns and operates the most bizarre manner of store anyone has yet visited.

Indeed, it is called the Bazaar. Imagine all the treasures of a marketplace under one large roof. And then imagine one cannot find a bar of soap nor a linen handkerchief, but instead be amused by brass elephants and silken draperies. Such is the exotic nature of her merchandise."

"Perhaps she has found a ready market in Illinois."

"Cincinnati is in Ohio, but no matter. Geoff tells me the town is best known for the slaughtering of hogs."

"I suspect it matters to the people of Cincinnati. And to the hogs."

He laughed out loud, and she realized she so much liked the warmth and depth of the sound, she ought to make him laugh more often. Not that she knew how to go about it. But if she were exposed—as eventually she would be—he would undoubtedly laugh very hard indeed.

"Excellent point," he conceded. "It is only a pity your friend is not as sympathetic to either. If she were, her business would possibly succeed."

"And does it not?" Verity asked curiously.

"By all reports, my lady, it is a dismal failure. Was it not your purpose in coming to America to assist her in her venture?"

Was it?

Verity could not imagine someone more ill-equipped to contribute something to a shop than Lady Verity, unless one wanted to only stock lacy corsets and frivolous gowns. Perhaps Lady Verity intended to invest in the venture and wished to approve of the operation.

But if such were the case, why would she bother to

be secretive about it? She always enjoyed flaunting her social superiority over that of her half sister. She would not have been reticent in this matter.

"My lady?" came the deep voice in the darkness. "Have you forgotten?"

"No, Mr. Bentley. I have forgotten nothing." Verity sighed once again. "But you are mistaken if you think I know anything at all about Mrs. Trollope's business. I only intended to visit her in friendship. As you can see, I cannot be helpful to you."

"I will not let you escape so easily," he said and put his large hand on her arm. She had no intention of escaping; in fact, she felt very desirous of staying here all night with him. "What I propose requires no knowledge of business matters, though it concerns them."

"You will have me faint from curiosity, sir," Verity said and turned to face him. His hand moved down her arm to catch her hand.

"As you know, I am a writer," he began. However little she knew of him, she certainly already knew this. "I have a modest income from my books, and the expectation that the next will also be profitable. However, the writing of travel books has become a very popular sport for gentlemen, and I find myself in a very crowded field. Mr. Marsh and I have wondered what I might do to stand head and shoulders above the rest."

Verity looked up at him, guessing he was being ironic, as he had to be aware of his impressive physical stature.

"And so you decided to write a book together, from different points of view?" she asked. "To compete with the likes of Benjamin Williams?"

"Like Benjamin Williams," he said solemnly. "I see you appreciate the possibilities. I believe readers, particularly female readers, will be intrigued by a book written by a man and a woman, together."

There was something in the way in which he said "together" that made Verity think he might not have been talking about business at all. She shivered.

"I see you are chilled, so I will not keep you. But perhaps you will think on my proposal."

"Proposal?" she squeaked. "Whatever do you mean?"

"Do you not see?"

"I do not see anything, sir!" Verity said a little desperately and tried to pull her hand away. Will Bentley played a game of seduction with her, though he would insist it was all about business. "I do not know what you want of me."

It was the wrong thing to say, she saw that at once. She knew it in the heated energy surrounding them, in the silence of the night, in his sudden intake of breath.

"I want for your name to appear as a joint author on my next book. I do not care if you do not write a single word, if I can only have your name." He spoke coolly, dispassionately, as was appropriate to a business transaction.

"I see. So this is somehow the reverse of a more ordinary proposal, as you would have my name, rather than I having yours." Verity considered herself very witty to have thought of this, but sobered upon remembering she already had someone else's name. "But why do you not ask Miss Marsh to partner with you, as you know her so much better?"

"I prefer an Englishwoman, so our views are as

disparate as possible."

"I see. And how would such an Englishwoman profit from such an arrangement?"

He laughed again, but as she knew he laughed at her, she was not as easily heartened as she was before.

"And you say you are too much a lady to be a businesswoman? You sell yourself short, dear Lady Verity. You never cease to surprise me."

Verity just thought the same thing of him but declined to say anything.

"I will grant you whatever you would like, be it a share of the profits or some other arrangement. Perhaps you would like for me to escort you home to England if you do not succeed in finding a traveling companion by the time you return."

"That would be most inappropriate, sir."

"Perhaps not so injudicious if we are…business associates."

She tried to see his face in the darkness, certain he was about to say something else. But the moonlight fell on his right shoulder, making the dark fabric silver.

"I believe I understand you, sir. But you say you require nothing but that I allow for you to use my name?"

"It is no ordinary name. It will attract the notice of a whole new audience of readers," he said.

"And what of the Marshes? Will they not be resentful?"

"It is not in their natures to be resentful. And, in any case, I have already discussed the possibility with Mr. Marsh and he approves. As my secretary, he profits from my success as well."

"This arrangement will be advantageous to

everyone, I see. I wish to understand one more thing, however." Verity wondered if she was treading into deep waters, into matters that should be of no concern to her. "I assume you are a man of means and have no necessity to profit from small volumes on the landscape of America and the manners of her people. Why, then, do you do it?"

"It will take more than an inheritance from my father to secure my happiness, my lady. Did you not just say how empty a home is without people within?"

Verity did not answer, too full of wonder about his frankness, his proposal, his expectations. She reflected on his need to do something useful with his life, and his pride, which perhaps would not allow him to admit pleasure in acquiring something he did not earn.

Perhaps that was what made him an American, more than the accident of his birth, for the people here seemed to believe one might seek advancement in nothing more than hard work. Entitlement was earned and not necessarily inherited.

Indeed, the idea was very seductive.

"Well, my lady? Have you forgotten what you said so recently? Or were your words only for Mr. Marsh's benefit? You need not bother, you know. He is already quite smitten with you."

Here was real surprise. Verity put a shaking hand to her cheek, wondering what Mr. Bentley hoped to gain by revealing so much. But her thoughts could not focus on this sudden, unexpected turn; they were tumbling down a roughly hewn, unfinished path.

"You say, sir, you require nothing more than my name affixed to the cover of your book," she recounted, ignoring his jibe. "Yet, even in this short time, I realize

I myself shall need something more than that."

"I thought you were insulted by the prospect of a financial arrangement…"

"I am as indifferent to it as you are to living in your New York home," Verity said recklessly. "What does matter, more than I first realized, is my participation in the project. I need something more than my name in print. I desire a greater share."

"Of the profits?" he asked, incredulously. "We have not even discussed terms."

"There is time enough for that. But I wish for a greater share of the work. If I should be an author, then I must be one in truth. I would have a hand in the preparation of this book." Verity heard her words as if another person spoke them, gathering strength as she went along.

"That is Geoffrey Marsh's job," Mr. Bentley said tersely.

"Oh," Verity said airily, "I do not intend to be your secretary. I have no desire to put myself in a position wherein I must take my orders from you. I propose to actually share authorship of your—our—book."

She did not need to ask why it took Will Bentley so long to answer her, nor did she need daylight to know he seethed as he sat beside her. She could hardly blame him; she herself only just arrived at the conclusion that such an arrangement was something she desired. Verity only knew a door had opened, allowing her to come closer to a man she was not even sure she liked, and at the same time, giving her a path to follow when her reckless masquerade ended. She could be a writer, like Mr. Bentley. It did not look so very hard. She would learn the rudiments from him and Mr. Marsh and set out on her own when circumstances made it necessary. In doing so, she would earn her right to remain in America.

"Do you know anything about the craft of writing, my lady?" he said nastily.

"Why do you doubt it, sir?" she challenged him, challenging herself at the same time.

"I cannot imagine. You do not profess to many skills, and so I can only speculate about your limitations. You do not play an instrument, you know nothing about business. You seem ignorant of your friend's affairs and seem oddly indecisive for someone who has traveled all the way to America. How do I know you are up to the task of writing?"

"How do you not? I am expert at many things," Verity said, and added to herself, *like cooking and polishing furniture and laying out a lady's nightclothes.* "But if you find I am deficient, I am sure you will not hesitate to give me stern and rude instruction."

"You can count on it," he said.

But Verity guessed she prevailed. "It is settled then? I will write, and you will write, and we will publish a book together."

"I must be a madman to agree to this scheme."

"It was your scheme, Mr. Bentley. But you do agree?"

He was silent, and Verity regretted she pinned him to the spot. Perhaps if she gave him time to consider, to think of advantages not yet apparent, to realize he had few choices if he wished to act at once…

"God help me, I do."

Verity felt her hand grasped again, and for one fleeting moment thought he would pull her into his arms and kiss her. She would necessarily have to act indignant, but she would first enjoy herself thoroughly. She closed her eyes and tilted her face up toward his.

But business was business. Mr. Bentley did nothing more than shake her hand vigorously, sealing their absurd bargain.

Will leaned close, tempted by her slightly parted lips and the inviting expression on her beautiful face. She must know what she presented to a man, for she was a most accomplished seductress. And yet, even if he did not already know how much she despised him, he might have taken all sorts of liberties with her just now. He denied being a romantic, but even a block of stone would be moved by the vision of Lady Verity Harwood.

So he did what any sensible man would do: he looked away and shook her hand as if she were a merchant at the docks.

"When shall we begin?" she asked.

Will caught his breath. He ought to have asked the same thing himself, assuming there would ever be a point at which another level of their relationship would begin. He supposed he would begin with her lips.

"Begin, my lady?"

"Of course, Mr. Bentley," she said crossly. "If we have a book to write, I propose we begin at once."

"Ah, yes," he said quickly. "In fact, I have already begun writing it. It is one of the things I did on board the *Andromeda*."

"When you were not flirting with ladies," she said.

"I do not believe it is any business of yours to know how I conducted my private affairs before we settled upon our current arrangement. I was at leave to flirt with whomever I chose."

"And now, sir?"

"I believe I still possess that liberty. We are only business associates, Lady Verity." And, he supposed, he could still flirt with her.

"Then I must be allowed the same liberty, sir."

"I would not think to deny you. What you do in your personal time is no affair of mine," he said, quite as if he were talking to his lawyer or banker. And yet, he imagined he would enjoy making her personal time entirely his affair.

"Then it is settled. Well, I should like to get to work at once. I suppose I ought to begin by looking over the leaves you have already written, so we will not repeat ourselves. If you will but get them for me, I will read them tonight."

Will's traitorous heart gave a little lurch. He thought about his written words, as intimate as any part of his body and soul, accompanying her to her chamber. The thought was absurd, entirely irrational, but almost beyond his immediate powers to control.

He struggled to make his voice sound calm. "Mr. Marsh is one of the few people capable of reading my hand, though I suppose you will soon be used to it. When we return to the dining room, I shall ask him to turn over my papers for your pleasure. But I do not think we need fear repeating any sentiments."

"Why not, Mr. Bentley?"

"I daresay we are as unlike as two people can be. There is nothing upon which we seem to agree, nothing we see in quite the same light."

"I thought we already agreed to work on this book together," she said in a small voice.

Will felt a moment's pity for her, suddenly realizing that, for some reason, this truly mattered to her. Why a lady, accustomed to every luxury and privilege, should want to soil herself with genuine work, he could not fathom. But somehow, it did matter to her.

He did not harbor any illusions she might be interested in working close to him.

"Oh, indeed. I only meant you and I could discourse on the identical theme and get quite the opposite results. No one would ever imagine we are looking at the same moon, for example."

He saw her gaze upward, and the pale light fell upon her fine cheekbones and pert nose. The shadow of her chin made a blurred triangle on her neck; below, the smooth skin of her breast glowed invitingly. Will knew his own thoughts rather too clearly, and therein demonstrated ample evidence for his theory. Whatever she thought just now had nothing to do with his own tumultuous desires.

"Poor Geoffrey will have quite a task assimilating our views, I fear," he said in a voice scarcely recognizable as his own.

"Why must he?"

Why indeed? "It is his job, my lady."

She made a gesture of impatience and turned away from the pale moon. "But why must we assimilate at all? I am a woman; you are a man. We will travel the same course, see the same things. Why do we not simply include both points of view, adjacent to each other? It will be quite the thing!"

It would be. Their perspectives might be set down in alternating chapters, with some interludes of commentary on each other's work. It was a novel idea and a very good one. Together they would attract a diverse readership, and undoubtedly do very well.

"It is not the way I planned it, Lady Verity," he said grudgingly, not yet willing to concede anything.

"And I did not plan to become an author when I set out for America, Mr. Bentley. I did not intend for Annie Merrill to die nor for me to travel with strangers to Cincinnati. But I have adjusted to difficult circumstances. Why can you not do the same?"

"The circumstances ought not be difficult; what I hitherto outlined was, in fact, quite simple to comprehend."

"And is that the way you like things, Mr. Bentley? Simple, expedient, exactly the way you planned? Do you never make provision for the unexpected?"

In all his life, Will was never given a more provocative invitation to act entirely out of character, to satisfy an impulse painful to suppress. Lady Verity Harwood sat not more than ten inches from him in the moonlight, her lips opened to him, waiting and watching.

He reached out and dared to touch her cheek.

The sea journey had played havoc with her complexion, as it did to them all. Though the skin looked smooth and clear in the light, his fingers felt a certain tautness there and the slight irregularities brought about by the daily spray of salt water. The same dichotomy might be noted of the lady herself: while she appeared soft and gentle, closer proximity revealed a somewhat rougher truth.

It did nothing to diminish her attractions.

"Lady Verity…" he began and leaned forward.

But with a little gasp, she pulled away and rose above him. In the uncompromising light, he saw her breast rise and fall, rise and fall.

He took a moment to steady himself, to school himself not to say anything he might regret later. Once again she seemed possessed of a greater wisdom, for she surely just now prevented them from making a mistake they both would heartily regret.

Though he waited too long to be proper, he finally stood next to her, looking down at her curling hair. He was suddenly reminded of the circumstances of their meeting on the *Andromeda*, with her face turned downward in thought, and the breeze ruffling through her hair. If he did not already know something about her, she would have seemed only honest and good.

"I hope Mr. Marsh can bring me your papers as soon as possible, my lord. It would benefit me greatly to give the project all my attention. I fear the long journey and the loss of my friend has made me victim to restlessness. I must have something to do."

As an excuse for evading his advances, it was very tidy. It did not make Will feel any better, nor any less frustrated, but it made absolute sense.

"Then let us find him at once," he said gallantly and bowed from the waist.

Lady Verity passed in front of him, apparently sure of her way in the shadows. Her gown brushed against his legs, and her footsteps barely made a sound against the slate walkway. The sweet smell of lavender wafted up from the nearby field of wildflowers, or so he thought until he realized they ought not yet be in season.

He followed her.

"Oh dear," she cried suddenly and stumbled again on the path. Will reached out and caught her by the elbow, believing she would have fallen. She first resisted, and then suddenly sank down in one fluid movement, to sit upon the stone wall.

"Are you hurt?" he asked, thinking she sprained an ankle on the irregular stones. It seemed to be a habit among those he knew. "If you lean on me, I will help you back to the house."

He was not sure she grimaced, or if it was a trick of the light that made her seem so dismissive, but she shook her head and started to rise again.

"It will not do," she said. "There is something embedded in my foot."

"What? And right through the slipper?" Will asked in surprise.

"Right through my skin," she said between clenched teeth. "There is blood too, I think."

Will stood as helplessly as he did only a few minutes before, wondering if he should give in to impulse or respond in an appropriate manner.

"Let me see." He dropped to one knee, in a position that would inspire entirely erroneous reactions by anyone coming upon them. He looked across at the lady's face and thought he saw tears on her cheeks.

Cautiously he reached for the hem of her gown, grappling a little awkwardly beneath the laces and silk. Her foot, small and smooth, slipped into the palm of his hand.

Warm, sticky liquid puddled in the cup he made. He rubbed a thumb over her knitted stocking and felt the sharp prick of something in her arch.

She rose slightly off her seat but, unlike most

ladies of his acquaintance, did not cry out.

"Do not do that, sir," she cautioned him. "Every touch seems to drive it in farther."

"It is a thorn, I think. The gardener must have done some trimming of the rose bushes and did not clean up after himself. I am surprised it went clear through your shoe." He felt around blindly for the missing item of her clothing. "Ah, where is your shoe?"

She did not answer, and he could only just see her face as she glanced away from him and toward the house. Could she be embarrassed? He could not comprehend why it should be so and wondered how he would manage to work alongside a woman whose sensibilities were decidedly so different from his own. He knew so little about her, about her temperament and interests, her passions and preferences, her habits and her flights of fancy. Suddenly an idea took hold, and he glanced up, amused, in the moonlight.

"Are you about to turn back into a scullery maid, and your carriage into a pumpkin?" he asked.

"What on earth do you mean?" she gasped.

Was it possible she did not know what he meant? "It is the old fairy tale, my lady. You know the one, in which the cinder girl turns into a princess and loses her slipper."

She turned back so quickly, a curl came loose. "Whatever I may be, sir, I do not fancy you a prince. You must be possessed of a keen romantic sense to imagine it for, believe me, I did not think it at all. There it seems we have another great divide between us, another strength for our collaborative venture."

Will felt a spurt of anger, desiring very much to put this little prig in her place. He was also, he realized, somewhat embarrassed. It was such an unusual feeling for him, he was not quite sure how to handle himself.

"I assure you, I am not inspired to romantic notions, though the garden is lovely and the moonlight very promising," he said ungallantly. "Nor would I wish to be a prince. I only wanted to know where you misplaced your damned slipper."

"Will!"

Lady Verity was so righteously indignant she did not seem to notice she used his name. No doubt she considered it appropriate for his loutish behavior.

Will stood up and brushed petals off his trousers, ready to abandon her. If she believed she could traverse a foreign country on her own, she certainly could manage to find her way to the drawing room. He turned away.

"It is in the dining room," she said in a very small voice.

He stopped and tried to collect himself. "What is?"

"My slipper, Will. Mr. Bentley. I left it under my seat at the dining room table. It is not alone, of course. The other is sitting by its side."

"You have been walking barefoot all this while, Lady Verity? Like the cinder girl you haughtily reject? Perhaps the affinity is closer than you imagine."

He heard her sharp intake of breath.

"I am no more romantic than you, Mr. Bentley."

"And now you hurt all the more," he added. "You have punished yourself by seeking relief."

"One could say it is a fault of mine," she said cryptically. "But, all the same, I should like to get to a comfortable chaise and relieve my present pain."

"But it will pain you even more to arrive at that

chaise if you have a thorn in your foot," he pointed out.

She sat on her stone wall, unmoving and silent. Behind her, down the hill, the dark waters of Fresh Pond lapped against the rocky shore. Some small creature cried out in the night, hunted and captured. And from the drawing room, the strains of harp music echoed in their garden.

Verity raised her arms.

Will said nothing, asking neither permission nor direction, as he caught her. She weighed almost nothing, though he knew the deed would be heavy upon him, and she fell easily against his chest. The delicate fabric of her gown gathered almost to her knees and the smooth texture of her stockings glimmered in the moon light.

He already saw too much, already wondered how it would be possible to work with her day after day with any degree of equanimity. Her patent indifference—even dislike—for him should provide a natural deterrent, but somehow he thought it would not.

She rested her hand on his chest as he walked through the garden, fiercely concentrating on not tripping over something himself. The harp music grew distinctly louder as he pushed against the door, and he followed it into the drawing room.

"What, again?" Geoffrey looked up amused. "You are making this sort of thing into a habit, my good man." And then he turned to his sister, who stopped playing her instrument and looked at the newcomers with surprise. "Will was pressed into precisely this sort of service when I injured my ankle on the ship. It was the same thing."

Wordlessly, Will eased Lady Verity down into a

nearby seat facing the hearth's fire. He was glad his friend was able to make light of the episode.

Because he knew it was not the same thing at all.

Chapter 5

Verity struggled to push out of Will Bentley's arms, but he wisely did not let her go: her embarrassment would have been even more acute if she lay in a tumble of silk and bows on the drawing room floor.

"What on earth happened?" Nell cried.

"Our friend dared to venture outdoors without her shoes. She does not yet know how rugged is the soil here, how dangerous is such a decision." Will made a great show of straightening his back, as if he ached from plowing the fields.

"If you do not recall, we have thorns in our English roses, as well as you have here," Verity said disagreeably.

"I believe we have ample evidence of that, my lady," he answered, leaving no question of his meaning. "But you must know there are also snakes and spiders here, and plants capable of leaving a nasty rash upon your skin."

"Will, do hush up!" Nell admonished. "You are likely to scare my new friend away. It is not only your talk of such things, but your presumption to talk about a lady's person."

Will Bentley scratched his head, apparently deep in thought. His bemused act did not fool Verity one bit.

"Then I am about to misbehave very badly. I

hardly think we need to send for the doctor for such a trifling a thing as a thorn. If the lady can bear the insult of giving me her foot—again—I shall attempt to extract it."

"Can you bear it, Lady Verity?" Nell asked anxiously. "It must be very painful."

Verity nodded, but knowing the pain was nothing to the touch of Will Bentley's hand upon even so distant an extremity. Reflexively, she bent her knee, bringing her foot higher beneath her gown. Unfortunately, that meant he needed to probe farther to bring it forth.

Verity caught her breath as he rubbed his thumb over her arch. She felt the little tickle of the thorn, and his hesitation as her body tensed.

"It is a trifle," she echoed through clenched teeth.

"So it appears, making it even harder to detect. Nell, would you bring the candle closer? And is there a needle in your sewing basket?"

"You know there is, Will, and you also know how clean it must be, since I am not likely to use it." Nell giggled and came closer.

Geoffrey Marsh remained quiet through the little operation, and Verity glanced curiously at him. His expression opened her eyes to a startling realization: as devoted as he was to his good friend, he did not like the idea of Will's familiarity with her. The two men seemed to share everything, but perhaps even the good-natured Mr. Marsh had certain limits.

"Ah, here it is," Mr. Bentley said after an eternity. Mr. Marsh seemed even more relieved than she and backed his chair away from the scene. "A nasty little thing. Who would expect such wickedness from a flower of such beauty?"

"I believe the rose has need to defend itself, sir. Powerless to speak, she must bear arms," Verity said firmly.

"Your eloquence is admirable, my lady," came Mr. Marsh's voice from the shadows. "You might expostulate as well as my verbose friend."

"She has already convinced me of it, Geoff. In fact, Lady Verity has accepted my proposal."

Nell's candle slipped out of her hand and onto the exquisite rug, missing Verity's gown by inches. Mr. Bentley quickly rose and stamped out the spray of sparks before any damage was done.

"Mr. Bentley has proposed that he and I write his current book together," she explained quickly. "He tells me it is for so practical a matter as increasing sales, but I believe I know the real reason."

Three sets of eyes turned to her.

"If Mr. Bentley oversees what I write, he will not allow me to include any harsh words against him. Which, of course, I have been tempted to record since we first met." Verity pulled her legs over the side of the chaise and sat up straight.

Mr. and Miss Marsh seemed visibly reassured by her words, and Will Bentley, predictably, scowled down at her.

"I did not realize you were a writer, Lady Verity," Nell apologized.

"She is not," interrupted Mr. Bentley rudely. "It only just occurred to her when we had words in the garden."

Verity assumed a pose of extreme boredom, wistfully recalling her half sister. "You may find I will surprise you, sir. There are many things about me you do not know."

"I daresay you will introduce me to each particular as we proceed on this journey," he said.

"I sincerely hope not," Verity remarked, as she rose, unassisted, to her tender feet.

\*\*\*\*

"You do not think this madness, Will?" Geoffrey asked from behind his desk. It was many hours later, and the ladies were already retired to their chambers. The two men sat alone, in the waning firelight, with nothing more than the chirping crickets for company. "I cannot imagine how you agreed to such a thing."

"Can you not? I wanted nothing more than her signature, the use of her cursed name. I would have generously paid her for it. But instead I have the harpy herself with which to contend, and her mistaken belief she can match me with her words."

"A hard bargain, indeed. Why, I have witnessed you matching your skills against peddlers in Jerusalem, and marketers in Florence, but do not recall you ever being bested. You must be losing your touch, man. A pity, since you already have lost all power of discretion."

Will turned sharply to his friend, nearly knocking over his abandoned glass.

"A harpy, you say? Her cursed name?" Geoff pressed on. "You must be mad. In all our travels I do not recall ever meeting a lady more tempting to my baser instincts."

"Then you are welcome to her. With my condolences."

"If this is to be your manner, I do not think we

ought travel with her after all. You are sworn to be her protector, and yet you would hand her over to the first man who fancies her."

"But you are that first man, Geoff, and I wish you well. You may be more in need of a protector than she."

"I believe I can handle the lady," Geoff said quietly, and those were the last words spoken in the room for a very long while.

Outdoors, the heavy limbs of the pine trees brushed against the clapboard shingles of the Marsh home, releasing an odor so sweet and so strong, its scent carried into the drawing room. The breeze caught a shutter and held it, whistling gently. And though closer to dawn than to sunset, a blue light still illumed the room, the moonglow even more intense for its reflection in the still waters of Fresh Pond.

All this felt familiar to Will, though he had been gone from America far longer than he'd desired. But neither the elegant gardens of England nor the wild openness of the Atlantic had invoked anything similar to this. Cambridge remained largely in a state of nature, and yet Will thought it entirely predictable. He knew the moods of its weather and the hallmarks of its landscape. He understood the nature of the people who lived here, who were much more forthcoming than the society in Europe. Friends like Geoff and Nell were reliable and trustworthy, and he anticipated their responses as well as he knew his own. Sometimes even his own kin in England remained a cipher to him, and strangers utterly unfathomable.

"She desires my manuscript. What little I already completed," he said, abruptly.

Geoff gave a little snort and shifted in his seat.

"Were you asleep?" Will asked, surprised. They were accustomed to staying awake all hours of the night, reviewing the events of the day. "I am sorry."

"Don't be, my good man." Geoff asked grumpily. "What did you say? Nell wants the manuscript?"

"Not Nell," Will answered, grumpy in his turn. "The other one. My partner."

"Ah, do you mean Lady Verity Harwood of Harwood Hall, lately of England? Is she the one?"

"You know she is. Well, we cannot continue to call her Lady Verity as we travel to Cincinnati. People will think she is a prostitute."

Geoff laughed out loud. "Considering she jumps like a cat any time you touch her, I do not think she could be mistaken for anyone in that profession. She is a true lady. Anyone could see that."

"Hmmm," Will mused, recognizing at least one source of his consternation. "I am not sure I do. Recall the manners of my English relations, if you will, and their attitude of barely concealed contempt for anyone of lower rank than a baron."

"You must forgive them. It is a mere thirty years since a New Yorker dared to marry your father and produce a potential heir to the precious Eastbourne estates. Give them time. At least your relatives have not yet shot at you as you rode past the gatehouse."

"Ah—there is what they would consider the quintessential American response. My relatives would never consider shooting me outright. But I am sure they thought about poison."

"What was it we ate when we dined with your Aunt Carolyn? Are you sure it was not poison?"

"We have eaten worse, I am sure. But wouldn't it

be just as effective to throw pretty and eligible young girls my way? The right Englishwoman could restore the family honor."

Geoffrey laughed.

"But they did, old friend. Or did you not notice it? Were you so preoccupied by the rethatching of Eastbourne's tenants' roofs, you could not be bothered with lovemaking?"

"The need of the tenants was greater. And now we will travel with an English lady who is already too well known to some of my relatives. And what they do not know is not likely to improve her reputation. Can you imagine any of them walking about barefoot in the garden? Or discussing the flavor of the meat with a servant? Or agreeing to a business proposition? Lady Verity is a very different sort of creature; I wonder if she has a bit of the New World in her blood."

"Consider it an asset for your joint endeavor."

"I daresay she has few others. I doubt she can string five words together in a sentence. Damn! I must have been drugged to agree to her ridiculous terms. Can I honorably dismiss her?" Will asked, hopefully.

"No," Geoff said. "If you were drugged, it must have been by her delicious scent. I would not mind a dose of it myself."

"So you shall have it, my friend, but do not say I did not warn you. And you can start on the morrow: the wretch wants to see what I have already written, no doubt so she can correct my grammar, or tell me that reticules are draped from the left hand rather than the right. Or something equally superior." Will stood and yawned loudly in the still room. A thought occurred to him, making him abruptly catch his breath. "But we will have to stall her, Geoff."

"To give her time to reconsider?"

"Of course not. To give me time to reconsider."

"I do not follow."

"After we met her so unceremoniously, it is possible I wrote a few harsh things about her in my notes. If Lady Verity reads them, she will skewer me over flames."

"Possible?"

"Definite."

"It would make for good reading," Geoff pointed out.

"But very awkward company. I think I ought to revise my manuscript."

"You sound as if you are afraid of the woman. For goodness' sake, Will, she is barely more than a girl."

Will cleared his throat. "Don't be ridiculous."

But he wished he didn't sound as if he were barely more than a boy.

****

Verity gripped the sides of her wide canopied bed, wondering why the ship no longer rocked. Outside, she heard the call of birds and the steady hum of insects. Disorientated, bemused, several moments passed before she realized she was no longer at sea and about to open her eyes onto a whole new world.

She was in America. In service to none but herself, a woman with the possibility of earning her own way, and surrounded by those who considered her their equal: she could scarcely dream of such things when she left Liverpool with Lady Verity.

Now she was Lady Verity, and she would be a better Verity than that lady ever was. She would exercise kindness, and compassion, and act responsibly, and do more with her life than attend dinner parties at night and sleep through the day.

"Lady Verity?" A gentle voice interrupted Verity's thoughts.

"Oh, Nell. Come in! Have I overslept?"

The door opened, and Nell slipped through. She wore a simple muslin gown with a white linen apron.

"It is not yet noon. But I could not wait to see you again. Will and Geoff went into town to buy new clothing and some supplies. Will is anxious to leave on our journey in the next few days, and Geoff will not say no to him."

"Does anyone?"

"I suppose not. Will is accustomed to having his own way in everything. But I believe you are capable of challenging him at every turn."

Verity looked at her in surprise, flattered to hear it.

"We are not friends, if that is what you mean," she said evasively. "He has none of your brother's affability."

"But Geoff is a darling. I am lucky to have him for a brother. A woman would be lucky to have him for a husband."

Verity pulled herself out of bed and winced as she stepped onto the floor.

"I think you ought to wear sturdier shoes to protect yourself, my lady."

Verity hesitated but wished to correct one of the several misconceptions about herself, the only one she dared. "You must call me Verity, now that I am in America. It is much easier because we are also friends."

Nell nodded, smiling.

"And another thing: I am not comfortable with the shoes I have brought with me. Perhaps I did not anticipate the rough terrain. Do you suppose I might purchase a pair locally?"

Nell clapped her hands together in delight. "Of course! I did want to take you into town! Now we have a perfect excuse to do so."

"Excellent," Verity said, and then immediately reconsidered. "Oh, but has Mr. Bentley left me work to do?"

Nell looked thoughtful. "I do not think so. He did not say anything to me at breakfast. I am sure he is not so cruel a taskmaster as to insist you work on the very morning after your arrival. Aside from anything else, he surely understands how unaccustomed you are to such rigors."

Verity smiled, and breathed in the fresh, pine-scented air of her new life. A vision of wash buckets and laundry tubs and rising breads flashed in her memory.

"And yet, I think I can grow accustomed to it very easily," she said.

Cambridge proved a surprise for Verity. The bustle of the market, the wild symphony of sound, the bright colors, even the dust of the road seemed utterly familiar to her, making her both homesick and comfortable at the same time.

"You will have little trouble finding shoes in our shops, Verity. Cambridge is known throughout the world for the excellence of its shoemakers," Nell said cheerfully. "Though of course, there will not be time to order shoes special for you."

Verity jingled her purloined purse and felt a wave

of disappointment. For the first time in her life, she was at luxury to have shoes made to fit her, and now her hopes were dashed.

"But I believe you will like the selection in this shop," Nell added.

An hour later, the two women watched as several boxes of purchases were loaded onto the carriage. Verity realized that what she sacrificed in custom quality she more than compensated for in quantity. But it had been so very difficult to resist temptation, and indeed, she made only a very little dent in the collection of coins Lady Verity was given by her father before setting out for America. Even so, it would be necessary to visit Lord Harwood's bank agent in Boston and present his cheques for additional funds. Their journey would be long, likely with unexpected expenses.

"I hope you do not intend to transport that all the way to Cincinnati," said a sardonic voice behind them.

Verity gritted her teeth in frustration. She knew but a handful of people on the whole continent, and yet her luck would have her unable to avoid this man. She turned on her heel.

"And if I do?" she asked.

Will Bentley stood before her, his hands deep in his pockets. He rocked on his heels and gave the illusion of being contemplative; Verity thought it all an act.

"Why, you might have to pay an extra fare for it on the ferry," he said.

Nell laughed. "Do not be ridiculous, Will! If you are not charged for your library, Verity will not be charged for a few pairs of sturdy shoes and some very pretty dresses. They will be far more appreciated than your boring books!"

Mr. Bentley did not answer, but Verity saw all she needed to know in the expression in his eyes. He did not think his books were boring and looked insulted that anyone else should feel they were. Nell would never gain his love when she mocked what was dear to him.

"And where is Mr. Marsh, sir?" Verity asked kindly, hoping to change the subject.

"Do you miss his company, my lady? He is just yonder, at the apothecary. By the by, we are in a hurry, because he promises to work this day on supplying you with what has already been written. As you requested."

"Of course. But I did not mean to intrude on Mr. Marsh's very first full day in his homeland."

"I see. And yet you would intrude on my time."

Verity wondered if it would ever be possible to make a simple statement to this man, and not have him give it a provocative interpretation. Nothing she said ever seemed to please him; nothing she did made him happy. The book they would write would necessarily be so argumentative, their readers would put it down in frustration.

"Of course, Will. I do not hesitate to intrude on you, because you have already convinced me you would have it no other way. I must confess: I purposely bought so much just now, because I knew it would displease you. And you see, you have proved yourself utterly predictable. I wonder if it is a trait common to American men? I shall make a note of it right away, so I might include it in our book."

For once, he had no answer, but he did not fool Verity into thinking him compliant as he helped her and

Nell up onto the seat of their carriage. Verity did not doubt he was already planning to retaliate, and that it would make for very unpleasant bedtime reading.

\*\*\*\*

*Unlike in America, in all things English there is a level of class awareness, so if you doubt the loftiness of a man's position, he is quick to put you in your humble place. It is not difficult to account for such notions among the aristocracy, but one often encounters instances of class identification among the common folk, as well.*

*Thus, one might meet a groom just returned from an outing. As you pass on the drive, you might sensibly ask him for directions to the nearest town.*

*"That I canna say, sir," might be his earnest reply. "For direction, ye must ask the gatekeeper."*

Verity turned the page impatiently, already formulating an indignant reply to Will Bentley's limited view of the universe. Indeed, is it possible the groom deferred the question because he did not know the answer? And what right has Mr. Bentley to be censorious, when he has never known what it is to be another man's servant?

*I believe such manners stem not from ignorance, nor from unwillingness to be of assistance. Rather, the man in the lowliest position understands from birth he must never step on the heels of the man just ahead of him. Even to speak in the place of the other is to risk censure.*

*For clarification of my hypothesis, I dared to question a lady of the highest order, an acquaintance on board ship. She, still mourning the loss of her compliant, excellent companion...*

Verity turned the page so quickly, she almost tore it in twain. She did not doubt the source of Mr. Bentley's next complaint and felt righteous anger just anticipating it. But, to her consternation, the following words described the moments when the *Andromeda* drifted gracefully into Massachusetts Bay and made no further mention of the "lady of the highest order." Is it possible the man left off a thought in mid-sentence?

She rubbed her weary eyes. Geoff Marsh had delivered the papers to her just after dinner, with very much the manner of someone offering up a delectable dessert, and Verity immediately sat down to the task. Indeed, there were some opinions within the pages about which she could scarcely argue, but many, many more she felt compelled to address.

Edgy, anxious, she knew her responses would not be so quick if she uncovered anything incriminating about herself. The thought of revenge, of attacking slander with insult, provided such a spur to righteous indignation, Verity's eyes raced across the bold strokes of ink upon each page.

And yet here, when she finally caught an intriguing personal reference, the opinionated Will Bentley quickly turned to another topic.

Rubbing her forehead, Verity wondered if she'd lost a page somewhere and glanced under her writing desk. Then a thought struck her, and she spread Mr. Bentley's pile of pages across the desk. In the upper left corner, he customarily numbered his pages; on close scrutiny, Verity identified at least twenty pages omitted in the present text.

A little ruffle of pleasure stirred Verity's sensibilities. Was it possible Mr. Bentley originally intended to devote so many pages of his manuscript to the subject of Lady Verity Harwood? It was terribly wrong of him.

But so delicious.

**** 

"I am still digesting the dessert you offered me, sir, but find it oddly incomplete," said Verity as she walked purposefully into Mr. Marsh's library. When Mr. Bentley did not raise his head, she dropped the pages she held onto his lap.

"Was it not sweet enough, Lady Verity? Do you desire more honey? Did I not already tell you my criticism might be harsh and uncompromising?"

"Indeed you did," she said and sat down. "Unfortunately, you neglected to tell me it might also be irrational and therefore so easy to refute. I can scarcely contain myself for all the cake you have served me."

"I am sure you cannot," he said dryly. "Pray, then, what compels you to waste such valuable time in my poor company? Has your inkwell run dry? Why not speak to one of the servants about it?"

"And thereby prove your very point? Do you not think ladies are capable of filling their own inkwells?"

"I do not yet know of what you are capable," Mr. Bentley said ominously. "But is that why you have interrupted us? To demonstrate your proficiency? You said something was lacking. I am sure you will delight in pointing out what it might be."

"Of course, sir," Verity said slowly, feeling out of breath, though he did almost all the talking. "I lack at least twenty pages of your text."

Looking for it, she did not miss his quick glance in

Mr. Marsh's direction. He pulled at his cravat and finally met her eyes.

"You understand there is a great deal of revision involved in the writing of a book, do you not?"

"I am not stupid, sir," Verity retorted, though the thought never occurred to her.

"Well, then, the omission is quite easy to understand. Having written those twenty pages, I decline to include them in the final chapters."

"Might they not be of interest to me, nevertheless?" Verity asked sweetly.

"I am sure they would be. But that does not mean I wish for you to read them," he answered in a like tone.

"And why not?"

"I daresay you would find certain items in my clothing closet of interest as well, my lady. But that does not mean I wish for you to inspect them."

Verity's cheeks grew warm, and she bit down on her lip.

"And do you also require a partner to make some sense of your arrangement of garments? I hope you will not be lacking in as many essentials as you lack in pages."

"It is the reason Geoff and I made purchases in town. Though I daresay we both can make do with a good deal less than you seem to require, my lady."

He gave her the answer she needed in his very criticism.

"By definition, a lady requires a good deal."

"I see," Mr. Bentley said thoughtfully, and Verity dared to hope she managed to have the final word. "But all women are ladies in America, and the needs of one ought not be more worthy than the rest of the group."

Geoffrey Marsh cleared his throat. "Will means no disrespect, Lady Verity—"

"Of course I do," Will said a little too cheerfully.

"Watch your words, my friend," Mr. Marsh cautioned.

"Oh, I allow you the same deference as I would any other woman of my acquaintance and have no intention of harming your reputation any more than it already suffers."

"I beg your pardon…" Verity began, wondering what on earth he knew of her reputation or, more likely, Lady Verity's.

"Ladies do not beg," he answered tersely. "But you do not imagine a young woman traveling through the countryside with two unmarried men will not be the subject of some speculation? And when you reveal, as eventually you must, you are the author of a book, do you not think the loftiest of the ton will not condemn you for it?"

Verity stood unhappily for several minutes, knowing the truth of his argument. For all her wish to establish an identity for the serving girl once known as Annie, she had scarcely considered the future of the lady who was now Lady Verity Harwood.

"I am not the first woman of my class to gainfully use my talents," she said with uncertainty. "Nor will I be the last."

"She has you there, Will," Geoff said.

Mr. Bentley sighed. "Perhaps she does. I concede the point, though I would like very much to witness the eventual reaction of her family and friends when she returns home."

"My future is none of your business, sir."

"It is not. We will concern ourselves with the present. Where you risk censure and gossip if you are introduced as Lady Verity while we are together. I propose we call you Miss Harwood."

"And yet the three of you are so familiar with each other you call each other by your given names. Might it not arouse suspicion if I am the only one who is a Miss?" And then, when neither man answered, "Geoffrey? Will?"

Mr. Bentley looked surprised "Verity? You would have us call you Verity?"

"It is as good a name as any other," she said slowly.

"It is settled, then," Will, agreed quickly. "Geoff and I have just decided we will leave in two days' time. We have hired a coach to take us west as far as the Hudson River, in New York. Then we will change to a larger vehicle, one of my own, in Albany."

"I will be ready," Verity began, turning toward the door.

"You will have finished your business in Boston? You may not be back for some months, perhaps before winter."

Verity paused, remembering full well there was some business to accomplish, something she hoped to put off as long as possible. But she could not continue on, relying solely on the generosity of people she hardly knew. Though she would be no better than a thief, it was necessary she present herself to her father's agent in Boston.

"There is a small matter to which I must attend," she said, while avoiding looking at either of them. "I must secure additional funds from a gentleman authorized to act on my father's behalf. I have an address for a Mr. Meldon, on Milk Street in Boston."

"You must not go alone," Geoff said quickly. "Nor do I like the thought of my sister riding alone with you when you are carrying a full purse of coins."

"Will you be able to accompany me, Geoffrey?" Verity asked, looking only at him.

"Geoff is busy just now with the affairs of his own household," said Will. "I will go with you myself."

"But you must be very busy, Will," Verity said, still watching Geoffrey.

"Not at all, Verity," he answered, emphasizing her name. "I think the outing will give us a splendid opportunity to get to know more about each other."

So she feared.

Chapter 6

The office of Mr. Josiah Meldon was small and dusty, precisely as Will expected. He watched the expression on Verity's face as he opened the door for her, expecting to witness some reaction of dismay or disgust on her elegant features, but she seemed to find nothing amiss in the cramped quarters of her father's American agent. Nor did she hesitate to plant her silk draped bottom onto a stained leather chair.

Will, not nearly so fastidious as a rule, preferred to stand.

From where he stood, he noticed her hand shook slightly as she offered a folded letter to the elderly man, and she sat rigidly on her seat. Will had never seen her like this, nervous and cautious and for the first time, he wondered what her father was like, and if she was, in fact, running away from him when she decided to come to America. Perhaps her father tried to punish her after her unseemly affair and intended to force her into a hateful, arranged marriage. What did anyone know of another's life?

With growing wisdom, Will studied Verity's face and form, the proud independent tilt of her chin and the faint shadows her long lashes left upon her cheeks. Indeed, why had such a beauty not yet married? There must have been dozens of young men pursuing her, offering her a life of luxury to which she was already accustomed, and which she owned every right to expect. Why make a risky and dangerous trip to a country where she would be a stranger and where the men she might meet would be exempt from her lofty consideration?

With the possible exception, of himself, Will wryly noted. How ironic the one potentially eligible man she was likely to meet in America was one she could barely tolerate? Whatever she was running from could not be much worse than the wall she now ran into.

"And how is your dear father, my lady?" Mr. Meldon asked solemnly. "When last I visited him, he seemed in some distress."

"And when was that, sir?" Verity asked softly.

"Do you not recall? We sat together on an evening, and I told you about the glories of this fair city."

For once, Verity seemed unsure of herself.

"I described the woodlands and the abundance of fresh water," Mr. Meldon pressed on.

"Ah yes, I recall it now. Were we not seated on the veranda, looking out over Harwood Park?" Verity asked somewhat tentatively.

"We were, indeed, my lady. I confess, you did not seem very impressed at the time. You did not take well to my proposal."

"Your proposal?" The lady leaned so far forward, she nearly fell off her chair.

"Of course. I said you must come to America and see it for yourself. I invited you to stay with Mrs. Meldon and myself in Beacon Hill. And yet here you are in the company of a stranger." Mr. Meldon studied Will. "A writer, you say? And are you settled, young man?"

"I am not in want of funds, if that is what you are asking, sir. I own property in New York and in England and am fairly successful at managing my interests. But this is not relevant to your business at hand."

"It is indeed, if you are a fortune hunter."

Will started, feeling a fool for not having thought of it first. Of course the man would want to inspect his credentials before handing over a cheque to an innocent like Lady Verity. But when Will glanced down at her face, he took heart in what he saw there.

She trusted him. He was not altogether sure why, but her open expression told him not to doubt it.

"I am not a fortune hunter, sir. I seek neither financial gain, nor fame, nor a wife. Your lady has nothing to fear from me."

"Mr. Bentley is a friend," Verity said quickly. "His intention is only to see me safely to Mrs. Trollope in Cincinnati. And I do recall our conversation, sir. Perhaps you proved more persuasive than you realized. I decided I would come to America and see it for myself."

"Your father would not let you come by yourself."

"Of course not. I traveled with Annie Merrill, my maid. She did not survive the journey."

"Miss Merrill, you say? She who is the daughter of Harwood's…"

"Indeed," Verity said quickly. "Her mother died this past winter. I beg you say no more on the subject. It pains me greatly."

Meldon nodded. "I remember the chit," he said with what sounded like genuine regret. He then looked across the table at her, and narrowed his eyes. "She looked very much like you."

"I feel the loss daily, Mr. Meldon. But I did not come to you to commiserate. There are practical concerns, matters I must complete before continuing on my journey."

"Of course. You require money."

"I do. My understanding from my father is that I need to apply to you for it. I hold his letter in my hand."

"I recognize his hand, even from here. I shall need proof of your identity, of course."

"What is it you need?" Will asked, his voice echoing in the still room. Did the man not already recognize her?

"Why, your personal witness will do very well here."

"Of course."

"You can attest the lady is who she says she is?"

"Why do you doubt it?" Will asked, and for no sensible reason, put his hand on her shoulder and she eased back against his touch. He recognized the sweet smell of lavender in her hair.

Mr. Meldon raised his brows and faintly smiled. "I do not doubt it, of course. I ask for only a formal statement. There is, after all, a rather considerable fortune involved. Since you are only friends, you might not be aware of it."

"It is no matter, Mr. Meldon," Verity said hurriedly. "I have many things to accomplish this morning; shall we proceed?"

Mr. Meldon sprang to action. Producing papers, envelopes, pockets of coins, and documents, he spread out everything on the desk before him. Verity accepted his pen and studied it for a moment before laboring over her signature. Will wondered why she should make such a business of it, and then realized she might very well have gotten out of the practice of holding a pen. Well, that would be remedied shortly. Soon she handed the pen to him, for it was apparently his moment to vouch for her. He raised the little vessel almost to his lips, lifting her fingers with it, and catching the surprised look on her face. She was still afraid of something.

"There you have it, my lady. You can appeal throughout your journey to gentlemen on the enclosed list, who will honor your transactions. And here is more immediate cash," said Mr. Meldon at last. "I trust Bentley will see you safely home."

"You can rely on me, sir," Will said graciously and caught Verity's elbow to lead her to the door. He felt drawn to her, frankly curious and undeniably attracted. He had never fully comprehended the power of a woman's dependency upon him as a mode of desire. And yet, there it was.

They stepped into the Boston sunshine, and Will breathed in the fresh air tinged with the smell of the sea. It was a potent tonic for his heated senses, a gulp of pure sanity.

The lady's slim arm slipped away from his, and she seemed interested in a shop across Milk Street. Will followed her gaze and saw a man duck through the doorway.

"Thank you for your assistance, Will, though I think I might have managed this transaction on my own." She glanced up at him. "I believe that was Mr. Reese entering the milliner's shop, by the by."

Will believed the same thing. "Perhaps he is buying a bonnet for his mother."

"Perhaps I shall buy one for myself," Verity mused. "Did you say we have an abundance of space for our baggage?"

"I believe it is quite the opposite. And let us stay away from Reese," Will said, helping her up into their waiting carriage. He felt the hard bone of her stays and wondered why such a slim form required them.

"You really are rather strict."

"No worse than Mr. Meldon," he said.

Surprisingly, Verity laughed. "He was rather fierce, was he not? Like a stern cook who discovers someone pilfering the eggs!"

Will raised his brows, but her mood was infectious. "Or a strict editor, questioning the loss of a few dozen pages?"

She caught her breath and leaned forward. Her face was very close to his, and he could see a sprinkling of freckles across her cheeks. That she did not bother to powder them seemed an endearing quality.

"Or a gentleman who finds a lady stands in the way of his assistance of a friend?" she asked.

He nodded, still wondering about the circumstances of the day when she sought help for the much lamented Annie Merrill.

"Or a man who is denied anything upon which his heart is set."

"Oh." A small sigh escaped her tempting lips.

He would have dared to kiss her right in the middle of Milk Street if he did not sense Mr. Meldon's eyes upon his back. As it was, they were giving him enough upon which to speculate.

"But that is something about which you must know very little. What has Lady Verity Harwood ever been denied? Why even the tough old gent within did not insist upon withholding your money. Though he did not trust me, he accepted me as a witness. I daresay other petitioners would have had to dance naked on Boston Common to achieve the same recognition."

Something flared in her bright eyes, though he dared not put a name to it. But if they were alone, sitting beside Fresh Pond perhaps, he might have put his riotous instincts to the test.

"A very provoking thought, Will," she said, her accent no longer quite as lofty. "If this is the sort of thing you are accustomed to doing, I entirely understand Mr. Meldon's reservations. Though I must confess, the idea of asking for a demonstration is very tempting."

Neither of them said anything for several minutes, and they must have appeared an odd spectacle on the busy street. Will only knew something had subtly changed in the lady's manner toward him, as if the old agent had liberated her of some prescribed inhibitions. He believed he, himself, did nothing to warrant such a change. Nor did he yet imagine it would liberate some of his own feelings as well.

Suddenly, she shifted in her seat, quite as if nothing happened between them. Indeed, Will thought with a moment's regret, nothing did.

"But you forget, Will, he recognized me. We enjoyed a lovely afternoon once at Harwood," she said in the manner of a delighted hostess.

Will hoisted himself up beside her, taking care not to brush against her. "It sounds like great fun. You must have been rapt with the description of the trees of Boston."

"Do not be sarcastic, Will. I would never be impolite to a guest in my father's house. I am sure I nodded and smiled most agreeably."

"I daresay you are capable of it when the occasional mood suits you," Will said a little brusquely. And yet she would be impolite even as a guest in someone else's house. "In any case, he remembered you quite well. I confess to some curiosity, however."

"And what is that?" she asked too quickly.

Will turned to study her and saw the look of fear that was both inexplicable and familiar.

"Why were you not able to remember him? Are elderly American men so common in your rarefied company, you could not recall a visitor of less than a year ago?"

Verity cleared her throat. "I meet many men socially."

Will could not understand why he should feel such a jolt of disappointment. With a lady in her position, it could not be otherwise, and yet he would have preferred to hear she had been locked in a tower at Harwood, speaking to none else.

"I see. I daresay you confused him with someone else. But I have another question, and this relates to a woman I did not meet, and never will."

He waited for her to respond but she said nothing, just stared directly in front of her.

"I am speaking of Miss Merrill," he ventured.

Still Verity did not answer.

"I realize it must be painful to speak of her," he continued, trying to sound casual, conversational, "but would it not relieve you of a burden to reflect upon her life? She must have been young and full of excitement about her journey to America. It seems such a pity she suffered and never reached these shores."

Will paused and turned in his seat. Verity was drawing in great gulps of air, and her eyes were closed.

"She was a wonderful person," she sobbed as if a great dam had opened. "She was common, with no expectations but to be a lady's maid all of her life, and yet there was a certain nobility about her, a generosity…"

"Surely it is not a coincidence, Lady Verity? You spent many hours together, I assume."

"Of course. We were like sisters."

"So I gather. Mr. Meldon is not the first to remark on your similarities of appearance."

"There is a good deal of Harwood blood in the neighborhood," she said vaguely, and wiped her tears on her silken sleeve.

Will reached into his vest pocket and handed her a linen handkerchief. "It must run very strong to create such a match," he said, relentlessly.

"You know how immediate it must be, so you may stop goading me, Will. My mother died when I was very young. But even before that sad event, my father looked elsewhere for…recreation."

"I suppose you mean sexual relations," Will said, most daringly.

Verity blushed so fiercely he felt immediately sorry to have taunted her. And yet, he felt compelled to push her further.

"Is it not a word you have heard in your sequestered society at Harwood? It means—"

"I know precisely what it means, Will," she said haughtily. "If I appear flustered, it is not from ignorance, but from indignation. A gentleman would never use such a word in the presence of a lady."

Will feigned regret, though he felt it not at all.

"But between us, dear Verity, the rules do not apply. We are partners; do you remember? Such a relationship demands absolute honesty between us, particularly in matters of language."

She did not answer, but he did not wish to rush her into a retort they might both regret. Instead, he lifted the reins and urged his team forward, toward Cambridge. They rode alone in silence, but when they approached the Charles, and Will saw the ferry already ten feet out in the river, he cursed briefly under his breath.

"But my understanding, at your insistence, was that it did not pertain to matters in our private lives," Verity said suddenly. Will, already diverted by the nuisance of the wait at the river crossing, did not understand what she meant. "And yet, I suppose there is no harm in frankness on this point. After all, poor Miss Merrill is dead."

"But your father is alive," Will said hurriedly, recovering himself.

"He is, but I do not know if I will ever see him again." She sighed.

Will pulled the carriage up to the end of the drive, guaranteeing they would be the first vehicle to board the ferry, and also the first to disembark. He gave a fleeting thought to the American spirit; he was only a few days back in Boston, and he already felt prepared to fight his way to the front of a line. In England, people in a line merely accepted their place and order. He made a mental note to include a commentary on this when he again sat down to write.

But, for now, he did not want to lose the confidences of the lady.

"Why do you think you will not see him again? I thought it always your intention to return to England. Are you not a great heiress? Mustn't you claim what is yours?"

Verity turned wide eyes upon him, making him wonder what she saw and he could not.

"When I claim what is mine, sir, it is because I no longer have the ability to see my father again. And, until such time, I am not altogether sure I desire a meeting. He is not the most doting of fathers."

Will studied her, thinking she appeared a good deal less emotional than when she had sobbed over the death of Annie Merrill.

"If we are to be honest with each other, you must know the truth, of course. My father enjoyed the company of his housekeeper, Mrs. Merrill, even before my mother, the countess, died. Both women were with child within a year of each other, and both infants were daughters. It must have been a very disappointing outcome for a man who desired a male heir, but not so awkward as if Lady Harwood were delivered of a girl, and Mrs. Merrill of a boy. You see what might have resulted, then."

"An illegitimate heir cannot displace a legitimate one—even if she is female," Will pointed out.

"No, but odder things have happened. Suppose Lord Harwood married his housekeeper, and acknowledged their son?" She sighed. "But I am just indulging in fairy tales. Since Mrs. Merrill conveniently had a daughter, Lord Harwood had no need to ever acknowledge either of them. Miss Merrill suffered the consequences of his neglect all of her life."

"Do you mean, she was in a somewhat weakened state? Might that have led to her death?"

Verity made a gesture of impatience. "I do not mean her physical health, Will. I refer to her emotional state. She lost her mother only months before and had no expectations of her father. I was her only friend and ally."

"How very good of you," Will said and immediately regretted that the words sounded sarcastic, even to himself. "But yet you were half sisters, and the bond is not one you would have regarded indifferently."

"Of course not," Verity said.

"You might have been twins, but for the circumstances of your births."

"An odd way of putting it, but yes, I suppose that is so."

"So alike were you, one could have been changed for the other."

Verity pulled slightly away from him. "We were not all that alike, you know. I considered poor Annie Merrill a great beauty."

He looked at her, considering her face one of infinite fascination, a symphony of the most attractive features. He wondered what it must have been like to gaze upon two such faces at once.

"Then there is justice in heaven, Verity. You have the wealth and all the honor of your position. Miss Merrill, unacknowledged by her father, had the beauty."

"Thank you very much. But is it justice? I am surprised at you, Will. Miss Merrill scarcely had time to live, to use her beauty to her advantage. Whereas I…"

"Have me," he finished wryly. "I suspect you will

continue to use me to your advantage whenever possible."

He braced himself for her inevitable retort, in this case, more than justified. But she closed her lips into a tight line and turned her eyes upon the nearby shore, where the damn ferry had just begun its return to Boston Landing.

**** 

Verity tried to remain calm by applying herself to a variety of tasks—none of them unpleasant.

How would she continue in his company if he would provoke her so easily and drive her to confession?

She dumped the contents of Mr. Meldon's purse upon her bed and knelt before it as if praying at a shrine. In a way, perhaps she was. Indeed, she had never before seen so much money.

She lifted a gold coin and hefted it in the palm of her hand. She as yet had no sense of what such a bounty might buy, but it must be considerable, even in such a market as America's. And here she had fifty such coins, shining like the gold of a child's curls. Or the glints in Will's dark eyes.

How close was he to uncovering the truth? Had she given anything away in their little duel of words?

A knock at the door broke into her thoughts.

"Do come in," Verity called out, before she realized the impropriety of anyone seeing all her assets splayed on the bed.

"Is this a bad time?" Nell asked. "Oh dear, I suppose it is. I do not wish to interrupt your counting of money."

"It is all done. I am trying to conserve my

resources, but I overspent when we shopped yesterday. Thank you for lending me coin when I fell short. I do have enough to repay you now."

"Oh, it was not so very much. Geoff gives me a generous allowance and granted me more with the instructions I was to see you properly dressed."

Verity smiled wickedly. "You do not think he liked the dress I wore to dinner the first night?"

"I think he liked it altogether too much. So did Will. If you had bent over the tea cart one more time, I believe they both would have fallen over. Perhaps your new wardrobe will protect them from foolishness." Nell spoke like a middle-aged schoolmistress. "It will not do any harm to me, either."

"Oh, my poor Nell! To you, I owe a full apology! I do not intend to displace you in any man's affections! Indeed, I would have none of them."

"Not even my brother, Geoff?" Nell asked.

Verity realized how much she would love to be able to say he interested her. But the truth, she realized a little belatedly, was he did not. He was kind, and good, and everything admirable, but she saw him undoubtedly very much as Nell did herself: as an older brother.

"Geoffrey is the best of men," Verity said diplomatically. In a corner of her mind, she wondered why she did not covet the best. But before her own doubts or Nell's inquisition could take hold, she changed the subject. "And you need not worry about my old wardrobe any longer. I shall prove no competition for any man's affection, for my new dresses are far more serviceable and not likely to attract undue attention."

Nell laughed. "They are far grander than what most women in Cambridge are accustomed to wearing. I guarantee, you will be noticed."

Verity sighed and started to untie the lace at her neckline. "I suppose I am a bit of a novelty just now. But that will change, no doubt. I believe one can assimilate into society very easily, if one chooses to do so."

Nell looked surprised. "Is that something you desire? Would you not feel as if you lost something of yourself?"

Verity knew, with dreaded certainty, it would be a casual moment such as this that would reveal her for the wicked person she truly was. She, who was perfectly happy to lose her identity and dress herself in another's, would say the wrong thing, not recognize someone she ought, write the wrong signature on a correspondence.

"Verity?"

Indeed, it was the name that was now hers. "I believe it ought to be my intent, if I am to write honestly about my experience in America," she said slowly, thinking it through. Amazingly, it made perfect sense. "How else might I intrusively observe and make acquaintances, and live among Americans? I want to sound knowing and convincing."

"You are very clever," Nell said, without a trace of irony.

"And you will help me, dear Nell. You must tell me when I overstep, or call too much attention to myself. I must attract no notice."

"I am sure that will be impossible. The gentlemen can scarcely take their eyes off you," Nell said, shaking her head. "Verity, what are you doing?"

Verity had fully unbuttoned herself to the waist, and slipped her arms out of her sleeves. The room was warm, and her senses entirely liberated.

"I wish to loosen my stays. Will you help me?"

"Of course. You must be accustomed to having a lady's maid, after all. We will have to serve each other during our travels, which I'm sure will be a new experience for you."

"I will do my best," Verity murmured, between gasps of breath.

"Why, what is this?" Nell asked. "It is a dreadful scar."

Verity had nearly forgotten that other souvenir from her lady. They were only girls when Lady Verity beat her across the back with her riding crop, for a reason so trivial Verity could no longer recall it.

"But it no longer pains me, and what I cannot see, I do not recall," Verity said lightly. "The person who did that to me can no longer harm me or anyone else."

Just then someone knocked at the door. Nell waved Verity away and opened it just a crack. Verity scarcely moved in time, and only caught Will's first words.

"That sounds perfectly delightful. When shall we leave?" Nell said. And then, after a vague sound of an answer, "We shall be ready."

She closed the door and turned to Verity, who stood with her back to a mirror, straining to see her own scar.

"I have reminded you of it, and I am sorry for it. I will not speak of it again." Nell pointed toward the door. "That was Will, by the way. We are to go to Mrs. Evans's house on Brattle Street this night. She is hosting a dinner and dance. You are not only invited, you are to be the guest of honor."

Verity turned away from the mirror. "I cannot possibly accept that honor. I know nothing about the custom of such a thing."

"Do you not? We may not be accustomed to French corsets, but we are not entirely barbaric here. It will not be very different from the dances you attended at home, I am sure."

Verity had a brief vision of barn dancing in the cool evening hours after the harvest, of drunken young men groping her breasts and planting wet kisses on her lips. She could almost hear the cranky strings of old Mr. Macy's violin and smell the roasting pigs and ducks on the large spit. The dance would end in the early hours of the morning, and no one would bother to sleep since the duties of the next day were already upon them.

"On the other hand, you might be very much surprised," Verity mused.

****

Verity herself was much surprised when the gentlemen pronounced themselves ready for the evening, and no carriage awaited them on the road. Will angled Geoff's chair down the stone steps of the house and wheeled him out onto the road. Nell handed Verity a soft wool shawl and reached for her hand so they might descend together.

"We cannot walk all the way, Nell!" Verity protested. "And in our formal gowns?"

"It is not so very far, and as we approach, we are likely to find friends to join us along the way. We are great walkers in America, you see. We would be considered a bit haughty if we were to fuss with the carriage and horses for a mere five-minute drive."

"And what of our return? Will it not be dark when we leave the party?"

"Oh, certainly. But Will and Geoff will carry torches to see us on our way. Do not worry so; we do it all the time."

"Would my lady prefer to ride in a wheeled chaise, like my friend Mr. Marsh?" a sarcastic voice asked. "Geoffrey, would you give your seat to a lady?"

"I would if I only could, Will. Lady Verity, let me be the first to tell you how lovely you look tonight."

"You are not the first, Geoff," Nell said lightly. "But I would not mind if you echoed your compliment for me."

"Let me say it then, and it shall be no echo," pronounced Will gallantly. "You look wonderfully grand, Nell. It is a pleasure to behold such beauty after so many weeks of deprivation."

Nell responded by squeezing Verity's fingers. "You must not mind him, you know. He says things like that to goad you."

"Oh, I do not mind Will's insults," Verity answered, when they were close enough for him to hear. "If only he had any skill at it, he might have the ability to offend. But as it is, they fall about me like light rain."

"I shall have to work at it," Will muttered under his breath.

Nell giggled. "But not tonight, I hope. Lady Verity is the guest of honor, and no one will allow any insults."

"Dear Nell, they have yet to meet her. For most of our neighbors, the expectations of the daughter of an earl are so grand, they are bound to be disappointed.

There is no hope for it," Will said, smiling too brightly.

"I daresay if I remain cheerful and friendly and do not deliver insults with each breath, I might pass muster. But whatever the popular expectation, I hope I will make myself worthy of attending with my new friends," answered Verity, buoyed by her conviction.

"I claim some of Nell's attention as we will dance together," Will said.

"By all means, you must," Verity said, "if she will have you."

She glanced across his broad back and saw by the expression on Nell's face that she would have him in an instant. Dear girl; she probably deserved better than this unpleasant man. But Verity's next thought was a slap on her own face: did she, a lady's maid masquerading as a dead woman and stealing the money intended for another, deserve half as much? She rather doubted it.

"Is that the best you can do, Verity? I fear you will certainly bore Geoff to tears this evening. After all, he will be your captive audience," said Will.

"You are incapable of boring me, Lady Verity, and I will be honored to spend the whole evening with you. But surely you will dance."

"I do not care so very much for dancing," Verity said.

"Impossible," Nell broke in. "You will be much in demand. Every gentleman will want to dance with you and every lady will insist on an audience. I am sorry to disappoint you, Geoff, but you are likely to spend the evening with Mrs. Whipple, the professor's mother."

"Is it possible the lady still lives? Was she not elderly and infirm when her son was our mentor in Greek and Roman antiquities?"

"We thought her as ancient a relic, as I recall." Will laughed.

"What kind boys the two of you must have been," Verity said tartly. "But at least one of you has outgrown your youthful propensity to disdain."

"And here are the Websters," Will said a little too loudly.

Verity looked up in surprise and realized they had come along much farther than she would have thought. The lights of large houses were already in view, and people strolled along a well graveled avenue. A small cabriolet made its way between them.

"Darlings! Is our destination one and the same?" a brightly dressed woman cried out.

"Good evening, Maudie," Nell cooed. "Allow me to introduce our new friend, Lady Verity Harwood. Maud and Richard Webster, our neighbors."

Verity held out her hand, and Mrs. Webster shook it heartily.

"I am only Miss Harwood here in America. Mr. Bentley informs me that the nobility hold no currency."

"You would not guess it when you see the crowd assembled at the Evans's home tonight. You are a rare bird in our midst, and do not allow someone as cynical as Will let you believe otherwise," Mrs. Webster reassured her.

Verity slanted a glance up at him and realized he was barely able to conceal his impatience. She could not read him any easier than she did his manuscript. If, as he would have her believe, he was a student of American manners, why could he not take pleasure in the evening's events? Why did he insist on being rude to his friends and neighbors?

Why did he not take pleasure in her company?

But her unsettling thoughts were quickly interrupted by the arrival of more party-goers, and introductions were passed about like sweetbreads on a platter. Verity smiled and nodded and held up her head like the lady she was not and was swept along with the enthusiastic crowd to a white clapboard house of generous proportions at the end of the street. From within, the strains of a violin and flute added to the gaiety, and she could hear people clapping in time.

She was drawn to Will's side. She already recognized his touch, could sense his large form, could breathe in the air that surrounded him, and thus recognize him without looking at him.

"You will enter with me," he said tersely.

"Is that not unkind to our friends?" she asked first, and then, "And I thought you preferred not to remain in my presence?"

"The servants will lift Geoff into the house, and Nell knows everyone here. However, an English lady is deserving of a formal introduction, and as I have English relations, it is expected that I do it myself."

Verity turned and faced him, gathering her thoughts around her as she gazed at his face. His hat was slightly askew, but otherwise he looked impossibly proper and dignified. His dark eyes reflected the glow from the candlelight within, but the rest of his face was in shadow. She knew how he would look, however, for his lips would be pressed together in a frown and his eyebrows would slant toward the bridge of his elegant nose.

"I wonder, do you ever hear yourself, Will? I mean, really hear yourself? How is it possible you have taken on the task of writing about your own countrymen, except to find blame and inferiority in everything they do?" He did not so much as blink at her words, and so she went on, determined to crack the surface of his polished veneer. "We are all equal here, are we not? Our titles mean nothing in the rarefied air of Cambridge, Massachusetts. I was not so very fond of my position when I lived at Harwood Hall, so it is certainly not something I would insist upon here."

"That is not what my cousin has said," he whispered.

Verity was grateful for the darkness and glad her back was to the windows. "If that is the case, then certainly Lord Eastbourne was not particularly mindful of his lofty position either, or of the fact he was a married man. It is beneath him to reveal to anyone the particulars of his relationship with another lady."

"You do not deny there was a relationship?" Will said.

"We were neighbors and occasionally saw each other in passing. That is all that need concern you." She realized they were now standing alone in the drive and dancing had started in the room closest to them. "But if this is a matter in which you feel you need to intrude, I suggest we break off our partnership right now, and go our separate ways. I am sure I will find my way to Illinois."

"Ohio," he corrected. "I am quite certain you could, Verity Harwood. But I believe that is no longer my biggest concern."

"Indeed? What is the matter now, Will Bentley?"

He pulled her arm through his and started up the drive. "I cannot let you out of my sight, Lady Verity.

Now that you are determined to write your way through America, I must keep you close, lest you slander my reputation from Illinois to Edinburgh."

"Ohio," Verity said softly, leaning against him.

"No matter. I am quite sure word will spread quickly enough."

"Honestly, I should think it would provide very good publicity for your own book. And aside from that, why should it matter what I write about you, or that I think about you at all?"

He turned to her very quickly, so that her arm was suddenly behind his back. Before she could pull away from him in protest, he lowered his head and kissed her. Whatever he would have answered no longer needed to be said, for this was answer enough.

His lips moved over hers gently, and then with greater pressure as he tightened his hold on her and brought her closer. Verity pressed against the length of him, wishing nothing so much as that he might have chosen another time, when they weren't wrapped in shawl and topcoat, and were in plain view of anyone looking out the window, wondering what delayed them. For her part, she was content to be delayed as long as it took to thoroughly savor this unexpected moment.

But he finally pulled away and stared down at her as if her identity quite surprised him.

"Are you trying to buy my silence, Will?" she asked, scarcely recognizing her own voice.

"If I were, it would require a good deal more than that, for I believe you are a lady accustomed to very fine things," he said.

Verity blinked, reasonably certain that was not a compliment. And yet, he seemed to speak with affection and not with his usual derision. But since she was not sure, she was prompted to meet fire with fire.

"And are you sure you are the man to provide them?"

Verity knew she had never said anything so provocative in her life and was grateful for the darkness, lest he see her flushed face.

"I suppose the next months will give us the opportunity find out," he said, just as a triangle of light fell across his nose and cheekbone.

"Will, are you still out there?" came a voice from the open doorway. "Maud Webster is concerned you might have gotten lost."

"Perhaps so," he said and turned them both toward the light. And to their host: "Here we are, John. I was merely preparing Miss Harwood for what she would find within."

"I hope it proves as interesting as what she finds without," came the cheerful rejoinder.

****

Will was not sure what the newcomer expected to find in a large wood frame house in Cambridge, but she seemed to adapt to American ways almost at once. While grand by New World standards, the house on Brattle Street was nothing to what she was accustomed at home and the company was brought together, not by social class, but by the advantage of geography. Most ladies of the ton would have found the whole business insupportable.

Verity seemed to think it all great fun.

She danced and flirted with every man in the house including—though he could not be certain of this—the servant who kept the fires burning. She laughed with the ladies, and at one point seemed to find the samplers framed on the wall to be inordinately fascinating. She demonstrated a few steps of some country dance Will never saw in his life and stood at the bottom of the stairway to greet the children of the house.

Will witnessed all this in silence, trying to pay attention to the women with whom he danced and the men who wanted to hear the latest news from England. Finally, it proved to be too much. When one of his partners begged off from a reel, and Verity had a rare idle moment, he caught her hand and pulled her onto the dance floor.

"I believe this is my dance," he said abruptly.

"I believe you said you would not dance with me," Verity said, as she took her place in the line.

"I go through several drafts of my words before I write down what I truly mean," he said

"Then I am never to trust you, I suppose?" she asked, as their right shoulders passed in the first movement of the dance.

"No more than I trust myself," he answered.

Chapter 7

*The good fine people of America Cambridge, Massachusetts, are very keen on the subject of politics and pleased proud of their roll role in the uprising that separated them from the King's government, yet are happy to admit an Englishwoman to their midst. Indeed, the party I attended featured an excellent dinner repaste and musicians from nearby Harvard College. The dancers were quite proficient keen remarkable.*

Verity frowned down at her creased paper, blotted with ink, and said aloud, "I wish you would not sneak up on me. It is very rude."

"I already know what you think of my manners, so it hardly matters. Besides, it is an excellent strategy for eavesdropping on conversations I am not supposed to hear," Will said cheerfully.

"Precisely! And an eavesdropper will never hear any good of himself."

"But I do not hope to hear good things, only those that will make for interesting reading," Will answered, looking over her shoulder. He hummed for a few minutes. "And you spelled 'repast' incorrectly. Do leave off the 'e.' "

He pulled up a chair as he continued to look over Verity's shoulder.

"You found me a remarkable partner, you say?"

Verity put her hand over her written words. "I did

not say I found you remarkable, only that there were some remarkable dancers. Some Americans do know the steps and formations and have excellent manners. Some, of course, do not."

"What would you say of my cousin Eastbourne's manners?"

Verity turned her head, but his eyes were still on her scribbled page.

"Eastbourne's manners are better admired when his attention is reserved for his wife and children," she said.

Now she had his full attention and saw his surprise.

"That is very good, coming from you," he said. "I believe you did everything possible to court his attention."

Verity was not altogether sure what Lady Verity did but was prepared to believe the worst. However, she was not prepared to take the blame for it.

"A fish is not obliged to seize the bait offered him," she said.

"A fish is a stupid thing," Will said. "But then, so is my cousin. I doubt intelligence and good sense played any part in this business."

Verity felt a little stupid at the moment as well.

"Indeed, the only intelligent thing you did was remove temptation. I only regret you have now placed it before me."

"Seducing you is not my plan, Will. But haven't you given me encouragement? After all, I might have muddled my way all the way to Cincinnati on my own. But you approached me with your enterprising scheme, and now we are partners. For me, the only temptation is to demonstrate I can work faster than you."

"On our book."

"Of what else could I be speaking?"

"Our book," he repeated. "Let me give you a little lesson."

"Whatever do you have in mind?" she asked, remembering his kiss.

He cleared his throat. "It is a fine thing to write how the Americans excel, but sales will be much stronger if you write about their utter wretchedness. They cannot dance, they are terrible hosts, their food is provincial and overcooked."

"That insults Geoff and Nell. It is probably true for you, however."

"Geoff is a man of business, and he understands what sells in the marketplace. A book pointing to the weaknesses in American society will guarantee us a success."

"It does not seem fair." Verity sighed. "And why slander your countrymen? Why not write on another subject? I am sure there are many of which you would prove to be quite expert, though I cannot think of a single thing."

She caught a hint of amusement in the line of his lips. "I am somewhat knowledgeable about natural history, as is your father. We had some conversation on the subject, as you may recall."

"Ah yes. Then you might discourse on birds or fish. It sounds rather diverting."

"Do you think so?"

"No, not really. I find human behavior far more interesting. If left to my own preferences, I daresay I would write about the distinctions of class and manner of expectations. I do know much about Annie Merrill's life, you know."

"But you know a good deal more about being the daughter of an earl and having everything you could ever desire."

"No, that is not altogether true," Verity said wistfully.

"I suppose you are speaking of my cousin. You would have saved everyone much trouble by marrying him before he and Mariah ever met."

"Eastbourne?" Verity asked before she could stop herself. Of course he meant Eastbourne, and she was a fool to ever forget the fact of their relationship. "But what has that to do with you, sir?"

Will looked surprised. "My father was Eastbourne's father's younger brother. Eastbourne is an only child, and I am an only son with five sisters. Eastbourne has three daughters."

"They are very pretty girls," Verity mused. "But I don't see how…Oh!"

"Oh, indeed," Will said. "I am an American, but my situation might change at any time. Eastbourne is habitually reckless and indifferent to his responsibilities."

"But you travel back and forth across dangerous seas and are soon embarking on another journey. Might that be construed as equally reckless? At least Lord Eastbourne remains at the Hall, where he risks little more than falling off his horse," Verity pointed out.

"Or being shot by an irate father, demanding justice for his daughter?" asked Will.

"My father…"

"Yes?" Will urged her on, and then relented. "Take heart, my dear. I may very well die before my cousin, and he might require another wife someday. Perhaps all might turn out as you desire."

"I certainly do not desire any harm to come to poor Mariah. And you cannot know what I desire. You have mistaken my relationship with your cousin, which is simply youthful flirtation." Verity hoped so much was true and that Will was as ignorant as she.

But it seemed she was wrong.

"Mariah might turn a blind eye to your behavior, but I find I cannot. I must ask: why did you escape Harwood Hall? Why were you so reclusive on board the *Andromeda*? Why did you need to purchase new gowns as soon as you made landfall in America?"

Verity blinked, trying to digest his words. Suddenly, an awful awareness fell upon her, seeming to weigh her down. Was it possible? Is this what the doctor meant by Lady Verity's condition?

Lady Verity was with child. She'd surely confided in Eastbourne, who sent his cousin after her, for Will would not make so offensive an accusation unless he was certain of it. Momentarily stupefied, Verity returned his questions with several of her own.

"Is it a coincidence that we found ourselves on the same ship? Did your cousin send you after me, to protect his interests?" Verity navigated her way through uncharted waters, wondering how she, of all people the closest to Lady Verity, never guessed the truth of the situation.

*Because I am a stupid, naïve girl, who will never be better than a servant.*

"No, he did not send me, and this is most certainly a strange coincidence. But you have just confirmed what I only guessed. Now it appears I have another reason to remain at your side, to fulfill a family obligation to one of our own, as your child will surely be. I suppose Mrs. Trollope has agreed you might remain with her?"

Verity had no idea what Mrs. Trollope knew or expected. She had no idea whom the woman was, other than someone who owned a shop.

She put her hand to her forehead, blocking out Will, wishing she could block out every sinful decision she made in the past few weeks. But Lady Verity and her unborn child were dead, and nothing could ever change that. And Annie Merrill's impossible dreams had not died; if anything, they had grown even stronger.

"You are not well?" he asked gently.

She was very well and not yet ready to walk away from the privilege and independence she had already tasted and enjoyed.

"I am not with child," she said at last. "The poor babe did not survive the wretched journey."

This, at least, was true.

"And I absolve you of our partnership, as you no longer need to be protective of your cousin's property," she continued. "I have no claim on Eastbourne, if I ever did."

"I will not let you off so easily," he said gently. "I am sorry for your loss, and your plans might very well change. But did I not already say that our audience will be more interested in everything that is wrong? From the moment of our meeting on the *Andromeda*, I knew you were censorious and uncompromising."

Then he did not sense the confusion and desperation.

"Sir, my companion was dying. Geoffrey seemed

far too cheerful for one who had just broken his ankle, and I claimed the right of urgency. As it turns out, I was completely justified." Verity nodded to herself. "And I am neither censorious nor uncompromising."

"It is true. You surprised me at the party. I wrongly guessed you'd avoid some of your partners, and I certainly did not expect you to converse with the servants."

"I was doing research, sir. How can you expect me to write about my experiences if I have none? There is so much I do not know."

*But if Lady Verity carried a child, she knew a great deal.*

He smiled. "What would you like to know?"

She did not doubt his intention and avoided his trap. "Many things," she said coyly, "but to begin: how shall I remove ink from my fingers? I cannot attend parties and appear in society with my hands looking like…"

"Mine? I have more or less given up on the business. But you will find that whiskey works better than water on those stains."

"Whiskey? And must I then walk about in public smelling like a public house?"

"I cannot imagine you smelling like anything other than lavender," he said. He caught her hand and seemed to study her fingers for several moments.

"I do not wear it for your benefit," she said firmly and pulled away.

Will stood quickly, nearly tipping the ink pot on the desk. "No, it most definitely is not for my benefit," he said and walked out of the room as silently as he had entered.

\*\*\*\*

"You doubt the advisability of this venture," Geoff said. He adeptly wheeled himself away from his writing desk and turned to face Will.

"The venture is sound. I am not sure I can say as much for my mind. The woman is driving me crazy."

"Nell?"

"You know I do not mean your sister. Verity has started to write, and she only has positive things to report. She enjoyed the food, the music, the damned provincial company."

"Well, so did we. We're damned provincials ourselves. At least, I am, and you are partly so. But it need not be a problem."

"Really? What is your solution?"

"Why, you need only explain to her that we wish for her to see the faults, not the grace, in society. It will sell better."

"Of course I explained it to her. And the problem is she actually accepted my advice."

"And how is that a problem?" Geoff asked.

"Because she is not whom I think she is. I cannot explain it. But when I met her last year, in the company of my cousin, she was selfish and rude, and completely inappropriate in her behavior by demanding Eastbourne's attention. Who was no better, of course." Will lowered his voice. "I thought them a perfect match, for all that he is already married."

"Perhaps he is a bad influence, and her father wanted them apart."

"Eastbourne is surely a bad influence. My own father wanted him and me apart when we were no more than boys. But Verity was also rude and demanding when we first met her on the ship."

"No more than you, my friend. "You all but attacked her. And if she seemed imperious, perhaps it was because you put her on her guard. She must have recognized you."

"And yet she did not. I am almost certain of it."

"Let us not forget she was agitated about Miss Merrill. If she needs an excuse, that surely is it."

Will shook his head. "I have been through all this over and over in my head. She cannot be anyone but Lady Verity Harwood. She told us her name before she had any reason to dissemble, and she looks like the woman I remember. Except, perhaps, for her hands."

"You have confused me, Will. She looks and sounds like Lady Verity, she knows your cousin and is familiar with the estate, but her hands belong to someone else?"

"I know it sounds absurd, but I have the feeling they are different."

"You are right, my friend."

"You see it too?"

"Yes. It is clear she has driven you mad. A woman might alter her appearance with a smudge of rouge or powder; she might even change the color of her hair or don a wig. But she cannot change her hands."

"I must be wrong, then."

"I cannot believe what I am hearing. You say you are wrong?"

"I do not have any other explanation, so it must be so. Certainly, you must allow me to be wrong once every two or three years?"

"Now I am not certain of your identity either."

Nell came through the door, and Will wondered if

she heard anything of their discussion. But it seemed she had other matters on her mind.

"Verity and I have been invited to lunch on Georges Island," she said. "Shall I take the carriage to the ferry, or will one of you escort us?"

"Georges Island is that great wasteland in the harbor, is it not? Do you intend to dine on beach plums with the gulls?"

"Verity and I intend to dine with Captain Warburton, who is the engineer designing the great fort being built there. You have been out of the country too long if you do not know of it." Nell's tone was mildly accusatory. "Or him."

Will shrugged. "Is this new fortification needed to keep the English out of Boston? The war is long over."

"As to that, I cannot say. I do know it is to be named for Dr. Warren, the surgeon who sent Dawes and Revere on their way to Lexington and Concord. So perhaps the spirit of that old conflict lives on," she said. "But I shall have the opportunity to ask Peter about it on the morrow."

"Peter? And how do you know this man?" Geoff asked.

Nell shook her head. "You are gone for an age, and do you not think me capable of making acquaintances or finding friends."

"I am not forbidding you friendship. I am only curious," said Geoff.

"Curious and somewhat forgetful. The two of you spoke to him at the party the other evening. Do you not recall? He is tall and blond haired and rather attractive. He wore a lovely uniform and danced twice with Verity."

"I shall escort you," Will said hurriedly.

Nell looked at him and shook her head. "On second thought, I believe we will take the carriage. I want to give Verity every chance that comes her way."

"Chance?" Will choked out. "You hardly know the man. He might be unkind, or unthinking, or absolutely tied to his work."

"Imagine such a thing," Nell said sarcastically. "I would not believe anything Verity or I did was of particular concern to you, Will Bentley."

Will brought himself up straight. "It was not. But she is my business partner now."

"And I am giving her a chance to observe something interesting about American life. That is what I meant, but you seem to be very touchy whenever I mention anything about her. I wonder why?"

Will had no desire to continue this discussion.

"Even so, I prefer to accompany you."

"Even so," Nell echoed. "I prefer you do not."

Having the last word, she left the room as suddenly as she had entered.

"She has a point, Will," Geoff said quietly. "I do not know what it is about Lady Verity that sets you off. You seem alternately to draw her closer, and then push her away. I have never seen you like this with any other person. I can only guess you fancy her."

"I do not," Will said. "I should not."

"Because she is acquainted with your cousin? You scarcely know the man, and it will be easy enough to avoid his company if you desire it. And clearly, Eastbourne and Lady Verity have broken it off, or she would not be taking off to Cincinnati in our company. There is nothing to stand in your way."

"It is not so simple as all that," Will confessed.

"No, it never is." Geoff sighed. "My sister will be disappointed."

"We never had an understanding, Nell and I. And just now, she looked like she might stick a fork in my chest."

"You are right. She also neglected to mention she danced twice with Warburton as well. So perhaps this little journey is more for her pleasure than Verity's education. It might be a good match for her."

"Surely you are not thinking of marrying her off?" Will said.

Geoff pushed himself away from the desk. "She is old enough to make her own decisions, as we just witnessed. And I would sooner have her settled than not, particularly before we return to England."

"You sound like a brother."

"I am a brother, and I do not envy your five sisters to my one. You have years of challenges ahead of you."

"I would be happy to survive the challenges of the next few weeks," Will murmured.

****

Verity and Nell set out the next morning for the harbor, managing the small carriage through Cambridge's busy streets. Nell drove with an expert hand, and Verity wrote down her observations in her journal, with a somewhat less expert hand. There was much to record as Nell kept up a continuing stream of commentary.

But it was all rather exciting, and something to which Verity was not at all accustomed. She had never felt so utterly unfettered and out on her own. The *Andromeda* had proved a prison for her and a wretched experience by anyone's tally. But it had brought her to this new country, where women rode freely in the streets, and where an invitation to dine with gentlemen on a harbor island aroused no particular interest.

Verity expected one of the men to travel with them, or at the very least, that Will would lecture them about the proprieties. But Will and Geoff were closeted in the study when she and Nell left Fresh Pond, not the least bit interested in this day's excursion.

"My dear friend, Mrs. Ellen, operates that little shop," Nell pointed out.

Verity followed her companion's finger to a small cottage with buckets of flowers beneath the windows.

"Is she a dressmaker?" Verity asked, watching two women came through the door.

"Oh, much better than that," Nell said. "It is a bookstore for ladies."

Verity's hand scribbled a line right off the page. "How is that possible?"

"Why, ladies read, do they not? And there are many books in which men are not at all interested, and of which they are even scornful. Why shouldn't ladies have a place where they can be quite comfortable purchasing books of interest and discussing them? On warm days such as this, Margaret Ellen serves tea in the garden, and ladies can have refreshment of the mind and body."

"How extraordinary," Verity said. "I could hardly comprehend it. Perhaps that is something I might do when I am settled in America."

"I do not understand. Are you not an heiress and able to marry where you choose? Surely there cannot be a reason for you to open a shop?" Nell looked straight ahead so that it seemed all her attention was for the road that led to the Charles River and beyond to the harbor.

"My friend, Mrs. Trollope, runs a shop," Verity said, though she had no notion of the lady's status or wealth. "And I think it would be a very fine idea for me to do something creative and exciting while I am able. I am ever known in society as an 'original.' " Indeed, Lady Verity did have that reputation, though it had more to do with her utter lack of discretion than any novel plans.

Nell merely nodded, which gave Verity hope that her absurd reasoning was somehow persuasive.

The road they traveled skirted along the shore of the river, at its widest point. Across the water, the impressive brick buildings of Boston rose above the trees, and people walked along a promenade nearer the shore. The wind picked up, making Verity's bonnet ribbons dance and blowing salt air into her eyes.

"There is the stable, and there is the ferry," Nell said.

"Will we have need of transport on the island?" Verity asked.

"I have never been there, myself," Nell said, and shrugged. "Very few people have, though I understand the Pequot inhabited the island before moving further south to Rhode Island, where the land is better for farming. But there are some folk who row out to pick the wild berries or dig for clams, and they have been most vocal against the building of the fort. This, Captain Warburton explained to me the other evening."

"Is another war likely?"

"I have no idea. We might ask the captain about

that. Perhaps they are concerned about an invasion from Canada."

"Truly?" Verity asked.

Nell laughed. "No, not truly. I daresay they are building it all for show."

If that was the intent, Captain Warburton did not intend to impress them today with anything other than a splendid excursion into a wilderness. Nell and Verity shared the ferry with a load of lumber and a case of nails, and several crates of squawking chickens. Verity couldn't bear to look at the poor things, imagining they were destined to appear at the luncheon table. But Nell was confident the captain and his guests would be dining on oysters.

"They are very dear," Verity cautioned her. "I doubt the American government allows its military officers to dine so splendidly."

"Oysters are not so very dear in Boston. They are sold in every market, for those who have neither the time nor the inclination to gather them themselves." Nell looked at her and made a little scribbling gesture with her hand, suggesting she write it all down. "As to the taste, you shall have to decide for yourself."

A group of uniformed men waited at the pier on Georges Island, though they seemed more interested in the lumber than in the two young women. But Captain Warburton quickly separated himself from the others.

"Welcome," he said as he extended his hands to help them down the plank. "I hope the harbor journey did not make you ill?"

Verity looked up at him. He was a very fine gentleman, equal in manners to those she witnessed in England.

"After my long voyage at sea, this little sail was nothing more than a gentle glide over the water, Captain Warburton," Verity murmured, as he pulled her onto the wooden pier.

"But I am not accustomed to a sea journey, and I am a bit unsteady on my feet," said Nell, falling gracefully against him. He released Verity's hand and held Nell by her shoulders until she smiled at him.

Verity blinked at this little performance, thinking there was material for yet another volume on American manners. So far, everything she already knew about Peter Warburton was in his favor, but they hardly knew him.

Though Verity doubted the same would be said when this day was over.

"Come see our headquarters on the island," he said, offering each of them an elbow. "It's a bit sandy here, but the path gets rocky as we go up the hill and easier to find traction."

"It is not so bad," said Verity, accustomed to walking the cinder path to the door of the Harwood kitchen. But their pace slowed, to allow for Nell's cautious steps.

"Do you live on the island, Peter?" Nell asked, as a small cottage came into view.

"It would be a very lonely existence, unless one prefers gulls and small rodents to people. And I much prefer people," he said, grinning down at her. "The men and I sail back to Boston each evening, unless the waves are too rough. I have a pleasant house on Beacon Hill."

"How lovely," Nell said. "And does your family await you?"

Verity rolled her eyes, thinking her friend could not be more obvious. But Captain Warburton did not seem to notice and played right into Nell's hands.

"My mother is often at home, though she is a tireless reformer. When she is lecturing or at a meeting, the cook provides company, though I believe she finds me somewhat dull. Certainly, she is not interested in my designs for Fort Warren." He led them through the open door and into a sparsely furnished but very pleasant room. Amidst volumes of books and maps on a large table were relics of the sea: starfish, shells, curious pieces of driftwood. "However, she was interested enough in the fact I was receiving lady visitors here today and prepared lunch for us. I hope you both enjoy oysters?"

Nell winked at Verity, who laughed out loud.

"Oh, I see," Captain Warburton said. "You have had your fill of oysters. There are also crab cakes with beach plum jelly."

"I am sure it all is excellent, sir," Verity said. "And the sea air has given us an appetite. But I am curious about your mother's activities. What is it she hopes to reform?"

Nell interrupted. "My friend is a writer, Peter. Do watch what you say, for she is likely to include it in a book she is writing with Mr. Bentley."

"My mother would undoubtedly appreciate the notice, and Will Bentley is a fine writer. You are lucky to be associated with him. My mother's cause is…" Here, he paused. "Everything."

Verity laughed. "Surely you exaggerate?"

"No, truly. She moves from one passion to the next. She has supported the causes of musicians and public libraries, and women's ownership of property and child rearing. Just now, she is concerned that the children of recent immigrants are not being taught to read."

"Surely that is not necessary? Very few people on the Harwood estate know how to read, and they manage just fine."

"I believe my mother would disagree with you, Miss Harwood. How could they ever hope to leave the Harwood estate if they cannot read and make their way in the world?"

"But they are happy at Harwood," Verity said, though even as she said the words, she knew their falseness. She was not happy at Harwood, even having advantages the other servants did not. She had been taught to read and write, however much she was unlikely to use those skills at home in England. But here, in America, there were possibilities, as strange and as promising as everything else about the place.

"Most people in America know how to read," Nell said, confirming Verity's conclusions.

"Several schools have been established for the children of slaves," Captain Warburton added.

"We have newspapers printed in several languages in Boston," Nell said.

"You have made a very fine point," Verity said, holding up her hand and laughing. "Reading is a noble cause, indeed, and I cannot argue with anything that allows my book to be shared by more people."

The point apparently settled, Captain Warburton and his guests sat down at a small table to begin their luncheon. And through the afternoon there was nothing at all with which Verity could argue. They toured the site, where the brush was already cleared for construction. They examined the architectural sketches, which allowed them to imagine how grand the fort would be. They gently examined the eggs of seagulls, hidden in the marsh on the bay side of the island. It was all perfectly congenial and pleasant.

And while Verity applied herself to her notes, Nell applied herself to Captain Warburton.

****

"Where are they, Geoff?" Will asked for perhaps the tenth time and stared out of the window. The shadows of the trees were long, and the sun was low in the sky over the pond. "They might have had a mishap. The carriage could lose a wheel, or the ferry sink into the harbor."

"Or Verity has decided to stay for dinner because Captain Warburton proves a most gracious host." Geoff pushed his chair to the window. "Perhaps they are already married."

"That is not amusing. You certainly would not think it so if I said the same of Nell."

"I know my sister too well. She will want a posh affair for her wedding and invite half the neighborhood. No, I am confident it is not Nell. But why not Verity? I suppose a captain is too far beneath her?"

"I believe we all are too far beneath her."

"Now it is you who is unkind. She has been nothing but generous and thoughtful. One would think she is the daughter of a vicar rather than the heiress of an earl."

Will turned from the window and stuffed his fists deep into his pockets.

"That is the strangest thing of all," he said.

Geoff shrugged. "Not so very strange. I have met your sisters, as you may recall. They are the granddaughters of an earl, and they are very sweet girls, despite having you for a relation."

"That is not to be helped," Will muttered. "And you know I do not mean that a title bestows good behavior on anyone on whom it strikes even a glancing blow. I speak only of Lady Verity Harwood, who seemed a perfect match in temperament and manners to Eastbourne."

"Which suggests why they had such great affinity," Geoff pointed out. "But if you knew this of her character, why would you have her with us? What could you have been thinking?"

"A lady of her unstable temperament might not be a good business partner, but her writing could reveal great wit. And I thought I might be of some service to my cousin by looking after the chit." It sounded reasonable, but Will wondered if Geoff believed even a word of it. Would he better believe what Will could hardly credit himself: that he was attracted to Verity Harwood from the moment he saw her on the *Andromeda*, for all her lofty disdain?

Now, any evidence of that disdain was held in reserve for him, only him.

"It is not too late to back away from the arrangement now, my friend. We need only put her on a stage to Cincinnati, and that's an end to it. As for your cousin, he seems less concerned about her than you are. Is he even aware that the two of you have met?" Geoff, as always, pulled away the wrapping to reveal the real contents of the parcel. "Perhaps he took your advice and turned his attention back to his wife."

"And perhaps when he did so, Lady Verity's character became what it had been before their liaison. Yes, I suppose that is possible. My cousin always had the ability to corrupt others, and the lady might have been his latest victim."

"Is she corrupted, Will?" Geoff asked, and their eyes met.

Will wondered how many people knew her secret. Eastbourne knew and, as always, took the coward's way out by sending her away. The Earl of Harwood certainly knew, for why else would he have allowed his daughter to set off on such an uncertain journey? And poor Annie Merrill must have known and took her secret to her watery grave.

But Geoff and Nell remained ignorant of the truth of the situation and must remain so.

"That remains to be seen, I suppose," Will said slowly. "Neither of us knows her well enough to pass judgment. But we will be close companions, and it is possible that what is revealed in the next weeks may make us regret this literary experiment."

"I believe the flaws in her character would have already made themselves apparent to us, and I am rather more concerned with her writing talents," Geoff said. "But if her words do not prove worthy to go alongside yours, she can find her own publisher."

Will thought about her first efforts on the page. "That is what I am afraid of. A lady might outsell me two to one. Ladies will want to read about the fashions and balls and society in America, and Verity has the advantage over me there, I believe."

"Yes," Geoff said speculatively. "I rather think so."

The dog began a great barking, which was as

effective a warning signal as a lighthouse on a dark night.

"Our adventurers have returned?" Geoff asked. "Do they bring the handsome captain with them?"

"They do not. And I do not think him handsome."

"No, I suppose you wouldn't. There is another example of what might interest ladies in a book and of which you know nothing."

"I have been to many balls and society events," Will defended himself.

"Only those you could not easily escape. And I've never known you to write your impressions about such things."

"Of course not. Who would read about such things?" Will asked though he already knew the answer. He looked down at Geoff and together they answered, "The ladies" as the ladies burst through the door in a very unladylike fashion.

They were laughing and out of breath. They had sand on the hems of their skirts, and their hair slipped untidily beneath their bonnets. Their noses and cheeks were sun reddened. And they held shells and pieces of driftwood in their hands.

"Good evening," Will said solemnly.

Verity looked up in surprise. "Why, hello. Is everything well?"

"Why should anything be amiss? I have been working all afternoon while the two of you were apparently—"

"Everything is well," Geoff interrupted. "We only hoped you hadn't missed the last ferry and would be left on Georges Island all night."

"Of course not, Geoffrey," his sister said. "We

would not have been alone, and Peter would have seen us safely to shore in his own boat."

"Peter? Some sailor perhaps?" Geoff asked.

"Peter is Captain Warburton, with whom we now have a passing familiarity," said Verity. She deposited her dirty shells on the fine Hitchcock table and wiped her hands on her wrinkled skirt. "He took very good care of us, and we discussed many things. You need not be concerned that I was wasting my time, for I learned many things this day. I have much to write about."

"And I will have much to write about as well," Nell said clearly, looking directly at Will. "He has asked that I correspond with him while we are traveling. And it sounds like an excellent idea."

"Captain Warburton is probably too busy for letters," Geoff said.

"Apparently, he is not. I suppose it is possible for some men to apply themselves to a project and still find the opportunity to write to a friend," Nell said. She continued to look at Will.

"He is a man of many talents," Will conceded.

"And he is quite handsome," Nell added.

**\*\*\*\***

*There's Theirs is a society in which there is much room possibility for improvement, but never have I seen heard of so many women people involved in projects for the publick good. Today I heard of an old a lady of some advanced years who is engaged in establishing education for newcomers to the country. The value of these efforts cannot be faulted. Those who can read have the potential to get a better improve themselves. Thus the maid can become a shoppkeeper. And the ferryman can build his own fleet.*

*Everyone reads in America. On nearly every streetcorner men and women stand with broadsides in hand and share the news of the day.*

"What do you think?" Verity asked, when Will looked up from her pages of neatly written prose. It was the first time she willingly offered her words to him, but it was also the first time she was excited about what she had to say.

" 'Shopkeeper' is spelled with only one 'p,' " he answered.

"And that is all? I thought very long and hard about this, and I expect some notice beyond my indifferent spelling," Verity said. "And I do try hard, even on that."

"So I see," he said.

"And what else?" she continued to push, until she found herself up against a wall.

"I did not think you would write about such things," he finally confessed. "I rather hoped your perspective would be all for parties and social events, and the ways of the people."

"I have written about the ways of the people. They read, and they know about many things. It is far more interesting to me, and I daresay far more interesting to readers to learn about this, rather than the color of ball gowns this season. Who will care about that in ten years? Or even in ten minutes, come to think of it."

"I thought all ladies cared about fashion. You seemed most concerned with such matters when I first met you at Eastbourne Hall."

Verity leaned back in her chair, wondering how she would ever be able to reconcile the foolish and reckless Lady Verity with her present character.

"I confess, I was a bored and silly girl then. I had

nothing to interest me, and no friends except for darling Annie Merrill. I came to America to mature, even to become another person. I am not here long, and already I have new friends, a new understanding, an avocation, and a partner."

*But no child.* He did not point out her omission but let it hang between them. They both knew why Lady Verity came to America; it did not need to be said.

"You mean Nell, with whom you can have adventures?" he asked.

She smiled, unable to help herself. There was something pleasurable about unsettling this man. "Truly, I mean you."

Will cleared his throat. "As we are partners, I would like for you to write about things of interest to ladies."

"As a lady, I think I have the best knowledge of what is of interest to ladies. And I assure you, they will be far more interested in Mrs.Warburton's social reforms than silly gowns and bonnets."

"I believe we agreed that we will write from different points of view."

"And so we shall," Verity said. "Why do you not write about wool jackets and men's undergarments? I am sure ladies will be interested in that, as well. That is, unless they spend all their waking hours washing them."

"I am not sure this partnership can work," Will said. His eyes challenged her to deny it.

She held up her hand. "It is too late. My fingers are quite stained with the wretched ink, and your whisky does nothing to help."

"I have often said that whisky does nothing to

help." He laughed quite unexpectedly, as he reached for her hand. "Perhaps this will work better."

He brought her fingers to his lips and tasted each one in turn. His mouth was warm, and his grasp on her was firm. She could say nothing, do nothing, but watch him in fascination and remind herself to breathe.

Finally, he paused and studied her wet fingers.

"No, it will not do at all," she said. "You will have to try harder."

He pulled her closer, and their lips met over the papers on the desk. His hands caught her at the elbows, and she both blessed and cursed the solid oak between them. Will Bentley's kisses were nothing like those quick smacks to which she was accustomed at Harwood, bestowed with an urgency that seemed more fitting to the stable yard or pantry where they often took place. Will's kiss promised finer things, things that went deeper and were meant to last.

She found herself kissing him in return, though she knew nothing of this, or if she ought to do such a thing. But they were partners, after all, and hadn't she just asserted her rights?

He stood without releasing her and pulled her to her feet. In one deft movement, he nudged the small desk out from between them and ignored the sound of papers fluttering to the floor. Verity lifted her arms to embrace him, deciding to ignore it as well.

She was lost, still adrift on the wide sea without direction, but gently, steadily, Will Bentley was easing her into his safe harbor. She imagined the scent of the salt air was still upon him, but he was warm and comforting, and as he navigated a course from her lips to her chin to her neck, she grew warm as well.

Indeed, she was burning for him, with him. All was improper, and yet felt very fine indeed.

"I do not recall discussion of this when you spoke about our partnership," she said against his lips.

"Sometimes the unexpected occurs, and it is necessary to renegotiate the terms of the agreement," he said, as his hands defined the shape of her body through the folds of her gown.

"What is unexpected, Will? You knew me for all I was back at Eastbourne Hall and guessed the reason why I escaped to America. I have gone along with your plans, but I have not embarrassed you and your friends. Nothing has changed, not really."

He caught her hands and ran his fingers over hers.

"Everything has changed, my dear. I have lived my life avoiding all alliances, of the heart and otherwise. I have dodged the schemes of matrons and their sweet offspring. I have managed to remain aloof from one young woman I know as well as my own sisters. But somehow, I find I cannot stay away from you."

Verity shook her head, denying her own desires as well as his.

"This will not end well," she said.

He drew in his breath. "Because of Eastbourne, you mean. Because of what people will say. We shall stay in America then, if you will accept that."

She pulled her hands out of his. What was he offering her? In accepting "that" was she also accepting "him?" As his wife? As his mistress? Surely not his business partner?

"And what of my father?' she asked bluntly, as Lady Verity would surely ask. For her part, she would be content to stay in America. After what she left in

England, she imagined she might be content to set up housekeeping on Georges Island and dine on oysters every night of her life. "Could he accept this, as well?"

Will stared at her as if he saw her for the first time and took several deep breaths.

"You have answered your own question by doing nothing more than reminding me of the great gulf that divides us. Your father knows nothing better than the natural history of things, of the order that governs all life. But he surely would be the first to admit that the machinations of man often have precedence over instinct. Whatever natural impulse has brought the two of us together must be overruled by social expediency. Lord Harwood would not accept this. He would not accept me as his daughter's suitor. You are quite right to remind me of it."

No, he was quite wrong, because there was nothing right about it at all. Her stupid, willful deception now proved to be her undoing in ways she never imagined. In America, Annie Merrill was as worthy as any other woman, with rights and possibilities never afforded to anyone of her class in England. It was Lady Verity, still bound by the laws of precedence and custom, who faced limits here. Annie could welcome Will Bentley's overtures; Verity could not. She had tied herself into one wretched knot with this business and had no idea how she might untangle it.

"I wish it were not so," she said, more to herself than to Will.

"So do I, but there it is," he said unhelpfully. "We must forget this ever happened and resist all temptation in the future."

Verity looked up at him and read the confusion and

unhappiness in his expression. Surely he did not know how very tempted she was to throw herself back into his arms.

"I will never speak of this again," she promised. "But do not imagine I will ever forget it."

## Chapter 8

The day of departure from Cambridge dawned rainy and cool, which seemed apt for Will's mood. He spent several days convincing himself that he would be able to deal with Verity as he would any other business partner and avoid personal entanglements, but when the small coach arrived at Geoff's door, he had reason to doubt his success.

In this modest space, he was expected to spend his days, in close proximity to two unmarried ladies who would require comforts which would crowd the coach, need frequent stops to see to their personal needs, and talk of many things, some requiring his answers.

He much preferred the company of a friend like Geoff, who would read and write and doze off and require nothing more than he did, himself. He liked traveling with Geoff.

Yet, he'd also like traveling with Verity, if circumstances were different. For sure, they'd have to be very different. How very grand a thing it would be to have her all to himself, to sit with her on a long journey and tell her about the American landscape, read each other's journals, allow her to sleep with her head on his shoulder and...do other things. If she were free to marry where she chose, and he was defiant enough to eschew all convention, how very fine a life they could have. He realized he did not care what recklessness brought her to American shores, if she would only stay here with him. He could make her forget his pompous idiot of a cousin.

But now he was doomed to a hell he himself had created, one of polite indifference and business etiquette, when all he wanted was to have Verity all to himself in the cursed coach, to do as they both pleased.

"Please use a parasol, Will. I doubt any of us will appreciate the odor of damp wool in our tight quarters."

He turned to see Verity at his side, well protected in a hooded cape buttoned right to her chin. She held out a tiny lace-trimmed parasol.

"My own hand, held aloft over my head, would provide as much protection as that thing," he said irritably.

"It is all I can offer," she said. He wondered if she realized how laden with meaning was that simple remark. "Though I imagine you must have an umbrella somewhere. It seems New England is not so very different from England, in the amount of rain you might expect here."

"It is not so very different, in that regard," he said. "When it rains or snows, we may be required to change our garments several times during the day. But I am certain you will manage, judging by the amount of luggage you have packed."

"I have packed enough to see me to Cincinnati. As my friend, Mrs. Trollope, operates an emporium, I am certain I will be able to replenish any of my needs."

"Will you be happy wearing and using American goods? They may not be as fine as to what you are accustomed."

"You have no idea to what I am accustomed, sir,"

she said softly. "Nor have I any intention of standing in this dreadful rain discussing my personal requirements for travel. If you feel they are subjects worthy of inclusion in our book, then do come and discuss it indoors."

He heard her footsteps splashing in the puddles along the walkway as she returned to the house. He refused to follow her and only succeeded in making himself more miserable than ever and getting wetter by the minute.

A horse and rider announced themselves on Fresh Pond Lane even before they loomed out of the mist. Will recognized that blasted Captain Warburton, who had proved so popular with the ladies. What was he about?

"How do you do, sir?" the man called out. "It is Mr. Bentley, as I recall?"

"And good day to you, Captain Warburton." Will raised his hand in greeting, and water dripped down his sleeve.

Warburton rode up to the post and slipped easily off his large horse. From beneath his cape, he retrieved a large bundle, neatly tied with twine.

"I am afraid you have come too late for a social call, sir, for we are about to depart from Cambridge."

"So it appears," Warburton said agreeably. "But I have come only to bid the ladies farewell, and to bring them small tokens of my appreciation. I promise I will not be long. And judging by the look of things, you may still need some time to change out of those wet clothes."

Will was inclined to give the fellow a token of his appreciation as well, but his ungenerous thoughts vanished when a flash of yellow caught his attention, and he turned full around to see Nell standing in the doorway. She was a lovely girl, and not for the first time, he realized how much simpler his life would be if he felt something for her other than the love of a brother. But then he caught the answering expression on Warburton's face and realized things are never as simple as one might hope.

Excusing himself, Warburton strode up the path toward Nell. And, at last, Will was willing to forego his pride and stubbornness, and just get out of the damned rain.

****

"Peter, your thoughtfulness will keep us warm throughout our journey," said Nell. She draped her knitted shawl about her shoulders.

"It truly was my mother's idea," Captain Warburton admitted. "If it were up to me, I would have brought along some oysters."

"But they would not travel half so well." Verity laughed. She held her own shawl in front of her, admiring the neat stitches. "But surely your mother did not knit these herself? She already sounds like the busiest woman in the city."

"That she is, but even she must be idle when she travels from one place to another. She carries her yarn and needles with her, wasting no moment. She surely gets more done in a day than most women do in a week."

"I should like to meet her," said Nell, with a forthrightness that Verity had come to recognize as characteristic of American women. Someone as young as Nell did not have to wait for an older woman to notice her and ask to make her acquaintance.

"I should like for her to meet you as well," Peter Warburton said softly, and Verity realized how strong a promise those few words offered.

Nell realized it as well. "We will not be gone so very long," she said. "How strange that after spending so much time longing for a real adventure, I find I am already anxious to be home again. I can hardly account for it."

Verity could account for it and envied her friend the possibility of joy. Captain Warburton was kind and attentive and undoubtedly would be waiting for her when they returned to Boston.

Will reminded her of his presence by clearing his throat. "It is a well-known adage that absence makes the heart grow fonder, Nell. You are only a bit precocious in feeling such a loss before we even set off on our journey."

Warburton leaned closer to Nell. "I hope the absence of some months will make you happier to return to me as well."

Nell sighed and wrapped the shawl even tighter about her.

Verity grinned and looked up at Will, who scowled.

"Oh, you are such a misanthrope," she said softly and waved him off with her hand. "If you cannot bear the sight of such happiness, go back into the rain and help the men with the trunks."

"Are those the words of Lady Verity, to someone beneath her notice?" he asked.

"You are absurd. Those are the words of plain Verity Harwood to a man who is determined to find fault with everything. It might do very well when one is writing a book but has no place in this pleasant company." She paused. "And you are certainly not beneath my notice, for I cannot avoid you."

"Would you have preferred that? Do you wish we never met on board the *Andromeda*, or that our chance meeting was nothing more than the blink of the eye?" Will said as he turned toward her. He raised his hand to rest on the door frame, and his body blocked Verity's view of Nell and Warburton.

Verity studied the solid lines of his chest and shoulders and bit down on the retort that was nearly on her lips. She'd never known someone like him, nor was it likely she ever would have if she had remained in the circumstances in which she had been born. Though better educated than a housemaid was likely to be and always wishful of an opportunity to better herself, in England she attracted no more interest than a coat rack and often got less respect.

She was far below Will Bentley in station. And now he believed he was below hers.

"I know what you are thinking," Will said, interrupting her thoughts.

"I think not," she whispered, resisting the fierce temptation to finally have the truth revealed.

"You disappoint me, then, Verity. I just offered you the perfect cue to respond that our first meeting was more like a cinder in the eye."

"How very clever, Will. But then, you think you know me so well." Verity leaned toward him, wishing his arms would pull her against him, against the dry, pine-scented worsted of his jacket.

For a moment, she thought she might have said it

aloud, for his hand slipped from the doorframe.

"With each passing day, I find I am less certain of that which I assume I know about you, my lady." His hand caught hers, and their fingers intertwined. "I believed I had your full measure when we met at Eastbourne, but clearly I was wrong. Something happened on board the *Andromeda*, and I would be a fool to imagine it had anything to do with our meeting. I suspect the death of your companion affected you more than you care to let on, perhaps bringing you face-to-face with your own mortality. I do nothing more than observe human behavior and write about it, but I believe you underwent what is often called a sea change. It is a metaphorical expression, to be sure, but in your case it seems quite literal."

*This is the moment,* Verity realized, and the need to unburden herself to one she now trusted was overwhelming. She looked down at her hand in his and realized his fingers were beating a tattoo against hers, as if he were counting them. *He knows.*

"What are you doing, Will?" she asked, her voice stammering over the words.

"What are you doing, Will?" echoed Nell, from the room behind him.

Verity had quite forgot Nell and Warburton were there. Will dropped her hand and turned to face them, while Verity was grateful he blocked the view of her own flushed face.

"We are puzzling out the next chapter of our book," Will said.

He was extraordinarily adept at lying, Verity realized. But then, so was she. Nell, however, was not so easily gulled and would not accept his excuse.

"Oh, that does not seem very likely," she said and laughed.

"Indeed, it is very likely," Will said solemnly. "Verity and I are at a bit of an impasse and have to better understand our purpose and design before we can go forward."

And Verity realized it was no lie.

****

As expected, the sheer quantity of requisites for a lady's journey added an additional challenge to readying for the journey, for it was some time before the grooms considered the coach well balanced under the weight of Nell and Verity's trunks. Geoff came burdened with the additional baggage of a wheeled chaise and crutches. But, for his part, Will managed to fit all his belongings into a good-sized leather bag. They were only journeying for a period of several weeks, possibly a couple of months, for goodness' sake.

One would not have guessed it by the warmth of the farewell between Nell and her blasted captain, however.

"I suspect you will soon lose the guardianship of your sister," Will said to Geoff as he helped him into the vehicle.

"Things are progressing so quickly between them, I can only wonder I haven't already lost her for the pleasure of this journey."

"It will not be such a pleasure if she spends her time sighing over his miniature or writing 'Mrs. Warburton' in her journal a thousand times over. Ladies do that sort of thing, you understand," Will said. "Are you quite comfortable?"

Geoff looked around at the close surroundings.

"More comfortable now than I will be in an hour. And what has made you such an expert in what ladies are apt to do?"

"Do not forget I have an abundance of sisters."

"With whom you spend as little time as possible," Geoff said pointedly. "Your perpetual absences will not recommend you to your future wife."

"Then I shall have to find a woman who is suited to travel," Will answered, letting Geoff draw his own conclusions.

An hour later, Geoff proved himself wrong but settled into a deep sleep, in which he looked very comfortable indeed. The two ladies, after a period of excited chatter that tempted Will to climb out onto the roof and sit on the trunks, spent a good deal of time arranging the cushions and lap robes around them until they each appeared to be seated in a nest of her own, with books and papers handy, and a hand mirror between them. Will did not think it very important to periodically check if their curls were still neatly arrayed, but they clearly felt it necessary.

His next chapter was shaping up very nicely, though thus far only in his mind. For all he had experienced travel, even in the company of other ladies, he did not fully appreciate what was required for a woman's journey. It was not possible to merely sit, or admire the passing scenery, or even engage in conversation. A lady found it necessary to nest, to replicate in some small measure the pleasures of her parlor.

Will tried hard not to appear so obviously fascinated as he studied his companions, but as they were no more than three feet from each other, the invisible barrier would eventually be shattered, for they could not ignore each other indefinitely.

"What is it you're writing, Will?" Verity finally asked. Nell seemed very intent on her book, and Geoff turned in his sleep.

Will looked up from his blank page. "I am writing about the ways in which ladies and gentlemen differ in their traveling habits. I do not know if you have observed this as well. If not, it might be helpful to take notes as we move along," he said.

"Are you reprimanding me for neglecting the business of our book?" Verity asked. "I assure you, there is very little that slips my notice, and I have an excellent memory."

"And yet you did not recognize me as someone who had been introduced to you before, when we met again on the *Andromeda*," Will pointed out.

But something in her expression changed as she looked at him across the interior of their coach. He expected her to straighten her back and raise her brow and pinch her delicate lips, in her usual manner of haughtiness. But instead she seemed diminished, younger, and more innocent than he knew her to be. She sank lower into her nest of cushions.

"But I did know you, Will," she said so softly, he could barely hear her over the rumble of the coach wheels. He leaned closer. "It is only that I never expected to know anyone on the ship or need to explain why I was escaping to America. I was embarrassed that you knew me and knew of my relationship with your cousin. I suppose we never want to be reminded of the errors we have made in our choices."

Will stared at her, for once not considering her

lovely eyes or pert nose but rather the limited choices of a young woman whose destiny was marked out for her from birth. He, who had the opportunities to be the master of his own universe, could only imagine what it might be like to be trapped by the circumstances of birth in a small provincial community.

Verity did not have a mother or sisters or a father willing to see to her social interests. Lord Eastbourne, the most imperfect and selfish of men, must have seemed like a god if she had few men with whom to compare him.

Will leaned back against his seat, full of his own regrets. He had not been any kinder to her; indeed he had been as rude and inconsiderate as a common lout. If he had only seen her then as he did now, their relationship might have progressed in an altogether different way. Her opinions of his family, of American men, and of him in particular would have evolved more favorably and very much to his credit.

"I have been guilty of errors as well," he said simply. "I am sorry that when you were suffering the loss of your dear companion, you were not able to call upon me as a friend."

"A friend?" she asked, and smiled. "Would it not have been rather presumptuous to lean on such a tenuous connection when there was another lady leaning rather heavily on you? I do mean that literally, you understand."

He wished he had the courage to smile about that. "I suppose you refer to Miss Compton? We were barely acquainted. She did not do much leaning."

"Oh, truly? She could barely keep her hands off you, Will. And I assume her balance on shipboard was no worse than anyone else's."

In the space of a moment, Will realized his regrets about his past were likely to remain in his past—and hers. The lady was jealous; he was as certain of it as anything in his life.

"Oh, do not look that way with me, sir."

"What if I tell you I was thinking of Miss Compton just now?" he asked, and instantly regretted it.

"I do not credit you with affection toward her now, for I believe it very unlikely. She is the type of lady some of us used to describe as a 'bubble,' light and full of air," Verity said dismissively, as she waved her hand.

"She might be deeper than either of us imagine, though we will likely never find the truth of it. But as long as we are being honest, do you not think there are those who might have considered Lady Verity Harwood a bubble, as you say?"

"Indeed, she was an infuriating example of..." Verity stopped suddenly and dropped her gaze before turning to the window.

Infuriating was an apt word, but not for the reasons the lady before him nearly articulated. Who would have been close enough to Lady Verity to comment on her frailties? Who would have been attracted to gossip about a young woman who never came to town and who was known to no one? And who was so alike to Harwood's daughter she could pass for the same? Will knew he had the lady now, if he only understood who she was, and who she was not.

But this little interlude had settled one thing for him; playing the confidante was more likely to produce results than playing the bully. He would gain much by stepping over this small bump and continuing on the more congenial path they seemed to be traveling.

"You are quite clever, my dear, to see yourself as others may have seen you, whether the portrait is true or not." Will paused, watching her shift her gaze slowly back to him. "But I am sure you exaggerate your faults."

"Why do you think I exaggerate my faults, sir? What would I gain by it?"

"I find you nothing like the bubble you claim to have been. Everything you do seems thoughtful, considerate, and kind. You are generous to others, right down to the servants. You spend time weighing your options and thinking toward your future. In quieter moments, I sense a deep gravity in your sensibilities that can easily be mistaken for sadness or regret." He reached for her hand, surprised by its warmth. "And for all that, you have gained a partner, someone who understands the literary value of exaggeration. I could not have worked with you in your former guise."

She started to pull away, but he would not release her.

"You are better than you were," he insisted, "better than when I met you at Eastbourne's home."

"And you are better than you were."

"How do you know this, Verity? You profess not to remember me."

Her eyes studied his features as if, having once forgotten him, she never would again. "But I do. The servants gossip, of course, and there was much interest in Eastbourne's American cousin. It was, and is, rumored that you will inherit the estate and title if Lady Eastbourne does not produce a son. I believe that is very likely."

"Why do you think it so? Is it possible circumstances have changed since you left for America?"

Now his hand warmed hers, as she turned quite pale.

"It is well known they are not compatible. I would not speak of such things to you or any other man, but I believe it might make a difference in your outlook or expectations. Forgive me."

"There is nothing to forgive, for I can only admire the rich spring of gossip that flows from the servants' quarters. How very clever of you to tap into that source, for it is an admirable trait for a writer," Will said artlessly.

But he tripped over the same bump she did moments before, and he wondered how a conversation with this woman was capable of making him forget himself so easily. As surely as he was the navigator on their road to Cincinnati, so must he guide them through this discussion.

"But I confess to some curiosity," he added.

"Yes?" she asked, a little too quickly.

"What did the servants have to say about me? The American cousin?"

"Oh, they laughed about your speech, your strange hat, your longish hair, your—"

"I am so glad I asked," Will muttered.

"But they also thought you very handsome and quite generous. They were touched by the gifts you brought."

"So it is possible to buy one's favors?"

"Of course. And you are speaking of servants, in any case."

"And they told you all this?"

She paused, but only slightly. "Yes, of course."

Neither of them said anything for several minutes. Verity seemed inordinately interested in some speck on her fingernail, and Will's imagination flickered with a possibility he had not truly considered until this very moment. When he finally spoke, his words were—he hoped—deceptively casual.

"I understand your relationship with Annie Merrill was unusually congenial, though I have observed that the English remain very aware of class and position in a very small household. Even when people live side by side in such a situation, they create boundaries by which they must adhere. Annie was your servant, but you mourned her like an equal. I can only guess that the confidences you enjoyed with the other servants made you receptive to this particular relationship. It is very admirable."

Verity did not look up from whatever fascinated her on her fingernail. Surely it could not be more fascinating than his growing speculation was for him.

"Her name was Anne," Verity said. "Anne Louise Merrill, named for her mother."

"And her mother was Harwood's housekeeper, I believe?" Will asked.

Verity dropped her hand into her lap in a gesture of frustration or impatience. "Both women are dead. Why could this possibly matter to you?"

Will shrugged. "I am curious about everything, as well you know, Lady Verity. If I am to write about the differences between the English and the Americans, I would like to know how the two daughters of the house came to share so much."

Verity pushed her way out of her nest and leaned toward him, her face flushed.

"There was only one daughter of the house. It did not matter that they were of an age and taught by the same tutor. It did not matter that Lord Harwood allowed both girls to help him with his experiments into the natural sciences. It did not matter that he was…"

"Yes?"

"Kind to them both," Verity said quickly. "There was still only one daughter of the house. She was the one born to privilege, and the other daughter was born to serve her."

"The housekeeper's daughter, of course."

"Of course." Verity looked puzzled.

"And yet you were so closely related to each other."

His partner swayed, but he could not be certain it was not caused by the rhythm of the coach.

"You already know that we were. But why could it matter now? Poor Annie is gone, and I am the only relation who now mourns her."

"And there is your father of course. Whatever secrets were kept by the family, the household will surely share his grief. If nothing else, neighbors and friends will assume some relationship between Lord Harwood and Annie Merrill, for housekeepers are often retained and trusted because they are a third cousin or impoverished in-law of the master or mistress of the house. If that is understood to be the case, one might expect the house to be in mourning. It is a sad occasion." For all his reasonable explanation, Will was nevertheless unconvinced of the truth of the situation. Something was yet missing. He looked at Verity for more, trying to read her expression. "I know you felt her loss very grievously."

"I did," Verity said. "I still do."

Will merely nodded.

"My father loved two women. I have always preferred to believe that, and hope Annie did as well."

Will saw tears on her lashes and regretted the inquisition. But they still had miles ahead of them, and many more opportunities to discuss matters that ought to be none of his business. And yet, increasingly, it seemed like they were.

When the coach pulled up to a small toll house some time later, Verity was eager to escape from the confining quarters. Indeed, she was eager to escape from everything. She stood on the slate terrace, studying the few travelers seated at benches and tables, and wondered if she dared to ask any of them for a ride to Cincinnati. On the other hand, perhaps she could manage to make her way on foot.

But woodlands surrounded them, and Verity had been warned about the people who lived in such places. They might be able to subsist in the wilderness, but she doubted she would be able to manage it. As uncomfortable as she was in Will Bentley's company, she at least had shelter and food and resources. If their travel book proved to be successful, she might be able to manage on her own in this new country. She was already too reckless for her own good; she would not jump blindly onto another path.

"Where is this place, Geoff?" she asked. "Are we anywhere near Cincinnati?'

Geoff Marsh rubbed his eyes and smiled ruefully. "As much as I would love to say we are nearly at our destination, we have not yet left the Commonwealth of Massachusetts. We are in Wayland, our first stop on the turnpike. There is a small toll to pay before we continue, for the privilege of traveling on this fine road."

"It does not look very fine to me," Verity said as they climbed out of the coach, nodding toward a deep rut filled with rainwater.

"It may be a good deal better than what awaits us. But the owners of the toll house have made the payment more congenial by offering excellent refreshment. They do a thriving trade here and have recently added more rooms to their inn. Most people come to enjoy the ale and biscuits, however."

"They must employ several cooks, then," Verity said. Here was a possibility for honest labor, she realized. She knew enough about housekeeping and cooking to make an honest wage. And in a place such as this, she was also likely to meet other people who could offer her opportunities.

But then she thought about Mr. Reese on board the *Andromeda,* who seemed honest and good until Will warned her about him. On the other hand, the man might have been a prince, for all she had was Will's testimony to the contrary.

She looked toward Will, who was laughing and talking with one of the men sitting at a bench. Though he saved all his good humor for others, she had to admit that thus far he had played fair with her. It was possible that what she took as an inquisition was nothing more than Will being conversational. At least, this was what she tried to convince herself.

He looked up and met her gaze. The seated man

continued to talk, but Verity knew that for better or worse, Will was still thinking about her.

"I am sure they do, for people arrive here at all hours and are usually hungry. A successful business is open at all hours," Geoff said.

"I daresay this business is successful because of their biscuits," Nell interrupted, as she pulled on Verity's arm. "They also have precisely what I require in the rear of the inn. Will you excuse us, Geoff?"

Verity heard her companions, though she continued to look at Will. She discarded her foolish thoughts of wandering off into the woods or finding work as a cook. She wanted to better herself, to be sure. But she also wanted Will Bentley.

"Where are you taking me?" she asked Nell, somewhat distractedly.

"Where do you think? I have warned my brother and Will that traveling with ladies is somewhat different from that to which they are accustomed, and we will insist they stop often. Geoff complained that our needs will add a year to our journey, but Will said nothing at all." Nell led Verity to an unusually long shed that contained three separate closets. She wished she knew what she might find to write about such an oddity, other than that it existed. "One would almost think that the coach ride was the adventure, and that the destination was irrelevant."

"I suppose that is the unique challenge of the travel writer?" Verity asked when they were finished with their business. "Will must intend to fill his volume with observations made along the way, perhaps noting the conversation with the man out in front, or the taste of the biscuit you mentioned."

"Though even here in New England people are now referring to them by the old Dutch name of *keuken*."

"*Keuken*," Verity repeated, savoring the new sound.

"No," Nell said, and Verity was correcting her pronunciation before she realized her friend lingered on other, more important matters. "I believe it is the unique challenge of Will Bentley to remain in your company as long as possible. He knows he is likely to lose you as soon as we arrive in Cincinnati and wishes to delay our progress as long as possible."

"I have already promised to be his partner," Verity murmured.

"That is not what he wants. I am sure of it," Nell said succinctly.

"Why, this does not sound like the girl I met only a few weeks ago. Has Will said something to you to make you so certain, so knowing of his desires?"

"Will would not say anything to me of such things, nor will my own brother betray a confidence. It is only that my friendship with Peter Warburton has made me wise. I cannot say that Will is in love with you, but it is clear to anyone who sees the two of you together that he is fascinated with you. Besotted."

"Vexed, more likely, Nell. We do not get on at all, really. We are doomed to make each other unhappy," said Verity. But to think Will Bentley found her fascinating? The notion was quite flattering, even if his attention was for all the wrong reasons.

The two men waited for them on the slate terrace, to escort them into the toll house. Even leaning on his crutches, Geoff had to duck his head to enter, and

Verity was surprised to find herself in a dark, low-ceilinged room. She supposed that most buildings in America were fairly modern, but the toll house might well be as old as some with which she was familiar in England. Perhaps she would write something about the architecture and mention that strange three-seater privy in the rear of the building.

"The toll house was built over a hundred years ago," Will said. "There have been some fires and accidents over time, but we stand in the original part of the building."

"Is it necessary to anticipate every question, Will? Should I simply rely on you for the answer to everything, or dare I question other people we meet?"

Will smiled, and she realized he took her questions in the right spirit. "It would not be altogether proper, even in America, for a lady to talk to a stranger. But it is true I have not yet found the answer to everything I wish to know."

Verity did not take that comment in the right spirit, however, for she knew he still reflected on their words spoken in the coach. No matter what happened, her deception would always be between them, whether fully revealed or not. And in a curious way, it would always divide her character as well, for she was no longer Annie Merrill, nor would she ever be Lady Verity Harwood. At some point, perhaps in Cincinnati, she might shrug off both identities.

"How far do we go tonight?" Nell asked. "Will we see Springfield?"

"I have already discussed this with Quint, and we will likely fall short of Springfield tonight," Will said. "It is a pleasant town, upriver from Hartford, and I would not mind staying there. My mother's cousins own a comfortable and popular inn along our way.

"You ask me often enough about my family connections, but it is rare you speak of your own," Verity pointed out, as their tea and *keuken* were served.

"I have an abundance of sisters," he offered.

"It must be a very nice thing to have sisters," Nell said pertly. "And have you any yourself, Verity?"

"I do not. Nor brothers, for that matter."

"Brothers," Geoff repeated. "That could make all the difference in one's life. Not so much here in America, but in your homeland. Our friend Will might find himself in an uncomfortable situation if his cousin Eastbourne does not produce a son. He will be known as the American earl who dared to publish words critical of his English cousins."

"I am content to be nothing more than an American cousin," Will said, irritably.

"What if you should marry wealthily?" Nell teased and kicked Verity under the table.

"I doubt I shall find a lady who would have me, a poor writer with a modest house on the Hudson River," Will said, looking across the table at Verity. "What would I have to offer her?"

"The answer to all her questions, perhaps?" Verity said softly.

Chapter 9

*Tho Though Americans are likely to tear down old buildings and build anew, there are nevertheless excellent examples of Colonial architecture in New England. The smaller communities of Massachusetts pride themselves on such structures, perhaps proud to demonstrate how well they all—people and houses—survived a war of Independence. There is much pride in statehood, and taverns and inns bare bear names that serve as remnants of that war. Tonight we stopped at a pleasant inn not many miles from Pittsfield, Massachusetts, called the Revere. Paul Revere warned the colonials of the advance of the English army, in 1775.*

Verity handed her pages over to Will, eager for his opinion and hopeful of his praise. He stood over her, reading through her paragraphs. When he raised his brows, looking surprised.

"You are much improved in your grammar, my dear," he said softly. "Geoff will be most happy about that, as his work will now be easier. But I think it very likely that our inn honored Revere because of his excellent silverwork, rather than his famous mission. Our chargers beneath our dinner plates were of very fine work, did you not notice?"

"I have learned to notice everything, Will," Verity said. *Including his increasing use of the endearment.*

"But I prefer to believe the owners of the inn honored an American hero than the value of their tableware. If they call too much attention to the service, the pieces are likely to leave the inn beneath the cloaks of dishonest guests."

"You have not paid much heed to the tribal nations that inhabited these lands before the English and Dutch came to these shores. And yet there is much to remind us of their presence, in the names of our towns, in the foods we favor, even in the harvest holiday we'll celebrate in the fall."

"I said I notice everything, did I not?" Verity smiled. "I have been reading much about the native Americans, including how unfairly they were dispossessed of their lands along the route we will follow across New York."

He pondered this and then shook his head. "I suspect our readers prefer to read about cultural appropriations rather than political injustices, however much they impact recent history, however."

"Do you think they would be indifferent? This from a man who insists on sharing the truth in everything?" Verity thought he would admire her initiative and sighed in disappointment. "I must have caught you in a weak moment."

"I believe you have," he said softly.

"Well, in that case, I should like to see what you have written, for you have not shown me nearly enough of it. Come, Will, what do you have for me?"

The air between them changed in some subtle way. He looked down at the papers in his hand, before placing them very deliberately next to her traveling desk. His arm brushed against hers, which she supposed was deliberate also.

"What do you want from me?" he asked, though whether it was an entreaty or an enticement, she neither knew nor cared. Verity stood into the circle of his arms as her chair tumbled to the floor behind her.

She knew how this kiss would be, for she had relived the first hundreds of times in her dreams, and Will did not disappoint. He pulled her close as his lips caressed hers, gently edging them apart. Her hands caught the broad lapels of his wool jacket and tugged. He released her for a moment as he hurriedly slid the jacket off his shoulders, and Verity's arms reached for him before the garment fell to the floor.

And yet she was the first to pause in this madness, when she finally pulled away, breathless. One hand remained on his heart.

"This is what I want from you, though it is very forward of me to say so," she admitted. "I think I started to imagine how it might be when I met you at Eastbourne Hall, and my feelings only grew stronger on the *Andromeda*. And now I am utterly distracted."

He laughed, pressing his nose against her hair. "I shall have to reconsider all my notions of courting, it seems. First, I should ignore the lady, then treat her with rudeness, and advance to studied indifference. If this is the effect such behavior has on gentlewomen, I shall have to inform the poor knaves who are still trying to attract a lady's interest with flowers and chocolates and sweet words."

She leaned her cheek against his chest. "I am not indifferent to such ploys, you understand. I would have given up the whole wretched experience of a sea journey for one small daisy." She closed her eyes, wishing this moment of pleasure could last a lifetime. Will's fingers combed through her hair, releasing her plaits and a dozen or so pins. Truly, whatever was in store for her for the future, she could always say that she had been to heaven.

But she tumbled to earth in a quick drop. She pushed slightly away and gazed up into his face.

"Will, you will not write…you will not make my love life the subject of an odious book? If you are doing research with this little display of passion, I shall have to murder you in your sleep."

He grinned, which truly was not a satisfactory answer.

"Will?" She pushed harder.

"My dear, have you not yet considered the wisdom of the old adage that those holding rapiers are nevertheless afraid of those armed with goose quills? You have the ability to hold me hostage by virtue of your own writing on the subject. I dare not reveal anything," he said. "Nor would I."

"I suppose I must trust you on that," she said.

"As I trust you," he added, to seal the bargain.

But it was a bad bargain, as only she knew. He thought he kissed Lady Verity Harwood, the wealthy daughter of an earl, not the illegitimate daughter of the earl and his housekeeper. Will Bentley, for all his American ways, was heir to an earl. Whereas Miss Annie Merrill had inherited a carpet bag and a few silver coins. In a moment of poignant irony, she realized the American might have to live the life of an Englishman, while the Englishwoman would forever be banished to America.

Perhaps Will saw the doubt and sadness in her

expression, though he could not guess its cause. But he responded in a way that allowed her to escape, for one more blessed interlude, the wretched reality of her situation.

"But did you just say my lovemaking was a 'little display of passion'?" he asked. "I must be somewhat out of practice, for I am not known to disappoint."

Through her misery, Verity somehow managed a giggle. "I did not mean to suggest…"

"Come back here, Verity. I shall endeavor to try harder."

"You must not…" she protested, even as she walked back into his arms. "I have no complaints."

And though she intended to apply herself to her writing this evening, and the air grew chill around them, and his day's beard scratched her cheeks, she did indeed have no complaints.

****

Verity avoided Nell's curious gaze when she arrived in the dining room the next morning. Though the two women shared a bed, they might have well been living on opposite ends of the earth. Nell was sound asleep by the time Verity stumbled, dazed with cooling desire, into their room last night. And when Verity opened her eyes this day, she was quite alone among the rumpled bedding. She hoped her restless, fitful night did not disturb her companion, causing her to escape at the first light.

But when she took a seat across from Nell in the large public room, her friend looked quite refreshed and beautiful. She, on the other hand, looked like she had spent the night lost in the wilderness and had the bleary eyes and tangled hair to show for it. Such was the price one paid for an illicit evening of passion.

"What have you done to your cheeks?' Nell asked, holding up the candle on their table. The small flash of light was painful to Verity's eyes, and she closed them. "Did you sleep on an old pillow, with tiny quills sticking through? Mine was quite comfortable. And what of your hair?"

"My hair?" Verity asked, as if she did not know her hurriedly plaited curls gave her the appearance of a milkmaid. "Oh, I neglected to put it up in wrappers before I went to bed, and I can scarcely comb it through this morning. It is nothing."

"Oh, no. It is something. We shall have to do something or cut the whole thing off." Nell said, twisting one of her own curls with her finger while she spoke.

"I thought I managed it quite well," Verity said, defensively.

"And up until this point, you did. There is no time to take care of it now, however, for Geoff and Will should be down shortly, and they will surely be impatient to leave. Perhaps I can brush it out for you while we ride in the coach, if the gentlemen do not mind."

Verity had a sudden image of her loose hair draped over her face and Will's when she was poised over him on the divan last night.

"They will probably not mind," she said and blushed.

Nell studied her for a few moments. "But before we leave, we will look around for some sassafras leaves, so we can wash your hair in an infusion this evening. It will make your hair soft and easier to care for. I learned how to go about it from one of our neighbors, whose family has always lived on the land."

"I have never heard of sassafras, though my father taught me a fair amount of the natural sciences."

"Perhaps you do not have such trees in England. Their leaves look like little mittens. They're quite charming, actually."

"As are you two ladies," said Geoff, as he approached them, catching the last few words. Verity wondered if he might recant his statement, as he stood over them, studying her hair and face.

"Oh, Geoff, sit down before you fall down," his sister said quickly. "Where are your crutches?"

"I believe I can manage without them," he said and took a little hop on his good foot. "Traveling by coach is rather sedentary and allows me sufficient rest."

"I believe the doctor said that you would need sufficient exercise, which is not to be gained simply by walking to and from the vehicle. Verity and I must take a short walk in the woods before we depart, and perhaps you would like to join us."

"Indeed?" Geoff said, looking surprised. "Are you looking for Will?"

"In the woods? Why on earth?" Nell said scornfully. "Do you think he is writing about our local fauna?"

"I have no idea what he is writing about, for he has not given me anything new in over a week. But I am quite busy with Verity's papers all the while, who seems to have found her muse, while my friend Will appears to have lost his."

Verity blushed again, wishing it possible she could just take every utterance at face value and not suppose it had anything to do with herself.

"Then perhaps he is looking for her in the woods," Nell said. "If Verity and I find him wandering about, searching under rocks and such, we will leave him quite alone."

"No, do not do that, for I would like to be underway. You may have to drag him kicking and screaming, however." Geoff turned to face Verity, nodding to himself. "On second thought, he will probably come most willingly."

This time, Verity knew that Geoff's words had much to do with herself, and that he might very well have a better awareness of Will's intentions than did she. But there was no time to put Geoff's theory to the test, for Will himself came through the door. He looked wonderful, curse the man, with not a hair out of place, and his cravat tied quite neatly. She imagined that after delivering her to her room, he wandered off to his own bed and slept soundly through the rest of the night.

Verity started toward the buffet on the sideboard, where Will intercepted her. She tried to act as casually as she could, nodding a greeting as she did every other morning. But Will would have none of that.

He reached for her thick plait trailing down her back and brushed its end against her cheek.

"I hope you slept well, my dear?" he asked.

"I will sleep better tonight if I am not thinking that everyone in this dining room can guess what is now between us," she said and stepped away. He still held her hair.

"They do not know us, and we do not know them. And one of the great advantages of travel is we move on, and they move on in another direction."

This was what she had hoped to do the night she made her irrevocable decision on board the *Andromeda*. And so she might have gone on and disappeared entirely, but for the ill fortune of a chance meeting with someone who already knew her. Verity turned to face Will, ignoring the slight tug on her plait. Ill fortune? No, whatever became of her because of her misdeeds, she would never consider it ill fortune that she found comfort and pleasure in Will Bentley's arms last night.

"Geoff and Nell will know," she said softly.

"I believe they already do. I suspect they knew before I did myself."

Verity was tempted to drop her plate on the floor and throw herself into his arms again and hear him say some of the things he murmured last night in her ear, against her breast, on her lips. She wanted to confess the whole wretched truth and hear him say it did not matter. She just wanted him.

"Do you prefer coffee or tea in the morning?" she asked instead.

"You will find New Englanders enjoy their tea. It was one of the reasons for the Revolution."

"And a very important one, indeed," she said. "If you will release my hair, I will bring a teapot to the table."

A few minutes later, they assembled as a foursome, and Verity did the honors of serving the dark, rich tea.

"You have a steady hand," Geoff said.

"I have had practice," Verity said, and added quickly, "since coming to America. It does not require great skill."

"And yet good servants are hard to find," Nell said earnestly. "No one wishes to be a servant, when everyone is capable of being a lady."

"Indeed," said Verity, praying it was possible.

\*\*\*\*

Some time later, while the men were settling the bill and seeing to the loading of the coach, Verity and Nell went down a marked trail, on the advice of the innkeeper. He had recently sawn a fallen sassafras for firewood and guessed that the ancient hardwood had offspring scattered about in the clearing.

"And here are chestnuts, which many people use for food. And here are young maples, which will give us the sweetest of syrups." Nell skipped along the path, making Verity feel foolish for worrying about venturing into the woods. All the same, she doubted she would get very far if she tried to escape.

"And these must be sassafras, for these leaves are just as you described."

"Oh, I am sorry you found it so quickly, Verity, for I would have liked to spend an hour here instead of getting back into the coach. But that is certainly sassafras. We will need eight or ten large leaves."

Verity brushed one leaf under her nose.

"You need not be afraid you will smell like a dead fish or something of that sort," Nell said, grinning. "Someone will be quite entranced once he gets a whiff of it."

"I do not wish to have strange men following me about like the Piper of Hamlin."

"I do not think him very strange at all. I do not know anyone kinder or more handsome than Will. Aside from my brother. And Peter, of course."

"Will?"

"Oh, please, you cannot continue this act with me.

I am certain he adores you, and I suspect you feel something of the same for him."

*She did not know the half of it.*

"But it is not meant to be, Nell. We are from different worlds and must simply remain friends. Certainly Will has not said or done anything for me to think otherwise."

"Really? I would have thought he could not have signaled his intentions more clearly than when he tugged on your plait in the dining room. Even in America, boys stop pulling on a girl's hair by the time they are ten or twelve. Will is well beyond that, which is quite lucky for both of you."

"Will is just a friend."

"Friends offer the loan of a book. The man was playing with your hair, which is a different matter altogether."

Verity looked up, surprised they had doubled back on the trail and were approaching the stables of the inn. Geoff seemed to be examining some paperwork with Quint, but Will just stood next to the coach, watching them approach.

"Besotted, that's what," Nell said.

"Confused, more like," Verity said, speaking more for herself than anyone else. She did not know what Will was truly thinking, but her own desperation had certainly gotten them both into a situation from which neither could gracefully escape. She went on anyway, scripting the story as she had from that fateful day on the *Andromeda*. "He thought to find a business partner, and now he is encumbered with two additional traveling companions who demand that Geoff and he stop the coach at regular intervals, and who crowd his space with baggage and an abundance of cushions."

"Well, I daresay the lad will just have to get used to it. Whatever the inconvenience to himself, he will not abandon us at a crossroad, waiting for the next ride." Nell smiled and waved at him. "But if he continues to scowl at me, perhaps we will leave him behind."

"Have you been waiting for us, Will?" Nell asked sweetly, as they came close.

"It seems to be both my burden and my pleasure," he answered.

"How well you disguise your displeasure with us, sir. And with nothing more than a turn of phrase. I believe you would do very well as a writer," Nell said.

Verity looked at him, thinking they both had talents at disguise, though she was not sure she could sustain hers much longer.

"What do you have for me, Will?" she asked, as he offered her a sheaf of papers. She guessed it was his long-awaited chapters.

"Anything you wish, my dear," he said and took her hand to help her into the coach. He offered assistance to Nell and then Geoff before joining them within.

"James Quint and I just examined the map," Geoff said. "And we intend to make excellent progress today."

"Then I shall do the same, for I have been given my work for the journey," Verity said. "You have written much, Will, and I wonder when you found the time."

Good God. Now she was being provocative as well.

"I have spent many a sleepless night recently," Will admitted, and grinned. "I intend to compensate for it while we ride along. That will also save me the discomfort of watching your face each time you find fault with my words on the page."

"You are very confident I will find fault. And yet, I don't believe I expressed lack of satisfaction for anything at all," she said softly. "At least, not in the last few days."

Geoff cleared his throat with the effort of one trying to dislodge a lump of coal. Nell reached over and started to pound him on the back.

"Then I hope my words are as good as my deeds," Will said softly.

Inasmuch as her own words failed her then, and her cheeks burned so hot she thought she would incinerate the coach, she only nodded and looked down at the papers in her lap. Quint called out a warning, and the coach lurched toward its western destination.

*There is something in the very atmosphere air of America that nurtures the spirit of enterprise, allowing even the most privileged of souls to seek opportunity. A gentleman, well accustomed to every advantage of birth, might well find himself contemplating opening a shop or building a house with his bare hands. A lady might don gloves but is willing to do very much the same. Dirtying one's hands—either literally or metaphorically—is a sign of healthy ambition in America, whereas in England it is viewed with disdain.*

Verity's eyes left the page and looked toward the roof of the coach, as Nell's comb tugged at her hair. The two of them had positioned themselves so they both faced the right side of the vehicle. They had not been riding for more than ten minutes when Nell suggested they get to work, each with her own project, and decided this position would suit. Geoff and Will watched them curiously, though Verity sensed something keener than curiosity when Nell started to unravel her plait. Out of the corner of her eye, she watched Will study her long tresses and once, when he caught a falling hair pin, he reached over to brush his hand against her curls.

"This will only take a moment," Nell murmured, as she tugged harder on the back of Verity's head. Verity feared the whole mess would have to be cut off, but Nell seemed to be doing wonders with nothing more than a jar of sweet-smelling pomade and a tortoiseshell comb. Later, when they reached this evening's destination, both women would wash their hair with Nell's sassafras infusion.

"It is no matter, Nell. It feels wonderful, and I do need a break from Will's observations on society." Verity closed her eyes, savoring the feel of Nell's hands.

They rode along in silence for some time, until the men's breathing became deeper.

"Do not be fooled into thinking they are actually asleep," Nell said. "I am sure they are waiting for us to say something, so they can take us to task for our opinions."

Verity turned her head slightly, and if Will was indeed awake, he did a very fine imitation of slumbering. She poked her finger at his knee and received no response, but that could have been part of his ruse as well.

"Well, in that case, I confess that I find Will's

words to be those of a visionary and scholar. How brilliant are his observations! How clever are his words!" Verity was sure such praise would cause him to stir, yet they did not. She ought to try harder. "They are so much wiser than my own!"

She thought she had him there, but he only shifted on his seat and leaned his head against the hard veneer of the window frame.

"I think he is well asleep, Nell," she admitted.

"That is how it should be. It is not truly proper to witness a lady's toilette, is it?" Nell asked. "Did you ever allow a man to see you with your hair down at Harwood Hall?"

"It was unusual for a gentleman to see me without my gloves, let alone in such a casual state." Verity answered as Lady Verity would. "But then, I did not have brothers or a husband."

"Did you have many beaux?" Nell asked. "You are an heiress and very beautiful. They must have been lining up in the hallway."

For the first time, Verity thought about the fact that Lady Verity was not sought after at all. She pursued Eastbourne, who surely encouraged her. But why did other gentlemen not come to call or engage her at the assembly balls she attended? Could it have been nothing more than the extra digit on her hand? Surely there were ladies with more grievous deformities than this, and Lady Verity's assets more than compensated for the peculiarity of her right hand.

Or was it something in her character that was off-putting? Lady Verity had been a beast to her servants, to be sure, but what if she treated her would-be suitors with similar contempt? Verity thought about that, realizing she was never a witness to such conversations, for which she ought to be very, very grateful.

"I did not, nor did I mind. After my mother died, my father and I stayed in the country, where he could follow his interests in the natural sciences. I often helped him with his little animals and helped to organize his notes. There were not many gentlemen whom my father admitted to his little sanctuary."

"And yet he allowed Will to come. I remember him describing it all to me. But how odd that he did not describe you. For surely, I do not think he could have avoided falling in love with you then."

"You are a dear, Nell. But you know it is never as simple as all that. Perhaps he was already told by his cousin that I was not to be trifled with."

"If that means he could not be allowed to fall in love with you, I wonder why that changed as soon as you stepped foot in America. Nay, even before that."

"Nell!" Verity protested, praying that Will did not overhear any of this.

"What?" Nell asked, sounding very innocent as she pinned up part of Verity's hair. "It is certainly the truth."

As to that, Verity could not really say. But Will's own words in the papers she held seemed to argue in their favor. Even a lady was transformed on American shores, willing to get her hands dirty while doing honest work. Was that not true for Frances Trollope? And here in America a maid could live like a lady, riding in a well-sprung coach while another combed the knots from her hair and patiently pinned it all up into a regal coronet.

Nell was quite right. The dream of America began

before reaching American shores. And it was a dream of possibility, only to be imagined once a person understood that an accident of birth did not doom one for life. Such was true for the well born as well as those who were common; those born with no hope of betterment were allowed to strive, and those born with every seeming advantage could escape unhappiness. Lady Verity, for all her gowns and riches, had never seemed to be happy.

In fact, it was quite the opposite. And in her perfect misery, she was able to infect others.

"Stop moving your head," Nell admonished her. "I am not a lady's maid, accustomed to such tasks. I am only your friend."

"Never say 'only,' dear Nell. A friend is worth twenty lady's maids."

"And I suppose you know the truth of that, better than the rest of us?" Nell asked, laughing.

"Indeed, I do," Verity said, not laughing at all.

*And yet, in America, one sacrifices the traditions that make a nation great. Where there is long, sustained history by native tribes, it is only scarcely acknowledged as the past, while the Europeans set a course for the future. This recent history is so brief, its narrative seems to have been invented and edited as suits one's purpose. For example, a large shade tree stands on Cambridge Common, under which General George Washington is reported to have taken command of the Continental Army. The elderly veterans of the War dispute that claim, however, and point to an ill formed and gnarled elm not very far distant and suggest the great moment occurred under its branches.*

*But no matter. A plaque will be nailed to the*

*grander tree, and Americans will celebrate it with flags and banners every year on the anniversary of the event.*

*The reinvention of history, to suit one's purposes, is the hallmark of what it is to be an American.*

Verity grew cold as she read Will's stark words, guessing he already knew the truth. Why did he not already expose her for the fraud she was? Did he hope to entrap her into making a full confession? Did he wait to have her arrested in Cincinnati? What was his wretched plan?

But there was something else here, for his words were oddly familiar. She closed her eyes and recalled where she had read—if not the identical words, then the identical sentiments—before. She had sat in the cramped library in the Marsh home, preparing for her journey by reading the words of those who came before her. Most illuminating were the travelogues of the American Benjamin Williams. And here was an echo of his words, though in Will Bentley's hand. Benjamin Williams. William Bentley.

She was a fool for not realizing with whom she bargained. But then, he was dishonest for neglecting to tell her something rather important.

She looked up from his page and saw Mr. Benjamin Williams, the renowned travel writer, was wide awake, watching her.

Whatever she read of his words had suddenly produced a profound effect, he realized. Will casually looked down, trying to see the page in her lap, but his own writing was so cramped he could not make any sense of it from this distance and reading it upside down. Was she bothered by his references to the English country house hierarchy? Did she frown upon his reflection on American ambitions? Or did he touch a sensitive nerve when he wrote of establishing an identity in the New World?

The pages suddenly fluttered to the floor of the coach, and he looked up to meet her gaze.

"Have a care, my dear," he said, as he gathered the papers and started to shuffle them back into order. "I spent a good deal of time on those paragraphs and despise the thought of chasing them down the road when the door opens."

"And yet I believe I read something similar not so long ago, though in the pages of a published journal. If you recreated these pages by copying them out of that book, no one would call you a plagiarist, I suppose?"

"Whatever do you mean?" he asked quietly.

"Because you are already the author of that other book, writing under a *nom de plume*. Did you imagine you would always be able to disguise your identity from me, Mr. Benjamin Williams? Were you concerned I would demand too great a price if you revealed that my partner was the most famous travel writer of the day?"

"Why does it matter?"

"How could it not?" Verity countered.

"I am one and the same, no matter my name. I think that is true of everyone, even those who would look to the New World for a new start." He hoped she recognized the door he just opened for her and would decide to walk through it. But this was not the moment, not the place.

Verity opened her mouth and closed it. She said nothing. Beside her, Nell's knitting had fallen into her lap and her hands were limp at her sides. Geoff slept on.

"Nell has made your hair most severe, which gives you the look of a strict governess. I think I prefer your hair loose about your face." He offered her a reprieve.

"Which would give me the look of a milkmaid, I suppose," Verity said, sarcastically. "Is that what you had in mind when you considered how America allows us the opportunity to change identities?"

"Not identities, for in many ways you shall always be Lady Verity Harwood, with her expectations and demeanor. I suspect this will be true even if you marry and change your name," Will said. "But even if the name stays the same, what you do with it may differ. That is the point of starting a new life here. A lady might decide to become a milkmaid, if it is something that interests her."

Verity was biting down on her lip so intently, he thought she would start to bleed from a wound.

"Or she might be a governess, or open a shop like Mrs. Trollope has," Will spoke reasonably.

"I ask you, Will, what would be the point of it all? Why would a lady, a person of privilege, decide to lower her own rank in society? Do you imagine it would be enjoyable for anything more than a day's lark? As an experiment to see how the common folk live? I would imagine that one night spent in a drafty thatched cottage would be more than enough to retire any romantic illusions."

"But what if the romance is not an illusion?" he asked.

"Do you mean, if I, that is, a lady, decides her life is much more pleasurable waking at dawn to work her poor fingers to soreness while milking a cow?"

"No, I mean what if she does it for love? What if she is willing to sacrifice everything for love?"

Nell suddenly opened her eyes.

"Then it would not be a sacrifice, would it?" Verity answered softly.

Nell sighed.

But she was a clever woman, his mysterious lady. The Lady Verity he had known would never have twisted his comments until she had the last word, would never have managed to get past looking like a governess. She would never have consented to ride all the way to Cincinnati with him and certainly would not have agreed to partner with him in the authorship of a book. Gone was the vain and foolish girl who could scarcely take her hands off a married man and who would not give his American cousin a second glance.

In her place, there was an intelligent and thoughtful soul and a young woman who kissed like a girl. Unless his cousin was a complete lout—and that was, of course, entirely possible—it did not seem possible that the woman he caressed and kissed the night before had managed to conceive a child not that many months ago. The Verity who sat across from him, scowling at his silence, was untutored in the arts of love.

"And what of yourself, Will?" she asked. "You are very settled in your American ways, it seems. You extol the virtues of this country, even while gently finding fault with its customs."

"I do not find that unusual. It is possible to be born and raised in a society and still understand its weaknesses," he said.

"Of course. But what will happen if you suddenly find yourself Lord Eastbourne? What will happen to the poor travel writer then?"

"I am not poor now, though I might be if I ever inherit Eastbourne's debts. My cousin is neither cautious nor wise with his investments. And if anything should happen to him, Lady Eastbourne and her daughters must be provided for," Will answered, before realizing how it might appear he had already considered the possibilities. He certainly was not wishing any ill upon his cousin, no matter how reckless the man might be. "But the likelihood of such a sad event is almost nil. I do not expect to ever be known as Lord Eastbourne and am quite satisfied with being plain Mr. Bentley."

"You might not be able to marry as you wish," Nell said and smiled.

Why did it seem like all their conversations came to the same end?

"Then I shall take care in deciding whom I wish to marry," he said, hoping he had once again dodged the thrust of their conversation.

Nell, the little vixen, smiled as she reached for her knitting. But Verity sat rigidly still, pale but for her bright lips.

"How far do you propose we journey today?" she asked.

He studied her for a moment, wondering if she was asking a coded message about their possibilities of after-dinner activities for this evening. But it was not a question that could be asked with an audience, and it was not a question that could be answered while her expression was so pained.

"Are you anxious to be at the end of the journey?" he asked. "Have you had quite enough of us, or of our meddling questions?"

"Our journey will be the story of our book, so I could hardly wish for it to end so soon. But I am asking for all practical purposes: I do not know the geography of this country and do not have a map. Perhaps I can borrow Geoff's, because without it I do not have any sense of our destination."

"Oh, please, do not get him started," Geoff murmured, uncurling his body from his position of sleep. "You would have been better off asking me for the details. I would show you the way. Will is likely to describe every scene in vast detail before you have the opportunity to see them for yourself."

"But I would not mind that so much. After all, much of what I write is in response to Will's words. I do not take anything at face value." She leaned across the coach to accept the scroll Geoff offered her and unrolled it in her lap.

"If the weather remains fair, we will arrive in Albany this evening. You can see it just there, on the far side of the Hudson River, in New York."

"The Hudson River? Is that where your estate is, Will?"

"It is on the wider part of the river, several hundred miles downstream. It is close to West Point and less than a day's ride from New York City."

"Do you not wish to travel there and visit your family? I daresay you have not seen them in some months."

"It is not on our way to Cincinnati. Though I might impose on Geoff and Nell to allow me that detour before we return to Cambridge."

"We are at your service, Will," Geoff reminded him. "And I never would complain about the opportunity to see any of your lovely sisters."

"I would like to see them as well," Nell said.

"As would I," Verity added, and then perhaps realized her error. "But where do we go after Albany?"

"We might not see Albany this evening; if the hour grows late, we will stay in Troy, which is on this side of the river. But in any case, we will then find ourselves on the broad plains of Western New York, past Amsterdam, Utica, Salina, and Rochester, where the great canal is being built."

"Tell me more about that," Verity asked, and he could see she was genuinely curious. "I heard nothing about it while I was in England."

"Oh, please don't ask him about it," Nell groaned. "It is all we read about in the newspapers."

Will ignored her, knowing he already had a captive audience.

"It may have been pure folly to build a waterway to connect the Mohawk River and the Hudson with Lake Erie, but the possibilities of its success are enormous. It will change the way of commerce from the port of New York to distant cities and serve to move passengers to places nearly inaccessible before."

"How is it proceeding?" Verity asked.

"We do not yet know how successful it will be," Will said, "although the groundbreaking occurred nearly four years ago. On July 4, as it happens. You will find it is a date that is much beloved to Americans."

"And so it was natural to use it for such an auspicious occasion," Verity said, nodding her head. "Shall we be able to mark its progress as we travel? I should think it would be interesting to observe. And I much prefer to travel alongside a waterway than on the waterway itself, as I learned on the *Andromeda*."

Geoff laughed. "Then let today's travelogue be enough for a while. You will not want to hear about our journey across Lake Erie to Ohio."

Verity looked surprised. "You have already mentioned it, but surely it will not be much of a journey? It is only a lake, after all."

"These are our Great Lakes, my dear," said Will. "They are so vast, one cannot see from one shore to the other. The ship will not roll as it does on the ocean, but we will have an adventure, just the same. Geoff has already booked our cabins."

Will sat back in his seat, enjoying the prospect of several days on ship with Verity Harwood. But his companions all looked at him strangely, and Geoff and Nell were clearly amused. What had he said?

Verity turned to the window, where the sun lit warm chestnut streaks in her hair and made her cheeks glow.

He cursed himself silently, realizing he revealed too much. And yet Geoff and Nell would have to be fools not to see how things were between him and Verity. They knew him too well not to guess what emotions moved beneath the still veneer he presented to the world but also would understand why circumstances made it impossible for him to publicly act on those emotions.

If only he understood it himself.

Surely his character was not so self-righteous that he could justify his reticence by proclaiming a union to Lady Verity Harwood to be a blow to his pride. He had no title, but he was the grandson of an English earl and a gentleman of property in America. Hudson Point was not Eastbourne Hall, but it was a tidy little estate with excellent fruit orchards and a grand prospect. Someone of Lady Verity's expectations would not be wholly disappointed with living along a great river, one that was about to become even greater as transportation routes opened to the west.

And he could not justify his reticence by asserting that a liaison with Lady Verity was an impeachment of his honor. If he and she were thrust together when he was in England, he would have vigorously resisted, for the little flirt made no secret of her affections for his cousin. But to marry Eastbourne's castoff would suggest a precedent, that Will was ready to take what his cousin could not own. It was a bad business, all around. And yet these affairs would not matter so much in America.

This left him with the lady herself, so unlike the Lady Verity he'd met and once reviled, that he should have known at once that she could not be the same person. Her perfect little hands, which he very much enjoyed on his body, were not those he remembered. Her even more perfect mind, lively and intelligent, was perhaps the most damning evidence of all. And therefore, in this more perfect form of Lady Verity was a woman who was deceitful and dishonest and had stolen the good name of another.

But Lady Verity's name was not very good as it was. Before him was the person who actually brought honor to the title and the family. So, in stealing another's name, she had managed to polish it up and make it respectable. Was there a crime in that?

Indeed, there was, if it was not hers to polish.

"Will, perhaps you would like to tell us about the Great Falls at Niagara?" Nell said sweetly. "It might be a perfect moment to bring them into the conversation."

"Why is that, Nell?" Will asked.

Verity still gazed out the window at the passing landscape.

"I have read that it is a very romantic place," Nell said. "And Captain Warburton has said very much the same."

Will quickly intercepted any comment Geoff might make about Nell's current favorite.

"It is very grand and very beautiful," he said. "But I have found it almost terrifying in its beauty. I do not think of it as a place for romance, but rather one of industry."

"Do you intend to open a shop there, Will?" asked Verity, still looking out the window.

"It would undoubtedly be a fine investment if I did, but I have no such intentions. But there are those who imagine that the energy of the falls can be harnessed to serve our needs. Imagine the output of the mills on all the rivers of England and increase it by a thousandfold. There, I suspect, is something akin to what is available to us."

"If that is true, then you are right. It is much better than romance," Verity said, nodding.

Suddenly it seemed as if she and he were quite alone in this small compartment, dancing politely about the patterns of conversation, when there was really only one thing on his mind and on hers. She wanted him. And he wanted her, far beyond any reason he conjured for thinking otherwise.

"There may not be anything better than romance,"

he said, before he could catch himself. Geoff slapped him on the knee, and he quickly brushed him off. "For it is romance that drives the progress in America, that makes men dig canals and harness water power. It is the spirit of romance that brought Europeans to these wild shores and continues to do so."

He thought he acquitted himself rather nicely.

"Well said, Will," Verity said. "I should like to use that in one of my chapters, if you do not mind. It helps to explain a great deal."

"Does it now?" Geoff asked. "I would have thought such a statement to be rather discouraging."

Verity seemed to ponder this for a moment before she spoke. "Yes, I suppose it would be discouraging for a person—man or woman—who had little on the mind except for lovemaking. And indeed, I know many people back home who seemed to care for little else. Estates went to ruin, and children were fearfully neglected, but it was all in the name of love. Is it not better to have ambition and see to society's improvement?"

"Hail! Hail!" Geoff said, tapping his finger against the map. "But for your odd turn of phrase, you could be a true daughter of the Revolution."

"Is that why you have come to America, Verity?" Nell asked eagerly. "You have never really quite told us your reasons."

"Yes, tell us, Verity," Will said. He knew she was too spry to be trapped into an admission, but he had a natural curiosity to see how her story was evolving.

"I came because I was bored, because there was nothing for me at Harwood Hall." She nodded to herself. "Yes, I suppose that it is. You might think of me as one of those little river mills in England, producing energy, but with no place to spend it. I had to go somewhere and do something."

"And if your and Will's book is a success, you will no longer be a little mill, but the great Niagara," Nell said gleefully.

"You are very optimistic, Nell." Verity grinned. "But I do hope it is a success. It will be worth everything."

Before Will could ask her what "everything" might be, Geoff interrupted.

"You will have to change your name, of course," he said.

Will did not imagine the look of terror on Verity's face, nor the sudden blanching of her skin. This promised to be more edifying than he imagined.

"Whatever do you mean?" she asked slowly.

"Fear not," Geoff said, seemingly oblivious to her pain. "I am not proposing marriage or anything of the sort. I am only suggesting you would do well to change your name, as our friend Will has. Has he already told you he is truly Mr. Williams, the travel writer? He can offend anyone he pleases and not pay the price for his honesty. And as you seem to remark very favorably on American manners, you may decide to eschew your title and choose another name. Otherwise, you may not find yourself very popular in England."

"Oh, yes…what fun!" Nell clapped her hands. "Let us find a good name for you. Miss London would do very nicely. Or what of Miss Shakespeare?"

"That could be extremely immodest of me, I believe," Verity said, though visibly relieved of her discomfort of moments before. "But I've only just learned our friend's other identity on this very journey, though I cannot imagine why he needed to be so secretive about it. Perhaps he was being modest."

"No, not at all," Will said. "Inasmuch as I didn't know if our partnership would succeed, I saw no reason to reveal the truth and compromise Benjamin Williams' reputation."

"I see," said Verity. "You would not compromise the reputation of someone who does not actually exist."

"But Verity will use her real name?" Nell asked.

"I expect that to be the case," Will said.

"It doesn't seem very fair," Nell said, and no one said anything for several moments.

"May I suggest…" Geoff began, and they turned to him. "Well, since we conceived this partnership with the design of improving sales, perhaps Verity should write as 'Mrs. Benjamin Williams'?"

"Perfect!" Nell agreed. "People will think you are married. And, of course, no one will know the truth of it."

"Indeed they will not," Will said. "But this scheme will never convince anyone."

"Why not?" asked Geoff. "You can present yourselves as a married couple, she of England and he of America, who happened to meet on board ship during an Atlantic passage."

"It is rather a fanciful idea," Verity murmured.

"It is rather a wonderful idea." Nell sighed.

"And no one will actually know who we are," Verity said, "but for the four of us? I suppose that a new identity is something one gets used to?"

"Oh, indeed. I am already quite accustomed to it, for I have been writing as Mr. Benjamin Williams for years. Soon you too will feel perfectly comfortable assuming a new identity."

He had her there. And as she sat studying him, he realized she might finally realize he guessed the truth.

"Congratulations are due to the two of you, then," Nell said gaily. "And you may kiss the bride."

As Will leaned slightly forward, the coach jolted and crashed to its side, and the two ladies screamed as they toppled into his and Geoff's laps.

Chapter 10

"What has happened?" Verity said, against Will's lapel. She had fallen forward, crashing against his chest, kneeling in his lap. His arms tightened as he seemed ready to ward off another catastrophe, but she started to pull away.

"Don't move yet," he said urgently. "I do not know where the coach has settled, and we do not want to shift the balance. I suspect we have lost a wheel."

Verity moved her head, just slightly, and saw that Nell's position was more precarious, as she apparently fell nearly head over heels onto her brother. She heeded Will's warning and didn't even dare to straighten her skirt.

"Mr. Bentley? Mr. Marsh? Are the ladies well?" James Quint appeared at the window.

"We have all survived, Quint," said Will in a clear but low voice. "Are you and the horses fine?"

"They are frightened but unharmed. I hit my shoulder as we went down but no lasting damage, I suspect."

"What is our predicament?" Will asked in the same tone.

"Not good, but certainly reparable," Quint said. "Do not move about, if possible, while I unharness the horses."

Will's chest rose and fell as he took a deep breath.

Verity decided there was nothing to be done but make herself comfortable against him, which was both perfectly delightful and perfectly unseemly.

"Does this sort of thing happen to you often?" she asked, lifting one arm around his neck.

"I am not sure what you mean, but the answer to all must be 'no.' " His free hand cupped the back of her head.

"My hair must smell of pomade, like a horse's tail."

"Your hair smells of some sort of flower. Roses, at a guess."

"Lilacs, Will," Nell interrupted. "If you are married to Verity, you ought to know that."

"I am not married to Verity; that is a fiction."

"Pardon my error. You are playing your parts very well." She giggled.

"Don't mind the girl, Will," Geoff said tightly. "We are busy with other things, like trying to extract her foot from my face."

"Geoffrey! You are lucky I don't stick you in the eye with my hat pin."

"Come now, children. Play nicely," Will said. And then to Verity, "Pay no attention."

"To your fingers in my hair? It is very hard to ignore that, Will."

"Not harder than having you sitting in my lap," he said against her ear. "If we don't topple over to our deaths, this shall remain a fine moment to remember."

"But one we ought not write about, I think," Verity said.

"It should make for very dull reading, except for those who enjoy lady's novels." Will sighed.

Verity slapped him gently on his chest. "I enjoy lady's novels, as do most ladies. If I am truly a partner in this arrangement, I should like for our book to sell very well. Therefore, there must be something for the ladies, beyond the current fashions in Boston."

"Do you suppose, while we are in this predicament, we might find something to discuss other than business?" Will asked.

Verity would have loved nothing more than to discuss business. But Will did not know that such matters were to be her only salvation. When the truth of her wickedness was revealed, he would reject her as quickly as any man ever hardened his heart against a women, and she would have to fend for herself in a new country.

"It is not so bad as all that, my dear?" he asked, wrongly guessing the source of her hesitation.

She pressed her hands against his chest, to look up at his face. But her movement was ill timed, for just then the carriage fell forward, and she nearly flew out of his arms.

"It is fine. Do you not hear the horses? They are glad to be free of their burden," Will reassured her, gathering her close again. "We will soon be free as well."

The door opened, and Quint stood there in the sunlight, looking a good deal worse than he had admitted. A crease of blood marked his forehead, and his hair stood nearly straight on end. One jacket sleeve was ripped, and his shirt was stained with water.

Though Verity felt she could manage on her own, Will lifted her and passed her to Quint's waiting arms. The driver put her down unceremoniously on the grass and turned his attention to where Nell was impatiently waiting at the door.

"If your shoulder is hurt, Mr. Quint, do not bother with me," Nell said, jumping to the ground. Will followed a moment later, and then they helped Geoff extricate himself from the damaged carriage.

Once they were all pronounced safe, Verity surveyed the scene. The horses seemed completely indifferent to their dangerous encounter and were off grazing on the side of the road. Boxes, blankets, and traveling trunks were strewn across the ground, and Quint's hat was in a puddle. Other carriages and travelers had stopped, offering assistance and advice. Feeling utterly useless, Verity just sat where she was, watching the others decide what must be done.

Suddenly, someone separated himself from the onlookers and started to walk toward her.

"Mr. Reese? Is that you? What on earth are you doing in New York? Is it possible you are a traveler on the same route?" Verity asked, as her surprise turned to suspicion. "You have only spoken of your work in Boston."

"Alas, my business partners have prevailed upon me to travel to Ohio," he said, though she sensed some hesitation in his voice. "How fortuitous, for I now may be of service."

John Reese held out her hand to her, and she accepted his assistance. She stood, pushing her hair away from her face.

"How fortuitous," she echoed.

"Allow me to offer my services, and my modest coach, to see you on your way."

When Will interrupted the conversation she had

with this man on the deck of the *Andromeda*, she was annoyed by his possessive manner and did not altogether believe Will's harsh criticism of a stranger. But now she knew Will and trusted him, and still did not know anything more about John Reese.

"I will not travel without my friends, Mr. Reese. Though I thank you for your kind offer."

"In that case, I extend my offer to all of you. We might be a bit close in the carriage, but we are good enough friends for that."

However, they were not friends at all. Verity already recognized the ways in which friends were made in America: a handshake, a shared drink at an inn, a conversation at a party. But she backed away from this acquaintance. Quite literally, for she bumped up against someone.

"What do you want, Reese?" Will asked.

Mr. Reese looked wounded and held his hand to his heart. "Only to see you all well, Bentley. I have a coach and am on the same route."

"How do you know our route?" Will crossed in front of her.

"Why, the lady told me of your plans weeks ago, when we met on the *Andromeda*."

Will turned back to look at her, giving her some idea of what he thought about her big mouth.

"Mr. Reese has extended the offer of a ride, Mr. Bentley," Verity said, enunciating each word sharply.

"How very kind of him. But it is not at all necessary, as Quint assures me that our own carriage can be easily repaired. We will be delayed, but not excessively so," Will said. "And there is another carriage awaiting us in Albany, in any case."

"But surely the lady is anxious to see her friend Mrs. Trollope in Cincinnati?"

Will looked at John Reese with equal parts dislike and distrust, and Verity was coming to see his point. She thought back to her conversation with the man, trying to remember what she had said. Her pleasure at meeting a congenial gentleman might have made her reveal more than she ought, but she really did not think she was as indiscreet as that. Could she have named the person of Mrs. Trollope to an absolute stranger?

"I have waited all this time, Mr. Reese. Surely another day or so could hardly matter. But if you do see my friend before I do, please tell her I am not far away," said Verity.

"At your service, my lady," Mr. Reese said and bowed.

"Are you acquainted with Mrs. Trollope, Reese?" Will asked. "The world is smaller than I otherwise thought."

Mr. Reese stared at Will, looking like he would just prefer to end this conversation by stabbing him in the heart. "I do not know Mrs. Trollope," he confessed. "But I would be happy to serve Lady Verity by seeking her out."

"How very kind," Will said again, making it plain his meaning was quite the opposite. "I know several people between here and Ohio, and perhaps I can prevail upon you to visit them as well. It would be a great service."

"No doubt, Mr. Bentley. But I only wish to please Lady Verity."

"Lady Verity would be pleased if you leave her alone," Will said and started to shrug himself out of his jacket.

"Lady Verity would be pleased if the two of you dropped the subject," Verity said, coming directly between them. "Thank you for your offer, Mr. Reese, but I shall wait until our carriage is repaired."

"You may have to wait many days," Mr. Reese continued to argue. "The carriage wheel is beyond repair. Are you certain you wish to remain in the company of this disagreeable person any longer than necessary?"

The prospect sounded Elysian. "I am quite certain, Mr. Reese," Verity said and stared at him until he finally gave up and walked away.

"I have already told you not to trust him," Will said, tugging on his jacket.

"I do not, though at the moment he seems to be the more reasonable of the two of you." She took a few steps closer to him and straightened his cravat. "What precisely did you intend to do? Fisticuffs in the apple orchard?"

Will caught her hand at his neck. "That is not a very ladylike thing to say."

Verity bit down on her lip before she would say something she would regret.

"But perhaps if I had him down on the ground with his face in the dirt, I would be able to get the information I want. Are you not suspicious that he has been following us all this time?"

"Perhaps he has been bewitched by my beauty since he saw me on the *Andromeda*," Verity tossed off, intending to be ironic.

But Will did not seem to see it like that. He looked down at the ground, drawing in deep breaths.

"Only promise me you will not be in that man's presence without others in the vicinity. Do not approach him. And do not step up into his carriage to examine his sketches of the countryside, or something as foolish as that."

Was it possible Will was jealous? No man had ever before offered to fight for her, to protect her, or be in the least concerned for her welfare. But she had never before been Lady Verity Harwood of Harwood Hall.

Will raised his head and met her eyes. What she saw there was even more unsettling than her current thoughts, for there was an intensity in his gaze that had nothing to do with her supposed title or position in society.

He wanted her as much as she wanted him.

Though they were surrounded by those curious about the mishap and those who actually tried to assist them, Verity had the strange sense they were quite alone in their own time and place. The noises of the men, of the horses, and of several barking dogs somehow dissipated into the clean country air, and Verity believed she heard the tattoo of Will's heart. She took a step forward.

He shook his head, barely perceptibly, reminding her that though she had escaped their world, he had not.

"I will not leave you, Will," Verity said. "We made a bargain, which you may soon regret, but I will abide by it. Do not fear that I will walk away from what we have already started."

"Many books remain unfinished, for want of a conclusion."

He was not talking about their blasted book.

"Books that go unfinished surely do so because

their authors will not see it to the end," Verity said. She was not talking about their book either. "Either party might decide to pull away, and begin anew. But it will not be me."

But once she told him the truth, it would be he.

"Do you not yet trust me?" he asked softly. "Are you able to step away from your Lady Verity role and trust your better instincts?"

"I have already stepped away from it, Will. Or else you would not have found me in a coach traveling with near strangers to a place I do not know. If that is not sufficient evidence of stepping away from a role, I do not know what is."

"I believe you have embraced the role. You have displayed courage and determination, uncommon spirit and ingenuity. If those are not the very hallmarks of a lady, I do not know what is."

It was impossible not to smile in the face of those compliments. Verity averted her gaze, knowing she blushed.

"Those are the hallmarks of an American woman, Will, which is quite a different thing from what you describe or that role to which I was born."

"What if you decide to become an American woman? Would it be so reprehensible, so impossible to imagine?"

"You know it would not," she said, for she imagined it all the time, but she also knew how impossible it truly was.

Will reached for her hand, but they kept a distance between them as they turned to face the chaos before them. Geoff had recruited several young men to help them, and he cheerfully gave them orders while he sat on one of Nell's leather chests. For her part, Nell endeavored to gather up all their strewn property, mostly papers, and collect them in a large basket. Quint was holding court with a group of older men, each apparently an expert on the fitting and replacement of coach wheels. Not far away, John Reese looked on, with apparent interest in the proceedings.

Pulling her forward, Will approached the circle of experts, rather pointedly turning his back on Mr. Reese.

"What say you, gentlemen?" he asked. "Do you think it possible we will be able to travel by the morrow?"

"If not tomorrow, then the next day," said James Quint. "I'm told there is an excellent smithy in these parts, who has much experience in the repair of wheels."

"And is there an inn nearby? If not, I will be happy to pay for rooms in a farmhouse or similar abode. Mr. Marsh and I might manage a good night's sleep in a field, but the ladies will want their comforts."

"The ladies are prepared to sacrifice as well," Verity spoke up and pulled her hand from his.

"You are in luck, ma'am," said one of the men. "There is an excellent lodging house not far from Albany, in Troy."

"Ah, I have always dreamed of finding Troy," Verity murmured, grateful for all those lessons she once shared with her mistress.

"Along the plains of New York, you will also discover Rome, Utica, and Iliom, though not necessarily the ones you dreamed of," Will said. "Though perhaps, years from now, you will remember them fondly."

She glanced at him, wanting to believe therein was a promise. Will was enigmatic, though surely it was not possible to be more so than she.

"What can we do here to help?" she asked, practically enough.

"Not a thing, Miss Harwood," said Quint. "Mr. Goodnow, this gentleman here, is ready with a carriage to transport you and Miss Marsh to Troy when you are ready. Mr. Marsh and Mr. Bentley could follow on the horses, and I will remain here and sleep above the blacksmith shop. It is all arranged."

Beside her, Will nodded. "That is a good plan, Quint. Though Mr. Marsh must go with them to arrange for the rooms."

A short time later, as Geoff, Nell, and Verity were helped into the carriage, Verity sought out Will, to bid him farewell. But his eyes were on Mr. Reese, whose own eyes were on the vehicle that would take them to their next destination.

\*\*\*\*

"Mr. Reese is a kind man, do you not think so?" Nell asked, many hours later. She stood over Verity, wearing a towel around her own hair, while running a comb through her friend's. The aroma of sassafras was sweet and strong.

Verity started, as she was thinking of the man just at that moment. She looked up at Nell's reflection in the mirror, but her friend seemed rather intent on her task.

"Why do you say so? Have you met him before?"

"Of course I have, Verity. He was in the breakfast room at the inn in Wayland and asked me about our travels. He said he knew you in England and that you were on the *Andromeda* together."

Was it possible John Reese knew Lady Verity before her journey? And her maid not know about it?

"Why didn't you tell me this before, Nell? It is something I might have liked to know."

"Mr. Reese told me you saw him and that you were well acquainted," Nell said, frowning.

"Do not believe everything a gentleman says," Verity said, a little too harshly. "I hardly know him, and I am a little suspicious of his behavior. He seems to be traveling a bit too close to our party."

"Perhaps he is another of your admirers, dear Verity. You do seem to gather them like rosebuds. But if that is the case with Mr. Reese, I doubt we will see him for much longer."

"Why do you say that?"

"Well, my friend, anyone who witnessed the scene between you and Will today could have little doubt about the direction of the wind. I thought I would incinerate by mere proximity to its heat."

Verity thought she would incinerate on the spot. "We didn't even touch each other."

"You didn't need to. It was as if the rest of us didn't exist."

"We scarcely know each other, Nell. It is not what it may seem."

"What does that matter, when you love each other? I have never seen Will behave as he did today, ready to challenge Mr. Reese in a fistfight. If it is somehow true that you scarcely know each other, then let me assure you that Will never raises his temper, nor his fists, nor does he allow anything to provoke him. No matter what happens, he remains rational and calm—sometimes too much so. I have never seen in him a passion."

"I have," said Verity, remembering their first meeting.

"I am not surprised," Nell said, laughing.

"He was very angry with me at the time," said Verity, smiling ruefully as she recalled her own anger as well. If not for that, she might never have assumed Lady Verity's identity and would not have embarked on an adventure that could only end with sadness and pain. And yet, in a moment of perfect clarity, she realized she had no regrets sacrificing all chances of future happiness for these extraordinary months of friendship and joy. Whatever else happened, these could not be taken from her. "It was our first meeting, and I came between him and Geoff."

Nell tugged at a snarl in Verity's hair. "And their manuscript, no doubt. Did you do something dreadful, like read a page over their shoulder, or something of that sort? One would think they discovered the location of the Holy Grail, rather than a pleasant beach on the coast of Rhode Island, so carefully do they covet their own pronouncements."

Verity laughed. "No, it was not so bad as that. We were all seeking the help of the ship's doctor, each assuming our needs were greater than the other's. It is a contest I would have preferred to lose."

Several moments passed, while the only sound in the room was that of the cabinet clock. Verity knew that in America it was called a "grandfather" clock, as if the very name would convey historical legacy and value. Americans liked that sort of thing.

"You have not said much about the girl, Annie Merrill, though you must miss her dreadfully. Here I am, trying to take her place, helping you, but I know she must have been infinitely dearer to you."

"I knew her all my life, Nell, but she was not dearer to me. We were destined to always be separated by our birth, though we shared so much. Annie was the bastard daughter of a housekeeper, and Lady Verity was a great lady, the legitimate daughter of an earl."

" 'Was,' you say? You may be roughing it on a journey with a group of commoners, but we never forget who you are. You are Lady Verity," Nell reminded her.

"I am not!" Verity blurted out. *It is done, all over.* "That is…I am not Lady Verity here, in this place, in this country. I am reinventing myself as a writer, a traveler, a woman no longer reliant on what fate has handed to me." *That much, at least, was true.* "I can never go back to what I was."

"Oh, dear, it seems that Will was quite right about you," Nell murmured.

"What has he said?" Verity asked anxiously.

"Why, that you are a romantic. Do you not recall the discussion? But I do not think your story is very original; it is a common enough tale of princesses disguising themselves as milkmaids and goddesses walking among the mortals. It would be much more clever if an ordinary person plays the part of a noblewoman."

*Yes, very clever. And utterly foolish.*

"It has been done, Nell. And while it may seem to be a good idea at the time, I am not convinced that any of those stories end very well. Do you suppose Cinderella was happy with her prince?"

"Of course she was," Nell said without hesitation. "Would you like me to braid your hair? It is nearly dry."

"No, let me wear it loose for a while. Before I go to bed, I will braid it myself," Verity said, glad to change the subject. "But now it is your turn."

And so they switched positions at the small dressing table, and Verity pulled the linen towel from Nell's hair. Combing another person's hair was a task she knew well, and she was glad she did not have to think much about it, for all her thoughts were elsewhere.

"Ouch!"

Verity saw she had a clump of Nell's hair in the tortoiseshell comb. "I'm sorry, Nell. I will be more careful."

"I suppose you will never be utterly persuasive as plain Verity Harwood, my friend. It is your lot in life to forever be a lady."

How cruel it was that the one thing Annie Merrill desired all her life seemed like a curse now that she attained it.

"You will enjoy having your own room tonight," Nell said, interrupting Verity's thoughts. "This inn is truly quite large and accommodating."

"It is."

"And you do not wish to talk, I believe."

Verity smiled. Nell did see a good deal. "But I am happy to listen," she said.

****

Nell was wrong about one thing: Verity did not relish the loneliness of her chamber, where her unsettling, confused thoughts intruded like an unwelcome guest. Her familiarity with her American friends made her careless, and one day soon she would betray herself with a spontaneous confession of the truth.

She would lose everything, including those friends. And yet there was something wretchedly tantalizing about finally unburdening herself and casting off the identity of a woman she'd never liked and never understood. If there was one consolation in her despair, it was that Lady Verity Harwood would be remembered by those who met her in America as a kinder, more generous person than the lady had ever been at Harwood.

Verity stood at the window, watching a small creature scurry through the shadows, and once again trifling with the idea of escape. When she heard a light tapping at the door, she guessed Nell returned.

But when she opened the door, Will stood in the hallway, dressed as he was when first they met, in loose jacket and open-necked shirt. His hair was wet and untidy, and he smelled of bay rum soap from the islands. He glanced behind him and slipped into her room.

"What is the matter? What do you want?" Verity whispered.

"You," he said, and pulled her into his embrace.

His mouth was warm and tasted of mint leaves, and his kisses left her without breath or sense. When his lips traveled over her cheekbone to her ear, she tried to protest, to point out the impropriety of his presence in her chamber, but no words came. And it was just as well, for he might accuse her of the same lapse of judgment.

Her hand escaped the prison between their bodies and lingered for a moment at the tantalizing V of his neckline. Her fingers found the smooth disk of his uppermost button, and slid it easily through the loop. She then went down to another, and another.

"Bay rum," she said, pressing her nose against his chest. The exotic scent mixed with the warmth of his skin was intoxicating.

"Sassafras," he murmured, as he lifted her long hair to kiss her neck.

"You should not be here," she said, tilting her head back.

"Tell me to leave."

"Leave the key on the desk," she said, as he turned briefly to lock the chamber door. "Leave the…"

"Leave it to me," he said, and startled her by lifting her into his arms and carrying her to the large four-poster bed.

And so she did, until much later in the evening, when she acted upon certain irresistible impulses.

\*\*\*\*

Will looked at his lady in the soft light of dawn, admiring her beauty and wondering how a woman as inexperienced as she could so quickly understand what gave him pleasure. When he first brought her to the bed, she was flushed and nervous, but as the night progressed, she followed his lead, touch to touch, inch to glorious inch. Now she slept contentedly, with a smile on her slightly swollen lips.

And he was utterly exhausted, unable to leave even though he ought.

This woman who was not Lady Verity Harwood captivated him, stripped him of his even-tempered manners and starched propriety. She made him look more closely at himself, laugh at his frailties, and realize there were greater pleasures than traveling about with a secretary and a pot of India ink. She made him remember what delights one could find in one's own home, particularly if she was waiting for him there.

She was not Lady Verity Harwood.

He suspected it from the first, watching her on the rolling deck of the *Andromeda*. He wondered at it when he held her hand, perfect in its form, and when he heard her speak. For while she reserved her wicked wit for him alone, she was kind and considerate of everyone else.

She was not Lady Verity Harwood.

He remembered his cousin's paramour, a lady who flaunted their affair and offered her temptations like a confection seller at a fair. She was not much of a lady in doing so, and Eastbourne proved himself not much of a gentleman for purchasing those wares while an embarrassed audience looked on.

The woman who slept beside Will was an innocent, or at least had been before this night's lovemaking. She knew little of kisses or of a man's weaknesses, and blushed when he gently pushed aside her nightdress to reveal her pale flesh.

Miss Annie Merrill, until this night, had been a virgin.

Of course she was Annie Merrill, and he wondered why he hadn't guessed it at once. He had scarcely noticed her in England—why would he?—but now recalled Eastbourne spoke of her when Will took his cousin to task for his unseemly behavior.

*"You are inflicting great insult upon your wife and daughters."*

*"I do not see it is any business of yours, unless you*

*imagine old Harwood might do me harm in a duel, avenging his child's honor. You would fare a good deal better than me in that case and be known in society as the American earl."*

*"I do not want to be an earl, nor do I want harm to come to you or that scholarly neighbor of yours. Let him keep to his books, as you should keep to your wife."*

*"Ah, but that is where you are wrong, dear cousin. Harwood put his marker in places other than his books. It is well known in these parts that his beloved wife and his even more beloved housekeeper were pregnant at the same time. The man has two daughters, equally lovely, equally tempting."*

But Lady Verity and Annie Merrill were not equally lovely, and Will was not all tempted by his cousin's lady. Until he bumped into her on the *Andromeda*, stunned and bothered by the coincidence, he had not thought about her at all. But there before him one moment was Lady Verity, yet when he blinked she was not there at all.

Instead, he saw someone very like her, but finer in all ways. She was Lady Verity, perfected.

Now Lady Verity was gone, wrapped in linen in her watery grave. She ought to be mourned by those who loved her and receive the respect she deserved. Her old father needed to be told the truth. With this turn of events, Eastbourne might even return his affections to his poor wife. And Annie Merrill must make amends for her willful deception.

But not yet. He was her partner now, in all ways that mattered. He would not allow her to be punished if no real harm was done. The money she withdrew in

Boston could be returned with the profits of their book. And he could keep her forever in America, where few would care if she once was in service in a great household and would think her brush with larceny a jolly good adventure.

All this was for a future that was still uncertain. He did not know if she would marry him, for she rather fancied herself an independent soul. He did not know if there would be real consequences for what was surely a crime, and if he could advocate for forgiveness. He only knew that he wished to marry her.

The journey to Cincinnati was still ahead of them. There was time to make decisions, to figure out what needed to be done. He would keep his own secrets and not reveal what he guessed and what he knew.

He glanced down at Verity, nestled against his shoulder, and was startled to realize she was awake and watching him. Her grayish blue eyes were hooded, and her quirky brows made her look like she was forever questioning him. But she smiled, as if everything had already been answered.

"Good morning, my dear. I hope you slept well," he said.

"You, of all people, know the truth of it," she answered, and brushed her fingers over the stubble of his beard. "But now I believe there are some things better than sleep."

Will pulled the wrinkled sheet away from her shoulder and traced the outline of a strawberry scar he noticed the night before. "I have heard it said that sleep is redemptive."

She pulled away, either not knowing or not caring that her breast was revealed. "Most say it is truth that is redemptive."

Will resisted one temptation to grasp at another. "There is nothing more honest than sleeping with the person you love."

She sighed, and said nothing for some time. Soon he felt dampness against his shoulder and realized she was crying.

"I hadn't realized my declaration would have such an effect on you. It's not so bad as all that, is it?"

"It is a good deal worse," she sniffed. "Will, there is much you do not know about me, but there is one thing above all others. I cannot bear the burden of it any longer, though I know you will hate me for it."

He knew, of course, what was coming. He did not expect this now, just when he settled himself into a comfortable delusion that they may go on with her deception a while longer.

"Do you love another, my lady?" he asked, knowing he was cruel in teasing her.

"I do not love another. But I am not your lady. I am not anyone's lady. I am not Lady Verity Harwood."

There it was, at last. And yet the earth didn't shake and the walls collapse. Nor did her beauty diminish, nor the love he felt for her.

"I know," he said.

Chapter 11

Verity shivered, though the morning air was warm, and drew the white sheet to her chin. *He knew? Was his intent to trifle with her or wait for her greatest vulnerability and expose her for a fraud?*

"You knew?" she said accusingly. "You knew what—and when?"

"I guessed almost from the start," he confessed. "But I did not know until this night."

She jabbed her fist into his side and struggled to escape. He responded by turning over and capturing her body beneath his and making her acutely aware that he might be interested in doing things other than arguing.

"Have a care, there," he said, releasing her wrists. "But please don't cry, for we will figure out what to do."

"I am not crying," she said, her voice wavering. "I am angry that you would use me in this despicable way and seduce me to confess. You have guessed the truth for weeks and yet bided your time, making me come to love you, before springing the trap. I would have thought you above such deception."

"One who is the mistress of deception ought to know better." He put a finger to her lips as they heard footsteps pass the door. "I have never before been accused of making someone love me and wonder if such a thing is even possible."

"Oh, hush. I take that back."

"It is too late, for I already heard your confession

and trust it to be true. That, and perhaps a few things uttered into the darkness last night."

Verity closed her eyes, wishing those things were not so vivid and so wonderful. "You are cruel to remind me of them now, when you have me at your mercy. I would take back everything since we met, if I had my choice."

"My love, you are quite mistaken, for you have me at your mercy. I was a cheerful soul, going about my business, writing my thoughtful tomes, playing chess every night with my friend. I provide for my mother and sisters and dutifully visit relatives in England every year or so. I would have been happy going on thus for years."

"And then you met Lady Verity," Verity said, grudgingly.

"No," he said and paused. When she didn't try to escape, he rolled off her and lay at her side. "I met you."

Verity closed her eyes. Who was she now? She was so lost in herself, in her stupid deception, she didn't know whom she ought to be. "How did you know?"

Without looking at her, his hand came up to cup her chin. "The lady I met at Eastbourne Abbey was so wrapped up in herself—and usually so wrapped around my cousin—that she bore little resemblance to the lady on the deck of the *Andromeda*. Lady Verity was not likely to brave the elements in the service of a prince, let alone a poor paid companion. She was selfish and a little foolish. You were neither."

"Perhaps I did have a sea change," she argued. "We already decided such a thing is possible."

"In books, perhaps. But there were other reasons I

had to doubt your identity. I could not recall if your eyes were darker or your hair more curly. I did not remember if the top of your head reached my shoulder or my nose. But there was one thing that remained most notable." He caught her right hand and wove his fingers between hers.

"When I first met Lady Verity, I noticed a rather singular feature," he said.

"It happens every so often, Will, as you must know. Her father, our father, hoped that surgeons might remove her extra digit. We were little children when one came to the house to examine her hands. She was frightened and told me to tell him I was she. You see how we practiced this deception at an early age, though always at her demand. But here was one switch in identity that could easily be discovered, as I suppose is still the case."

"Having six fingers on one's hand is difficult to disguise," he said. "He wished to remove the extra digit, of course."

"Of course. I can still hear her screams, and remember my mother comforting me, telling me Lady Verity would be happier if her hand looked like everyone else's hands. But our father sent the surgeon away, and I believe Lady Verity realized how persuasive she could be. In the weeks after, she continued to test everyone, but especially me, to see how far she could go in getting what she wanted." Verity wiped her eyes on the bedsheet. "But she was never happy, about anything."

"She might have been happier with a scar than a deformity."

"My lady wore gloves at all times. Even on her

deathbed." Will brought her hand to his lips. "Will, why do such things happen?"

"The death of a young lady, do you mean?" he asked, pausing between kisses.

"I understand death, as is my misfortune. But what of deformity?"

"There are some who believe that those too closely related by blood may produce an unwanted effect on their children. Lord and Lady Harwood were first cousins, I believe."

"They were. I recall one of the maids telling me theirs was an arranged marriage and not a happy one. It was, I believe, her way of reassuring me that he loved my mother more. They were also somewhat related, though distantly. It is surely why Lady Verity and I looked so much alike."

"And yet I can say with some authority that you are quite perfect."

Verity blushed for thinking of what they did last night and tried to remember that she was supposed to be angry at this man.

"What will you do now?" she asked sadly.

"What are we to do, do you mean? Are we not partners—in everything?"

"It cannot be, as well you know." She turned to face him, tangling herself in the warm sheets. "We shall remain business partners, if you will still have me. But anything else between us is impossible."

He pulled the sheets down to her waist, and the warmth of the sun on her bare skin was somehow both divine and heathenish.

"Nothing is impossible, as we amply demonstrated last night."

"Oh dear." Verity sighed. He was right in that, but wrong in everything else. "But it is not what I mean, as well you know. All these weeks I thought you were reticent because you did not feel yourself worthy of an alliance with Lady Verity. But since you guessed the truth almost from the start, perhaps you held me in abeyance because an illegitimate servant is not worthy of you."

She finally pulled herself away, wrapping the sheet around her as she stood over him. "And I have proved myself as indiscreet as my mother."

"Your mother had a daughter with someone who loved her, and perhaps she loved him as well. The only indiscretion I see is loving where it is sometimes not easy or convenient. But such is not the case for us. We will work through this tangle, and we will marry. There is no such thing as being worthy or unworthy here."

They had trod this path before, and still he was not reasonable. Verity pushed her hair out of her eyes, and looked for her garments. If they did not hurry, Nell would be knocking at the door, and then the tangle would be knotted beyond any redemption.

"If Eastbourne does not father a son, you are heir to his title and fortune," she said.

"I desire neither," he said. "It is quite fortunate since it is unlikely they will ever be mine."

"It does not matter. You will have no choice in the matter, if such a thing comes to pass. And then you will be shunned because your countess will have been a servant in your neighbor's house."

"More likely, I will be shunned because I am an American. We shall be invited nowhere, receive no visitors, and people will scarcely dare to utter our names in polite company. Truly, it does not sound so very bad." Will sat up in bed and pulled Verity's chemise out from under him. "Here, you may need this."

She snatched it from him.

"Eastbourne is not going to die. He may be a fool, but he is not going to gamble with the advantages of his birth. Perhaps, with Lady Verity no longer offering temptation, he will return to his wife and have many sons with her. In any case, I will not have us ruin our chances of happiness because of something that may not even come to be." Will stood up, walked to the window, and stretched his arms. He was not wearing a thing.

"Will! Step away! Must you advertise what we have done?" Verity cried.

He looked over his shoulder and smiled at her. "There is no one in the garden to see me, and I was very careful coming here last night."

"You will have to be even more careful this morning. People are already up and about."

He nodded, finally surrendering to sense. He dressed silently, requiring no assistance; as much as Verity would have liked to put her hands on his body once again, she preferred watching him do such an ordinary, familiar thing as dressing himself. But when he was quite done, she gave in to temptation and stepped closer to brush her hand over his cheek and chin.

"I will undress again, in order to shave," he said, thoughtfully.

"And I will dress and attempt to appear as if nothing out of the ordinary has happened."

"But it has. Everything has changed. It is a new world," Will said, and kissed her forehead.

"A new world in the new world?" Verity laughed despite her uncertainty. "What are we going to do, Will?"

"Today? We are not able to continue our journey yet, so we can explore the neighborhood. Or I can write an essay on the hazards of traveling, which may be of interest to no one but me."

"Then I suppose I shall write as well, and to no larger an audience." Verity took a deep breath, knowing how difficult the task would be. "I shall write to my father and sadly inform him of the death of his beloved child, Lady Verity."

Will kissed her again, before turning to the door. The floorboards in the hall creaked as someone walked past Verity's chamber and then stepped more heavily on the wooden stairs. Will nodded his head, as if counting the steps, and silently slipped through the door, leaving Verity alone with her conscience.

*Troy, New York State*

*16 June 1821*

*Dear Lord Harwood,*

*It is my sad duty to inform you of the death at sea of your devoted daughter, Lady Verity. She took ill several weeks into our journey and went into a very rapid decline. The ship's doctor, a good man, did all he could for her, but to no avail. She faded very quickly, to my infinite despair.*

*The captain of the* Andromeda, *as is his custom, presided over her burial in the Atlantic and was attended by many of the ship's passengers. They offer their respects to you, along with my own.*

*I regret not informing you of these sad tidings when we first made landfall in Boston, but grief has distracted me from my responsibilities. However, I am set upon a course to Cincinnati now, to meet with Lady Verity's friend. I am hopeful Mrs. Frances Trollope might be able to advise and guide me as I intend to remain in America.*

*It has ever been a privilege for the Merrills to serve your illustrious family, but as I have no current prospects in England, I do not intend to return. Through Mrs. Trollope, I hope to arrange for a courier to deliver Lady Verity's possessions to you, included among them the gold locket she wore every day. Along with her property, I shall enclose funds that I borrowed from her account when first arriving in Boston, as I had no other means by which to live. Please forgive me this deception, my lord, as I did not know what else to do. I behaved very foolishly, and you are surely pleased you will never have to see my face again.*

*Please accept my deepest regrets at your grievous loss.*

*Yours sincerely, I am,*
*Miss Anne Merrill*

Will reread Verity's letter.

"You reveal your lessons learned as a writer, my love. You do not say too much, nor do you indemnify yourself, nor do you allow your deeds to be anything other than the natural consequence of great sadness. It is a great talent."

"Do you think me evasive, then?" Verity asked. "Should I instead tell Lord Harwood that I shall surrender to the nearest constable and do penance in prison?"

"Taking one's identity is a crime, but I do not see that much harm was done. You offer to pay back the sums that were advanced, though I should not be surprised if Harwood simply dismissed that. And you can explain the rest of your behavior, as you do here, by describing your fear and indecision. Your lady died, after all, and it is a grievous event. Most maids would have no resources to recover from such a predicament." Will paused and rubbed his forehead. "But you are not like most maids and hit upon a solution almost immediately. If Lord Harwood appreciates that you are far too clever and clear-thinking to walk about in a stupor after the death of your lady, then he will not believe this letter. But let us stir that kettle when it starts to boil."

"I was confused, Will, truly. And I was angry, which also drives impulse to make stupid decisions."

"Do you mean to accuse me of making you take another's identity?" he asked, calmly. "I am not sure it would make a good defensive case in a court of law."

"I was angry at many things, which simply came to a head when you so arrogantly obstructed my way on the *Andromeda*'s deck," she said. "I was angry to be on that dreadful ship. I was angry that my lady treated me like trash beneath her feet. I was angry that circumstances set her on a platform so high above mine and that I was forever doomed to remain there. I was angry that my father never married my mother, though he had opportunity to do so and loved her for so many years. And so, I was angry with all these things, when we met on the *Andromeda*, and you so imperiously told me to get out of your way. Who were you—an American, after all—to treat me as rudely as you would a servant? That I was, in fact, a servant, was of no consequence in that confrontation."

"I was an American who was greatly distressed about my friend. Anxiety made me rude to you, and I apologize."

"As anger made me assume the name and authority of another because I, too, was distressed about a friend. Lady Verity might not have treated me well, but she was all I had."

"If you had known what possibilities awaited in America, would you have done the same thing?"

"Do you mean that I would come to love you?" she asked.

"Perhaps. But surely you realize you would have managed very well without my assistance."

She looked up then and narrowed her gaze. "Oh, truly? Did you not make it clear to me that Mr. Reese was likely to sell me into slavery or something of that sort?"

"I may have exaggerated his intent somewhat. But not so much that you could ever trust him."

"Why not? He seems pleasant enough. He offered to help us yesterday, when we lost the wheel."

"Oh, indeed, he is always near. In fact, when you seal this letter, you might as well hand it directly to him."

"Whatever do you mean?"

"I have given a great deal of thought to the fact he is always about and seems inordinately interested in you. I suspect John Reese is an agent of your father, never letting you out of his sight. Lord Harwood is getting a very bad bargain, for I doubt Reese is aware he is now spying on Annie Merrill and not Lady Verity.

But I daresay you can hand him this letter and ask him to enclose it with his weekly report back to England."

"Say never!" Verity cried. "And you have known this all the time?"

"No," Will said, shaking his head. "And I still cannot be certain. But how do we account for the man's presence wherever we go?"

"I am his guarantor of payment?" Verity guessed. "But it is not I; it is Lady Verity."

"Indeed. If John Reese discovers the content of your letter, he will realize he has been duped and will not be paid. So it is to his advantage to keep Lady Verity alive for as long as possible."

"Whatever shall I do?" she asked quietly.

"First, prepare a copy of your letter, for it shall be sent twice. Sign and seal the first one and, as Mr. Reese is prepared to be your lap dog, ask if he would be so good as to post it for you. He will undoubtedly see the Merrill name on the return address. If we lose him in Albany, we can hope that he has finally learned the truth and has given up. If he continues to follow you, we can assume that he knows the truth but intends to pick Lord Harwood's pocket just the same. At the same time, you may post the second letter, so your father finally learns the truth of it all. And he can then catch Reese in his deception."

Verity pressed her fingers against her forehead. "But Will, his deception is not worse than mine. And Reese is doing a job for which he has been hired by my father. He need not be punished for it, for all your dislike of him."

"Let it suffice to say I bear him a grudge, and this would give me great satisfaction."

"This is most peculiar revenge," Verity said sternly. "And at my expense?"

"Consider it a redemption, of sorts. What you do this day will save other young women from Reese's business ventures."

"He explained to me that he finds them jobs in Boston and New York."

"That he does," Will said. "And I shall forever be grateful that I found you before you agreed to go along with him to see what jobs he offers."

"But he would not have harmed me, for then he would not receive payment from my father."

"By offering Lady Verity Harwood to his customers, he would have been amply recompensed." Will watched the spread of emotions across her features until he was certain she understood his meaning.

****

"Something has changed about you, Verity," said Nell, as she and Verity sat beneath a spreading chestnut tree. The blacksmith promised the carriage would be ready for their journey the next day, but the afternoon was far too warm to do much more than sit about in the shade and work on their embroidery.

"Yes, there is something, Nell. I would like to confess it to you before we set forth again on our way to Cincinnati."

"You do not have to confess a thing, for I have guessed it already."

"You have?" Verity pricked her finger on the needle and looked up.

"Of course. There is something different about your eyes, and the color of your cheeks, and the way you smile. You and Will see nothing but each other."

"Oh, that," Verity said, more relieved than she ought to be.

"Yes, that. Please tell me: was it quite wonderful?"

It took several moments before Verity understood what her friend meant, and then she felt as if her cheeks were on fire.

"Oh, dear, surely you do not believe that we behaved in an inappropriate manner or..." Verity paused, realizing it was precisely what Nell meant. "Indeed, it was wonderful. Will often seems gruff or uncaring, but he is exactly the opposite in certain circumstances. Let that be all I will say on the matter."

"You have told me nothing but have certainly whetted my curiosity," Nell said, and pouted very prettily.

Verity smiled, suddenly feeling very mature and worldly. "There are some things that ought not be discussed, with the expectation that one should be allowed to draw one's own conclusions. But there is something I will confess, on quite another matter."

"What will it be, then?" Nell sighed, handing her a folded linen. "Please do not bleed all over your needlework. It is much easier to launder a handkerchief. But I suppose you do not know about such things."

Verity looked down at her finger as she wrapped the linen around it, and a small dot of blood appeared on the cloth.

"That is just the thing. I do know all about those things: laundering, ironing, styling a lady's hair. I have lied to the three of you by pretending to be someone I am not."

"You are already married," Nell gasped. "I feared it!"

"Why would you think so?" Verity asked, surprised. "But no matter. What I have to confess is infinitely worse. I am not Lady Verity Harwood."

Nell looked like a schoolgirl working through a particularly thorny arithmetic problem; and yet Nell was not a stupid girl

"I am Annie Merrill, her companion."

"This is a day of extraordinary tidings," she said in a hoarse voice. "However did you manage this? Did you kill the real Lady Verity?"

Now it was Verity's turn to be shocked. "Nell! However can you say such a thing! My poor lady died of some illness on the *Andromeda*. I did everything I could to comfort her."

Nell continued to stare at her, goading her into a fuller confession.

"However, I cannot say I never thought of it," Verity confessed.

Nell laughed out loud. "More and more extraordinary!"

"But I met your brother and Will while I was seeking the ship's doctor, as well you know. I did not want her dead, and I did not care for her riches or romantic conquests. I acted quickly and foolishly."

"What made you change your mind? About being a lady, I mean."

"I never really intended to remain Verity. I would never be able to fool my father, you see, or the other people at Harwood Hall. And Lady Verity would have to return someday and marry and inherit her share of the Harwood wealth. So I only intended to carry on the charade until I could figure out what to do here in America and how to make my own way."

"Did Will guess?"

"He did," Verity said, nodding. "He suspected me almost at once."

Nell shrugged. "He would say that, of course. All men do."

"I told Will the truth this morning. You are second to hear it from my lips."

"I am honored, I think." Nell shrugged again. "But I am confused about one thing."

"And only one? Things must be a good deal clearer to you than to me, my dear."

"I doubt it. But much is of no consequence, except: did you just refer to Lord Harwood as your father?"

Verity unwrapped her finger and twisted the handkerchief into a knot. "Ah, yes. I am becoming careless in this business of confession. There is another truth to be told, and I suppose it no longer matters who knows it. In fact, I have long known that I am his child, as he and my mother, his housekeeper, were intimate for many years. Lady Verity and I are—were—half sisters. We were the same age and looked very much alike. This is not the first time we traded places, but never were there such dire circumstances."

Nell said nothing.

"I am very sorry, Nell. I am sorry I lied to everyone. I am sorry I let the masquerade continue as long as it has. I am sorry I am not whom you thought me to be."

Nell shook her head. "You are quite wrong. You are everything I thought you would be. You are generous and funny and kind and considerate of everyone—and now you have demonstrated that you are unfailingly honest, as well. I have never had a better

271

friend nor would I want anything to be different."

Verity leaned back against the tree and realized she felt equally grateful for what she had. After years of unhappiness, knowing she would never change her situation, she had somehow emerged as a butterfly from her chrysalis. Nothing was settled, and her future was by no means ensured, but she would always be comforted by the fact that she knew keen friendship and the love of a good man. No, Will was infinitely more than that, for she suddenly knew she wanted to be with him more than anything else in life.

"Have I made you unhappy?" Nell asked.

"No, you have done everything to reassure me, though I little deserve it. I have made a great muddle of everything."

Nell leaned back as well, so their heads were touching. "You have done what any other woman with a taste for adventure and a normal curiosity would have done in the same circumstances. Do you not remember the first night we met? I only wanted to know about your life in England and such wonders as you enjoyed. Even in America, the life of an aristocrat is a dream we hardly dare imagine. Who would not have seized such an opportunity?"

"An honest woman?"

"Oh, please! The most virtuous among us has the slightest touch of larceny about her. Martha Washington would have done the very same thing."

"Who is Martha Washington?"

"No matter. The only question at hand is who are you? What shall we call you now?

Verity had laced herself so tightly into Lady Verity's identity, she had not yet considered this. "I think I became Lady Verity on the *Andromeda*, but I surely became Verity once I took my first steps on American soil."

"Then that's settled," said Nell. "You are Verity, though may find yourself losing the Harwood name some time soon."

"As to that…" Verity began, her voice trailing off when Geoff and Will came down a gentle slope toward them.

"I have excellent news of a party, ladies," Geoff said, when they close by. "We are invited to the home of Mr. and Mrs. Anthony Schuyler this evening, for dinner and dancing. Mr. Schyler is a prominent man of business in Troy and when he heard of our predicament, extended a kind invitation. Would you enjoy this opportunity to gather more information about our modest social events, Lady Verity?"

"Remember, she is Miss Verity Harwood here in America," Nell said.

"As I shall be if I ever return to England," Verity said.

"Your father may have something to say about that," Geoff said and laughed.

"Indeed, he might," said Verity and thought he ought to hear the truth from her. "Come, Geoff, I should like to talk with you on a matter that can be put off no longer." She glanced at Will, who revealed nothing in his steady gaze and raised her hand for his assistance in standing. His hand grasped hers, warm and steadying.

****

Of her three friends, Geoffrey Marsh seemed most uncomfortable with her deception, though not for the reasons she would have expected. He, who was so open and generous, explained how he had remained aloof from her because of her social standing and his utter lack in that regard. Will, owning some expectations, no matter how unlikely, was better positioned to make a conquest. And so, Geoff had deferred to his good friend.

"Did I not have any say in the matter? You were much kinder than he at our first meeting, though you were the one in most distress," Verity pointed out.

"You had every right to avoid him and consider his attention officious—as I believe you did. But I saw the way it was with poor Will almost from the start. I understand him too well. If I came between you, I risked being flung over the deck railing."

"He acted as if he despised me," Verity murmured.

"If you believe that, his deception must have been as good as your own. But everything is now illuminated."

"Is it? Has Will spoken to you?"

"He does not have to. I know things are as they should be, and I only have regrets that I did not risk all when we first met and might have been a happy man today."

Verity put her hand on his arm. "You are very good, Geoff. I was not so enamored of anyone else that I did not see that at once."

"But it is too late now."

"It is," Verity admitted. "But I am grateful to have you for a friend."

"Such is my lot in life—to forever be a friend."

"I do not think you are so very old as to give up on your chances for things to be otherwise. Perhaps you will meet a lady who will change your mind this very night."

"A lady of Troy? I think that epic has already been written, and it did not turn out very well."

"Perhaps you will be given the opportunity to write a new story, to reinvent an old one."

"As you have. Let us consider that Lady Verity was not ready to die, and you carried her name to bring her to the shores of America. You granted her time when the sand in her hourglass had run out."

Verity mused over this notion, so unlikely, and yet so elegant. "You should be a writer, Geoff, and not merely edit another's words. You have the soul of a poet."

"I have the soul of a realist," he said. "My position is not so very different from what yours had been. Do you not think I would seize on an opportunity to be my own man? To have my success in life predicated on my own accomplishments and not on those of another?"

"It is not the same, Geoff. Truly it is not. Will respects you as a friend and a partner. Lady Verity Harwood always treated me like the lowliest creature. I was no one, a woman whose opinions were worth nothing, whose future was dependent on her whims and schemes. I prefer to believe that once she found her way to Cincinnati, I might have found the courage to bid her farewell and set off on my own course."

"You must have been contemplating it already, or you would not have seized the opportunity afforded you on the *Andromeda*."

"I did think about it, in such rare moments when I wasn't scurrying about, tending to my lady's demands. She was an uncompromising, selfish person, but I did not wish her dead."

"And yet her death opened the door of possibilities for you," Geoff said.

"Your sister wondered if I murdered her," Verity said. "I hope that is not your plan for Will, by the way."

"I can't say I haven't been tempted," he said, echoing her own wry sentiments of a few moments before. "No, do not look at me that way. If I tolerated his bad temper during all these weeks when he was mooning about for want of your attention, I can survive anything. His suffering was pathetic, truly."

"You are saying that to make me feel better, and I love you for it. But I doubt Will Bentley ever mooned over anything, and especially not over a woman," Verity said lightly, though a giddy joy was bubbling through her veins.

"Did you not say he and I are partners and friends? I assure you, I know everything about the lad, including the fact that he talks in his sleep."

Verity already noticed that, but thought it indelicate to mention it, even to Will's best friend.

"Thank you for understanding how it is, Geoff. I thought this day of confession would be the hardest of my life, but you have all reassured me." Verity looked up at his plain and honest face and stood on her toes to kiss him on the cheek. "Come, let us return, for I am sure Will and Nell are curious to know how it turned out between us."

Geoff offered his arm, though she supported him as much as he did her, and they walked back to the chestnut tree.

"You two look like you have had a pleasant conversation," Will said. "Have you anything in particular to tell us?"

"Is there anything in particular you'd like to hear?" Verity asked, withdrawing from Geoff and placing her hand on Will's arm. "Geoff has given me a complete list of your faults."

Will said something under his breath, and then, "If you truly desire a complete list, you must speak to my mother and sisters."

"I should love to do so. Do you suppose I shall have the opportunity?"

"Not if you stay in Cincinnati," Nell said. "We will visit at Hudson Point on the return to Boston."

"I do not think I will remain in Cincinnati. Though my future is somewhat uncertain," Verity said, though Will had already made it somewhat less uncertain.

"Perhaps you might make your decision after you see Cincinnati," he said, which was not helpful at all.

"Perhaps I will," Verity said, removing her hand from his sleeve.

\*\*\*\*

Troy proved to be an attractive town close to the famed Hudson River. As their hired carriage made its way through the main thoroughfares of the town, Verity admired the well-tended gardens and many shops. As in Cambridge, there were many people out and about, though it was well past the dinner hour, and people seemed to be holding court on their verandas.

"Do we know anything about the Schuylers?" Nell asked, more interested in straightening the lace at her neckline than in observing the passing scene. "Are they good people?"

"You do not think we would have accepted an invitation from a household of ruffians, do you?" Geoff asked and patted her hand. "The Schuylers are an old Dutch family, distantly related to old Will here."

Verity turned to Will. Now that the relationship between them had grown into something closer than business partners, they found themselves next to each other in the carriage, rather than facing one another. Each time the carriage turned, they were pressed against each other, and the situation was far more intimate. Verity wanted to know everything about him. "Is your family Dutch?"

"You know my father's family is not," he reminded her of the obvious. "But my mother's family settled in the Hudson Valley a hundred years ago. I still have cousins in Den Haag, whom I visit when I am on the Continent."

"Or when he has a fancy for herring," Geoff added.

"There is nothing wrong with Zuider Zee herring. Or with Amsterdam ale, for that matter. There are many who consider the Dutch palate a good deal more adventurous than the English one. My mother, however, is perfectly happy with her English cook at Hudson Point." Will opened a book, which effectively signaled the end of the conversation. "Of course, the family heritage is much diluted after all these years."

He turned a few pages, and Verity, looking over his shoulder, thought it might be in Italian.

"You will not get very far with that," Verity murmured.

Will turned his head to look at her. "I assure you, I am literate in Spanish."

More so than herself, clearly. "I do not doubt your talents, Will, only the time allotted for you to demonstrate them. Surely we will be at the party shortly?"

They were now in a queue of several carriages and likely close to their destination. Their driver pulled into a neatly marked circular drive and they saw a fine stone house, distinctive for its stepped roof.

"This is a style popular in Holland and the Hudson Valley," Geoff said.

"Then I am surprised this town was named Troy and not Utrecht or Haarlem," Verity said.

"You will find both farther downriver," Geoff said, and then, "Here we are."

The carriage came to an abrupt stop, and Will dropped his book so he could put an arm across Verity's breast, like a brace against her falling off her seat. He glanced at her, and she knew he was not indifferent to the stolen intimacy; his dark eyes suggested it only a precursor to what would follow in this night of dancing and perhaps afterward.

The door opened, and their apologetic driver explained that a dog dashed across the road, necessitating the suddenness of their arrival.

"I will be waiting for you just yonder," he added. "Do not concern yourselves on my account, for the Schuylers always remember to bring out food and drink to the drivers and grooms."

"I shall make a note of that," Verity murmured, as she accepted his hand to help her down the small steps of the carriage. The driver looked at her in surprise, and she realized he could not know she meant it quite literally.

But by the end of the evening, there was much more of interest to observe and report. The house, as gracious as the one in Cambridge where she first danced with Will, was as different inside as it appeared outside. Blue patterned china, known for its provenance in Delft, framed the mantle and lined the walls of the entrance foyer. Paintings of landscapes wild and wonderful hung throughout the formal rooms, contrasting with woven rugs that Verity guessed were of Indian workmanship. The musicians were dressed in the casual garb of country laborers, which must have allowed them more mobility than the stiff jackets most often worn by English players, and their melodies reflected a certain freedom as well.

Verity stood in the corner of the small ballroom, admiring the massive stone fireplace and one particularly dramatic painting that might have been a scene of Eden.

"That is called *The Birth of the Hudson*, I believe," Will said, coming up behind her. "Mr. Schuyler has already told me that the artist himself is here, and he painted this just last year."

"Are there truly lions and tigers in New York?" Verity asked, fearing for their safety.

"There may be mountain lions about, and certainly bear and moose. But nothing like these beasts here. I would guess that Mr. Raymond Anders, the artist, is much prone to exaggeration."

Verity smiled, and watched as a short man wearing a loose shirt made his way across the room toward them. As he was not carrying an instrument nor a tray of drinks, she supposed he must be one of the guests.

"Any lady who admires such a painting must be one of refined tastes. And as she is truly the most beautiful woman in the room, I must learn her name," he said.

"I am Miss Harwood, sir. But there are many lovely ladies here."

"None so lovely as you, dear lady," the man said and bowed very low.

"And will you make us free with your name?" Will asked, though not offering his own.

"I am the artist, Mr. Anders, of course," he said.

Of course.

"Prone to exaggeration," Will said under his breath, and Verity shot him a nasty look. If Mr. Anders preferred to believe her the most beautiful woman here, so be it.

Mr. Anders looked him up and down, perhaps sizing him up for his next painting. "I never exaggerate beauty, sir. Do you have any claim on this lady?"

Will's moment of indecision was revealing. He was not ready to claim her, and yet told her things no man would ever say to a woman with whom he ever expected to be separated.

"I do not," he said.

"Then, dear lady, would you be so generous as to dance with me? You would make me the happiest man in all America."

"You do exaggerate." Verity laughed. "But I will not take you to task for it. Yes, of course, I will dance with you."

She accepted his hand as he pulled her away from his painting and Will. But she thought she felt Will's finger on one of her curls, tugging just slightly before he released her. As they walked through the crowd to the very small center of the room, Verity was grateful they were not to waltz together. For one, it would prove impossible to avoid bumping into the other dancers. But more compelling was the fact that Mr. Anders, a man of great ego, was of small stature. He just barely came up to her nose.

He also danced very poorly. Verity was hardly a proficient herself but knew her skills were sharpened when she danced with a man of some talent. Like Will, for example. She looked around her, with each turn of the steps, but he was not to be seen.

"Well done," said another man when the music stopped. He reminded Verity somewhat of her father. "You make a wonderful couple."

Dear God, but these Americans were prone to exaggeration. Who was he?

"I do not think we've met, but I want to welcome you to my home. I am Anthony Schuyler, and you must be either Miss Marsh or Miss Harwood."

"I am Miss Harwood," she said. "On behalf of my friends, I would like to thank you for including us this evening. It is very generous of you to take in stranded travelers."

"It is my pleasure, Miss Harwood. But you are not altogether strangers to me, you understand. One of your friends vouched for you," said Mr. Schuyler.

"Mr. Bentley, of course," Verity murmured. "I only just learned that his family has been in these parts for many years."

"Oh, he is a fine enough fellow, but I just met him. No, it is Mr. John Reese who spoke of you when I saw him yesterday in town. He explained your predicament, and I thought an evening away from the inn would be most pleasurable."

"Mr. Reese! And is he here as well?"

"Oh, certainly. He looks to be coming our way."

John Reese was dressed in very fine clothes, though they fitted him poorly. Was it possible he did not own formal wear or lost them in transit? Verity had not the time to ponder this, for he was rather intent in his purpose.

"Lady Verity," he said, and Mr. Anders gasped. Verity guessed the story of his dancing with a lady would be told all over town by the morning. "If you are not already taken, might I beg your acceptance of my hand for the next dance?"

His speech was as peculiar as his costume, but Verity's desire to part from Mr. Anders made Mr. Reese's request more compelling.

"I am not already taken and would enjoy this dance," she said politely, as she took his hand.

Now, Will suddenly appeared on the stairs, where he could watch her very well. It would have been a comfort to know he wished to protect her, but she had a feeling his intent gaze had more to do with feelings of possessiveness than anything else.

John Reese was a fine dancer, if one did not mind the fact he counted his steps. As such, it was difficult to engage in conversation, for which Verity was grateful. And yet, when the fifth repetition of the steps allowed Mr. Reese the confidence to cease his reckoning, it was Verity who spoke first.

"I have a favor to ask of you, Mr. Reese," she said.

He looked at her in surprise. "Anything you wish."

Verity turned away and bowed to the man in the opposite corner of their set. A moment later, she faced Mr. Reese again. "I understand we are to leave quite early tomorrow, and I have an important missive to post to Lord Harwood. Could I prevail upon you to send it off for me? It is signed and sealed and shall be waiting for you at the desk at the inn. I will pay for your trouble, of course."

"It is no trouble, and you do not have to pay me. You can trust me to do your bidding."

"Oh, of course I must compensate you, Mr. Reese. You have no connection to my father, and this is somewhat irregular, is it not?"

"Yes, I see," he said, and nodded. He missed two steps of the dance, causing the opposite lady much pain. "Shall we consider this dance compensation enough?"

"Thank you, Mr. Reese, but it is a trifle," Verity said, and smiled so broadly, she thought her lips would crack. "I shall leave it for your safekeeping."

Mr. Reese was so pleased that he stepped on both her feet at the same moment.

"Forgive me, Lady Verity. I do not dance very often."

"And I am months out of practice, so we are a fine pair."

"Do you truly believe so, my lady?" Mr. Reese asked, with a curious glint in his eye.

*Good heavens, no.*

"As I am Lady Verity Harwood, if you tell me that you can be trusted, I declare us a fair match."

Verity supposed she should not be surprised he was confused by all this, but at the same time she felt compelled to advise her father to hire a better man in the future. The poor fellow had not yet managed to figure out what Will claimed to have realized so soon after their meeting on the *Andromeda*. Her father would have gotten a better bargain if he'd hired Will.

*If he'd hired Will.*

What if he had? Will was a guest at Eastbourne Abbey only months before she and Lady Verity left for America, and he'd already confessed that he met with her father. What if, upon hearing that Lord Eastbourne's cousin was to make the return journey to America, Lord Harwood asked him to spy upon his daughter? He certainly seemed to know about things of which she, herself, had been unaware.

"You do not look very happy about the prospect, my lady," Mr. Reese said, interrupting her troubling thoughts. "I assure you, you can trust me to do this for you. I am a better messenger than I am a dancer."

"You are a fine dancer, Mr. Reese," she said kindly, if not sincerely. "And I do trust you."

It was a foolish thing to say, for she immediately saw the smug look of satisfaction on John Reese's face. It was the expression of a man who knew he had gained advantage.

Over his shoulder, Verity watched Will Bentley bow very low to a lady in a dreadful pink gown and then whisper something in her ear. He then glanced over to Verity, wearing that selfsame smug look.

This whole business was getting very tiresome.

Until Mr. Reese stepped away to allow Will his turn to dance with her. Despite the tight quarters, it looked as if couples were taking their places for the waltz. Because of the tight quarters, Will held her perhaps a bit too closely.

"Will Reese do as you asked?" Will said bluntly.

Verity stared up at him, utterly confident of her own powers of persuasion. "Did you doubt me, sir?"

Will seemed to consider this for a few moments, before he offered his so-rarely-seen smile. It transformed his whole face, making him seem younger and a bit rakish. He did not answer in words, but he pulled her even closer, which answered just as effectively.

"Do you ruffians in America know how to dance the waltz?"

"If we do not, you shall regret accepting me, for we are likely to be trampled to death in such small quarters. Besides, did we not waltz back in Cambridge?"

"We did, but I did not feel so far removed from England there. Here it is quite a different story." Indeed, the narrative had shifted in curious ways. "I know you ever so much better, now."

"Yes, there is that, of course. You know all my warts and imperfections quite intimately," he said casually, leading her into the first steps. "If you had any, I would know them as well."

Verity barely knew how to respond when he said such things, for she was certain no one had ever before looked upon her with such a loving and prejudiced eye. She did know, however, that for all his self-effacing words, she thought his body the very image of perfection.

But that was not what worried her.

"You need not look so concerned, my love. I have already seen that strawberry scar on your back and think it enhances your beauty," Will said.

"My lady told me it was the mark of the devil," Verity said. "She put it there herself."

"I daresay the lady spoke with some authority."

"She is dead, poor thing."

"Then with even more authority," Will said.

"You are truly horrible," Verity said.

"That is not what you told me last night," he reminded her. "But if you have changed your mind, I shall have to endeavor to regain your good opinion in a few hours' time."

Whatever Verity ever imagined about love, she never dreamed that a preoccupied man's words could leave her breathless and aching. She was a fool for harboring the slightest doubt about him, for she now understood what they shared was good and true.

"If you continue to look like that at me, I shall have to order the carriage be brought around at once, and we beg off from the rest of the night in polite society," he said.

"I am not doing anything to intentionally provoke you, Will," Verity said, wishing she did not sound like she was gasping for air. Surely it had to do with the rigors of the dance.

"For someone able to construct a new identity for herself, you are amazingly artless at times," he said. "You are a woman of many surprises."

"And yet you already told me you were not surprised at all, so I daresay your talents are even keener than mine."

"I am older than you and have had that many more years of practice," he said, as his hand slipped lower on her hip. "But I intend to teach you everything I know."

All her doubts banished, Verity hoped it was a promise.

Chapter 12

The journey across the fertile plains of New York, west of Albany, was uneventful, for which Will was grateful. They saw no more of that bounder Reese, and the people they met were mostly farmers, not altogether pleased with the anticipated influx of strangers into their communities. They also met several members of the Iroquoian-speaking tribes who already knew what such an influx would represent and were frankly distrustful. But the success of the new canal was by no means guaranteed, inasmuch as a gentleman of little experience had overseen the whole business. The plan had been ambitious from the start, and some of the waterways and locks had already opened to great fanfare. Still, there was much yet to be determined.

*The Europeans who farm the land west of the Hudson River are as concerned about the arrival of newcomers near their lands as the Seneca, Mohawk, and Oneida Indians must have been concerned about them, many years before. However, there is much land available and it looks to be fertile, if somewhat rocky. We traveled along the route of a deep ditch that is to be known as the Erie Canal, through towns with illustrious names. There is much anticipation and some trepidation, but one thing is certain: the land will never look the same again.*

Will looked down at Verity, who was sleeping

quite soundly on his shoulder. The rocking of the carriage was an invitation to close one's eyes, and they had gotten into the splendid habit of spending their nighttime hours in more active endeavors than sleeping. It was tempting for him to do the same, but there was a book to be considered and a publisher anxiously waiting for its completion.

It was also his luck, he supposed, to have fallen for the one woman who wished to make her own way through life. He meant to have her and did not intend to allow his wife to earn her own wages, but he suspected she would not accept his hand until he was able to meet her on her own terms. She intended to be his partner, in all ways.

She certainly worked hard at it. He recalled her first drafts and the uncertainty of her words, as revealed in the blotchy handwriting on the first pages she gave him. He was hard on her and now felt replete with guilt about that. But she did become a better writer and an acute observer of all they witnessed. She saw some things he did not and made him see other things in an altogether different light.

Gently, so as not to disturb her sleep, he pulled his own pages out of his leather portfolio. He also wrote about the great canal that would someday connect the placid Hudson with the great lakes to the west, but he had not considered the people. His commentary was concerned with the challenges of engineering a waterway through a landscape with hundreds of feet in disparity from start to finish, of building locks and bridges, of providing port towns along the way. What did Verity know of the Seneca Indians, anyway?

More than he did, apparently. For all his assurance

that he would teach her all he knew, she had much to teach him as well. When he woke each morning with her warm body folded against his, he felt like a new person and approached the start of each day with a joy hitherto unimagined. Had it been like this for his cousin?

But of course it had not, for Eastbourne had not had Verity. Or, at least, he had not had this Verity, this enigma of a woman. But Will was not Eastbourne and most likely never would be, so perhaps they each had the woman they deserved.

Truly, he was becoming a sentimental idiot. And he had a book to write with his partner.

She moved against him and said something in her sleep. Will glanced across the carriage at Geoff and Nell, hoping they did not hear her. But they both seemed rather intent—perhaps too intent—on their own reading, and did not even look up.

"What do you think?" Verity murmured, her eyes still closed. "Do you like what I wrote?"

"Do you believe the farmers terribly inconvenienced?" he asked. "Do you not think they will find benefit in the ease with which they may, someday, bring their products to market?"

"No one likes change," she said, "even if people know it will be to their betterment."

"And yet you changed the course of your own life with as much drama and upheaval as can be imagined. You left the security of a position and a home on a great estate and joined the company of vagabonds, making their way across the country."

Geoff and Nell, in unison, settled their books in their laps.

"I have left nothing, Will. Surely you realize that. I was on the land but not of it. I belonged to nothing, to no one. Even if one could claim a connection to Lady Verity, it was tenuous at best. I never doubted that if she did not like the way I styled her hair one morning, or if she found her bathwater too chilly, I would be out on the road, searching for work in another great house. Without references, I would be unlikely to find it."

"But your father would not have allowed that," Nell protested.

"You did not know my father," Verity sighed. "No one could. He was a private man, uninterested in society, unwilling to reveal his thoughts. What was your opinion of him, Will?"

"I hardly know what to say, Verity. When I met your father, he showed me his model for a new light machine, and his stuffed albino starling, but we did not discuss his paternal responsibilities."

"No, I suppose not, since it was a topic of little interest to him. I might have been gone for days before my father even noticed my absence."

"Would he have not noticed your absence at the dinner table?" Nell persisted.

Verity said nothing, and Will knew it because there was nothing to be said. She never would have dined with the family, never have been allowed to call Lord Harwood her father, never could have expected the slightest consideration from him, either in money or affection. No wonder she was so desperate to escape such a life.

"I believe he often dined alone." Will stepped in, wishing to ease Verity's embarrassment. "I know my cousin saw him but rarely and was pleasantly surprised when Lord Harwood joined us one night for dinner. I must have made a good impression, because I was then invited to his private sanctuary the next day."

"You did, indeed, make a good impression, for very few others are permitted there," Verity said.

"But you said you were often there, Verity," said Nell. "Do you remember you described it to me?"

"Oh, yes, Lord Harwood did not seem to mind having two little girls about, as long as they were quiet and took care when touching his treasures. I wonder if things would have been different if he had had a son, who might have been heir not only to his estate, but to his intellectual passions. I do think he once harbored hopes that Lord Eastbourne might be his protege, but it seems there were other things on the Harwood estate that interested Eastbourne more."

"And he is Will's cousin," Nell said. "How curious it all is. To think you should meet on the Atlantic crossing and not realize how intertwined were your lives. It is an excellent coincidence."

"Oh, indeed. Is it not, Will?" Verity asked, moving a bit away from him and questioning him rather pointedly.

"It was a coincidence, as I've already explained once before," he said slowly, wondering if she doubted him.

"And of course you recognized not me, but the person you thought I was."

Nell laughed out loud. "Do you see? It is all a wonderful tangle, just like a romance."

*And romances always ended well*, he thought. "What do you have to say about it, Geoff?"

Geoff looked surprised that they bothered to bring

him into this conversation at all, though he sat two feet away. "I have only one question, and it is for Will."

"Anything at all, my friend, assuming I know the answer."

"On this, only you can respond." Geoff cleared his throat. "Do you really think we are vagabonds?"

They spent several more nights in inns along the path of the deepening canal. Some of these were quite new, and the proprietors scarcely knew what to do with their guests. But there was a conviction that money was to be made from the workers and tourists who now flocked to the plains of New York, and farmers and anyone who owned a bit of property hung a sign on the road advertising rooms for rent. Verity used the opportunity to interview some of the men and women in the households but remained envious of Will and Geoff, who were able to join the canal workmen in the makeshift bar after dinner and thus find out more about their plans and ambitions.

Still, as Will came to her room every night, she was able to question him in his quiet moments. She already discovered that when he was exhausted from lovemaking, and just about to drift off to sleep, he was likely to be off his guard.

One afternoon, as Verity sat in the carriage, reading through her pages about Rome and Salina and Waterloo, she became aware of a steady hum, of some great noise in the distance.

"Do I hear work on the canal?" she asked no one in particular. "I thought they did not yet progress this far."

"Can you not guess what it is?" Will asked, and Geoff nodded knowingly.

"Of course we cannot guess, or Verity would not

have asked," Nell said impatiently. "I thought it thunder, but it does not seem to stop."

"It is the great cataract that all the world wishes to see; it is Niagara." Will opened the door, though the carriage was moving briskly. "We are yet miles away, and we can already taste the moisture on our lips."

"Will we see it by tonight?" Verity asked excitedly. Here was something she read about in every journal describing travels through America, including one of Will's own books. In a country best known for its industry, here was one of the glories of the natural landscape.

"Certainly we will. But the marvel is best appreciated in the daylight hours, and I believe we will have time this day for that as well. But, if not, it is no matter, for we shall remain here until Thursday, at least," Will announced.

"Is there so much to see and do?" Verity asked. They had not spent so much time in Albany, which was regrettable, for it was an excellent little city.

"The wonder of Niagara can be admired for days on end. But I rather thought we would enjoy speaking to fellow travelers, who flock here as ravens do to the Tower of London." Will briefly consulted a printed announcement. "And we do not meet our ferry to Ohio until Friday."

"Well, Verity? What do you say to this adventure? Did you expect to see the greatest of all natural wonders when you set forth from Harwood Hall?" Geoff asked.

"I did not. But if we are able to hear the roar of it from miles away, I wonder if it shall prove to be the most terrifying of natural wonders as well."

****

It was. Truly, it was.

Will tugged on her arm some time later, when they arrived at the promenade below the falls, where the Niagara River crashed into whirlpools and eddies. Nell dashed on ahead with Geoff, shrieking excitedly at the spectacle. But Verity could not move from the spot, paralyzed by a fear so great she scarcely recognized herself.

"Come, Verity! I promise I will not let go of your hand!" Will shouted above the roar of the falls. "Nothing will happen!"

Still she would not move. How could he know they would not be swept away and torn to bits on the rocks? How could people stand about and gape at something so fearsome?

Will seemed to find it all very amusing. Still clutching her arm, he circled behind, fully embracing her so he could speak quietly. "It is perfectly safe, my love. Would all these people be right at the edge if they feared a river monster might swallow them?" he said into her ear.

She said nothing.

"Will you not always regret coming so close, and missing the best view of Niagara? Come, I will not let go of you and will protect you. You can trust me."

Verity turned her head. "Truly?"

"Yes, you can," he said. His hand slipped under her cape and pressed against her heart. "Always."

She allowed him to push her gently forward, but again resisted when she felt the first spray of the water. "This is as far as I go, Will. I can see perfectly well from here," said Verity. She also could see that Nell was so giddy it was all Geoff could do to keep her from diving in.

"And here I thought you were a brave, adventurous girl. How will you write your chapter about Niagara Falls? Will you invent it all?"

"As you know, I'm very good about that as well," she said wryly. "But I will leave you to write about the direction of the water, the height of the falls, the number of people who have been foolish enough to try boating on the river and have their feeble brains dashed out on the rocks below. For my part, I will consider what draws people to this place, when they could be perfectly happy in a rowboat in Boston Harbor."

Nell ran up just then, her face damp and her curls dripping.

"There is a boat!" she cried. "We can hire a boat to take us under the falls!"

"Oh, good heavens." Verity sighed.

*Niagara Falls may be compared to some startling qualities in the American character. Americans seem quietly industrious and often reticent about revealing too much about their lives. And yet, suddenly they burst forth with an energy that is almost terrifying, making plans and gathering support even when their projects seem misguided. There is a great thunder of voices and expense of activity, and many observers who will speculate as to the results. So it is the same with the great spectacle of Niagara Falls. It is the destination of every traveler, and yet it is nothing more than a waterfall of uncommon size and strength. One cannot swim in the waters, or grow harvests along the banks. It is great because it is great, and it is something about which a traveler can say, "I have seen it."*

*Gentle readers, I have seen it, and it is very large*

*indeed. But as it is with a boisterous guest at a dinner party, one feels the need to move on...*

Will looked up from the page. "What do you think is misguided about our projects?" he asked.

Verity looked across the room to where he sat at a sturdy desk. The glow of candlelight cast dramatic shadow across his face, dramatizing his straight nose and high cheekbones. She took pleasure just looking at him, until he scowled at her.

"The canal, for one thing," she answered. "How many people will travel along its route when there is snow on the ground, and the river is caked with ice?"

He did not answer and returned to his reading. And she returned to hers.

*The potential to harness the energy of Niagara Falls is very great. If one imagines how effectively a rushing river drives a flour mill, the power of the Niagara River, as it roars over the magnificent falls, must be calculated at a thousandfold. Situated as it is, the growing city of Buffalo, New York, will stand to benefit. The city is not named for the bullish creatures that dot the plains of the Western territories but is derived from the slurring of the French words* Beau Fleuve, *or Beautiful River. As Buffalo businessmen pull strength from Niagara, it will be a very beautiful thing, indeed.*

"I do not think it necessary to boast about your knowledge of other languages, for it has little to do with the point of your paragraph," Verity said. "It just makes you appear like a conceited oaf."

"Is it so very bad, do you think?" Will asked, grinning.

"It is. You would do better to calculate the actual

strength of the waterfall."

"That is an excellent point. Do you know how one might go about it?"

Verity put down his pages. Really, did he intend for her to write this whole book?

"I don't think it ever came up in my studies," she answered truthfully.

"And yet I suppose you learned French?" Will asked. "Do you speak it?"

"*Un peu*," she said, naturally enough. "But mine is not the French of the schoolroom. Lord Harwood had a French cook, and I spent a good deal of time with her. Some things are best learned in the kitchen."

"I see," Will said thoughtfully. "Are you suggesting that in addition to your other skills, I may find myself with a wife capable of making crepes *jambon*? I will be getting a very good bargain, indeed."

"If I am transported to Australia as a criminal, you will get neither a bargain nor a wife."

"I shall chance the consequences. And I understand Australia is a rugged, yet beautiful place. My mother and sisters will miss me, however."

"It does not seem to me that they see you all that often, in any case." Verity stifled a yawn, for the business of merely observing the falls was enough to exhaust her.

"They see me as required." Will folded his papers and set them down carefully on the table next to him. "Did you say there are things that could be learned in the kitchen?"

Verity was no longer tired. "Would you like a lesson in kneading bread, perhaps? To see how quickly it will rise?"

"I believe I prefer a dessert buffet, at which I could taste all manner of sweet things. What can you offer, by way of a sampling?" He stood and smoothed down the crease in his trousers.

"Are Nell and Geoff already abed?"

"They have been very cooperative about accommodating our new work schedule and do seem to retire quite early. I told them we were exploring the possibilities of our partnership."

"Oh, surely, that will fool them into thinking us quite proper and chaste," Verity said, sarcastically.

"Even a stranger would guess by the way I look at you that there is nothing proper or chaste about this partnership, my love."

"Are we so very obvious? Does this mean you were not serious about sampling desserts?"

"I am dead serious. In fact, if they were any sweeter, my body would go into shock. And yet, I would die a happy man." Will punctuated his words with kisses to her eyes and nose. "But I would rather die in bed, than on Mr. and Mrs. Worthing's parlor floor."

Verity paused in unfastening his shirt buttons. "Then let us find one, and quickly."

\*\*\*\*

The ropes beneath the mattress on the bed in Will's chamber were not as tight as those to which they had more or less become accustomed, and some time later, Will and Verity lay comfortably in the center of the mattress, thrown together as if they lay in a hammock. She fingered a thin white line that ran from one nipple to his collarbone.

"Is this a battle scar?" she asked. "Did a reviewer

of one of your books attack you with his pen?"

"You have a very poor opinion of my abilities," he murmured.

"I believe I just gave you sufficient evidence that my opinion is quite the opposite," Verity said and rested her wandering hand on his chest.

"As a matter of fact, I won the battle that earned me that scar. It was with your old neighbor, Eastbourne, though he was just my cousin Goodwell then. He tried to kill me."

"You jest."

"I never jest about matters of life or death…or love, for that matter." He paused, and shifted against her. "He went after me with a pitchfork, claiming I had cheated at cards.

"He was always known as a bad loser. But then, so was Lady Verity, whose scar I bear as well. They were a fine pair."

"Except they were not," Will pointed out. "They should have married each other and saved us all a lot of trouble."

"We would not have met if that were the case." Verity stared into the darkness, listening to the sounds of the night, and the ever-present hum of the falls. "Will, where will this all end?"

"Not in Cincinnati," he said. "I hope you do not intend to set up shopkeeping with your friend Mrs. Trollope, or whatever it was Lady Verity intended to do."

"It may be the best thing, if that was the plan. With every night we spend together, I am another step closer to perdition. I have no money, no name, no resources."

"And here I thought that with each night we are

another step closer to heaven. You will have money, honestly earned from the sales of our book. You can have any name you wish, though I hope you choose Mrs. William Bentley. And you have resources that would be the envy of any woman."

Verity closed her eyes, trying to believe everything he said would come true.

"And you have love, stronger than any I ever believed possible," he said, barely audibly.

Would he remember all he just said, what promise was sealed by his words?

Perhaps not. After all, she knew he was apt to talk in his sleep.

Will managed to get Verity five steps closer to Niagara Falls the next afternoon, though he thought she'd pierce his skin through his sleeve, so tightly was she holding him.

"The rock at the edge of the falls is very strong, but even the firmest of bedrock is no match for the power of water. And so, I am told, the edge of the falls retreats several inches every year," he said.

"Who tells you such things, Will?" Nell asked. "I don't know how such a thing can be reckoned."

"I do not know how to do it myself, but I trust others to understand such things. Your Captain Warburton surely knows about it, if he is entrusted to engineer the fort in Boston Harbor."

Nell turned away, but he knew she was quite taken with the captain. For all he said about him, while they were still in Cambridge, Will could not help but be happy with the way things turned out. He knew he had hurt Nell when they first made landfall at the wharf in Boston and announced to Nell that she had a new companion. But Nell took to Verity right away, though she must have realized how he felt about the newcomer. Geoff claimed to have understood how it was within hours of their first meeting.

And yet, while Verity gave freely of herself, he sensed she held something back. She remained watchful of him, waiting for him to disappoint her or give her pain.

He supposed such thoughts were justified by the rude manner of his treatment toward her when first they met. He could not deny he treated her poorly then, but how could it have been otherwise? She presented herself as a person he suspected of very bad behavior, and he felt some shred of loyalty to his cousin, from whom Lady Verity might have been running. At the same time, for all Eastbourne's claim on the real Verity Harwood and evidence that this other woman was somehow also involved in the whole sordid mess, Will felt himself drawn to her. Her beauty was compelling but not enough to bewitch him, as indeed she did.

If he was honest, he had to admit he was drawn to her sense of adventure and determination, and her opportunistic scheme to create a destiny that would never have been hers but for the unexpected circumstances of Lady Verity's death. His Verity was an original, a true creation of the new country.

And she loved him.

He had other lovers before he met her and was a gallant player in the arts of flirtation. But he never before felt as if a woman approached him as an equal and made demands that caused him to rethink his presumptions and even his knowledge. There were other women he thought he loved through the years, but none he admired so very much.

He loved her.

He already told her as much and spent every night demonstrating it in ways he'd only imagined before. He shared his ideas and respected hers and admitted her as a partner in all things. Why did she still hold back from him? Surely he gave her every reason to trust him.

"I will not let anything happen to you, Verity," he said.

"I know you won't, Will," she said, her eyes still fixed on the great falls.

"And for all he says about the erosion of the stone, we are not about to be washed away by the torrent," said Geoff and winked at Will.

"You cannot know that, Geoff," said Nell, unhelpfully. Did she not understand how terrified was her friend?

But perhaps she did not. In fact, perhaps no one understood Verity as well as he did.

And then Will realized that her doubts and fears might have nothing to do with himself but might very well be the result of a lifetime of disappointments and reversals. He considered what little he knew about her life, but it all made perfect sense. After all, she was the unacknowledged daughter of an earl but was maid to her sister. Her father loved her mother but never married her, preferring that she be a servant as well. And even as she assumed the guise of another lady, she had inherited a defeated disposition. Lady Verity was pregnant with a married man's child, for she had cast her lot with one who was cruel and indifferent and used her as he used everyone else.

No wonder Verity withheld that last bit of trust in

him or anyone else. He might wish it otherwise, but he could not altogether blame her. She needed time. Time, or a resolution of her present tangle of identity.

She had lulled him to sleep last night with a question of how it might all end. But she got it wrong. The real question was when would it all be allowed to begin?

Her hand slipped off his arm, and she pushed mist-dampened hair off her forehead. He looked down and saw her expression, one he was becoming to know well. She had a desire to do something and would not be dissuaded from her objective. He only hoped he was a part of it.

"Did you say there was a boat that goes beneath the falls?" Verity asked.

Nell squealed in delight. "You will do it?"

Verity looked up at Will.

"Will you come with me?" she asked.

"We will all come," Geoff said. "You will need someone to rescue you when my friend is too busy to notice you've gone overboard because of his need to write all about it, in the moment."

"But I shall be doing the same," she said. "And if I go overboard, it will only add to the novelty of the adventure."

"And if we all go overboard, we will become famous for the manner of our deaths," Nell added. "It will all be very romantic and sad."

"I would much prefer to become famous by other means, Nell. Preferably ones by which I will be able to live and tell others," Verity said. "But let us go soon, before I lose my courage."

She turned to face him. "Do you think me mad?"

"Utterly mad," Will said. "And absolutely divine."

Absolutely crazy, he ought to have said. Will helped Geoff onto the sturdy boat first, then reached for Nell so that he could deliver her to her brother's care. Verity waited patiently at the little quay, wondering once again if a wild dash was still possible. Her hands shook and just as she thought her knees would give way, Will caught her hand and coaxed her onto the boat.

"Thank you very much," she said, wishing her voice did not tremble so.

"Ah, the lady is from foreign parts?" asked the boatsman. "We get many of your countrymen here at Niagara and haven't lost one yet."

"Thank you, sir, that is very reassuring," Verity said.

Perhaps this truly was the start of a new life. Whereas every day at Harwood was spent in ironing and sewing and styling hair and indulging Lady Verity's whims, every day since Lady Verity's death was spent in doing something different, unexpected, and exhilarating. If this was where it all ended, it could be said that Annie Merrill died fulfilled.

Will, who had stepped up on a barrel to study the opposite shore, jumped down next to her. Oh, yes, she already knew much about being fulfilled.

"Do not worry, my dear. We shall not die this day," he said, reading her thoughts. He surprised her, not by his words, but by his emphatic insistence upon them. He meant everything he said, she realized. How extraordinary he was.

They were joined by other passengers and were briefly lectured on the rules of the journey and what might be expected. Verity thought they were to go beyond the falls, through the whirlpools and eddies that violently swirled at the base. But the crewman told them otherwise, for they were to go behind the great cataract, where the rock was already worn to form a cave of sorts and where they would have a gentler ride. If any among them hoped to defect from the tour, it was already too late, for they had cast off from the shore.

Will pulled her away from the canopy and to the rail at the boat's deck.

"So long as we are doing this, we might as well do it right. And I refuse to sit like one of the matrons beneath the oilcloth and listen to others describe the sight," said Will. Nell and Geoff were already at the rail.

Verity held her ground but knew she would take the dare.

"But I would like to live long enough to be an elderly matron," she protested weakly. "It sounds like a fine way to spend one's dotage."

"There will be time enough for that many years from now. But on this day, you will dare enough to give our readers—and perhaps our grandchildren—a good story."

And those were the last words Verity heard for some time, for the roar of the falls drowned out all other sound. They moved precariously close to the first shower of water, and then the boat dodged the storm and edged between the wall of water and the glistening rock.

"Is it not wonderful?" Nell screamed, her hair plastered against her face.

Will's arms tightened. "Yes," he said, though only

Verity could hear him.

And then, just when she thought she could endure this indefinitely, they came out of the falls near the opposite shore. Verity twisted around and, for the first time in her life, spied a rainbow.

Nell leaned over the deck, intent on something near the quay.

"Have a care, sister," Geoff said and put out a stiff arm in front of her. "It is only a rainbow."

"I do not care for the rainbow," Nell said excitedly.

Verity looked at her friend, wondering at her indifference in the face of a small miracle. Then she, too, looked at the shore, and studied the throng of people until she could identify just one among the many.

"Well, of all wonders," she said. "I believe that is your Captain Warburton."

Chapter 13

The parlor in the Worthings' guesthouse was large enough for at least twenty visitors, but when Will, Geoff, and Peter Warburton entered in the late afternoon, the other guests promptly left.

"I am the problem, I suspect," Warburton said, as he picked up a book and examined its spine. "I am in uniform, after all, and this morning asked about town as to where I could find you. Perhaps I did not make myself well understood, and they must believe I have apprehended you in some wrongdoing."

"And have you?" Will asked.

"Have I what?" Warburton looked up from the book. Will recognized the volume he held.

"Have you apprehended us in some wrongdoing?"

Warburton laughed good naturedly. "Why? What have you done? Have you abducted Lady Verity against her will? Have you pilfered Mrs. Worthing's silver?"

"Not yet," Will answered. "I have no need of the silver, but the thought of capturing Lady Verity is very tempting. By the by, she is now known as Miss Harwood."

Warburton settled into a sturdy chair by the window. The light was bright enough for him to continue to examine the book. "She wishes to be recognized along with the common folk, then. I applaud her decision, for in doing so, she may gain more in friendship than she might lose in stature."

"I have said something of the same thing myself," said Will.

"I confess those are not my words, but those of Benjamin Williams, the travel writer. Here is one of his books, if you have not yet had the privilege of reading him." Warburton held out the book to Will, who settled in a seat close by.

"I have had the privilege," Will said softly. "That is my book."

Geoff laughed out loud. "Oh, stuff it, Will. Warburton, Will is the author of those books, and I am not only his friend, but his secretary."

Warburton looked from Will to Geoff, perhaps assessing the truth of it. "If this is true, then my luck is even greater for having found you. I have considered penning a work of my own on the subject of America's engineering marvels and have not known how to truly go about it."

"I am happy to offer some advice," said Will. "But you haven't traveled all the way from Boston just to receive editorial advice?"

Warburton narrowed his gaze and frowned. "As a matter of fact, I have orders to see to harbor development near Toledo."

"But you did seek us out?" Will asked.

Warburton turned toward Geoff, who had managed to remain aloof from the conversation. "I am in pursuit of a lady."

Will sat up in his chair. "She is already spoken for."

"That is not what she told me just an hour ago back on the dock. Mr. Marsh, is this true? Does Miss Eleanor already have a suitor?"

"Miss Eleanor does not," Geoff said, with apparent satisfaction.

Warburton turned back to Will. "I considered it the happiest of coincidences when I received my assignment and knew my journey would parallel your own. Of course, I had much time to make up and sometimes rode right through the night, making few stops along the way."

"How did you know where we would be?" Geoff asked. "Is it possible all those letters my sister penned along the way were not intended for our Aunt Evangeline and were addressed to you instead?"

"Quite possible." Warburton grinned. "It seems Mr. Bentley is not the only writer on this journey."

"It is no wonder Nell appeared so pleased with herself and did not complain about any delays along the route. She must have known you were on your way." Geoff looked rather pleased himself.

"Indeed. Some of the particulars of your travel were also relayed to me by Mr. John Reese, with whom, I believe you are well acquainted," Captain Warburton added.

Geoff glanced at Will. "Not very well. He seems rather more interested in our affairs than we are in his."

"But of course. He shadows Lady Verity, on her father's behalf."

Will shot upright in his seat. "You know that? Or is that an assumption? Miss Harwood is not aware of his interference with her business."

"Do you serve as her protector, Bentley?" Warburton asked.

"I do."

"Allow me to offer congratulations, then," Warburton said. "Though Miss Harwood has changed her name, she is no less a lady of England. It is a very fine thing, for all our nations' political squabbles."

Will reflected that whatever Reese revealed, he had said nothing on the truth about Verity, though he had surely read her letter to Lord Harwood. That was some consolation, at the very least.

"Let me offer you luck in return, Warburton. I have always respected the beauty and intelligence of my good friend's little sister," said Will.

"Thank you. But I would not court her if I thought of her as someone's little sister. She is a woman, in her own right."

"So she is," Geoff said cheerfully. "But I still appreciate your speaking to me before things went any further. That is, I assume they have not gone very far?"

"Far enough to make me believe I will win her affections, if you allow me to do so."

"Let us talk, then," said Geoff.

Will saw that as good as any opportunity to take his leave. He stood and pointed to the book Warburton still held.

"You should read it through, my good man. There is much made of American impressions of construction going on all around them. Not everyone is so pleased by the results."

"Then we are lucky to be citizens of a very large country," Warburton said. "If one is unhappy with his circumstances, then it is time for him to move on."

"No one ever had a better cue, though I am rather pleased with the present circumstances. I will leave you two," he said. "I am sure you have important things to discuss, as you soon may be brothers."

As he walked away, he realized he also had come to think of Geoff as his brother, for they'd remained in close proximity for so many years. Having no natural brothers of his own, and only the barely tolerable Eastbourne as his male cousin, he realized he was just a tad possessive. It surprised him.

"Please tell me things are not so bad as all that?"

Will looked up and saw Verity poised on the stairway. She took a few steps down, until she was just at his height. "You look quite solemn, as if you lost your best friend."

"I was just thinking it myself," Will said, and offered his hand.

She surprised him by holding it against her heart.

"We will not lose them, for true friends are always with us," she said. "And, after all, they must believe they are about to lose us, as well."

"Geoff has been with me for many years."

Verity smiled and continued down the stairs. "Geoff will surely marry someday, and his wife will not tolerate such traveling as he is accustomed to doing with you."

"I will need a secretary," he said, wrapping his arms around her and pressing her close.

"I happily accept."

"As my secretary, or my wife? My partner in every way," he said. "But you will not like it. Once you deem yourself an author, you are not going to want to spend your hours turning over the words of another."

He nodded. "After all, after feeling your freedom in the weeks since Lady Verity was lost at sea, could you ever again be a lady's maid? Once you've seen the other side of the mountain, there is no going back. Geoff will remain as my secretary, perhaps for many more years. But he shall be your secretary as well. Would that do?"

Verity put her head back and gazed at him. "I wish all our problems could be solved so easily. For we have them in abundance."

Will thought about John Reese, the message he carried for Lord Harwood, and the information he so freely imparted to Warburton. What was his plan?

"They will be solved," Will said gently, hoping he sounded more certain of it than he felt.

*Europeans, accustomed to crowded cities and small quarters, are quite unprepared for the boundless land and resources of the new continent. And yet, even with such possibilities for settlement, many Americans live in Boston, New York, and Philadelphia, or the great cities of the South, and seem contented there. Others move on to the West, establishing more cities from small towns, looking for farm land and property to call their own. It is certain that once one gets a taste of this sort of unbounded freedom, it is very hard to look back.*

Verity looked at the vast expanse of Lake Erie, and it did not seem possible that a lake could be this large. Erie was not even as large as Superior, Captain Warburton had told her. She should have guessed, like everything else in America, the lake's proportions were overly large and yet dwarfed by its neighbor next door.

"I look forward to landing in Toledo," she said to her companion. "Thank you for arranging for our accommodations."

Captain Warburton nodded. "Yes, indeed, I am

acquainted with a family there, who run a very fine house. The O'Neils settled in Boston when they first arrived in America but found better opportunities in Ohio. They are familiar with your part of Sussex, as they are related to several families there. I believe they know your father. Mrs. O'Neil is hopeful that you might take their daughter under your wing, and perhaps sponsor her when they travel to England next year. She believes you will be a very fine influence."

Then Mrs. O'Neil certainly did not know much about Lady Verity Harwood.

"I should be happy to help in whatever way I can," Verity said. "But I should not want to give them false hope. After all, it is very possible I shall remain in America and never return to my father's home."

"I wish you well, whatever you choose," he said, watching the gulls hovering above them.

Verity watched as he reached into his pocket and pulled out half a loaf of bread.

"I say, sir, is that your breakfast?" she asked, relieved to turn the topic.

Warburton cracked the loaf against the rail. "It was once someone's breakfast. The cook was ready to dispose of it when I asked if I might feed the gulls. I suppose I am too accustomed to living on my little island in Boston Harbor."

Verity laughed. "You will not lack for good companionship soon, I hope."

He looked very serious as he handed her a wedge of the hard bread.

"No, indeed. If Nell will have me, I shall be the happiest man in America. I believe I am to also wish you well, Miss Harwood, for I understand you and Mr.

Bentley have come to some sort of an understanding." A gull alighted on the rail between them and began to peck at the brick of hard bread in Warburton's hand. "He is a very lucky man."

Verity, warmed by his words, leaned toward him but was rebuffed by the very large bird.

"And I am a lucky woman," she said. "I have known only the greatest joy since coming to your country."

Surprisingly, Warburton laughed. "It is hard to believe that a lady who has known only the greatest privileges and a life of every advantage should find joy in such company as we provide and on vessels such as this."

Indeed, the ship looked like it had plied the waters of the Great Lakes for far too many years and, by comparison, made the *Andromeda* look like the royal yacht.

"And yet I feel like I never knew myself until I came to America, and that I never breathed such air as this."

Unfortunately, the ship's engine coughed out a cloud of black smoke at that very minute, sending the gull off to glide along a fresh breeze and sending Verity into a spasm of coughing. Captain Warburton gently patted her between the shoulders with his left hand.

The air cleared, and Nell appeared on his right. She cocked her head, observing the intimate scene, and cast Verity a quizzing look.

"I am happy you two are getting to know each other better," Nell said.

"We have just offered each other congratulations. And as you and I shall remain friends, so it appears

Captain Warburton and I shall be able to remain friends as well."

Warburton turned to the object of his affection. "Miss Harwood tells me she may not return to England, which has very much surprised me."

"Perhaps those of us who have never had a title or were born to privilege cannot imagine how anyone could abandon all that. And yet I understand how it might be a burden." Nell drew her arm under his elbow and knocked the bread into the waters of the lake. "You have a title, Captain Warburton, but you desired it and earned it. It must be quite a different thing."

Verity knew her friend spoke the truth and made a mental note to include such a sentiment in her present chapter, for it seemed very wise.

"And that is why our own Mr. Bentley ignores the possibility that a great estate and title might be his one day. He does not desire it and has done nothing at all to earn it," Nell said. *Better and better*.

"Truly?" Captain Warburton asked. "Is he the second or third son, perhaps? The sun always seem to shine on that gentleman."

"The sun does not shine all that brightly, Captain Warburton," Verity said. "Our friend, Mr. Bentley is only a first cousin to an earl, the son of a younger brother. His hopes of ascendancy are rather slim, as his cousin is of the same age and has already produced several children."

"But they are all females," Nell said. "It does not seem very fair, but if something should happen to their father, Will immediately owns the ground beneath their feet."

"Such are our laws of inheritance. If something

should happen to Lord Harwood, my father, the property and title will go to…" Verity paused, realizing she was not at all certain how the estate would be disposed. What expectations did Lady Verity have, other than to marry someone with an estimable rank?

"Verity?" Nell asked.

Verity suddenly recalled a young man who came to visit Harwood Hall some years ago, greeted like a conquering hero. Lord Harwood was very much taken with him, and though he was pushed in front of Lady Verity at every opportunity, she was somewhat less taken. He was a cousin, or a nephew, or a cousin's nephew. It suddenly occurred to Verity that he likely was the heir.

"My father has a distant relation, who will also stand to gain a great deal if my father dies without a son. Just now, it looks likely that will be the case. Such things are not uncommon."

"Which is why we may permit Mr. Bentley to harbor some hopes in that direction," Captain Warburton said and looked at Verity. "But as an American, he marries where he chooses, without any regard for title or wealth. After all, the affairs of the heart are difficult enough without having to worry about class and inheritance. Here, to love is enough."

He turned to Nell, and the expression on his face revealed everything. Verity ached with pleasure for her friend, whose life promised such joy and so few complications. "Might I interest you two ladies in a stroll about the deck? We are likely to see other vessels on the lake, and I should be happy to tell you all about them."

Nell would have responded with equal enthusiasm

had he suggested they get married on the spot and hold a great ball in their honor upon reaching the distant shores of Ohio. As such, Verity decided that she would make her friend even happier by declining the offer.

"I have much to write in my journal this day, Captain Warburton. You will forgive me for not joining you, but I am sure Nell will share your insights on the seaworthiness of the various ships in the area. It is a subject about which I know so little." She smiled broadly, without the slightest hint of regret.

But as Nell and her captain strolled off together, Verity wondered if he would now be compelled to speak of such things, if only so Nell could impart information. For indeed, she doubted that riggings and sails were what he really had on his mind when in the company of the woman he loved.

****

In the years since Will had ventured this far west, much had been done to improve the first impression one had of the territory. When they arrived in Toledo, he realized the city, while nothing to Boston or New York or Buffalo, had grown in height and depth, and the waterfront was reasonably lively. He noticed Verity's delight as they walked along the quay and bought her a sprig of flowers from a cart laden with farm produce.

Warburton, Geoff, and Nell walked several paces behind them, after Warburton arranged for their trunks to be transported to the home of his friends, the O'Neils. The distance to their destination was not very great, and the five of them decided to walk while the light was good, and their spirits even better.

"I believe the captain is enamored of our friend

Nell," Will said, after glancing back to see them arm in arm.

"Yes, I am very happy for her," Verity said. "I hope she is not going to be disappointed, however."

"In him? He seems a resolute fellow, and he adores her." Will suddenly realized why Verity might have any misgivings about the captain. "I regret anything I may have said about him that appeared ungenerous. To be fair, I thought he was interested in you."

"I see," Verity said and looked at him far too solemnly for a woman who had just heard her lover was jealous of other men. "But Nell was interested in you, and only shifted her allegiance when she sensed you would not return her affections. What if I am arrested or imprisoned for what I have done? You would not have me then, and Nell…and Nell—"

He realized she could not bear to say it.

"I will not allow anything to happen to you; surely you already know that?" he murmured.

"There will be precious little you could do to protect me in a British court of law, Will. You are no more Lord Eastbourne than I am Lady Verity Harwood. And my father will never forgive me."

"Lord Harwood ought to find forgiveness for his own deeds before he sits in judgment of another," Will said. "But it will never come to that. You have written to him and safeguarded the letter by sending it twice, for good measure. You will earn money from the sales of our book and will pay the estate the small sums you have already borrowed against it. Surely, Lord Harwood can forgive you that."

"But Mr. Meldon will know I lied to him."

"Mr. Meldon is entrusted to dispense money, and

he did only after reading your letter. The man could not know that Harwood would have two daughters nearly identical in appearance. Though, quite honestly, I doubt if Meldon's myopic eyes could have seen the difference between Lady Verity Harwood and a Jersey cow."

"Thank you very much, Will. How kind of you to note that," Verity said sarcastically.

"It is past time you heard this, my dear, and I am not sure what else I must do to convince you," he said.

"Of what?"

"Your poor sister, for all her grandeur, did not hold a candle to you. You are more beautiful, infinitely kinder, and far more clever than she. Is there any justice in heaven if she was the anointed one, and you were born to serve her? I am very sorry she died—for the death of a young woman must always be tragic—but I am not certain what else would have released you from such unjust bondage." Will heard the voices of their companions behind him and decided to move on before they would be obliged to share in the conversation. "Though I suppose you might have married well," he added, grudgingly.

"Well, indeed," Verity mused. "I would have been lucky to marry a groom or my father's valet. I might have met a farmer on the estate and considered myself quite lucky to be the mistress of chickens and a few sheep."

"I am not sure you are doing much better by marrying a poor writer," he said. "I will never be Lord Eastbourne, my dear."

"And I would never marry Lord Eastbourne, as the association is quite odious to me."

"In fact, it is to me as well. I am duty-bound to

visit my cousin on occasion but have never taken pleasure in his company, as well you know." They walked together in silence for several moments, hearing the odd word from the conversation behind them. "But I have a confession to make, as well."

Verity looked up at him, her eyes narrowed against the late afternoon sun.

"I am not poor," he confessed.

Surprisingly, she laughed. "Oh, dear, Will. I thought you were about to tell me that you had a wife and four children waiting for you at Hudson Point. Or you murdered someone back in Boston. But I never believed you were without means."

"What tipped you off?" he asked.

"I read your books, you recall, and I knew you could not possibly support a household on those slim words. In short, you need me as a partner. Our book will do very well."

"I find I need you as a partner in many things, my dearest Verity. At the very least, I need to be humbled every so often. So I gather that when you agree to marry me it will not be for my money."

"Certainly not." She smiled in that way she had before she flung out a witticism. "In fact, I felt I must marry you so your fortune might be assured. I took pity on you, poor man."

Will decided he deserved that, for he had been rather imperious with her. "In that case, should you ever find your inkwell dry, so to speak, do you agree to accept my money? What is mine shall be yours."

"As your wife? That is the usual arrangement." She looked flustered, as if she had not yet considered it. What a prize he had won; every other woman of his acquaintance sized up his accounts and property moments after their first meeting, it seemed.

"What is less usual is your acceptance of some funds before we are married. Will it ease your conscience if I advance you the funds you need to repay your father, in expectation of the money we will receive from our book? It would be purely a business agreement."

"As your partner," she reminded him.

"And it is for love, of course. Though I rather hoped you would accept a ring, as well."

She looked up at him, surely about to say something wonderful, when they were interrupted by Captain Warburton.

"You have passed our destination, Will!"

Will stopped in front of an elegant clapboard home, neatly appointed and freshly painted. Indeed, he hadn't noticed the wagon laden with their trunks on the gravel drive nor the sign near the front door. Warburton's announcement also alerted their hostess to their arrival, for the door opened as Will and Verity retraced their steps.

"Peter Warburton, is that you?" the woman called out. "I would not have recognized you in an audience of ten."

"Mrs. O'Neil has known me for many years," Warburton said in an undertone to his friends. "Yes, it is I! With warm regards from my mother and greetings from my fellow travelers."

Introductions were made as they made their way up the walkway. Mrs. O'Neil was joined by her daughter Heather, who seemed of an age with Nell, and Mr. O'Neil came to the door with a broadsheet in hand.

"There has been an accident along the canal," he said without preamble, waving the sheet of newsprint. "The project probably needs men like yourself, Peter, with engineering skills. Are they doing a good job on the project?"

"I did not stop to examine the works along the way," Warburton said. "I had more compelling business and wished to travel to Buffalo as quickly as possible."

Mrs. O'Neil cleared her throat. "I am sure this conversation can wait until we are within, Jerry. The ladies have traveled far and surely need their rest."

"The gentlemen have traveled far as well," Mr. O'Neil observed, as he bid them all enter.

Will was happy to see that Warburton had not exaggerated the comforts of the O'Neil home or the warmth with which they would be received. Although most of the innkeepers along the way were pleasant enough, few were exceptional. But here, in the elegant and well aired rooms in Toledo, he knew that everything would be to their satisfaction.

"Your trunks are just now being brought up the back stairs," Mrs. O'Neil explained, "so perhaps you would enjoy some tea in the parlor before Heather shows you to your rooms."

She did not wait for their assent but led them into a well-appointed room facing Lake Erie. Will paused before sitting down and studied the way the afternoon sun danced upon the water, and the slow progress of several barges, laden with cargo. Once the canal was complete, the city would necessarily accommodate four times the traffic.

"I hope you intend to stay in Toledo for some time," said Mrs. O'Neil. A young maid already delivered a tray of steaming tea and small sandwiches. "Miss Harwood, you will be surprised to know that there is a large community of your countrymen here, and you will feel quite at home."

"Thank you, Mrs. O'Neil," Verity said, and seemed hesitant about continuing. "Just now, I feel I should be quite content to remain here forever, but I have a call to make on Mrs. Frances Trollope, of Cincinnati."

"Mrs. Trollope," Mrs. O'Neil said and looked off toward the window. "Oh, dear, not that dreadful woman who heaps fault on everyone and everything she encounters? But forgive me, for she must be your friend, Miss Harwood. You will discover that she does not enjoy a fine reputation."

"It is quite all right, Mrs. O'Neil. I do not know her very well. I believe her husband's uncle was acquainted with my father and that Mrs. Trollope came to America to secure the family's finances. She has a rather grand emporium, you know."

Heather O'Neil leaned forward. "Truly?"

Mrs. O'Neil sniffed. "I have heard of it. It is said that the lady has imported goods from throughout the world, bringing to Cincinnati the sorts of things one could usually only find in New York and Boston and Philadelphia. And London, of course."

"Your gown is very lovely, Miss Harwood," Miss O'Neil said and glanced at her mother. Some understanding passed between them.

Will, having a generous supply of sisters at home, understood the message and groaned.

"We should like to join you when you are ready to travel to Cincinnati," Mrs. O'Neil said emphatically. "I have not enjoyed a good shopping excursion in some years, and I believe our fashions are woefully out of date."

"That would be lovely!" Nell said happily. "It is much more fun to shop as a party, and I am certain Mrs. Trollope would appreciate the patronage."

Will smiled when he saw the expressions on Geoff's and Warburton's faces, which were nearly identical. Geoff would bear the cost of it while his sister was a spinster, but the captain could expect to meet such extravagances for the rest of his life. Will hoped Warburton had deep pockets and rather suspected he did.

He turned to Verity, wondering if she would have some fashion requirements as well, and hoping she would accept his assistance. But she seemed preoccupied with other things, and he considered how accounts of several sorts were going to be settled in Cincinnati.

****

Will did not come to her bed that night, and Verity thought she ought to be grateful for that. On one hand, she would have been happy for the pleasure and diversion of his lovemaking, and the quiet conversation they usually had in its aftermath. But on the other, things seemed to be happening too quickly, and she had much to consider before meeting the notorious Frances Trollope, who might already know more about her than she did herself.

That is, she might know more about Lady Verity and what she planned to do in Cincinnati and what she had already revealed in private correspondences in which Annie Merrill played no part. Mrs. Trollope might have offered a refuge for Lady Verity's confinement or a home for her child or the opportunity to invest in her emporium. She might be planning to abandon the business altogether and travel with Lady Verity throughout the country. She might have promised nothing more than a few days' respite from a weary journey.

Verity was very much in the dark about it all and wondered if going to Cincinnati was a huge mistake. She had started this journey with three others, and they were now joined by another three. Could she count on their discretion? Could she hope for Mrs. Trollope's? From all accounts, the lady was rather haughty and censorious of all society, American and British. What would she have to say if she discovered the lofty British lady who was to visit her was the illegitimate daughter of Harwood's housekeeper?

Truly, she wished Will was here with her now, for it was impossible to sleep.

Verity dropped her legs off the side of the mattress and felt about for her slippers. She had work to do.

*Though Americans may revel in the spirit of adventure that is likely to take them to small outposts of civilization in their vast continent, it is certain that many of them long for the cultural graces that bless the large cities of the East, and even further, to the sophisticated populace of Europe. In their fledgling opera houses, one is as likely to watch a man playing the fiddle as see a production of* Hamlet. *Some libraries have been built but have yet to install books. And while every lady seems to have some skills with a needle, she nevertheless studies the styles in outdated publications, to catch a rare glimpse of what other ladies in more habitable climes were wearing one or more seasons before.*

*Mrs. Frances Trollope may be one of the visionaries of the new country. Her emporium is reputed to be one filled with artifacts and fabrics and fashions exotic to Ohio, but rather commonplace in London. She has decided to bring high culture to the West, and I daresay she is quite successful in her venture.*

"What do you think of this?" Verity asked Will the following morning. She thrust several pages between his eyes and his breakfast plate. He had scarcely touched his fish and toast, and his eyelids drooped in a rather appealing fashion. She dared imagine that his night, alone in his room, was as restless as hers.

"Did you write this while sitting astride a galloping horse?" he asked. "I can scarcely read it."

"Open your eyes, and you may find my penmanship much improved."

He looked up and smiled at her. "I think I can see everything to my satisfaction. When did you write this?"

"Perhaps it was a bit dark in my room. The light from my fireplace was all but gone, and I relied on some tapers I found in the drawer at my bedside."

He looked back down at her pages. "Did you have trouble falling asleep?" he quietly asked.

"I confess I did. Perhaps I am too accustomed to dropping off to the sonorous sound of your snoring."

"I shall keep that in mind," he said, not looking up from the page.

Verity reached under the paper to snatch a slice of cold toast from his plate. She was hungry, even if he was not.

"Are you truly speaking for all American women when you wrote this? Or are you answering your own call for art and fashion?" he asked.

Verity sat back in her chair. "Will you never accept the very humble manner of my upbringing? I am a woman accustomed to cast-offs, and country dances in the stable yard. For me, a small party in a lovely warm house in Cambridge is the epitome of society."

"And yet there has never been anything lacking in your sensibilities, I believe. Surely they are a good deal finer than those of my cousin Eastbourne. And perhaps of Lady Verity, as well."

"Is that one of the reasons you are willing to marry me?"

"Willing? There is no coercion here, my love. I love the whole package of everything you are. Your worldliness is just a part of it."

He cast off the compliment as if it could not possibly matter and resumed his reading of her chapter.

Verity spread some marmalade on her toast and sampled the flavor. It was not very sweet but was pleasing to the palate.

"I hope your expectations of the mysterious Mrs. Trollope do not run too high. Her emporium could be nothing more than a few market stalls, and her accounts could be perfectly dismal. You may have to retract these words," Will said.

"And so I shall," Verity said between bites of his breakfast. "It shall not be the first time I have had to revise my story."

"No, it is not," Will said and caught her hand. He studied her fingers carefully as he raised them to his lips and licked off a sticky little pat of marmalade. "I confess to a hope that the Bazaar is not at all impressive."

"But why? Do you think an Englishwoman incapable of succeeding in this country?"

"I believe an Englishwoman can manage very well, as you have amply demonstrated, my love," he said.

"I would not have managed very well at all, if not for your intervention in my affairs. As officious as I found them at the time, I am now grateful for your help, Will."

"You were a very determined woman," he said. "That you bumped into Geoff and me on that stormy day might have been the intervention of Fate, but that you sought us out and agreed to join us in our travels was your own doing. If not with us, you would have found your way to Cincinnati with others."

"Do you not think you had something to do with it? Would you believe me if I said that I wanted to be with you?"

"I treated you abominably."

"I will not disagree with you. I might have been a little high-handed myself. But of course I was Lady Verity then."

"Not to me." He still held her hand and ran a finger over the slopes and five peaks of this incriminating part of her anatomy. "I did not quite realize what was wrong, but even when I realized you were not Lady Verity, I had no idea whom you might be. I confess I was—and am—very intrigued."

"Still?" Verity laughed and pulled her hand away. "But you know everything about me, Will."

Will pushed away her pages and looked down at his empty plate, clearly surprised that his toast was now gone. He looked at her plate, with its sprinkling of crumbs and drops of marmalade.

"If we live to be a hundred, and I hope we do, I will still not know everything about you."

Verity smiled, feeling a satisfaction so deep she finally allowed herself to believe all this was going to work out. They would go to Cincinnati. Mrs. Trollope would greet them politely and show them around town and send them on their way. Lord Harwood would properly mourn his daughter and forgive Verity her short-lived masquerade. She and Will would return to Hudson Point, or wherever he wished to go in this vast country, and they would be finally married and contented for all those hundred years he spoke about. The prospect was at last in sight.

"What do the two of you have in mind?" Mrs. O'Neil asked as she put another plate of toast down between them.

Verity blinked, quite forgetting where she was for a moment.

"I thought we might take a walk along the waterfront," Will interceded, very smoothly. "Do you have any particular recommendations, Mrs. O'Neil?"

"Many," she said, leaning forward on her elbows. "None of which are particularly remarkable or unique. We are quite happy in Toledo, Ohio, but I daresay the sights are infinitely more engaging in Toledo, Spain. I have not been there, myself, you understand."

"I have," Will said. "They have some very fine churches there, built centuries ago as synagogues."

"And we have some very fine churches here, built years ago as churches," said Mrs. O'Neil. "But I am not referring to your plans for this day."

Verity rather thought she did not and glanced at Will.

"I am asking if the two of you have a mind to marriage," Mrs. O'Neil asked. "Because if you are, you might wish to marry here and travel more economically throughout the rest of your journey. In one room."

"It would be very practical," Verity murmured, but one look from Will silenced her on the subject.

"Thank you for your kind offer, Mrs. O'Neil, but my mother and sisters would be most disappointed if a marriage takes place before they have had the opportunity to meet the bride. Miss Harwood and I have not known each other very long, you see."

"I see a great deal, Mr. Bentley. And I also know that sometimes one does not need much time to recognize when something is meant to be."

Will nodded his assent. "We will proceed to Cincinnati and on our return go to my family home in New York. I have already written to my mother to ask her to anticipate a small reception, at which time my wife can be introduced to all the Bentleys. If possible, we hope that you and Mr. O'Neil and Miss O'Neil can join us."

Mrs. O'Neil looked quite satisfied. "As to that, I cannot say. Our business is here, in Toledo, and Mr. O'Neil is quite put off by the fact that Heather and I are going to Cincinnati for a week. But if we cannot attend, we will nevertheless send our blessings and best wishes."

Verity looked from one to the other and found that she could not say anything, either.

\*\*\*\*

"You might have said something to me about the

matter!" Verity said, as they walked along the lake promenade.

Will looked down at her, wondering why she was so agitated. Had they not already agreed on everything that mattered?

"What if I wish to stay in Cincinnati?" she argued. "What if it proves to be the most beautiful place on earth?"

"It will not," Will said. "I have already been there to the most beautiful place, and it is not there. But if you find Cincinnati particularly pleases you, we shall return there and buy a home."

"As simple as that?" Verity asked.

Will shrugged in confusion. "You already know that I am capable of living a comfortable life, when it suits me. We can buy or rent a house wherever you'd like to live. Hudson Point is already ours. But we can live anywhere at all."

"I must meet your family first. What if they don't like me?"

"They will. My mother has nearly given up on me and will be perfectly delighted. And my sisters will desire so much of your time that I will hardly get to see you. They will all love you as much as I do."

Verity seemed much taken by the words. The morning sun was not enough to account for the blush on her cheeks, and the breeze insufficient to bring tears to her eyes.

"Do you prefer to be married in England?" he asked, though he already knew her answer.

"There is nothing for me there. Lord Harwood shall surely never forgive me, and I certainly cannot face Lord Eastbourne ever again."

"Is there no other family? On your mother's side, perhaps?"

"No, we were quite alone. If things had turned out differently, I might have had brothers and sisters, I suppose. I would not have been in service to a lady, my skin would be freckled and tan, and I would likely have been married with several children of my own by now."

"You would not have traveled to America, you would not have been educated, you would not have dared to work a deception." Will caught his breath, thinking of all the extraordinary possibilities that went into the construction of a life. "You would not have met me."

"No." She sighed. "I would have only seen you taking an evening stroll on the Eastbourne estate. I would have wondered who you were and why you were about. I might have dared to nod my head to you in greeting but never to speak."

"All in all, I suppose we are very lucky indeed. Think of all I would have missed if I never heard you speak," Will said and meant it.

But perhaps Verity thought he did not, for she did not speak for the length of a mile. By this time, they were quite removed from the bustling center of Toledo, and the houses were little more than cottages, with rustic roofs and isinglass windows. Fishermen stood along the shore, occasionally flapping their arms to ward off the curious gulls who would challenge them for their day's catch.

"Where is that place, Will?" Verity asked suddenly. "The place that is the most beautiful on earth?"

"You have already been there with me," he said

softly, pulling her close. They turned in their path, to make their way back to the O'Neils'. "It is not on any map."

His words were coming to take a romantic turn, he realized. But Verity, as always, returned him to earth.

"I suppose you mean Albany," she said, grinning happily. "Yes, it was quite beautiful."

Chapter 14

The fog was heavy on the Maumee River when the band of travelers left Toledo by boat for the next leg of their journey toward Cincinnati, but Verity remained on the deck, breathing in the cool, damp air. It reminded her of her childhood days at Harwood Hall, when her life was carefully prescribed, and she only took risks in her dreams. She did not complain then; it was all for which she dared hope. But now, after climbing the mountain and gazing out upon the vistas on the other side, she wondered if she had ever been truly happy.

Surely she was? She'd had the love of her mother and the occasional attention of her father and the companionship of a girl who was just her age. She had her own little room on the fourth storey of the Hall and several books shelved along one wall. She wanted for nothing.

But once she met Will, even when he was most rude and uncompromising to her, she realized she'd wanted for everything. She was sorry that she teased him a few days ago, when he told her that being with her was the most beautiful place on earth.

For, truly, she felt the same about him.

When, a few moments later, she heard him talking to someone on the narrow deck of the boat, she turned to greet him as she guessed he might be looking for her

"Verity," he murmured, as he kissed her on the

forehead. "At last."

"I am never far away," she reminded him.

"True. And yet I somehow feel quite lost without you. I thought I might find you in the lounge with the rest of the women. Nell and the O'Neils are there, playing whist with a Canadian lady, and they told me they did not know where you were."

"You need not have worried, Will. I have been admiring the scenery and contemplating the strange journey my life has taken since leaving England," she said. "It has been extraordinary, wholly unexpected and, I fear, undeserved."

"The proverbial sea change, as we've said. But why this sudden change of heart? Have you not already convinced me that it is entirely deserved, and what you have always wished for yourself?"

Verity sighed, wishing she had half his confidence in her own merits. "But I am soon to meet someone who will likely judge me most harshly. The lady who is expecting Lady Verity Harwood will want to know everything that has happened and why a servant has come in her stead. I think I will be very happy if the boat runs aground, and we must return to Toledo. Why did you not convince me that going on to Cincinnati was a bad idea? Why did I think otherwise?"

"You were most persuasive, and Geoff and I thought it would be a fine chapter for our book. We might have been satisfied to turn back in Buffalo, but you seemed quite determined to continue. It is not altogether a bad thing. After all, if you do not meet Mrs. Trollope, you may forever wonder what brought you to America in the first place. And did you not say this journey offered some homage to Lady Verity? Her life was cut short, but you will continue in her stead."

"Please do not make it sound as noble as all that, Will. I am reluctant to take it even so far as Cincinnati, so there it must end. I intend to close the book on this chapter once all is resolved and allow my new life to begin."

"I thought it already has," Will said, as he turned her around to face the near shore, barely visible through the fog, and rested his chin on her head.

*While it is often noted, even by the great Shakespeare, that a city is naught without its people, I believe the native people and all those who followed would not have settled into a cluster of homes and community in the first place if not for the convenience of its waterways. Rivers and lakes are the livelihood of a society, and it would do the British much good to be reminded of this fact. In London, I have heard people complain bitterly about the great inconvenience of the river that divides the city, and the Thames is thus treated as a great garbage pit. Every so often, a fisherman pulls up a Roman sword or some souvenir of antiquity from the depths of the river, and we are reminded that it has served this function for many centuries.*

*In America, this lesson has yet to be learned. For now, the rivers are clean and unscarred with crumbling waterfront warehouses, and they are the pride of the community. In New York, we witnessed the progress of construction in the Erie Canal. And in Ohio, there is talk of another canal, the Miami and Erie, to be dug parallel to the Maumee River. There is no doubt that these projects will deliver people, goods, and culture to the budding inland communities.*

While the travelers and their many bags were transferred to two coaches that awaited them for the overland transport to Dayton, and then to Cincinnati, Verity handed her pages to Captain Warburton. She knew Will watched this little transaction and saw that it bothered him. Well, he would set eyes on her words soon enough, and why should she not take advantage of the company of an engineer to comment upon her assessment of civic development?

After all, if Will chose to write about shopping at Mrs. Trollope's emporium, would he not ask her?

No, she quickly decided. He would ask Mrs. O'Neil, who seemed as fine a shopper as ever was. Just now, the lady was overseeing the placement of her trunks to the roof of the coach, and demanding that they be covered in oilcloth. The drivers, told to expect four people and now receiving seven, were a bit surly.

"I will help her," Peter Warburton said. "After all, I have made these arrangements more difficult by intruding on your party and then complicating matters by introducing you to two ladies who decided to make the journey as well."

"But that is a very good thing, for we were quite getting tired of our own company."

Peter laughed. "Spoken like a true lady! I am sure there is nothing you and Will would have preferred than a quiet tête-à-tête each evening."

"But my friend Nell was truly bored, with only her brother for conversation. You have done much to make her trip truly enjoyable. And I hope you are pleased as well; surely our society is much better than the gulls and oysters on your little island in Boston Harbor?"

Peter smiled and looked to where Nell stood by one

of the coaches. She looked like she was about to hit Geoff with her carpetbag.

"I confess, it was a very peaceful, contemplative life, a bit like being sequestered in a monastery but without the necessity of frequent prayers. However, I suspect my mother never stopped praying that one of the women she paraded about during her calling hours would make me return to the mainland. And so, she has succeeded. I met Nell last winter."

"I do not envision Nell as one who would parade."

"Oh, do not misunderstand me, Miss Harwood. Nell attracted me because she was one of the few who had no interest in doing so. It was rumored she was waiting on the return of another gentleman."

"I hurt her very badly, and I shall always regret it," Verity murmured.

"I, for one, shall never regret it. And she would not have been happy with Will."

"How can you say that?" Verity asked.

Peter shrugged. "I suppose it is because I am an engineer. I know how things work."

Verity laughed out loud. "That is absurd."

"And what is that, Verity?" Nell asked, coming close.

Peter covered their tracks very neatly. "I told Verity we might take up housekeeping on our little island in Boston Harbor."

"It is not so very absurd," Nell said, looking at him. "I would live with you anywhere."

"I did not doubt it, my dear. But you have not yet seen Riverrun, Ohio."

"If you fine folks are finished joking about, we'll be on our way to Riverrun in a moment," called one of the grooms.

"We shall see," said Nell and slipped her arm through Peter's.

\*\*\*\*

"I should like to see you get away from the construction matters in your pages and return to the people," Will said, handing Verity's pages back to her. The coaches were covering rough terrain, and the carriage rocked back and forth in a tiresome manner.

"And I should like to see you write less about the doctors, lawyers, and military men in town society and speak to the farmers and tradespeople instead," Verity retorted. "There is where one finds the real story."

Geoff laughed. "Spoken like an American!"

"American or English, I was getting weary of masquerading as a lady, in either case."

Will shook his head. "This is something we did not expect when we first made our bargain. I believe the whole point is that we are looking at the same landscape but through different eyes. You are the English lady and ought to be slightly disdainful of what you see. I am the American and rejoice in the industry of the common man. This is what will sell books."

"Will we sell any less if it is I who rejoice in canal digging, and you look forward to the prospect of a dance?" Verity asked.

"It is all very ironic, is it not?" Geoff asked.

"What?" Will and Verity said in unison.

"Well, consider the facts. Verity, whom we believed a proper lady, is not an aristocrat at all. And Will, who prefers to shamble along as a common man, may find himself an earl someday."

"It is not very likely. And do I really shamble? Can

common men not walk with some dignity?" Will argued.

"Well, I only know that I cannot," Geoff said. "Every time I walk into a room, I fear I might fall flat on my face."

"Then you ought to write the damned book," Will said.

"If the two of you cannot agree on your approach, then I may have to do so. And I will not be the first secretary to rise to the task." Geoff stretched out his legs in the cramped coach. "And please apologize to the lady for your language, Will."

"Yes, do apologize," said Verity sweetly.

Whose side was Geoff on? And what gave him the right to interfere with what a man said in the company of his lover?

"I apologize for my words, Miss Harwood," Will said formally.

"Thank you, Mr. Bentley," Verity answered. "Now please tell us what is bothering you so. Surely it is not about the book?"

"No. It will all turn out well in the end. Mr. Benjamin Williams and Mrs...."

"Sophronia," Verity said promptly.

"Sophronia Williams? Where the hell did you come up with that?" Will asked.

"It was the name of the milliner in Toledo. I rather like it," Verity said. "And you owe me another apology."

"If you intend to put Sophronia Williams on the cover on my next book, I believe you would owe me an apology. Can you not be Anne or Verity? I would think you already have a surplus of names."

"But none so fine, my dear Benjamin. You have already established a reputation for your books, and thus no one would be apt to notice me. I daresay with Sophronia, people will take some notice."

"She has a point there, Will," said Geoff. "I like it. And it is nearly of the same length, so will be well balanced on the cover and flyleaf."

Verity, or Annie, or Sophronia, or whomever she was, just stared at him across the carriage, running her tongue over her lips. Did she know what effect that had on him?

Of course she did, the little vixen.

\*\*\*\*

Verity rather doubted that her friend Nell would have found much happiness in Riverrun, even in the same house as her beloved Captain Warburton. And this evening they found themselves in Hillandale, which did not seem much better. However, the night was full of promise.

The O'Neil ladies convinced Peter and Nell to join them at a concert in the park that evening, and they left after they all enjoyed a simple dinner. Geoff begged off, saying he had much reading to do. And Verity, having already considered the large tub behind the screen in her bedroom, decided she would be most happy soaking away the dust of travel.

She did not doubt Will would find some fine excuse to remain behind as well.

She also anticipated he would not be very patient; indeed, her hair was barely dry when she heard a light tapping at the door. Verity looked up as the handle moved and the door opened just enough to let him in.

Will looked as if he had just bathed as well, and

there remained a spot of shaving cream on his chin.

Verity met him halfway across the braided rug and rubbed it off with the edge of her sleeve.

"You must have been in a hurry to get here," she murmured.

He kissed her before answering. "I don't deny it. But haste combined with a looking glass just big enough to reflect my nose allows for some carelessness in my appearance."

Verity stood back for a moment to gaze upon his face. "And it is such a fine nose. But I see nothing wanting in your appearance."

"No, there is nothing wanting," he said as he pulled her very close. "I have already made love to Verity and Annie, but what of Sophronia? She sounds a bit shrewish."

Verity drew him to the bed, where she already pulled down the counterpane. She wore nothing under her light robe, but revealed herself very slowly as she unbuttoned the fastenings.

"Why don't you wait to be surprised? American ladies can be very enterprising."

"I am not going to be able to wait much longer," he said and slipped her robe off her shoulders before she had quite finished. "And I am not very fond of surprises."

****

The moon was high in the sky when Verity was awakened by the sound of their friends returning to the inn. She knew there was no reason for any of them to enter her room, but she pulled the quilts up and around Will's sleeping body and tucked the overstitched edging under her arms.

Will said something in his sleep, and Verity promptly put her hand over his mouth.

"What?" he said, startled into wakefulness and pulling the quilt off her as he sat upright. The moonlight shimmered across his wide, damp shoulders.

"Shhh," Verity whispered. "It is nothing. I just wanted to keep you quiet so our friends would not be suspicious."

He rubbed his eyes and then ran his fingers through his hair, so it stood on end. "Suspicious of what?"

"Of what we are doing and where you are at night," Verity said firmly and pulled him down next to her, for warmth and so she did not have to raise her voice.

"Oh, that," he said and slipped his arm under her neck, pulling her closer. "I doubt it is much of a mystery. Mrs. O'Neil's disappointment when Geoff said he wouldn't be going with them tonight suggested she has already written me off as a prospect for Miss O'Neil."

"Perhaps she doesn't like you," Verity said. "After all, I thought you were completely odious when I met you on the *Andromeda*. Geoff was the gentleman then, for all his pain of an injured ankle."

Will sighed, lifting the hair that curled by her ear. "I may have been a tad rude. I did not think you odious at all."

"No, you thought me pushy and imperious. But I was Lady Verity then, or in the process of becoming so." Casting off her false identity was liberating, allowing her possibilities the real Lady Verity would never have known or exploited. "And, by the by, what do you think of Sophronia Williams? Is she worthy of your consideration as a partner?"

"I have not yet made up my mind. I think I must experiment more before reaching any sort of conclusion."

Verity turned her head and looked into his dark eyes. The moon cast a deep shadow across his face, but she saw he was smiling even as his free hand moved beneath the quilt.

"But do have a care, sir. This bed creaks most dreadfully, and our neighbors might come storming in, thinking I am having a nightmare."

Will paused for a moment. "But with what little I already know of Sophronia, she will undoubtedly use the incident for a most amusing chapter in her book."

"I cannot imagine who would be amused," Verity pointed out and then said nothing else for quite some time.

****

Though Will would not admit it to Verity, he was nearly as agitated as she about their reception in Cincinnati. Mrs. Trollope was reputed to be a headstrong and uncompromising woman, who had been censorious of nearly everything in her American experience and littered her path to Cincinnati with resentment and contempt. Verity, drawn to this woman for no other reason than that Lady Verity had some connection to her, might well be a lamb going to slaughter. Was Mrs. Trollope a friend? An ally? A paid accomplice? Did she know Lady Verity had nearly disgraced herself in England and was now, or ought to have been, with child?

Was she expecting a haughty, selfish girl and would find a cheerful and generous lady in her stead?

Even if Lord Harwood or his agents chose not to

pursue the fact of a lady's maid's deception, Mrs. Trollope might not be so discreet. If her nasty description of the District of Columbia was lively enough to be quoted in every magazine in America, what power would she yield with a story of a masquerade and a gentleman duped by a lady?

Will shook his head. And yet, he was not duped, for he knew something was amiss when first he met Lady Verity. But if he argued that he knew the truth all along, Mrs. Trollope would brand him for either a fool or a rogue, someone who went along with the deception so he would gain access to Lord Harwood's fortune.

All in all, it would be better if Verity sent a letter to Mrs. Trollope declining the invitation. But her sense of honor was a good deal stronger than that of her half sister, and so this pilgrimage would be made, no matter if redemption was impossible at the end of the journey.

"You do not look very happy, Will," said Verity, beside him. They stood in the small courtyard of the inn, watching the familiar process of their bags being loaded onto the coaches. "Was Sophronia a disappointment to you?"

"Sophronia was willing to learn from one somewhat more experienced than she. I wish she would do the same when she puts her pen to paper," he said.

"Oh, truly?" Verity asked, her eyes still on the coach. "I suppose one should be open to learning new skills, of all sorts. One might find unexpected pleasures."

"One did," he said succinctly.

"Does Mrs. Trollope know when we are due to arrive?" Peter Warburton asked.

"I have written to the lady," Verity said. "I let her

know our numbers have increased, and she has recommended a guest house that is just a brief walk from her emporium. Originally, she only expected me and...my maid and me."

"Will you stay with her long, Miss Harwood?" Peter persisted. "I confess I am not certain of our plans once we reach Cincinnati."

"That does not sound like you, sir. You are always rather precise in your expectations."

He grinned a little sheepishly. "I have been distracted of late. I was so pleased to reach your party while you remained in Buffalo, I have not thought much beyond it. But we will be in Cincinnati today, and I thought I should let my superiors know when to expect me back in Boston. My mother would be happy to know that, as well."

"Perhaps we will have a better idea by the end of this day." Verity turned to Will. "Cincinnati is not very large, is it? We shall be able to see it all in a matter of a day or two?"

"Oh, certainly. But it will not be our sightseeing that will pose any difficulty. Our time spent in the city is most likely dependent on your—our —obligations to Frances Trollope."

Verity said nothing to this, but when he reached for her hand to help her into the coach, he could feel the iciness of her flesh through her cotton gloves.

They were scarcely settled in when the driver urged his team forward, and Will wondered if they had somehow left Geoff behind, for they were so accustomed to his company for all these weeks. Instead, Mrs. O'Neil was their companion, and she reassured them immediately.

"I thought I would like to ride with the two of you for this part of our journey," she said. "My daughter has been reading a particularly difficult history, and Mr. Marsh agreed to explain certain passages to her."

"And yet Miss O'Neil seems a very bright lady," Verity murmured.

"Oh, that she is. But she has not traveled, you see, whereas the gentlemen have traveled a good deal. Since Mr. Bentley was already well situated in this coach, Mr. Marsh generously changed places with me."

"Mr. Bentley is well situated," Verity agreed.

"And Mr. Marsh is well traveled," added Will.

"Then it has all worked out for the best," Mrs. O'Neil said, and reached into her carpetbag for her knitting.

As her needles clicked comfortably in the coach, Will hoped that her words would carry them through their sojourn in Cincinnati. Perhaps it would all work out for the best, whatever that might be. He had the uncomfortable feeling it would largely be out of his control.

The landscape from Hillandale to Cincinnati was fairly flat, and sprawling farmhouses dotted the fields. Every so often, their coach would be passed by a horse and rider, a wagon, or another coach. But the traffic on the road was not what Will would have expected en route to a growing city, and for the first time, he wondered what compelled an English lady with large prospects to invest in such a business in Cincinnati.

He did not know but hoped she'd explored other possibilities before putting down roots.

"Miss Harwood is very tired," Mrs. O'Neil said softly. "I hope it is not our conversation that has bored her."

Will looked at her in surprise and then realized Verity's head was resting on his shoulder. He gently took her book from between her fingers and put it on the seat beside him.

"I believe she is anxious about our upcoming visit, for she does not quite know what to expect. Mrs. Trollope and she only had a passing acquaintance in England, you understand."

"Then why is she visiting the lady?"

Will truly wished he knew the answer. "Well, it is always a pleasure for countrymen to visit each other and deliver news of their homeland. It must be lonely for Mrs. Trollope."

"My dear Mr. Bentley. There must be thousands of English citizens between New York and Cincinnati. In Boston one cannot walk five steps without bumping into a native of London. It is very kind of Miss Harwood to feel so loyal but truly unnecessary."

"I daresay you are correct, Mrs. O'Neil. I shall rely on you to tell her that when she awakens." Will smiled and hoped the matter was resolved.

Indeed, it seemed to be so. The hours wore on, the needles clicked away, Verity slept soundly, and the landscape held no greater promise than it did the hour before.

But Will was tired as well. Though he would have sworn he slept for a mere ten minutes, when he opened his eyes, he saw clusters of buildings that grew larger and more expansive with each passing mile. They had arrived in a city. The rough dirt beneath their coach wheels shifted to cobblestones, and passersby observed them with some interest.

This, then, was Cincinnati.

Over Verity's sleeping shoulder, Will spied a large hexagonal building, glistening under a fresh coat of white paint. A porch surrounded the building and was replete with barrels and boxes and items that were likely to endure the elements.

He nudged Verity gently.

"We have arrived," he said.

Verity stretched and yawned, and their companion tossed her needles and yarn into her open bag.

"We are in Cincinnati," Mrs. O'Neil said.

"Oh, dear." Verity sighed and reached for her hair.

"You look lovely as is, Miss Harwood," said Mrs. O'Neil.

"And yet I undoubtedly do not look as good as I ought. Mrs. Trollope is likely to be disappointed when she sees me."

Mrs. O'Neil shrugged. "Then we shall do our shopping and leave."

Will renewed his respect for the lady, for it seemed like an excellent idea.

Ten minutes later, they arrived at the guest house that was to be their living quarters while in Cincinnati. The travelers disembarked from the two carriages, and Will and Peter went inside to make arrangements for their visit and sent a messenger to Mrs. Trollope that her visitors would be arriving.

And soon they set off, falling naturally into groups, the gentlemen walking on the outside of the pathways as they followed the directions to the Bazaar. As they came close, Will thought it looked much better from a distance, when one did not see the cracks in the plaster or the mud in the street. There were no people or horses in front of the building, and he wondered if the emporium was closed for business today.

It was not; perhaps it simply did not have any business today. The staff seemed ready for customers, however.

A man dressed as a cross between an Eastern pasha and a Scotsman greeted them at the door and bowed.

"May I be of service?" he asked, in the nasal tones of a New Yorker.

Will closed his eyes briefly, trying to fix this bit of pretense into memory, for it would be a glorious thing to write about.

"We are here to see Mrs. Frances Trollope," said Verity, beside him. Her voice sounded firm and slightly impatient. "We are expected."

"We are also here to examine your merchandise," said Mrs. O'Neil, to whom the exotic Scot gave a grateful nod.

"What is it, Anthony? What is the cause of this uproar?" came a voice from the deep shadows of the Bazaar.

Will reflected that if the conversation of a few people could be considered an uproar, then business was very bad indeed.

A large woman emerged from the shadows, dressed for an evening's dinner party, though it was only late afternoon. Her hair was elaborately styled, with strings of pearls woven in and out. In her arms she held a most unusual cat, until she came close enough for Will to see that it was actually a very small dog.

Verity stepped forward and gracefully curtseyed.

"Mrs. Trollope," she said softly. "Allow me to introduce my friends. Mr. William Bentley of New

York and his friend Mr. Geoffrey Marsh of Boston. Mr. Marsh's sister, Miss Marsh. Our friend Captain Warburton of Boston. Mrs. O'Neil and Miss O'Neil of Toledo, Ohio. We have only just arrived in Cincinnati."

Mrs. Trollope cleared her throat. "You have forgotten one thing, miss, and it is of utmost importance."

She lowered her dog onto a velvet settee and reached for Verity's hands, exploring the graceful fingers.

Will winced. *She knows. She knows what is lacking on those perfect hands.*

"You have forgotten to tell me one thing," she repeated.

"Mrs. Trollope?" Verity asked.

The lady deliberately looked her up and down before dropping her hands.

"Who the bloody hell are you?"

Chapter 15

Verity heard her friends gasp behind her but refused to cower before their ridiculously rude hostess. No wonder the shopping hall was bereft of customers, if this was the way guests were greeted. But then, she was not any guest, and Mrs. Trollope seemed to be already sure she was not whom she was expecting.

"I am Miss Harwood, lately arrived from England. I traveled across the Atlantic with Lady Verity Harwood, whose intention it was to visit you here. As my lady did not survive the journey, I have come in her stead." Verity took a deep breath. "Her father, and mine, is already aware of the tragic and unexpected events."

"And your father is?" Mrs. Trollope asked, ignoring what was already implicit in Verity's words.

"Lord Percival Harwood," Verity said, nearly choking on the name.

"Well, my dear, Lord Percival Harwood does not know about this or anything else."

Perhaps the woman did not understand what she was saying. "I have sent word to him of the situation, and he surely is already in mourning."

Absurdly, the lady laughed. "The household, perhaps, but not poor Percy."

"I beg your pardon."

"Lord Harwood is dead. The letter from his

solicitor reached me here weeks ago, as this is one direction he knew would find Lady Verity. I took the liberty of reading the letter, having no idea when you intended to arrive. Lord Harwood is dead. My sympathies, Miss Harwood, even though I have no idea who you really are." Mrs. Trollope paused and pulled Verity into the brighter light. "Perhaps I do have some idea, after all. You are very like Lady Verity, close enough to be sisters."

"I am the daughter of Lord Harwood's housekeeper."

"I am prepared to believe it."

Behind them, Nell gently coughed, and Peter said something in a low voice.

Mrs. Trollope looked over Verity's shoulder, assessing either the audience or the potential for customers. "Come with me to my office, Miss Harwood, for we have much to discuss."

"I am the lady's betrothed and shall accompany her," Will said.

Mrs. Trollope glared at him. "You shall not, sir, for Miss Harwood and I are our own keepers. Men have caused us enough troubles in our lives." She scooped up her dog and turned in the direction from which she had come. "Well, Miss Harwood? I am waiting!"

Verity turned a little helplessly to Will and shrugged.

"You go on, my dear," said Mrs. O'Neil. "We will determine if the merchandise here is truly worth a journey from Toledo. Do not worry about us."

But Verity thought they should rather worry about her. The consequences of her deception merited far worse than a private tongue-lashing, and she steeled herself to take whatever punishment Mrs. Trollope would mete out. She put a hand on Will's forearm and smiled a little bleakly.

"I shall be fine, you know. I have weathered far worse than this in my life, and I am prepared to hear a litany of grievances. Perhaps you can help me by looking about the Bazaar for a new writing set for me? If I survive this interview, I shall have much to write about." Verity's smile brightened as her confidence increased. "Perhaps I shall start a whole new book."

"We have one to finish before you do so. So whatever the lady demands, do remember that I need you," Will said, and put his hand over hers.

"Miss Harwood?' echoed the stern voice behind her. "And Anthony? Where are you?"

Verity nearly collided with the Scotsman as they rushed the door at the same moment, but Anthony remembered his manners and allowed Verity to precede him into the room. She expected to see a stark and efficient business office but was both surprised and delighted to enter a room even more elaborate than the stalls of the Bazaar. Oriental rugs hung along the walls, and ropes of sparkling crystals dangled at the window. The skin of a massive tiger spread before a fireplace that was embedded in a wall of Delft tiles. Enormous porcelain pots held orange trees, and the sweet smell of their blossoms nearly masked the spicy incense burning in a small bronze bowl.

"Anthony, we should enjoy a pot of tea, for Miss Harwood has surely missed the luxury whilst traveling through the country." She glanced at Verity but did not give her a chance to respond. "And do bring us some of Lucy's tartlets, for I believe I can smell them baking in the oven. If Miss Harwood's friends are hungry, feed them as well, for there must be some other food about."

Verity raised her brow, about to suggest that her friends merited fine tea and fresh pastries as well, but Mrs. Trollope raised her hand to silence her as she watched Anthony leave the room.

"He is a fine man," Mrs. Trollope said. "He reminds me of my own son, which is why I named him Anthony."

"I am sorry for the loss of your son," Verity said softly. She took a seat, waiting for Mrs. Trollope to argue with her.

"The loss of my son? Whatever can you mean? My Anthony is at home with his father and other people, when he is not at school. I certainly have no desire for any of them to come here." Mrs. Trollope scowled and then brightened. "That is why I named my man Anthony, so I will always be reminded of what I have sacrificed for the benefit of my family."

"Does he not mind using the name of another?" Verity asked, regretting her words at once and with good reason.

"Do you? I daresay it has opened doors for you and has provided you with an avenue of escape that would not have been available to you back at Harwood Hall."

"It did, for a very short while. I did not have a plan to deceive anyone, but it is possible I would have left service once Lady Verity and I arrived safely here. It was not meant to be." Verity's voice shook slightly. "My lady died of an ailment on board the ship. By the time we reached Boston, I was already known to all as Lady Verity."

Mrs. Trollope snorted. "Your scheme did not take

very long to be implemented."

"I borrowed my lady's name because it allowed me to claim attention and some respect when it was needed. In truth, my lady was very ill, and I thought if I demanded the services of the doctor, using her name, my request would be heeded. It was, of course, no use. She died that very night."

"Did she already have an understanding with Mr. Bentley? Did you step into her love affair as well as her identity?"

"No, my lady did not, though they'd met several times, I believe. Mr. Bentley is the cousin and heir to Lord Eastbourne, owner of an estate adjacent to Harwood Hall."

Mrs. Trollope cupped her hands under her chin. "Is that so? Then you are a fortune hunter as well."

Verity grew tired of this game. "If there is a fortune to be had, it will be achieved by my own hand. Mr. Bentley has taken me on as his partner, and we are writing a book together. It is about the manners of the Americans. He has some experience in publishing endeavors and has assured me that it will do very well."

"Ha! I have never heard of him and read many books of that sort. Everyone knows of de Toqueville, of course. And there is Mr. Stoddard and Mr. Williams."

Verity said nothing.

"Mr. Williams? Benjamin Williams? It is he? The author of *A River Tour of New York*?" Mrs. Trollope clasped her hand to her bosom. "Here in my Bazaar?"

To her surprise, Verity realized she was coming to enjoy this. "I regret he is not so very exotic as you might prefer."

"He is handsome, which is much more desirable as

a commodity. But what on earth does he want with you?"

She deserved that, she supposed. If Mrs. Trollope did not intend to kill her outright, she could whittle away at her with a blunt knife.

"I am not so very plain, and I am educated and willing to learn more. Mr. Bentley thought a lady's point of view would offer readers something new and appealing. A more desirable commodity, as you say."

"I see." Mrs. Trollope did see something, but Verity was not sure what it was. The lady looked off into the distance, perhaps imagining the savannah of Africa or the pages of a book in her own name. She moved her fingers slightly, as if calculating something, and nodded thoughtfully.

"Yes, you might be right about that. A lady's perspective on American manners and matters of domesticity; I daresay it would sell very well to an English audience. Undoubtedly better than Russian nested dolls sell to the people of Cincinnati." She paused as Anthony entered the office with a tray of strongly brewed tea and browned tarts. "How are our guests enjoying themselves, Anthony?"

The man looked up in surprise. "The men are looking at whips, and the ladies have found the display of peacock feathers."

"Yes, that sounds about right." Mrs. Trollope sighed, and waved him away. "You will serve me, Miss Harwood, as you must be accustomed to that sort of thing."

Verity did as she was told, for she suddenly lacked the energy to continue to assert her own authority.

"You most certainly are not plain, Miss Harwood.

In fact, you are rather beautiful, even more so than Lady Verity. There was always something sharp and cutting about that lady, and she was not a pleasant creature to be around. I nearly detested her, in fact."

Verity handed Mrs. Trollope a cup of tea. "If that is the case, I wonder you wished her to come here."

"What else could I do? Her mother was one of my dearest friends, and when Lady Verity appealed for help, I could not refuse her. She told me how things stood, and how she must leave England before scandal erupted."

"That was very kind of you."

"Indeed it was. In exchange for my kindness, Lady Verity was willing to underwrite some of my expenses in this business. I was also to receive a commission for arranging for her child to be raised by a family in the vicinity. They will be very disappointed. Unless, of course, you are with child as well?"

"I am not," Verity said firmly. Goodness, but this lady was possessed of a hunger.

"Then you deserve more credit than your mother. No, do not bother to justify her behavior, or how she gave in to temptation. Percy was irresistible; I could hardly avoid him either. No woman could. But he was destined for his cousin, even while they cared little for each other. When Lady Verity was born, and her tiny hand was revealed, it was viewed as punishment against the grandparents for forcing such a marriage upon the parents. Percival and Sarah had no more children, and my poor friend died far too young. Percival grieved appropriately enough, but it was known he'd already sought comfort with his housekeeper, your mother. She was a cousin too, of course." Mrs. Trollope studied

Verity, looking for defects, perhaps. "Not a very close one, however."

"Now my mother is dead, as is Lady Harwood, Lady Verity, and my father. How did he die? I assume you know, as you seem to know everything else."

Mrs. Trollope narrowed her eyes, and a strand of beads slipped down over the bridge of her nose. "He was in a riding accident, apparently."

"Impossible. He did not ride," Verity argued.

"Well, I do not think it was he who was riding." Mrs. Trollope shuffled a pile of papers on her desk, holding up each to the light. "Yes, here it is. It seems he was conducting an experiment of some sort and walked into the path of a group of riders. It appears Lord Eastbourne ran over him. I suppose one could make a case that Mr. Bentley's position as Eastbourne's heir, and your own assumption of Lady Verity's identity makes things very suspicious indeed."

Verity put down her teacup and leaned forward. "How so?"

"I am not sure. But certainly, I could resolve those curious circumstances into the pages of a novel. I am writing one, you know. There is little else to do in Cincinnati. Though I confess you have intrigued me sufficiently to think about writing a travel book."

"Do be considerate and use false names in your novel, Mrs. Trollope. Mr. Bentley has no interest in Eastbourne's estate. And I will soon be quite settled and require nothing from my father's, nor do I expect it."

"But that is just the thing, my dear." Mrs. Trollope spread the papers about on her desk, spilling tea over them. "Lord Harwood has left you a tidy sum."

"He has endowed Lady Verity, surely not me."

"I am a very fine reader and am not in the least bit mistaken. The estate and title go to a cousin. But he has something for you as well. Ah, here it is."

Verity held out her hand. "Mrs. Trollope, are those papers addressed to you or to me?"

"Whyever would a lawyer address such matters to me?"

"That is an excellent question. I might also ask, why would you read them?"

Mrs. Trollope made some rude noises as she handed over the papers to Verity.

"You have become a bossy little thing since your elevation to…ah…the middle class. I am sure Lady Verity would not have endured such rudeness."

"And yet there was no finer authority on the subject of rudeness than my lady."

Mrs. Trollope sighed and dropped her hands to the desk. "You have become one of them, an accursed American. I cannot abide them, you know. I daresay if I write a book, the population here would not be very happy."

"I shall have to let you know, for I intend to remain here and be happy. And my children will be Americans as well."

"I suppose there is no hope for it."

"No, there is not." Verity stood and looked down at her critic.

"There is one thing, my girl," Mrs. Trollope asked. "Do I ask too much if I request a small loan from you? I have a shipment arriving from Belgium, and as you may know, the Flemish require very punctual payment. Perhaps I shall write a book about them as well."

\*\*\*\*

For a man of impeccable control and dignity, a gentleman who ordered his life as neatly as the chapters of a book, Will Bentley felt as if his affairs were spinning out of control. Before he met Verity, he'd expected to marry a sweet biddable miss like Nell, who would agree with everything he had to say and make his life even more comfortable than it was. But then he realized he was in love with Verity, who provided comforts in equal measure to challenges.

For the rest of his life, it would be like this. His need of her was paired with what he hoped was her need of him. And yet, while he had no doubt she loved him and desired him, she was prepared to do such things that would make him frustrated and even fearful. He only wished to protect her and give her a very different life than what she knew in her first twenty years. But the things he loved about her were the very things that also unnerved him, for she proved willful and brave and utterly capable.

So he now stood, holding an Indian whip in one hand and tapping the handle on the other, watching the door through which Verity disappeared some half hour before. She was in the dragon's cave, and there was little he could do but listen to the rise and fall of feminine voices and the occasional sound of thumping. This did not sound particularly threatening, but much harm could be done in relative silence.

"Who is that fellow?" asked Geoff. "The one she calls Anthony. He is standing at the door, listening to all their words."

"I have no idea who this Anthony fellow is. I suspect he is intended to be part of the scenery."

"Yes, it is quite a place. Though it would be much

improved if there were any people about. Mrs. Trollope must be very confident about her prospects." Geoff picked up a carved ivory statue of an elephant with a stunted trunk. "Where does she find such things?"

"I do not know, nor do I really care. It is possible most people hereabouts do not know what an elephant looks like."

"Perhaps that is the point. Mrs. Trollope has furnished her Bazaar with items to spur the imagination and make people think about the world beyond Cincinnati. You do much the same thing in your books."

Will said nothing as he continued to watch the closed door and hammer away at his hand with the handle of the whip.

"She will manage just fine in this, as she does in everything," Geoff said quietly.

"She thinks she can, but what if she confronts an obstacle too big to surmount? She has made it clear she does not need me to help her."

"And that is where you are utterly wrong, my friend. If she seems to be confident, it is because you have made her so. You have given her purpose and direction. And you have given her love, which is not to be regarded lightly."

Will considered Geoff's words. "You seem to know a good deal about it."

"Well, I know a good deal about you, my friend. And your effect on the lady has been clear from the moment you nearly knocked her overboard on the *Andromeda*."

"I would have saved myself a lot of worry if we just walked on from there, ignoring the little wench."

"And include the episode in one of your books? Like everything else you sample and savor and walk away from?" Geoff took the whip from his hand and put it on top of a display case. "You will not walk away from her. She is the one who will finally bring you home."

Will suddenly had nothing to do with his hands and stuffed them into his pockets. From the closed room, he heard the sound of a chair being pushed on a wood floor.

"She has said she will travel with me."

"And wherever she is will be home to you."

Will knew his friend was right. He imagined new reasons to be at Hudson Point, homecomings and family gatherings, children running about the place as he and his sisters did so many years ago, finding peace and pleasure in a quiet evening. And for all these things, Verity would be at his side, pursuing her own interests as she allowed him his.

"It will be a very fine place," he said softly.

"Oh, indeed," Geoff said casually. "It may only want for an ivory elephant, or one of those beaded things. What are they, anyway?"

"Drapery for doorways, like they use in harems," Anthony said, walking past them. A new customer had arrived, silhouetted by the window behind him. Will knew him.

"A harem, indeed." Geoff laughed out loud. "Do you think your wife would tolerate such a thing?"

Will was ready to point out that his wife would be intrigued by anything novel and curious. But then he remembered the look on her face when he danced with other women, when he flirted with Nell, when he walked with Annabel Compton on the deck of the *Andromeda*. She was also a lady who lived with the consequences of her father's folly in housing his wife and his mistress under the same roof. "No, I doubt Verity would tolerate it. And since I would not tolerate walking through a shower of beads every time I entered my bedroom, I believe we stand in perfect accord." He watched as Anthony's customer came toward them, into the soft light of the Bazaar. "Why, what's this?"

"Good day, Mr. Bentley, Mr. Marsh. I did not expect to find you here, still traveling with Lady Verity."

"Mr. Reese," Will said tersely. What was the scoundrel doing here?

"Or should I say, 'Annie Merrill?' Yes, I can see you are quite surprised, but I have uncovered the unpleasant truth. The lady you are traveling with is an imposter, having assumed the title of her ladyship while we were still on board the *Andromeda*."

"If I show any measure of surprise, it is because I only wonder that you have so lately come to the realization that this is so. Miss Merrill revealed all to us some time ago. Indeed, I suspected it from the very beginning." Will pulled his hands out of his pockets and crossed his arms. "Tell us, Mr. Reese, what tipped you off?"

"Well, I have been correspondence with his lordship and…and I see no reason to tell this to you."

"No, indeed, for you are not in *my* employ," Will said. "Was it the matter of the lady's hand? Or the lack of evidence that the lady's condition is, in any way, delicate? Or perhaps you studied her character, for Miss Merrill is nothing like the temperamental shrew we know Lady Verity to be."

"It is the matter of the lady's hand. That is, more rightly, it is evidence by her own hand."

"I see. You admit you opened a sealed letter written to Lord Harwood by Miss Merrill."

"I see no reason to tell this to you," Reese repeated.

"And yet you will. What do you intend to do with the incriminating letter that is now in your possession?"

"I have sent it on to Mr. Meldon in Boston, who has already assured me that he has directed it to Lord Harwood."

"Has he indeed? If he said it, he is as dishonest as you, sir."

"I will not tolerate a strike upon my honor!"

"You have already admitted opening a letter not intended for your eyes. And I suspect you never heard from Mr. Meldon for you did not bother to write to him. But if you had, he would have contradicted your words."

"What do you know about it? I fully intend to take Miss Merrill with me back to Harwood Hall. She deserves to be punished."

"Punishment? And by whom?" he said slowly.

"By Lord Harwood, of course. She is but a maid in his employ. He could do what he wishes with her."

"I thought that was your intention," Will said. "To do what you wish with her."

"Will," Geoff said, putting a restraining hand on his arm.

Will shook him off.

"You will not get any satisfaction, if that is your aim, from Lord Harwood," Will said.

"What do you know of it?" Reese asked, grinning

unpleasantly.

"Because the man is dead. The new Lord Harwood, whoever he is, will not likely care about an errant maid. Indeed, he might even rejoice, because Lady Verity's inheritance might revert back to his estate."

"What do you mean, he is dead?" John Reese asked.

"For a man of your extraordinary discernment, you seem very dense. Do you not understand me?"

Will knew he went too far, even before Reese reacted to this news. He made a guttural sound and reached for the whip that Geoff had only recently pried from Will's fingers. Will, having nothing but his fists, looked around for a weapon. There was nothing but that damned ivory elephant.

Reese raised the whip, and Will lunged for his legs, pushing him to the ground. He felt the whip crack over his back, doing no harm to him but, by the sound of it, destroying some of Mrs. Trollope's merchandise. As white feathers snowed down upon them, Will grabbed Reese's hand and slammed it against the ground until he released the whip. But anger was a strong driver, and Will raised his body with his left hand to pummel Reese's chest with the right.

Reese twisted beneath him and gained enough momentum to spin them both into the legs of the display case, which collapsed around them.

"Enough, enough," Geoff shouted, before Reese knocked him off his feet. He cursed as he went down on the broken glass.

A gun went off, and Reese collapsed beneath them.

Gasping for breath, Will wiped blood from his eye with his sleeve and looked down at the man. What happened? Where was he shot?

"What is this about?" shouted a voice.

"Will, are you injured?" Verity cried.

He rolled off Reese and turned his face toward the ceiling. Between a red silk flag and a gold chandelier, he saw Verity's face.

"Will!" she cried. Her voice grew louder. "What has happened?"

He closed his eyes. "I think I am well, but there is a weight on my chest. Perhaps it is my heart?"

"Oh, that is me," she said and slipped off his chest to the floor. She pulled him to a seated position, and he thought his head would explode. "What have you done to Mr. Reese?"

Painfully, he turned his head to look down at his assailant. "Who shot him?"

"No one shot him, though I should have shot you all. Look what you have done to my shop," said Mrs. Trollope.

She came to stand above them, and smoke wafted from the pistol she held.

"I shot at the floor and will bill you for that damage as well. And look at my lovely elephant, carved in Persia. Oh, dear, and my eiderdown pillows."

Will coughed up a feather and started to fall back to the ground. But Peter caught him and pulled him to his feet, while Nell and Miss O'Neil did the same for Geoff. Mrs. O'Neil did not seem inclined to do the same for Reese, who groaned at their feet.

"This woman is an imposter," he spit out.

"So I was, but briefly. I have already confessed all to everyone for whom the truth could possibly matter." Verity knelt above the prone Reese but did nothing to ease his pain. "Have you the letter I gave you?"

Reese nodded and pulled a much-creased envelope from his jacket. "It is no use to your father now, if he is dead, as Bentley says."

"It is indeed too late for my father, in this and many things. But it is of use to me, for I shall always remember my fatal misstep and how I was rescued by the kindness of friends. It has given me hope, not as a lady privileged by wealth, but as one privileged by love."

Mrs. O'Neil applauded. "Very well said, Miss Harwood."

Will walked a bit shakily to Verity and reached for her hand. "It is over here," he said.

"What do you mean by that, young man?" Mrs. Trollope argued. "My Bazaar is in ruins. Something must be done."

Will looked around at the exotic merchandise on display all around them, at a grand enterprise with no customers. "I am happy to replace what you have lost, Mrs. Trollope. There are some wrongs that can be righted by dollars or pounds, but they ultimately prove to be of little consequence. Words and deeds matter more and can endure forever."

Again, Mrs. O'Neil applauded.

****

Hours later, Verity and Will remained at the large table where their friends had joined them for dinner. The O'Neils were enjoying a walk with Geoff, while Peter and Nell joined Mrs. Trollope back at the Bazaar to examine her collection of teaspoons.

"You must think me a man only capable of mental exertions," he said over his third cup of tea. He laced it liberally with rum. "And yet I'll have you know that I'm a fair wrestler and fencer. My brief battle with Reese was never in doubt."

"The man had a whip," said Verity. "Surely that changes the odds? But you need not convince me of your physical prowess."

He closed his eyes for several moments, in contemplation of either pain or pleasure, she guessed.

"Nor do you need to keep your confessional letter to the late Lord Harwood," he said. "Surely you do not require a reminder of the events of these past few months, when you will have me reminding you of them for the rest of our lives?"

"I shall have to behave myself, then," she said.

"Please do not. You are much more interesting when you misbehave."

"And I shall remain Verity, myself when I met you. It suits me, I think."

"What of Sophronia?"

"I thought we settled that. She is my *nom de plume*, a good partner to Benjamin Williams."

"Yes, that is all settled," Will said, and sipped his tea.

"I fear we may have some competition, Will."

"There is always competition, but we will have the advantage of a woman's perspective."

Verity could not meet his eyes. "That's just it. I believe Mrs. Trollope plans to write a book as well. The Bazaar isn't doing that well, you realize."

"I realize."

"Mrs. Trollope did ask me what we do, and how we go about it. I confess, I may have told her too much. She hates living in America, you know. Contempt is a strong impetus to a writer."

"Is that why you agreed to be my partner? Will asked.

"Contempt is a strong impetus, but it is not the only one. I believe love inspires even more passion."

"Then we shall have enough to drive us for a lifetime."

Verity mused over the extraordinary turns her life had taken in only a few months, how she went from servant to lady to business partner to a woman of some means. How she lost a sister and father but gained a coterie of loyal friends and, soon, a husband. How her life had revolved around the needs of another and how she now dictated her own history.

"Shall it always be like this?" she asked, more to herself than for Will's avowals. But he was ready for her, as she suspected he always would be. He put down his cup, and reached for her.

"Yes," he said. And it was all she ever wanted to hear.

****

*Americans are so curious to learn about the trappings of the titled and privileged, that one would think that they, like the English, would hold people of rank in highest esteem. Yet they do not. My husband's mother and sisters, situated in a lovely home on the Hudson River in New York State, want to hear every detail about life on a great estate but shrug off any suggestion that their son and brother—heir to an earl— might do a good deal better than marry a former servant with modest means.*

*Perhaps their interest was spurred on by the desire to plan a fine wedding at Hudson Point, and in this they succeeded. The farms of the Hudson Valley provided the provisions, the libations, and the splendid flowers for our autumn wedding, and the tastes and sensations of that blessed Sunday afternoon linger to this day, when snow sits upon our pine forest.*

*Much has happened since the day I was introduced to my new family.*

*My dearest friend, Nell Marsh, is now married to her beloved Captain Warburton, and my husband and I and two of his sisters traveled to Boston for the event. While there, his friend Geoffrey Marsh seemed quite taken with his sister Leonie Bentley, and we have high hopes for their happiness.*

*Our hostess in Cincinnati, Mrs. Frances Trollope, may delay the start of her expository tome on the manners of the Americans, for she is to have help in her business venture from our fellow traveler, Mrs. O'Neil. The lady has a fine taste in textiles and paintings and is more familiar with the local craftspeople. Thus, she may bring together several tradesmen under the single roof of the Bazaar, and the business may, at last, see a profit.*

*Though I wish the best for our dear friends, I am most satisfied when I reflect on the fruits of my own labor. Mr. and Mrs. Benjamin Williams have enjoyed great success after the publication of* The Meeting of Two Worlds *and have been contracted to write three more books of a similar nature. The audience has been most enthusiastic in England, but the rewards are greater in America, where nearly every person is taught to read. It is really an extraordinary circumstance and is a very promising prospect for authors.*

*For now, my adventurous days of travel are at an*

*end, and it is not merely due to the harsh weather. I spend many hours writing at my desk and am attempting to compensate for the time in the near future, when I will necessarily be busy with other things. But my new sisters and mother have assured me that they will lavish upon a new family member more attention than any tiny baby could possibly need or desire, and I am grateful for it.*

*My husband, defined for so many years by his restless curiosity, at last seems to have found peace in his own home. Perhaps he just awaits the day when he can travel about with several children in tow. Or perhaps he has discovered a new sort of contentment. Certainly, our lives are never boring, and it is very likely that adventure will come to us, rather than the need for us to quest after it.*

*If I have learned one thing since leaving Harwood Hall in Sussex, it is that journeys are taken in a myriad of ways. Certainly, ships and coaches are the vehicles that transport us from one destination to the next. But there is also the journey of the soul, set on its path by the unexpectedness of opportunity, fueled by desire, and encouraged all the long way by friendship and hope. With such things, one can go very far without ever leaving one's home.*

*Mrs. Sophronia Williams*
*Preface to* My Private Journey
*January 1, 1823*

## A word about the author...

A writer for most of her life, Sharon Sobel is the author of seventeen published novels, novellas and short stories. She earned a PhD in English and American Literature from Brandeis University and is currently a professor of English at the University of Connecticut and at Connecticut State College. She was Chapter Liaison and Secretary of the Board of Directors of Romance Writers of America, a founding member of its Connecticut and Lower New York chapter, was twice President of The Beau Monde, the national chapter devoted to the interests of writers of the Regency period and is currently Secretary of Regency Fiction Writers.

A native New Yorker, Sharon also lived in Boston and The Hague before moving to an eighteenth century farm in Connecticut with her husband and family.

Connect with Sharon at
SharonSobelAuthor.com
Facebook.com/p/Sharon-Sobel-Books

Thank you for purchasing
this publication of The Wild Rose Press, Inc.

For questions or more information
contact us at
info@thewildrosepress.com.

The Wild Rose Press, Inc.
www.thewildrosepress.com